STOKER

a dark romance

Cover & Interior: The Red Fox Creative
Editing : Lauren Cann

STOKER

a dark romance

Stoker is a dark romance intended for readers 18+ with topics that may be uncomfortable for some readers. This work of fiction is completely different than my previous two novels, Given the Chance and Letters to Olive. There are themes and topics discussed in this novel that may be triggering for some, please proceed with caution. If anything listed below sounds like it may be a trigger for you, I advice you to stop now and consider your mental health.

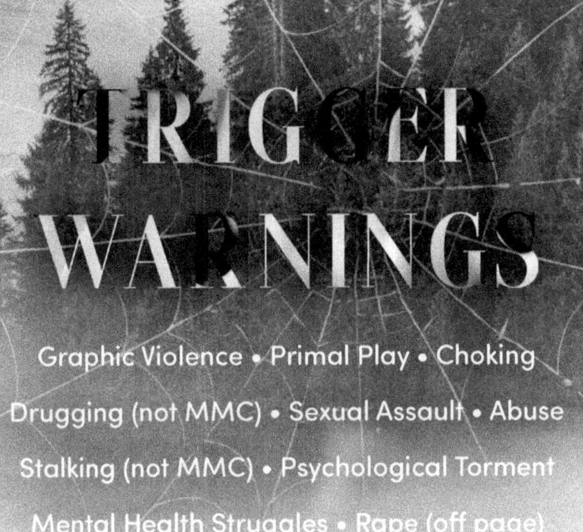

TRIGGER WARNINGS

Graphic Violence • Primal Play • Choking

Drugging (not MMC) • Sexual Assault • Abuse

Stalking (not MMC) • Psychological Torment

Mental Health Struggles • Rape (off page)

Death of a Loved One

PLAYLIST

Enjoy this chapter-by-chapter playlist I've created to set the mood as you read through.

Use your phone to scan the code below so you can listen on Spotify!

CHAPTER 1
Lovely • Billie Eilish

CHAPTER 2
Indigo • Sam Barber

CHAPTER 3
Sparks • Coldplay

CHAPTER 4
Lithium • Evanescence

Not every little girl dreams of Prince Charming. This is for the women who dream of the morally grey men covered in tattoos and aren't ashamed to say they wouldn't mind being called a filthy slut.

ISOLDE

chapter one

I've grown so used to the feeling of fear, I didn't think I could reach a new level. The kind of fear that snakes throughout your body resting in the very marrow of your bones. That's what this feeling is right now, as I race down the steps of my home in a silent panic, hoping, *praying*, he doesn't hear me escape. Because I need to escape. I can't stand the fear anymore, I'm afraid if I don't leave now there won't be anything left of me.

My heart thunders in my chest with each step I take, quietly, but effectively down the stairs I've used a million times. In this moment I know, this will be the very last time I take these stairs. It *has* to be. I can't go back now. Not after everything.

With one swift turn, I have the door open and am slipping past the threshold. Taking the stairs two at a time from the top floor apartment I've called home the last four years. As soon as my feet hit the last landing I realize I'm running, unable to hold back my need to escape any longer. The steps to my car feel heavy as wind whips at my hair like a vortex around my face, the scent of my lavender shampoo invading my senses. Clasping my hair in one hand, wrapping it around my fist, I unlock my car and hop in.

All I have to do is drive away from this godforsaken place. This town that has offered me little to nothing in the last six years, and drive until my eyes are weary and I know for certain I'm safe. That little voice buried in the back of my brain laughs, snidely reminding me, *you'll never be truly safe, Isolde.*

I crank the engine, thanking whoever it is watching over me, that my car makes little to no sound. Not like the clunker my neighbors from my childhood home have been driving for more years than seems safe. How they manage to get it past inspection is beyond me. Probably illegally. I laugh at myself for the thought, how silly a fake inspection sounds in the grand scheme of other crimes people commit. The ones I'm currently running from, not my own, but ones I've had to bear witness to. Ones I've had to *experience.*

A shiver runs down my spine as I blast the heat and I back out of the cobble driveway, chancing one last look at the house to ensure he isn't coming after me. My skin prickles as I reign in my panic when the smell of his cologne wafts around me, eyes wide and searching, when I remember he was in my car just a few hours ago. The lingering scent makes my stomach churn, like overly fresh linens and the ever lingering scent of vodka. Might as well get used to this feeling of paranoia. Looking over my shoulder is likely going to be my newest, most prominent hobby, and I have the distinct feeling everything about him will follow me like a ghost.

My turn signal is the only sound echoing inside the cab of my car, the repeating click offering the small comfort I need to keep my breathing in check. My heart rate has slowed significantly, matching that of my blinker, but the fear remains. Fear I may never be able to outrun - no matter how hard I try. That realization hits when I remind myself for the hundredth time that not all monster hide in the darkness. Sometimes they're the man who promised to always keep you safe.

What a fucking joke.

Not intending to listen to nothing but my thoughts on however long this ride lasts, I put on some music. *'lovely'* by Billie Eilish fills the space and I sink into my seat a little, allowing the soft opening of the song to settle my wild thoughts.

Twenty minutes into the drive I try to rationalize the last six years, how I managed to let so many things slide - how I could ignore so many red flags. Red flags seen by not only me at times, but family and friends as well. My relationship with my parents has faltered, something I promised myself I would never let happen. I don't even have that many close friends anymore, all of the ones I had got too tired of watching me waste my life away I suppose.

Can't say I blame them.

I heave a sad sigh, knowing that it's my fault things escalated the way they did, but also knowing the victim always blames themselves. I can't bring myself to relive what happened tonight, because if I do I'll probably vomit. Nausea rolls in my stomach again, and I know I need to stop somewhere soon to check my wound.

A wound that wouldn't be there if you had left a long time ago.

Before quietly sneaking out of the house, I managed to grab a few necessities and my purse, forgoing everything else. Everything in that house is tainted, my clothes - the ones he always picked out for me to wear, and my perfume - which I never liked the smell of anyways. He told me he loved Japanese cherry blossoms the most, so that's what I wore. The furniture - that he bought and always reminded me was his, a not so secret enjoyment he held over me. Even the cat was a cranky old bastard who would hiss at me every time I walked past.

One of the first red flags was meeting said cat and hearing that his name was Lucifer. Like the modern day version of Scar from *The Lion King* - little fucker was bound to be an asshole.

Nothing in that house, or that town, is worth keeping, and unfortunately the one thing I wish I could leave behind is forever burned into my brain. The very marrow of my bones can't get rid of the memories, the *trauma*. The only thing I needed to take with me, aside from the detailed notebook I kept to document the abuse, was the hope that some of my sanity is still intact and that I can in fact walk away from this only partly scathed.

The dishrag blotted under my shirt is soaked, and even though I know it needs tending to, I keep driving. I can't take the chance of him catching up to me and dragging me back to hell. Kicking and screaming wouldn't stop him either, the maniac got off on scaring me.

Some things may look like heaven on the outside, when lurking beneath the perfect facade is a grim reality that life is not always pretty. My relationship with Grant the last six years has been the perfect depiction of that line in one of Taylor Swift's songs, *'cause darling I'm a nightmare dressed like a daydream.'* Ha, if only people really knew.

Two hours after leaving, the sun is slowly rising, casting a warm glow on the car as I race down the highway. Taking a few minutes to bask in it, I focus on the sun warming my face, rather than the blood soaking through my shirt. I check the back seat and thank God I have a back up sweatshirt in here. Wouldn't want to walk out covered in my own blood like a neon sign that says 'hey, look at me!' That kind of negative attention will guarantee me the one thing I wish to avoid. Cops. Most of the ones in town were friends with Grant, so even if I ever tried to press charges against him, they never would have gotten me any reassurance. It would have done more damage than good.

Signaling, I take the exit off to the right and pull into a gas station, choosing this one only because there's hardly anyone here. Could be because this town seems quiet, or it could be because it's only five in the morning. Either way, it seems like the safest option and I really can't put off cleaning this wound any longer. If I do, it'll for sure reach the hem of my jeans and I don't have any other clothes aside from the ones I'm wearing.

Easing into the little store - bells jingling above me startling me slightly - I make my way down the aisles looking for medical supplies. Junk food and candy grabs my attention, causing my stomach to growl just by proximity. I can't even remember the last time I ate anything. By the time Grant finally passed out it was well past midnight. I sat in a chair watching him for hours before I got the courage to quietly leave, hoping I could get away before him waking.

With a handful of snacks and a few bottles of water I gaze around feeling the eye of the cashier on me as I go. I hate this fear instilled in me, like every man I come across is out to hurt me. It's what I get for putting so much trust, so much of my life, in the hands of the wrong man. I don't want to live my life in fear, but uneasiness settles in my belly, the hairs on my neck coming to stand at attention. It always feels like I'm being watched.

After a few minutes perusing the aisles I realize all the first aid supplies are kept behind the counter where the grumpy old man with wandering eyes sits, watching me like I'm a criminal. If only I could spew my thoughts to him, tell him about the man I've just escaped. Tell him about the terrible things I've had to endure these last four years. Because the first two with Grant were bliss, almost as if he was reeling me in, earning my trust and vulnerability just to crush me. Once he had me, he knew, and only then did the abuse begin.

I should be happy this man is looking at me with contempt rather than interest. That thought has my skin crawling faster than the centipede skating across the grimy tiled floors of the bathroom in this place.

Clenching the hem of my sweatshirt between shaky fingers, I round the corner heading for the register. After placing my items down, I point to the top shelf where I see a dusty first aid kit. Even if the contents are expired, it has to be better than letting the wound I'm sporting under my shirt right now fester. If I don't do something soon, infection will set in and I'll wish I had done anything besides letting it be.

"T-the uh, first aid kit up there, p-please." I glance down, trying to reel in my emotions so I don't appear as spooked as I feel. This man has seen a lot in his days, judging by his rugged exterior. I'm sure a frail looking woman like myself doesn't raise any concerns for him.

As I look up, he's already turning and reaching for the first aid kit, placing it on the counter before ringing up my other items. "Nine seventy-two young lady." He drawls, and my eyebrows pinch. I look over my items again, mentally doing the math knowing he missed something. But before I can protest, he kindly glides the first aid kit towards me and glances back at the contents of my junk food in the brown paper bag. Nodding his head in understanding, he simply repeats, "nine seventy-two."

Tears build behind my bruised eyelids, here I was fearful of this man, thinking he was eyeballing me or sizing me up as some criminal. Turns out he's just another human being, maybe someone who has seen his fair share of wounded travelers, stopping into his small town gas station for a small slice of solace. Running from whatever ghosts haunt them in life, looking for something to keep them moving forward.

Whatever look was on my face as I walked into his establishment gave him all the words I could never speak. All the information he needed as I requested the one and only first aid kit he has stocked on his shelves. No one stops into a store like this in the middle of nowhere in search of a kit this size. If someone needed a bandaid they could either tough it out, or just buy a small box. What I need is actual medical attention, something I can't get right now, and this is the closest thing to it.

Swiping at the phantom tears under my eyes that thankfully haven't fallen, I pull out a ten dollar bill handing it over with a soft smile. As he goes to make the change, I grab my items and nod my head, almost like we have a silent understanding of the other. Turning on my heels, I move toward the front door and stop when I hear the man clear his throat.

"You be careful out there, young lady." That's all he says before I nod once more and slip through the door, making my way back to my car. My image is visibly scarred, a massacred portrait of anguish painted into my features on display for viewers of all kind. As I pull out of the gravel lot, I remind myself that the next time I come in contact with someone, I'll need to hide my canvas of pain a little better.

————

Long car rides have never been something I enjoy, and in this particular case, I loathe them. I've been driving nearly eight hours straight, aside from my quick pit stop at the gas station. After pulling away, I drove a few miles before idling on the side of the road to clean the cut on my stomach. The stinging has subsided a bit, but in it's place is a nagging throbbing sensation radiating from my belly button up to between my breasts. I need to keep going, but I just can't bear the thought of any more driving.

Portland is a good eight hour drive from here, so even though Grant knows I'm gone by now, he would never be able to figure out which direction I went. I hope.

I was careful not to leave a paper trail, paying only cash for the snacks and gas I needed to get me here, Chelan County Washington. Or more specifically, Stehekin Washington, *the heart of the North Cascades*, as the sign in front of me reads.

I've never been this far north before, or anywhere for that matter. Once I met Grant, he was careful to keep me close to him at all times. Which is why I haven't visited my parents in years. Even our phone calls became infrequent over time. Once I'm settled, wherever the fuck that is, I'll find a way to contact them. Aside from my living arrangements, I need to get a new phone. Before hightailing it out of my house in the middle of the night, I removed my sim card and smashed my phone on the front steps. A clear sign to Grant that I planned on drifting away with the wind and that he shouldn't come looking for me.

That inner bitch voice of mine sneers at me, knowing for damn sure, he will in fact come looking for me, and he won't give up until I'm his again. "Fuck that," I mutter to myself.

Fear and paranoia roll through my stomach, something I need to acquaint myself with, because after the hell I've been through, those two things are going to be my most prominent personality traits.

Four hours into the drive I kept thinking about how weak I've allowed myself to become. Because of a man, no less. My parents raised me to be an independent, strong woman. The one good thing about cutting contact with them, is they didn't have to see their little girl deteriorate into this shell I've become. Angry tears poured from my eyes in rivulets, dripping from my chin and soaking into my shirt, mixing with the blood stains. As the two liquids pooled together the anger became more intense. But myself, and my inner monologue, know the only way to fight back is to be the strongest version of myself.

This is not it.

In the midst of all the chaos, I hadn't even thought as far ahead as my job. My only thoughts at the time were "get out".

Easing into the quant little town off the interstate, I see a cafe and make my way inside for something to eat. Junk food is great in theory, but not when it becomes your only source of sustenance for two days. Blissful Brews, small but cozy, layered with the aroma of coffee beans and cinnamon, wraps me in a warm hug of comfort. I may stay here just to frequent this coffee shop regularly.

People chatter all around me, only a few glancing up to gaze at me as I walk past, slowly, I might add. My steps feel heavy, like my sneakers are caked in concrete, keeping me from walking with confidence and sureness. As I take a seat on one of the worn stools at the counter, creaking as I pivot my body to lean on the counter, an older lady approaches me. Her smile is warm, with wispy gray hair swirling around her as she moves with ease behind the counter, refilling coffee and chatting as she goes.

She reminds me of my grandma, her demeanor radiates with warmth and kindness, and she hasn't even spoken a word yet. I can just see it in her eyes, a person who has been through shit herself in life and has managed to keep a genuine smile painted on her wrinkled face. If I could hug her without coming across like a maniac who traipsed in here with blood stained clothes, mascara smudged eyes and a nasty bruise blooming on my cheekbone, I would.

If she senses any discomfort or hesitation in my eyes, she doesn't acknowledge it, simply smiles and places a coffee mug down in front of me as she fills it. "You look like you need a nice cup of hot coffee, dear." Jesus, even her voice is like those velvety caramel candies my grandma always carried around in her purse. I wonder if she'd let me adopt her as my new Grams.

Smiling, I pull the hot mug towards me, ignoring the creamer and sugar sitting right in front of me. Inhaling a deep breath, I allow the steam from the coffee to penetrate my senses, drinking me in as much as I plan to drink it in.

"Thank you," I whisper sheepishly. I don't even remember how to interact with people normally, something else Grant took from me. He smothered any capabilities I had to converse with people, preferring to speak for me in public places. I wasn't even allowed to order my own food at restaurants towards the end. I became too afraid to protest whatever choice he made for me, even if I didn't like it, for fear of his backlash. All speaking up ever did for me was earn myself a new bruise.

Reaching behind her, she grabs a menu and tells me to take my time and to choose whatever I want. I feel tears brim my eyes, and choke down the emotion before she, or anyone else notices. "First time customers are on the house, so you go on and choose as much as you like," she pats my hand with a gentleness and a knowing look that tells me I'm not hiding my turmoil as much as I think I am. So much for hiding my canvas of pain.

"Names June, dear, holler when you're ready."

She whisks to the back as a bell dings, indicating the next order is ready. The menu is small, focusing on the classics, and my stomach growls at the anticipation of a hot meal. Deciding on eggs, scrambled, with toast and bacon on the side, I wait for her to reappear, the thought of yelling for her never coming to mind. In fact, I would sit here for an hour waiting quietly if that's what it took to place my order.

"All set?" She asks, startling me as she bustles up to me pad and pen in hand ready.

"Yes, I…" I'm cut off briefly as a younger guy strolls in, demanding attention from all the patrons present as he yells out June's name. I hide my chuckle when I notice her slight eye roll at the intrusion, before she glances back to me with an apologetic smile.

"Alex, keep your voice down, this young lady here was just about to place her order. Oh, and no one enjoys your antics anymore, you punk." June doesn't even glance over at him, just keeps her playful gaze on me, almost as if she's silently letting me in on their little banter.

Leaning both elbows on the counter next to me, he smirks at her before speaking up once more. "Aunt June, you and I both know you love when I come in here causing a ruckus. Just like the old days," he winks at her and I don't miss the way she shakes her head in denial, but smiles as if it's nothing but the truth.

"Shut it," she swats, then focuses back on me. "Don't mind him, what'll you have, dear?"

"The eggs and bacon please, scrambled if that's not too much trouble." I glide the menu back towards her, cursing myself for not mentioning the toast when she pipes up, asking what kind of toast I want. An angel. That's what this woman is.

"It's on the house, remember? I don't want you fussing over money, you hear me?" I nod, accepting the kind gesture just as Alex, I assume since that's what June called him, looks at me. My skin tightens against my frail body, and I feel perspiration form on my brows. Men were not allowed to look at me, if Grant ever caught one gazing at me, *I* was the one who would pay the price.

He had this delusion that it was my fault for being too beautiful, and that's why other men wanted me. Each time that happened, I would wake up the next morning with new bruises to wear, so that any man who took one look at me knew to look away immediately. As if I was damaged goods, and the markings were my Scarlett letter. The look in their eyes ranged from disgust to pity, and each time it tore me down just a little more.

This man looks at me with nothing but kindness, and it almost freaks me out more than if he looked at me with contempt. What could he possibly see in me right now that would cause him to smile like that? His voice startles me at first, a deep timbre, laced with utter happiness. This man is an optimist, happy to be alive.

I gave up on that feeling a long time ago.

"I haven't seen you around before. You new in town or just passing through? And before you think that's a pick up line, it's not," he winks then smirks with the most adorable dimple I've ever seen.

June comes out with my food already, steam billowing out of the eggs in a silent beacon. My mouth waters instantly, and I momentarily forget the company to my left. "Oh, don't lie to the poor girl, you menace. Anyone in the world can tell what that was. Leave her be and let her enjoy her meal, while it's hot." She fixes him with a *"don't mess with me"* stare and I hide my smile, again.

Holding his hands up in mock surrender, Alex just smiles and nudges my shoulder until I give him my attention. "I'm harmless, and she knows it," he slides off the stool and waves to a gentleman down the end of the counter as he heads for the door, turning back just once to connect those bright blue eyes with me. My face heats and I look down at my hands, wringing them in my lap, until I hear the bell above the door chime and the tension in the room lessens significantly.

He smelt like sunshine. Like the kind of man who works outside with strong veined hands. Judging by the tan he was rocking, even on a cloudy day like today, his skin glistened with a touch of sun. Sunshine and something else I can't quite put my finger on, cedar maybe, is now burned into my senses. The most alluring combination, and one I most definitely don't want to be close enough to smell again.

Everything about him screamed soft, sweet. His face was smooth under the sweeping of dark blonde hair, and that dimple reminded me of an innocent young boy finding worms in the dirt. Sure he comes off as a flirt, but in the harmless sense. Surely a woman like June who has offered me my first real meal in days, for free, wouldn't look so at ease if he were trouble. I feel oddly at peace in here, something that's become so foreign to me.

My battered heart and soul shouldn't even register the smell of another man, and the way his muscles rippled beneath the hem of his grey t-shirt as he laughed. But I'll just chalk it up to a physical reaction, nothing more.

The eggs have cooled a little, and I chance my first bite. These eggs could be the most basic display of breakfast foods, with no salt or cheese, and I would devour them like a five star meal. As my tongue tastes the first pop of flavor, I feel my eyes bug, dancing with the sound of the groan my body unwillingly lets slip free. Embarrassment coats my cheeks, and I chance a look up to see if anyone near me just heard my food orgasm. The man at the end of the counter Alex waved at is the only person within a few feet of me, and he seems unfazed.

In two minutes, my plate is more than half empty as June makes her way over to refill my coffee cup. "I'd be willing to bet you enjoyed those," she remarks as she pivots her gaze to my nearly empty plate. I cover my full mouth with the back of my hand as I smile through the wad of toast currently occupying the small space, nodding my head.

On a swallow, I wipe my mouth with a napkin and praise the eggs that once graced my plate before I ate them like a starved man. "I think those were the best eggs I've ever had," I admit. "Could also be because I've been eating vending machine junk the last two days, but something tells me that's not it."

My cheeks flush again when June says nothing but smiles at me knowingly. I feel like I may have just said some kind of back handed compliment, and now I feel the need to scramble backwards and correct myself. Another tick in the cons column of things Grant has instilled in me.

Fucking asshole.

"I'm sorry, I didn't mean to imply they weren't actually very good. They really were exceptional, please tell the cook." My ramble ends on a whisper as June squeezes my hand reassuringly again.

"Oh honey, workin' yourself up over silly things will give you grays. I should know," she winks at me and shouts over her shoulder to the cook. "Hey Len! This young lady here says those eggs were the best she's ever had. Try not to let that information go straight to your head."

"Thank you. It's been a long few days, my mind is clearly too tired to keep up with my mouth."

"Well your manners seem to be in the front seat, which is always good in my book, hon." She starts collecting my dirty dishes, placing them in a bucket for the kitchen person to clean. "I noticed Alex was asking about your traveling plans. I don't mean to eavesdrop, but if you are plannin' to stay, there's an inn just down the road. Good place to rest that mind of yours," she smiles knowingly.

Seriously, would it be too weird to ask this woman to take me in? I only just met her and something tells me I'd feel more safe in her presence after one hour, than I have in the last six years. I'm too afraid to admit that staying at the inn would only draw attention to myself, attention I can't have on me. I had enough cash in my purse to get me here, but certainly not enough to pay for a hotel room.

Sensing my hesitation, she pipes up again. "Tell you what, why don't you come to my house after my shift here ends in an hour. I've got an ancient computer, but it still works and maybe we can figure out your next move."

"I-I couldn't possibly impose." I want to say more, but I don't even know what else to say. I really do need help. As much as I wish I could pride myself on getting out of this shit situation I've gotten myself into, I don't think I have it in me.

"Hush now. We take care of people in this town, and Alex there is one of the good ones. As much as that boy gets under my skin, he's a good kid with a heart of gold. His brother on the other hand…" she waves her hand dismissively. "Well, let's just say he's not a bad apple as much as he's just quiet."

As much as it kills me to say, I'm intrigued by that. June has a knowing look, again. Jesus is this woman psychic? Fuck. No. This is how I got into my previous predicament, if you can call it that, with Grant. He was charming, and that intrigued me so much in the beginning. I felt like he was too good to be true, and turns out my gut was right. If I have any smarts left in me, I'll stay away from the mystery man known as Alex's brother.

I don't even know their last name, which is definitely a good thing. Plus, I'm not staying here.

I'm not.

———

Leaning against my car, I wait for June to finish work and exit the front doors. A set of doors that have changed my whole life somehow. I could have kept driving, past this town, until I fell asleep at the wheel and ended it all. Morbid, I know, but the thought did cross my mind.

Just like she said, an hour later she's shuffling out the door with a large bag that reminds me of *Mary Poppins* and her ever present smile. "Ready to go, darlin'?" She asks in that honey sweet voice of hers. I know she has a rough edge to her, probably a side not many have seen, and if they have, they won't want to again. June is a no bullshit kind of woman, and I respect the hell out of that. Maybe she can teach me a thing or two about standing up for myself.

"Are you sure you're alright with this, June? I really don't mean to impose." My polite mouth is getting an internal kicking from my brain that's currently screaming for it to shut the fuck up. I need the help right now, more than ever, and if June somehow decided this wasn't a good idea, I'd be royally fucked.

Despite the disconnect with my parents, I had a really good childhood and upbringing. They raised me to be respectful and inclusive to all, especially the ones who seemed to not fit in. When I met Grant and saw how kindly he treated other people, it felt like a welcoming beacon home. A place with a safe person who cared about the well being of others. Turns out he truly does, just not the woman he's in a romantic relationship with.

It took months before the possessive behavior started coming out, and even longer for the actual abuse to begin. By then he already had his hooks in me so deep, I was hopeful he would change if I loved him enough. Stupid little girl.

June clears her throat lightly, pulling me from my thoughts and tugs my arm. "Why don't you ride with me, yeah? We can come back for your car later." She's leading me to her cute little Honda sedan and unlocking it before I have a second to protest. If she turns out to be some cunning serial killer, that would be the ultimate plot twist in the fucked up story that is my life.

She puts the key in the ignition turning the car over, and slowly pulls out of the cafe lot. On my way into town I hadn't noticed too much in the surrounding area, my eyes were tired and I knew I need something to eat, fast.

As I look around outside I realize how charming and quaint this little town truly is. It feels almost like a storybook, the kind where the air is always a little dense from the fog and cloud coverage, giving it an eerie vibe. I used to love fairytales as a little girl, in some ways I still do, just darker now. My life having taken such a dark turn must be the reason behind that.

June is chattering on about who lives here and there, comforting me in ways she can't know. Just the simplicity of a normal conversation, without the fear of pissing off Grant, is like warm honey. I use to pray I was invisible, that no one would notice me. Because when they did, it never went well for me. But here, talking animatedly with a woman I know nothing about, feels like the first piece of normalcy I've had in years.

"How long have you lived here?" I ask as we pass a gravel parking lot with a scenic outlook, it's breathtaking here. It's drizzling out, and the cloud coverage is low, hiding the tops of the mountains. But it's serene in it's own spooky way. I'm not sure I'd ever get used to living in a place like this.

"Born and raised. Once you live in a town like this, it's impossible to leave. I've done some travelin' here and there, but nothing outside the US. Isn't that somethin'?" She wonders more to herself, keeping her gaze fixed on the winding road ahead. "An old lady like me, never leaving the country. Ah, probably for the best. I was needed here."

That admission has a dozen questions floating around my head, all of them pertaining to Alex and his mystery brother. I keep telling myself I don't care, and I don't. But for some reason, I know that's a lie. I must be a masochist, wanting to put myself in dangerous situations. I should have some tests done, clearly I'm not well.

Pulling myself from my thoughts to keep conversing with her, so I don't seem odd going radio silent every time she speaks, I comment on the beauty of Stehekin. "I can see why you love it here, or why you stayed at the very least. The scenery alone is amazing. And if most people around here act like you, then I imagine it's a pleasant place to be."

"Sweet of you to say, dear. It is a great place to live, but like everywhere, it has it's secrets." Okay? Ominous comment count is rising with each passing minute

I spend with this woman. June is exactly what you'd expect a sweet toffee eating Grandma to look like, but underneath is a story.

"What do you mean, exactly?" I ask, even though a part of me doesn't want to know. I have enough secrets lurking beneath my skin, ready to spill out at any minute. I don't need to be the keeper of anyone else's secrets.

"Nothing important, just a saying," she chuckles to herself, and even though I know there's more to that than she's letting on, I drop it.

We drive down a heavily wooded street, the tall pine trees intimidating in their nature. I've never seen woods like this, eerie, yet oddly peaceful. I don't think about weather too much, or how it makes me feel, but being here makes me want to reevaluate myself more and more. The things I thought I knew and liked, seem foreign to me. The people I thought I could trust and were safe with, betrayed that. Like these trees, I need to find my place and put down roots.

It may not be here, but I'll find a place to belong someday. I hope.

"Well, here we are," June declares, putting the car in park and cutting the engine. Her house it a quaint little cottage, nestled between massive trees. God, I wouldn't want to be here in case one of these monsters falls down.

The front path weaves up to cobble stone steps, flanked by beautiful rose bushes and other plants. June unlocks the front door, opening it up to reveal a cozy space, the smell of wood burning in the air. Inhaling deeply, I feel my muscles relax for the first time in who knows how long. The space is an open concept, her living room shifting right into a dining area and kitchen, with an island and stools in between. There's no clutter, not a mess of knick knacks lining the shelves, just vintage pictures in brass frames. You would think I'd feel some uneasiness walking into a strangers home, but my gut tells me this woman is one of the good ones.

"Your home is lovely," I tell her, meaning it genuinely. I could spend forever here, reading by the fire in comfy clothes, wrapped in a blanket with hot cocoa in hand. If someone wanted to get away from their problems and every day life, it would be to June's place. It reminds me a lot of Kate Winslet's house in *The Holiday*. A Maine coon cat wanders over, stretching once before brushing up against my legs, purring louder than an old car.

"Thank you honey, that there is Melvin. He's about as laid back as a cat can be, if you can believe that. Pretty sure he's more of a dog, but what the hell would I know." I giggle to myself picturing June walking into a vet's office saying her cat is acting strange, and might actually be a dog.

"I've never been much of a cat or dog person, my dad was allergic so we didn't have pets growing up." I curse myself for mentioning my parents, I don't want to dive into that deep hole just yet. Again, my relationship with them has always been good, but now that we're estranged, I don't know if they even miss me. How sad is that? I ruined more relationships than I can count, just to save the *one* that never should have counted in the first place.

June busies herself in the kitchen, putting on a kettle of tea. I don't miss the bottle of whiskey she pulls down from a cabinet above, though, and I laugh a little. Age is just a number, and thank god for that, because June might just be my new best friend. As she goes about getting the tea ready, I look around her living space, noticing lots of framed photographs littering the walls and furniture. June is clearly family oriented, I would hate to imagine what her thoughts about my current family status would be. Then again, she doesn't seem like the type of woman to judge another's life choices.

The wallpaper adorning the walls is light and cheery, which works beautifully with the dark wood trim and beams above. Her home is lived in, and every square inch is warm and inviting. Glancing out one of the back windows through the kitchen, I notice two other houses. One small and humble, like June's, and the other larger in size, with a gothic vibe to it.

The rambling victorian was probably black in it's early years, but has now faded to a dark gray. Large windows take place around a grand front door, and I have to wonder why June lives here, instead of there. Sure, it's creepy on the outside, but I'm willing to bet the interior has more charm than a southern man picking up women at a bar.

"June, I'm sorry if this is forward, but why don't you live in that house there?" I ask as I look back out the window. I got the sense this whole property is hers, so why wouldn't the house behind her be hers as well?

"Oh gosh, that mess? The bones are good, but that house fell into disrepair so many years ago, I could never devote the time to fixing it up. A damn shame too, it was beautiful in it's prime." The tea pot whistles on the stove, stealing June's attention once again. Staying rooted to the spot, I watch the house for several minutes. What I wouldn't give to see it fixed up to it's potential.

"Tea?" June says from beside me as she sits down at the small round table centered in her kitchen. I take the seat across from her, noticing there's three seats, rather than four like most set ups have.

"Yes, please," I respond while holding a mug between my hands for the warmth. I can't get rid of the chill that has embedded itself so far into my bones, I'm like a walking ice cap. "Thank you again, June, I truly can't express my gratitude enough. You've been so kind."

"People ought to be kinder, you never know what someone is going through these days," she eyes my over the rim of her glasses holding up the bottle of whiskey. I nod my agreement and focus on the steam billowing out of the mug as June reaches over and subtly slips some honey whiskey into my mug.

"At my age I've learned to be frank, say what's on my mind and get the tough shit out of the way first and foremost. That alright with you?"

My eyes meet hers over the brim of the mug as I'm about to take a slow sip. I knew she was smart, there was no way she missed my deer in headlights eyes when I first walked into the cafe, or how I had a shake that had nothing to do with the cold.

"Honey, I've seen a lot in my days. I can tell you're running from something. Now, whether that be literally or figuratively, I'd like to help," she sips her tea, rustling through the stacks of newspaper on the table, pushing them aside into a neat pile.

"You don't need to get into the dirty details, but you've been through some shit, could sense it the minute you walked into my place. It ain't always easy accepting help, especially from a stranger, no less. But when I was young, I had my fair share of shit thrown at me, and I had to climb out all on my own. I don't want you to have to do the same."

Silent tears slip down my cheeks, and I can't even feel embarrassment from them. These tears are entirely different from the ones I've been shedding the last few years. Maybe everything I went through was to get me here, to this town with this woman. I don't believe in fate, but the warmth spreading through my chest at her kindness just might make me a believer after all.

ISOLDE

chapter two

Indigo • Sam Barber

I wake up to the sound of birds chirping in the nearby trees, and as I focus even more, I can hear a babbling stream not far away. The room is quaint and cozy, and as soon as my head hit the pillow last night, I was out. Blame it on exhaustion and sleeping in the car for the better part of twenty four hours, or the emotional trip I took with June.

I opened up about everything with Grant, telling her more things than I've probably ever told my own mother. Guilt gnaws at me for that, but I try to tell myself it's better to tell a stranger than the woman who birthed me. Hearing the grave details will just hurt my parents, and that is the last thing I want to do.

June insisted I stay with her until we get something more permanent figured out for me. Just the thought of her kindness and hospitality has tears springing to my eyes as I lay here in her spare bedroom. The queen is a soft mattress with the perfect amount of firmness, topped with a down comforter to ward against the chill of the morning. I want nothing more than to burrow down, hiding in this room for the foreseeable future, but that's not how I want to live my life.

Hiding will only do one thing. Prove that he won. That he was able to get beneath my skin and steal everything of meaning, everything I value. I don't want to allow him to take *me*.

Forcing myself up, I move to the bathroom connected between this room and June's, giving the door a soft knock before stepping in and flicking on the lights. I'm immediately struck with my appearance in the mirror above the vanity. The girl standing there looking at me, looks nothing like the woman I once knew. This girl is weathered and weak. Tears pool in my eyes, but I refuse to let them fall.

Squaring my shoulders, inhaling deeply, I brush my teeth, splash water on my face and decide here and now that I want a change, whatever that may be. I need it now more than ever.

Considering I left in such a hurry, I wasn't able to pack a bag of clothes or toiletries. June was kind enough to loan me some of her nieces things that got left here from years of visits. Guess it was my luck we happen to be similar sizes.

Slipping on the jeans and oversized sweater, careful not to bump the bandaged cut on my stomach, I make my way down the hallway, inhaling the fresh aroma of coffee and bacon. "June, it smells amazing in…" my words cut off when I see a man already helping himself to a stack of bacon.

Swatting him with her spatula, June faces me as she reminds him of his manners. "Good morning dear! Sorry, he's a bit of an animal, as you can see," she says pointedly at him before turning back to the stove.

"It's okay," I chuckle as I take the seat across from him. "Alex, right?"

"In the flesh," he grins widely, flashing me his perfectly straight white teeth. When I met him in the cafe yesterday, I was so flustered and embarrassed about my situation, I didn't get a good look at him. He's handsome, insanely handsome now that I'm close enough to study his features. Strong and confident bright blue eyes stare back at me as I take him in. When he clears his throat I blush, embarrassed that I was caught staring. I was checking him out and he knows it.

"Like what you see darlin'?"

"Alex," June warns from at the stove where she flips pancakes. "You keep those man whore comments to yourself, Isolde doesn't need you flirting with her every time she turns a corner."

He laughs as he looks back to his plate before shoveling a mouthful of bacon in, holding his hands up in surrender like he meant no harm. I should feel uncomfortable, but oddly, I don't. I can tell he doesn't mean anything by his comment, that it's just in his nature.

"It's fine, I can handle a little playfulness," I concede before sipping on my cup of coffee. The warmth from the mug travels from my hands down my chest and the liquid finds it's way through me. An odd thing to think about, but that first sip is always the best.

"Careful what you wish for, dear. Alex here is known as the ladies man around town."

"Jesus, Aunt June, at least keep it a secret until she learns for herself," he replies with a wink.

"Honey, you walk by a woman and she can practically smell it on you," June laughs, and I can't help but join in. Sitting here with them, the whole setting, is oddly comforting and for once I feel like I belong in a sense, like I'm welcome.

Alex focuses back on me, squaring his shoulders and quirking a brow, I just know he has questions formulating in that brain of his. "So, Isolde huh? That's quite an old school name."

"Yeah, you could say that. My parents wanted something unique for me, not a name every other girl in school had. I gotta say, it didn't help me win any popularity contests, though," my laughter sounds sad. It's true, when I was little I loved my name. But as soon as I made it to grade school, the comments started. I felt like the real life version of Chrysanthemum, the little mouse from that children's book.

Some were innocent, where kids would purposefully pronounce it wrong just to irritate me, then they got worse once some girls figured out the meaning of Isolde. I would get called the Ice Queen, cold hearted and all kinds of other things. Some kids even went as far as pretending to turn to ice if I even touched them slightly.

I'm pulled from my thoughts when Alex places a gentle hand over my trembling one. Memories from the past stir up a lot of emotions for me, and lately I can't afford anymore breakdowns. "For the record, I think it's beautiful."

His comment sounds like another attempt at flirting, but something in his eyes tells me he's being sincere. Like maybe he understands in a way. That's all I can hope for these days, someone to just understand me. Isn't that all any of us hopes for? To be understood and seen?

A blush creeps over my fair skin, giving me away instantly, and Alex's eyes light up like Christmas morning. I must have missed the part where men like to make women blush and take it as a conquest. What the hell would I know? I wasn't even aloud to speak to other guys while dating Grant.

June comes over with a steaming plate of pancakes, making my mouth water instantly. I can't even remember the last time I had pancakes and bacon. My body is used to consuming mostly organic and healthy choices, my mind is having a hard time understanding that amazing smell isn't just a tease. I used to be more tone and strong, but over the years my body has taken on a frail look, my skin so fair I'm practically translucent.

"I can't even remember the last time I had pancakes. If these are anything like the breakfast I had at your diner yesterday, I think I'll stay a while." Grabbing my knife and fork, I cut a good size piece of pancake watching the steam billow out from the middle, and take a bite. The involuntary groan that leaves my mouth catches both Alex and June's attention, and I'd be more embarrassed if I wasn't so focused on the flavor erupting on my tongue. Yeah, I could get used to eating like this.

"Guess I don't need to ask how they are," June grins, turning away from us so she's focused at the stove again.

"June makes the best pancakes. I've tried asking her the secret, or what she puts in them even, but she's a vault." Alex shovels heaping amounts of food in his mouth like it's his last meal, sparing me a glance every so often. Other than that one comment, we eat mostly in silence. Just the sound of June humming by the stove as she flips pancakes.

There's a giant stack sitting on the counter, and I hope to God she doesn't expect me to eat all of those. Alex probably could, but I've had three and my stomach already feels distended. Not to mention, the cut running up my abdomen isn't feeling all to great as it is.

Sensing my slight discomfort, Alex looks down to where I'm holding the wounded spot, and his eyes bulge out slightly before he fixes his expression.

"Did you know you have blood on your shirt?" His voice is calm, but his body is tense. Maybe blood makes him queasy. As I'm about to formulate a lie, June whips around placing more food in front of him.

"Don't go asking questions you don't want the answers to. Now, eat up and get out of here. Aren't you meeting up with your brother today?"

June winks at me and I release a relieved breath, thankful she distracted Alex just enough that I didn't have to go into detail about the blood on my shirt. Time to change the bandage again, I suppose.

"Yeah, yeah. I'm in no rush."

"What are you boys up to today?" June wonders as she finally takes a seat to join us at the table.

I can't imagine another man like Alex. Maybe they're nothing alike, but if they share any similarities in the slightest, then this town sure has it's fill of eye candy wandering around.

"The Whitaker's barn needs a new roof, so we're heading that way this morning. Meeting him there in..," he trials off, reaching into his pocket for his phone to check the time, "now." Standing up, he places his dirty dishes in the sink just as the rumbling of an engine sounds outside.

I crane my head to try and see outside, but it's futile. A large rose bush covers half the window making it difficult to make out the figure resting against what appears to be a motorcycle. His back is turned towards the house and smoke billows off to the side of his head as he lights a cigarette. I wait for him to turn around, hoping to see his face, but he doesn't budge. Just stands next to his bike, waiting.

I've never been on a motorcycle before, but it's secretly on my bucket list. Things on my bucket list aren't exactly thrilling to some, like skydiving or cliff jumping. But growing up in a quiet little town with no siblings and helicopter parents didn't exactly give me a lot of chances to tango with the dangerous side of myself.

Honestly, it's a part of me that I've buried so deep, I don't think it even exists anymore. When I was younger, I used to yearn for some kind of adventure, of any kind. My parents are amazing people, loving and protective, but sometimes I wish I could have escaped the bubble.

In a way, I guess I did. But instead of finding that fun adrenaline people look for, I found the actual dangerous kind. In the form of a charismatic man who turned out to be a cunning asshole.

I watch as Alex rinses his plate in the sink, before stepping over and placing a soft kiss on top of June's head. "Pancakes were great, as usual. One of these days I'm gonna get you to cave and share that damn recipe, June."

Chuckling into her coffee mug, she fixes him with a smirk, "fat chance, now get out of here, punk."

Approaching the front door, Alex turns back to me and winks. "See you soon, Isolde." And with that he's out the front door and quickly starting up his truck. I listen to both vehicles moving down the dirt road farther away from the house, until gone completely, only to turn around and find June looking at me with a knowing grin.

"What?" I ask, though I already know. "Did I spill syrup on myself?" Looking down to check, I remember my blood stained shirt and blush, feeling embarrassed for whatever reason.

June just shakes her head lightly, placing her mug on the table. "Come on dear, let's get that cleaned up."

***

June brings me to her doctor in town, a young nurse practitioner, who looks to be the same age as me. A pang of jealousy runs through me, feeling like a failure for not doing more with my life or career. I could have gone into medicine, I had the grades for it, but as soon as I met Grant in college, all plans went out the window.

He made me feel like I'd never have to lift a finger, I could live a comfortable life with him as his trophy wife. I can't even remember why that sounded good in the first place, and thinking about it again now makes me feel even dumber than back then.

"You must be Isolde, I'm Dr. Lennox. June told me a little about your situation over the phone. Do you mind if we take a look?" Her hand shake is firm, but soft, giving me a calming feeling instantly.

Years of abuse made me really good at detecting a persons aura, and if they seem trustworthy from the get go. Probably sounds a little hippie dippy, but I go with my gut more than anything these days. My head and heart got me nowhere.

"Yes, thank you for seeing me on short notice. I'm sure you're busy with other patients." God, can I sound any more pathetic? It's like meeting June in the diner all over again.

"Never too busy for someone who needs help, part of why I love my job," she smiles as she leads us down the hall into a small room with a medical bed and a wooden chair in the corner. A part of me was hoping June would come in, but the other part of me wants to act like an adult and handle my shit by myself. Even if June is the reason I'm being seen right now.

Hopping up on the table, enjoying the crinkle from the paper, I lean back so Dr. Lennox can assess my cut. As soon as she lifts the hem, exposing the tender and abused skin, her brows pull together. I knew it looked bad, but I'm not a doctor so I just figured I was overreacting. Seeing the look on her face right now tells me everything I need to know, without the words.

"When did this happen?" She asks as she pulls on a pair of gloves.

"A few days ago," I admit, turning scarlet from my ears down my chest, no doubt. "I wasn't exactly in a position to get medical attention right away." Not a lie, but also not entirely the truth. I left out the part where I'm currently running from my abusive ex boyfriend for assaulting me and tearing into my skin with his pocket knife while he raped me. That was the only detail I left out when I spilled my guts to June.

She rustles around in cabinets, pulling a numbing medicine and the supplies needed for stitches. My stomach twists with anticipation. I'm not afraid of the pain, that's something I've unwillingly grown accustomed to, but I've never had stitches before. The thought is unsettling.

"I'm going to clean it thoroughly, though I can tell you've done a decent job keeping it clean, so that's good. But if we don't stitch it up, infection can set in and that will make this feel like a paper cut," she laughs lightly at her own joke and I can't help but smile in return. She's making a shitty situation seem less drastic for my sake, and I appreciate the hell out of it.

"Once it's clean, I'll stitch from here," she lightly taps the top of the gash just below my breast line, "to here." Her fingers gently touch the torn skin just above my belly button.

"Since the length is pretty significant, you're going to need about thirty stitches." My eyes bulge out of my head and my tongue has dried so much it feels like it's lodged in my throat. Fucking hell, I knew it was bad, but my mind never went to this extreme. I downplayed this a lot more than I should have. The look on June's face when I showed her should have been a bigger wake up call than it was.

"I know that sounds like a lot, and it is, but I promise it'll be quick," she starts numbing the area, giving it a few minutes to set in, and my body relaxes. This is the first time in three days I haven't felt any kind of pain or throbbing in that spot. I was beginning to get used to it, but now that it's practically gone, I'm more than ready to get this going.

Forty five minutes and thirty two stitches later, I'm walking back into the waiting room where June sits reading. As soon as she sees me enter, she's dropping the book and rushing over to me. "Christ, you were back there so long I was starting to worry a little." She admits and my heart swells.

"I asked the nurse if I could go back and she said no, so I paced for a few minutes before getting sucked into a dirty romance novel." I laugh, feeling lighter than I have in years and on impulse lean in to hug her. She doesn't falter for a second, and returns the hug causing tears to gather in my eyes. I want to keep them at bay, refusing to let them fall like I'm so used to doing, but in this moment, I let them fall freely.

When she pulls back to look at me, she gently wipes the tears away and smiles. I can't help my smile in return and we both look to Dr. Lennox as she joins us in the waiting area.

Writing something down on her clipboard, she faces us with a small smile. "I'd like to see you again in a week and we can asses how the stitches look. If the wound is healing properly we can remove them, or wait a few more days. We'll see in a week, okay?"

"Yes, thank you so much Dr. Lennox, I don't know what I would have done if it wasn't for both of you," I murmur as I look to June again.

"None of that, now," she says as she wipes my tears away with her thumb. "I told you already, we take care of people around here."

"Agreed. And please, call me Hailey." I shake her hand once more and head to the front desk to make my appointment for next week. I don't know how the hell I plan to pay for this, since I'm still too afraid to access my accounts. I can't give Grant any idea where I am, because here is the first place he'll come, ready to drag me back.

To my surprise though, the nurse at reception doesn't ask me for any form of payment. I'm still frowning as we exit the building, walking back to June's car. She said she would bring me by the cafe to get mine, and that I can stay with her until I figure out my next move. Either she really is jut a fallen angel, or I'm beginning to think she's enjoying the company.

Buckling in, I look at June as she starts the car. "June?" She hums in response as she backs out of the parking spot, signaling left on the main road towards Blissful Brews. "Why didn't they ask for a form of payment?"

"Caught that, did ya?" That's all she says, focusing on the road without an explanation.

"Uh, yeah, it's kind of hard to miss. Dr. Lennox gave me thirty two stitches, a prescription for pain meds and I have another appointment in a week. They didn't even ask for my insurance card," I let the sentence hang in the air, hoping June will talk about this, because I still don't understand.

She doesn't say so much as a grunt of acknowledgment and a shrug of her shoulders. I know she said people around here look out for one another, and I'm grateful, but this is taking kindness to a whole other level. "June," I press, a little more firm, and she looks at me as she pulls in the cafe parking lot. "This is more than neighbors looking out for each other, we both know that. Care to fill in the blanks for me? Because I'm having a hard time accepting people are just this nice."

She cuts the engine and swivels in her seat to face me. I'm hoping for just a little insight, if nothing else. "That practice is in the family."

"In the family? As in it's yours?" She smiles sheepishly at me and I have to wonder if June is the founder of this damn town. She owns a large plot of land with multiple houses. She owns Blissful Brews and helps keep things running smoothly daily. Now she's telling me she owns the local medical practice? Where the hell did I wind up?

"Don't work yourself up over it, dear. My husband was the head doctor here, and when he died we kept it going. The doctors and nurse practitioners are practically family, and they all stepped up when Charles died."

"I'm so sorry, I had no idea," I whisper, feeling bad I said anything at all. "June this is so generous, but please, I don't feel right accepting free health care. Is there anything I can do to pay you for it?" I want to tell her I have money, I have health insurance too. But if I try to access any of that right now, it'll lead Grant right to me. And at this point, I don't believe he would just harm me. I get the feeling he would hurt anyone to get back at me.

"I've been thinking about your situation actually, and I think I've come up with a plan," she goes to exit the car, and I scramble with my own seat belt to catch up to her. The bell dings on the door above us as we enter the cafe. It's right before the lunch rush, so there's no one here yet. I follow June to the office in the back, closing the door behind me.

She sits at her desk, and waits for me to take the seat across from her. "What would you say if I had a way for you to stay here, have a private place to live, and a job?"

My jaw drops and I'm well aware that I'm openly gaping at her. There's no way this is happening. I'm the girl with bad luck, not *'meet the nicest woman on earth who turns outs to be my long lost fairy godmother.'* I slap my face lightly a few times, eliciting a chuckle from June. She's so calm and laid back, like my answer won't offend or bother her either way.

"You're getting in that head of yours again, dear. It's ultimately your choice, but

I'd really like to help you. And I really think you'd like my help, but are too afraid to ask for it. That asshole stole it from you, but I intend on helping you get it back."

I don't notice the tears gliding down my cheeks until June hands me a tissue. Wiping them away, I suck in a deep breath, holding it for a moment before nodding my head. My voice is too weak right now, so a nod is all I can manage.

"I was up late last night thinking of the perfect solution. Nothing was coming to mind, other than offering you a job at the cafe. Well, that's still part of the plan, but I wanted you to have some sense of independence. As I was rinsing my plate in the sink, I looked out the window and it struck me. The house!"

Her jubilant expression startles me slightly in this small space, and we both laugh. I'm still jumpy, so she lowers her voice to a normal decibel and begins explaining her plan.

"I don't know what experience you have in fixing up houses, but you mentioned it the other day and how you wish you could see it back up to it's potential. Well, I think you're just the person for the job!" She's so excited, I don't have the heart to tell her I've never even used a hammer.

"June, I'm honored you want me to fix up that beautiful house, but I don't have the slightest clue about construction. I'd end up tearing the house down accidentally before making it better."

"Not to worry about that. The boys can handle the heavy lifting and more complex situations. You can be in charge of repairing, stripping the wallpaper and decorating. I think it would be good for you to get your hands on a project that has meaning, and in the meantime, you can stay with me."

It makes sense, the wheels in my mind are turning, ideas bouncing around. Thinking of all the things I can do make the space feel like home. Maybe she's right, working hard towards something might bring me a kind of peace I've been missing for so long. I'm still worried about the renovations, and not knowing what the hell I should be doing, but she said the boys would help, so. Wait. *What boys?*

Clearing my throat, leaning forward on her desk, I lower my voice to ask. "What boys?" Surely she doesn't mean Alex and his mysterious brother, does she?

"Alex and Abram. They run a construction company together. Abram stays focused on the work and craftsmanship, Alex usually handles the clients, it's better that way," she adds and immediately I want to know what that means. Why is it better to have Alex handle their clients? I haven't even met his brother, who I now know is Abram, but already I get the sense he isn't a people person.

"Is he the one who rode up on the bike this morning?" I ask before I realize what I'm doing. Making it known to June that I'm intrigued, even just a little. The look on her face though isn't the same as it was earlier when Alex playfully flirted with me. That face was relaxed and at ease. The face she wears now is pinched, like it pains her to discuss him in a way.

Even though she brought up the possibility of me working with them. What would make her feel less inclined to answer questions about him? Every day I'm here I unravel another layer of information. These are good people, I can feel it in my gut, but they've been through some shit. I just don't know how bad or how long ago it might have been.

***

Until I can figure out a way to transfer my money to a bank here, June has given me a debit card to use from one of her accounts. Not going to lie, that took some strong arming to get me to agree, but ultimately she reminded me that I don't have another option right now. My only other option would result in Grant finding me, and she reminded me that was not a possibility she would allow.

I almost want to see how she would react if she came face to face with him, probably pull a gun from her purse and shoot him on the spot. I chuckle at the idea as I walk into the pharmacy, enjoying the feel of happiness for once. Even if said happiness stems from the pain of my abusive ex.

Now that I've been here for a few days, I need some necessities of my own to feel more balanced. It's been helpful staying with June and her loaning me whatever I need, but it's time I have my own stuff again. Like deodorant.

Pursuing the feminine hygiene aisle, I grab deodorant, a box of tampons because I'm due any day now, and a new toothbrush and toothpaste. I'll need to hit a clothing store too, but for right now I'm focusing on the basics. Again, it's not like I'm broke completely, but I don't want to take advantage of June's money. She's worked really hard to be where she is, and while I know now how well off she is, it still doesn't sit right with me to keep taking handouts.

Grabbing a few more things on my way to checkout, like chocolate covered pretzels, I notice a man at the counter with his back to me. Obviously I've never met him, because aside from June and Alex, I haven't met anyone yet. But as I get closer my skin tingles slightly, this must be Abram. The leather jacket looks just like the one I saw on him this morning as he leaned against his bike. Now that I'm close enough to him I can smell the leather and mint from his cigarettes, with a hint of smoke from a fire.

Fucking hell, he smells amazing. Turn around, I chant in my head over and over. I just want to see what he looks like, then I'll drop this whole being intrigued by him thing. I don't need to know anything else about him, or him in general. I just want to get a peak at his features, see how much him and Alex look alike. Maybe even get a feeling of why June wore that pinched expression earlier when she mentioned him.

The cashier quickly hands him his receipt without making eye contact, and I brace myself for him to turn around. Just as he's about to leave, I ready myself, waiting to lock eyes, if only momentarily. But I can't shake the feeling of disappointment when he doesn't even turn to acknowledge someone is behind him. Surely he can sense I was standing there, and at the very least turn around like any normal person would do.

I catch a glimpse of his profile, but just barely, as he makes his way for the door, striding outside and hefting one leg over his bike before speeding off. What the fuck? I don't even know why I care so much about this guy. Maybe because he hasn't made himself known like Alex did, and that mystery intrigues me more than I care to admit. I'm still staring at the door he left out of when the cashier politely clears her throat. "All set?"

Dropping my basket on the counter, quickly righting myself, I apologize and wait for her to ring in my items while I obsess over Abram. I've never cared so much about meeting one person before this, so why do I care now? I go over the small details I have about him as I walk back to my car with the bag of toiletries. Alex barely mentioned he had a brother, other than that they work together in construction. June also said next to nothing, but her facial expression said more than words ever could anyways.

He rides a motorcycle, handles the renovations on projects and steers clear of the clients. Oh, and he clearly isn't phased by my presence or the nervous energy rolling off the cashier as she rang him out. With Grant, he was charming and seemed to be smitten right from the get go, and look where that got me. Alex is playful, and though he too is charming, it's different than how it was with Grant. I don't get a slimy feeling covering my skin every time he looks at me.

Maybe my judgment of people is just too far off to even tell anymore. I'd like to think June really is as amazing as she appears to be, but I still know practically nothing about this family or this town. Deciding my next move, I turn into the grocery store parking lot a few blocks down, ready to put together a home cooked meal to express my gratitude. It's time I learn more about the people who selflessly took me in.

***

I'm close to the finishing touches as June walks through the door, dropping her bag and keys on the entryway table. I hear her shoes hit the floor then the shuffling of her slippers as she rounds the corner into the kitchen. The look on her face is all the satisfaction I need, especially if this dinner turned out like shit.

"Welcome home!" I squeal in excitement. I hope she isn't mad I took the liberty of cooking dinner in her home, with practically every dish and pan she had. But the slow smile spreading across her face as she clasps her hands in front of her tells me everything I hoped she'd feel. She's constantly doing so much for everyone else, me included now, and I wanted to give something back to her. I can't do much right now, but making her feel appreciated is something I can do.

"Please, have a seat. Everything is just about ready."

"Isolde, my dear. What have you done here?" She says lowering herself into her chair at the table, holding her wine glass steady as I pour a stream of red to fill it up.

"I already know what you're going to say, *'why did I work myself up'*, but I *wanted* to do something nice for you. Something to show you how grateful I am for these last few days. I haven't felt this at peace in such a long time, that alone is worth me making you dinner until my last breath."

Chuckling, she takes a healthy sip of wine and leans back in her chair, suddenly looking lost. "I don't even know what I'm suppose to do right now. I'm the one always cooking, so it's a little unnerving to just sit here."

"I figured you'd say that, so I brought in reinforcements." Just as the last words leave my mouth, Alex is kicking off his boots at the back door and making his way to the fridge for the beer June always has on hand for him.

"Damn, it smells great in here. I thought you said you were cooking tonight, Isolde." I catch the wink just as he settle in next to June, proud of his joke I'm sure. Even June can't help the smile on her face, though I'm hoping his appearance is only part of the reason.

"Very funny. It's a family recipe and I had to go off memory, so it'll either be delicious or I fucked it up. There likely isn't an in between."

"Well, I am spoiled by June's cooking, so that already sets the bar pretty high," he stands, making his way over to the stovetop to inspect my masterpiece. Leaning in, he inhales deeply, closing his eyes to the aroma of garlic. "But, judging by how this smells, I'd say we're in for something delicious." A breath of relief leaves me, even if he's just being nice, his acceptance is heartwarming, and slightly foreign to me.

"I haven't cooked for anyone since…well, in a very long time." I chance a quick glance at June but she didn't miss my stutter of words. Just smiles at me reassuringly and pulls Alex's attention back to the table while I begin plating food.

"How did the renovation go today at the Whitaker's?"

"Good, good. Stoker was able to get most of the work done and we just have a few things to touch up tomorrow. On to the next after that." Who the hell is Stoker? I'm about to ask when the back door swings open, making me jump. We all look to the man who just walked in without a word, making his way to June to place a soft kiss on top of her head before grabbing one of the beers in the fridge and sitting down in the seat next to me.

"Speak of the devil," Alex laughs and now I'm really confused. I thought he said his brothers name was Abram? Technically June said it, but still.

"Well well, look what the cat dragged in," June snickers from her seat, but Stoker doesn't say a word and barely even looks at her. I don't miss the subtle twitch of his lips though, as if he wanted to smile but thought better of it.

"Ha!" Alex exclaims, filling the room with his laughter. "Like Melvin could ever drag this man's ass in here. He can barely tote his own ass around this house."

"You leave him alone, he's a gentle soul. Unlike you reckless idiots." Shaking her head, she looks up to me. "Isolde, please excuse my boys here, they seem to have misplaced their manners these days." I giggle as I watch her fix them both with a stern glare not scary enough to spook even a mouse.

"Aww come on June, I may have misplaced mine, but Stoker here doesn't posses any and we all know it. Better off Isolde figures that out sooner rather than later."

When he first walked in, Stoker didn't even glance in my direction. As soon as June said my name though, his head snapped up real quick, causing my skin to break out in goosebumps. He's so intense, from the sharp lines of his jaw, to the sparking way his light gray eyes sear into my own. An odd contrast against the rest of him, which is unmistakably dark. His hair is buzzed short on the sides, but fuller on top, causing some of it to slip in front of his eyes. And good lord, the tattoos on this man. He's like a walking advertisement for a tattoo parlor.

"Dear, this is Alex's older brother, Abram. Abram, this is Isolde. She was just passing through but we managed to convince her to stay."

"You can try and say it was because of your food, your kindness or your never-ending hospitality, June. But we all know she stayed for *all* this." Alex runs his hands from his head down the front of his body, and I can't help but laugh. He's a flirt and probably a womanizer, but he's harmless and fun. I like how easy it is to be around him and his playfulness.

A snort comes from across the table and I glance up to see Abram, or Stoker, I don't even know what the hell to call this guy, as he rolls his eyes. He still hasn't spoken a word, and I've never wanted to hear someone's voice as badly as I want to hear his. Is it rough like his exterior, or is smooth like a chilled glass of whiskey? So many questions.

Alex begins chattering on about the renovations from earlier, holding Stoker's attention for a moment so I can study his features without being caught. His jawline is sharp and strong, like he could bite the leg off a wild animal.His hair, like I already noticed is longer on top, and the contrast against the buzzed sides has my fingers itching to test the different textures. The bell on the stove dings, and I quickly jump up, pleased I wasn't caught staring, and pull the lasagna from the oven, along with the garlic bread.

The salad is already on the table with a greek seasoning and olive oil dressing, I just need to add salt and pepper. Both of which are right in front of Abram, and now I'm afraid to approach the table. Images of nights with Grant come rushing to the forefront of my mind, and I feel my hands begin to sweat.

'What are you doing?' he snaps as I reach for the pepper.

'Oh, I was just going to season the salad before serving it. You like pepper, don't you?'

His gaze bores into me, making me feel small. 'That's not the point, is it Isolde?' I already know what he means, I didn't ask him if he wanted it, I just assumed. Something he hates.

'I, I'm sorry, I forgot. Grant, would you like any pepper on your salad?' Before I have a chance to look back up at him, I feel his hand come across my cheek. I feel the burn before I feel the impending tears, and try to wipe them away before he sees. Tears just piss him off even more.

'I'm so sick of your excuses, you bitch. Forget dinner, I don't want this crap anyways.' He excuses himself from the table, grabbing his keys as he heads out the door. I used to worry where he went when he'd leave, now I don't even care. He could be doing anything, as long as he's not here tormenting me.

The second the click of the front door sounds, I feel the tears fall freely. All of this because I didn't ask if he wanted pepper on his salad.

A soft hand lands on my forearm and I jump back. June looks at me with concern, as does Alex. "Are you alright, dear?" She asks in that soothing voice of hers, reminding me that I'm not back in that apartment, that I'm safe.

"Y-yes, I'm so sorry. I must have spaced out. Please, forgive me." There's a touch of pain in my voice, and as much as I try to hide it, I don't miss the way Abram looks at me. I can't meet his gaze, so with my eyes cast down towards the table I politely ask if he would hand me the pepper. His presence is intimidating, and while I don't get the icky feeling around him the way I did with Grant, something still screams in my gut, *dangerous*.

Holding the pepper up in front of me, I reach for it, touching the tips of his fingers slightly. Only then do I look up to see his eyes devouring mine, in a way I've never experienced. He hasn't spoken a word, yet his eyes say so many things. "Thank you," I whisper, "would anyone like pepper on their salad?" I ask as I carefully lower myself into my seat, knees wobbling as I do.

Dinner carries on normally after my momentary trip down memory lane. Alex fills us in on the job from today, while Abram stays perfectly silent, focusing more on his food than the conversation.

Once everyone is finished, plates completely cleared, I resist the urge to ask if it was good or if they were all just being polite to spare my feelings. Though, I can't imagine Abram would pretend to like something if he didn't.

"Damn Aunt June, she's gonna give you a run for your money if all her meals taste like that," he pats his stomach in delight, and a warmth spreads through me. Even if he is lying, I'll take this gratification.

"Like I said earlier, I haven't cooked for anyone in a long time. So even if you hated it, please keep pretending it was good."

"I don't fake satisfaction babe," Alex winks at me and stands to clear his and June's plates. I'm about to get up and clear my own, when a tattooed hand reaches out and grabs my plate. His eyes are blazing again, and I'd give anything to know what he's thinking. Grabbing our plates, he makes his way to the sink to rinse them off. I expect him to walk away without a word, but instead he starts loading the dishwasher. What is up with this guy? Everything about him screams *'I don't give a fuck,'* but his actions say something else.

I made dinner with every intention of cleaning up too, I don't want anyone to feel like just because I cooked I'm not going to clean up the mess. Mess is an understatement, actually. Meeting him at the sink, shaking only slightly, I offer to help, but he just looks at me with a slight shake of his head and nods back in the direction of the table. Okay?

"You cooked dear, come join me on the couch for some wine," June declares as she makes her way to the parlor. With one last look at Abram, I scurry off to follow June. Alex is already wrapping up what little leftovers there are, while Abram continues rinsing and loading dishes.

Standing in the doorway, wringing my hands together, I look at June who settles into the couch. "I didn't want anyone to have to clean up after me. I made a bit of a mess in there."

"That's the rules around here. Whoever cooks dinner, doesn't clean up. The boys are well aware, so don't go worrying that head of yours again," she pats the spot next to her on the sofa, so I make my way over to join her. "The dinner was wonderful, Isolde. I know you don't need to hear that, cause we all ate practically everything, but I want you to know anyways."

I may not need to hear it, but the way that praise penetrates my skin and absorbs into the very marrow of my bones has a smile breaking free, and I'm glad she let me know.

"Something tells me you didn't hear that too often. It's time you stop second guessing yourself, and putting yourself down. That ends here and now, understand?"

Closing my eyes, I take a deep breath before nodding. I understand what she's saying, that people around here don't just take care of their neighbors in the literal sense of loaning someone sugar if they run out. It runs deeper than stopping to fix a flat, or loaning a friend money when they need it. It goes as deep as someone needs, and in my case, we're talking the deepest depths of the ocean. I need help to my core, I need help finding my way back to my old self. Normally I would pride myself on getting there without any help, but even my pride is misplaced these days.

"I don't even know where to start," I whisper softly. "I feel damaged on such a deep level, it's like trying to clean a cluttered mess, where do you even begin?"

June sets down her wine glass, clasping my hands between her own and gives me the look a mother would give their child. "We just find a spot and start there. Okay?"

I lean into her without realizing and she wraps her arms around me, hugging more than just my frame. A part of me knows she's hugging all the wounded parts of my mind and soul, and I want nothing more than to accept this help and find *me* again. I look up to see Abram watching us intently, and without any more hesitation, I lock eyes with him, nod my head and say, "okay".

ISOLDE

chapter three

Sparks • Coldplay

The next morning I wake up early, ready to start my day. I accepted June's offer to fix up the house behind hers and I already know I want to keep it's gothic vibe. It reminds me of a smaller version of the house in the Addams Family. I'm expecting to find cobwebs in every nook and cranny, along with some wildlife. Considering where we are, there's dense woods all around.

June had to be at the cafe early, so she left the keys to the house and reminded me to use the charge card for whatever I need during renovations. When she said it last night as we discussed possibilities for the house, I outwardly cringed, allowing her to see how difficult this is for me. June has this special way of reassuring me not to stress over the small stuff. I feel like this isn't exactly a *small* situation, but I chose not to argue about it.

Once the renovations are done, she can sell the house or rent it out to tenants or even post it on Air BnB. That is, if I do a well enough job other people might actually want to stay here. That's a big *if.*

Standing outside the house, looking up at it's size, is making me suddenly feel very small. I have no confidence in myself, or any of my abilities, if last night's dinner was any indication. But this is something I *want* to do. Like June said, I need to do something to keep my mind and hands busy. What better way than to throw myself into a creative project where I have no prior experience and quite honestly, am scared shitless.

The house, or small manor might be more appropriate, is twice the size of June's place, maybe bigger. There has to be at least fourteen rooms, and that alone has me shaking with nerves. She warned me the space has been unoccupied for years now, so there's no telling what kind of condition the interior is in.

With shaky hands, I unlock the front door and push it open with a satisfying creak. Definitely a movie moment. I'm immediately smacked in the face with a musky smell, and before anything else, I need to open up every single window in this place.

After dinner last night, Abram came out here to turn the power on so I'd have electricity. He never came back in the house after that, so I assume his participation for the night was done. I'm surprised he came for dinner at all, I certainly didn't invite him, not that he wasn't welcome, but I have no way to contact him and still haven't heard him speak.

Maybe he doesn't speak. I hadn't considered that as a possibility, but surely June or Alex would have mentioned that beforehand, right? He's not deaf, cause I haven't once seen him use sign language, and he seemed to hear everything around the dinner table just fine. He probably tried to hide it, but I caught the subtle smirks a few times something funny was said.

He's going to be a tough egg to crack, like this house. Dark and mysterious yet so intriguing, I can't help but feel compelled to open it up and discover all it's secrets. People always judge the outside of something, without ever knowing what could be hiding just beneath the surface. This house has good bones. I'm just not sure if the memories I plan to uncover are.

Once all the windows are open, and blinds drawn, I take in the main level. The foyer is open, beautifully displaying the grand staircase leading to the second floor. At first glance, the stairs look to be in decent shape, just needs to be sanded and repainted. It probably sounds crazy, but I already know I want them painted black. The thought causes me to involuntarily start humming the beat of that song by The Rolling Stones.

Past the staircase is a long hallway that leads to the kitchen and formal dining room. Large window panes take up the wall above the sink, giving way to a beautiful view of the backyard, and the woods just past that. We could open up the space in here by knocking down the wall connecting the kitchen to the dining room, as long as it isn't load bearing, that much I know. It could create an open floor plan, with lots of natural light.

Just as I'm about to inspect the dining room, to see if such a plan is doable, a small cottage catches my eye, must be the one I saw that first day. It's pushed back towards the woods more, so I don't notice it often. There's so much of June's property that's gone unused over the years, I wonder if it makes her sad the way it's making me right now. With so much property on this plot of land, June could be cashing in big time. Judging by her current situation though, I'd say she's already pretty well off. I can't help but picture a secluded rustic resort back here, hosting people to have either a quiet peaceful weekend alone, or a bigger function with how much space is here.

Finding the back door, I slip outside to get a closer look just as the door to the cottage opens, and a dark figure exits. My breathing grows rapid, a million scenarios running through my mind. Someone could be squatting there, and now I'm witness to them sneaking around on June's land. I should call her, let her know something is going on, but instead I'm frozen to the spot. The figure moves around the bush that was blocking their full image from me, and as he comes into view my breathing stops altogether.

It's Abram.

Why would he be sneaking out of that cottage? Another thought occurs to me just as quickly as the first, maybe he *lives* there. The cottage itself is well kept, definitely smaller than June's with more vines wrapping around the stone front. Smoke lightly billows out of the chimney above, and from here I can practically smell the scent of burning wood on him. The same smell I got off him the first day I saw him at the store.

God he's beautiful to look at, especially from this distance. I can watch him without feeling ashamed of being caught staring. There's tattoos all the way down his arms, ones I didn't see last night at dinner. They're usually covered by his jacket, or a long sleeve ripped henley. I wish I was closer so I could see them more clearly, maybe even lightly trace my fingers along them, but I'm still too afraid to move. If he were to turn around, he would catch me frozen in place staring at him. I feel like such a creep. I would be embarrassed at the idea of someone watching me so intently without me knowing, but still, I can't look away.

He grabs a tool box and starts tinkering with his motorcycle, looking like a sexy calendar shoot come to life. I'd hang him up in my room and never change the calendar. Okay, I'm embarrassing myself now, I just need to go back inside and keep assessing the house and figure out what I can do myself, and what I'll need help with.

What I'll need *his* help with. A tingle runs up my spine with mental images of him working alongside me. How am I supposed to work with someone who never speaks to me though? Alex is a more jubilant person to be around, and every time I talk to him more I realize why he's the one who handles the clients. Abram is a complete mystery, even after spending a dinner with him. I thought maybe then he would say something, *anything*. I don't get the sense he's rude, reserved might be a better word, but it still intrigues the hell out of me.

I hate the idea of asking June about him because I don't want her, or Alex, to know I'm even remotely interested in this guy. She knows I'm coming out of an abusive relationship, and I sure as hell don't want to give her the idea I'm the kind of girl to jump into something else right away.

Chancing one last look at Abram, I back away slowly without looking where I'm going. I bump right into a wrought iron table with some dead potted plants, both of which tumble to the tiled patio and shatter. My body stills as I gape at the broken terracotta pots just as my arms feel the chill of an icy stare. I'm afraid to look up, knowing his eyes are already on me. I'm afraid to look up and see them filled with whatever emotion has my skin prickling. And I especially hate that my body is all too aware of his gaze penetrating every inch of me.

Taking the coward way out, I bend down to gather the bigger pieces, holding as many as I can in my hands before tossing them in the garbage bins around the side of the house. I'm pretty sure that's where I saw it anyways. Standing upright, I adjust the pieces in my hold as the heavier one digs into my hand, cutting a decent size gash along the sensitive flesh of my palm. Before I can think better of it, I drop all the pieces, clattering to the tile once again, and curse loudly. Blood spills from the wound at a rate I'm uncomfortable with. I've dealt with enough blood and cuts over the years, but it hasn't lessened my queasiness in the slightest.

As I turn to head back in the house, hoping to find a cloth of any kind that's clean enough to wrap it, a firm hand grabs my elbow, spinning me around. Immediately I'm hit with his scent, that woodsy smell with a tinge of cigarette smoke, an intoxicating blend. I've never cared for smokers, but on him it doesn't seem so bad. I'm about to tell him I'm okay, that I can clean it up myself, but he just tugs me in the direction of his cottage.

Oh, so I will get to see inside. Not how I imagined it happening, but beggars can't be choosers. At this moment I'm desperate just to stop the puddle of blood forming in my hand. He walks briskly, pulling me behind him as I stumble to step over the tall grass leading to his front door. He clearly appreciates his privacy and I feel guilty now that I was spying on him just minutes ago. "I'm sorry, I didn't mean to distract you from your work. I can take care of this myself." I sound breathy, like a little kid trying to get out of trouble.

Abram just looks at me, continuing up the walkway until we step inside his space. I'm taken aback instantly. I don't know exactly what I expected, but it wasn't this. Judging by his appearance, I was expecting to find a dozen empty beer cans littered around, dirty clothes piled in the corner and a sink full of dishes. For the second time in the matter of minutes, I feel guilty for something pertaining to Abram Stoker.

His space is dark and moody, a low fire burns in the hearth nestled under a beautiful hand crafted mantel. There aren't any family photos lining the shelves like in June's place, but it still feels homey in it's own way. A large leather couch sits right in front of the stone fireplace, and in the left corner of the room is a floor to ceiling built in bookshelf. My fingers itch to touch the spines and see what kind of books he enjoys. I'd say as many as possible considering I don't even see a tv in the space. I don't realize he dropped my elbow until the sound of a cabinet closing gains my attention. I shift so that I'm facing him standing by the kitchen island, and tentatively make my way over.

He doesn't look at me as he rips open a bandaid placing it next to the peroxide and Neosporin. When he looks up, he holds out a hand waiting for me to place my hurt one in his. I do with only a moments hesitation. The second our flesh connects, I feel that tingle from before run through me and settle low in my belly. His eyes meet mine in a flash, and I know he felt it too. I clear my throat, ready to apologize once again but the words get lodged in my throat. He's so goddamn intimidating.

With gentle fingers, he cleans all the blood away and applies a hefty amount of Neosporin before placing a bandage over the sensitive skin. His presence screams danger, but his actions are gentle, kind almost. He's just intimidating with that gaze and his quiet demeanor. Even his space has similar energy. Wanting to appear intimidating and off-putting, but on the inside is warm and almost *safe*.

"Why did you apologize?" His deep timbre hits my ears in a pleasant symphony of masculinity. It takes me a moment to register he finally spoke to me. I was lost in thoughts of how he made this space a home and how cool the concrete countertops are. He's looking at me as I stare at him with a deer in headlights look, no doubt. Oh shit, he asked me something.

"I, um, I don't know. I felt bad I made you stop what you were doing to come help me," I admit.

"You didn't *make* me do anything," he counters.

I laugh at that. "No, I suppose I didn't. But I don't want you to think of me as some damsel in distress, I'm not as weak as I look, I swear." I sure as fuck sound like a weak little child.

He smirks briefly before restoring his features back to that stern look again. Abram begins cleaning up the counter, putting the first aid kit back into a cabinet while I stand there wondering what the hell I'm supposed to do now. Should I just say thank you and leave? He doesn't seem like the type to engage in small talk. When he doesn't turn around after putting away the first aid supplies, I go to leave, offering up a quiet thank you. Just as I reach the front door, ready to slip out his voice startles me from behind.

Standing just feet away, his voice lowers as he looks into my eyes, holding me captive. "Just because you feel weak, doesn't mean you aren't strong." And with that I stumble backwards as he closes the door in my face. I'm not sure what he meant by that, but I wish I could see what he sees. My mind is still fuzzy by the time I make it back to the manor, and as I continue my walk through the house, I'm only partly focused on what I came here to do.

***

The hardware store in town is stocked surprisingly well, and the owner was helpful in more ways than one. Since he knows June so well, having grown up with her, he said I can start a tab with the store and not have to pay for anything right away. That way I can work on the house without making so many charges on June's card all the time.

I still want to talk to her about it tonight and make sure she's okay with that, and give her a rundown of my ideas for fixing up the manor. I feel like it needs a name, something to make it stand out even more, but I think I'm going to have to get my hands dirty and get a feel for the space before I name it.

Alex is supposed to come by today and do a walk through with me to assess the space himself. He said it'll give him and Abram a better idea of what supplies they need coming into a project like this. Plus I haven't seen him since dinner a few nights ago. There's something about Alex that is calming, almost as if he knows I need that kind of energy in my life right now. I doubt June has told him anything, mainly because she doesn't seem like a gossip, and also because I pleaded with her not to.

I'll never forget the way she smiled sadly when I asked her to keep this between us. The look on her face wasn't so much pity, but just sadness. That the idea of me being nervous she would spill my secrets, physically hurt her. She knew I had been through a lot in the last few years, but the evidence was right in front of us both, I clearly didn't have many friends I could confide in. If any.

A month ago if you would have asked me if I'd somehow find the courage to escape my abusive boyfriend, drive hours away and end up in a town just south of Canada, I would have laughed without humor. The idea seemed so far fetched for years, the idea of leaving him. But every time I thought I could do it, something would stop me. Usually Grant's fist, but also the fact that I didn't know where I would go.

I never wanted to run to my parents because that could have put them in danger. I realized very early into the abuse that there wasn't much Grant wouldn't do to keep me locked away as his little secret punching bag. People suspected the abuse, I'm sure, but what would they say? In public Grant was kind and attentive, always keeping close watch over me in a way that screamed caring and protective. Little did anyone know, it was stemming from possessive and territorial, like I was his property.

He just learned how to hide that from everyone else.

I tried going to the police, after one of the first really bad incidents. I had no idea at the time Grant's connection to the police and what filing a report would do. It didn't take long to figure that out, though. If I had known the original abuse wasn't nearly as bad as it would get, I would have kept my mouth shut. My first attempt to turn him in was also the first time I was hospitalized.

I've tried so hard to repress those memories, but somehow they always slip back to the front of my brain, each time worse and more vivid. It's like the longer I try to shut out the memories, the harsher they come back. Opening up to June, knowing she wasn't going to judge me, was the first and only time I've been able to talk about everything without completely shutting down. I've found solace in such an unlikely friendship, and I don't think I could leave this place if I wanted to. Not without feeling the sting of losing more family. In such a short time that's what June has felt like. It's sort of like love at first sight but friendship instead.

Having been so lost in thought, I wasn't paying attention and am surprised by how quickly I made it home. The roads here are winding and often covered with a thick layer of fog and drizzle. The sun hardly shines in these parts of the mountains, and if I'm being honest, I love it. In the past, I've felt like I need to match the weather's energy to my own. On sunny days, even if I was struggling, I always kept a smile on my face. Here, I can be in a more moody state of mind and match the weather without feeling guilty.

Funniest thing about it though is, since I've been here, I've never felt like smiling more than I do now. I'm finally *happy*. A lone tear slides down my cheek freely, dripping onto my soft gray t-shirt. Too distracted by my feelings, I miss the greeting that must have come from the front of the house and am scared shit when Alex comes around the corner in his usual loud optimistic self. I let out a scream and am met with Alex bending at the waist to laugh hysterically.

"I'm so glad my fear amuses you, Alex. Jesus, you could have announced yourself!" I yell as I throw a dirty rag at his chest. I've been up to my elbows in dirt and grime for the better part of the day, covered in years of dust. He still finds this funny, but has straightened himself and is trying to take deep breaths to stifle his laughter.

"I did! That's what makes it that much more funny," he drops a few bags on the counter and rounds the island to stand in front of me. "Isolde, please accept my sincerest apology for scaring you, even though I did knock and announce myself upon arriving. It will *never* happen again." With a hand over his chest, he looks down at me with dramatic puppy dog eyes. I don't think it's possible to stay mad at him, especially when he looks like that.

Shoving him aside, I go back to wiping down the doorframes and baseboards. I want everything in here to be sparkling clean before painting. Most of the rooms just need to be deep cleaned and painted, maybe some new light fixtures. The real work is needed in all three bathrooms, the kitchen and dining room, and probably the basement. I have yet to venture down there, because while I may not be chickenshit, I'm smart enough to know all horror movies have a naive girl wondering into the basement alone to ultimately get butchered.

I refuse to go out that way.

Since Alex is here, I decide now is the time to check out the space, allowing him to go down there first in case there happens to be an axe wielding psychopath. "I haven't had a chance to check out the basement yet…" I let the words linger in the air and Alex glances at me over his shoulder as he kneels above his toolbox on the floor. His smirk is basically a neon sign saying he can read me like a book and knows I'm scared to go down there.

"What's the matter, Is? Afraid of a dusty old basement?" Jackass. He knows that's the reason, but I won't admit that to him.

"Why would I be afraid of an old basement with cold concrete walls and flickering light fixtures lining the descent? It's not like this house has been vacant for over a decade or anything. I'm sure there's nothing sketchy down there at all." I finish my sarcastic rant with an eye roll. Alex stands up, grabbing his tool box as he does and makes his way to the basement, flipping on the light before opening the door with a creak.

"Of course not," he says with a shrug and a wink. If I didn't know any better I'd say he's a little nervous too. But I do know better, and nothing about his current demeanor alludes to him being scared in the slightest. Why did he have to go and make me feel like a little kid?

He starts heading down and about halfway looks up at me. "You coming, scaredy-cat?" I should wait until he turns around and trip him so he falls on his ass at the bottom. Lucky for him, I'm classier than that, so I just follow him with a heavy sigh. One he knows is for him.

I don't miss the way he smiles, and releases a soft laugh like he's actually enjoying his time with me. When I asked him to come over this afternoon and check out some things, I assumed he would be busy and blow me off. He texted back almost immediately saying he'd be over in half an hour. I hope he wasn't working on a project with Abram, and left him to do the work alone.

I want to ask him, but again, that makes it seem like I care about what he's doing. And I don't.

I don't.

The basement is just as creepy as I imagined it would be. I try not to let Alex know that part, but the way I hover close to him as we inspect each room probably gives it away. "Why are there so many rooms down here?" I ask, accidentally brushing up against his shoulder.

He chuckles lightly, but doesn't move away which I find oddly comforting considering our circumstances. "Well most of them were for storage, like all houses. But sometimes smaller rooms, like this one, were used as panic rooms," he points towards a small room to the left, bigger than a closet, but roughly the same size as a half bathroom.

I don't even want to know why people needed panic rooms, but the idea that I could have had one to escape Grant makes me want to keep this room as it was intended.

Not realizing my internal monologue happening, Alex peruses the rest of the space before coming back to stand with me, hands on his hips. "So, boss. What were you thinking of doing down here? I mean, I get if you don't know yet since you were too scared to come down until now."

"Very funny," I shove him and do a slow spin, taking in the space all together. "I think we should open it up so it's one large rec room. We could have an entertainment section just over there," I say, pointing to the large area on the right. "Maybe even have a gaming section, with fuse ball and a pool table."

"I like the way you think, girl," Alex says, jotting down measurements in a notebook, probably to show Abram since he isn't here. "The electrical panel needs some updating and we might need to replace the pipes, but other than that this shouldn't be too difficult."

I turn around and face the panic room again, thoughts running through my mind on why we should keep it here. I don't know what forces the words out, but suddenly they're tumbling out before I can think better of it. "I want to keep the panic room."

Alex just looks at me, probably hoping I'll elaborate. But he fixes his face to not look so eager before he answers and just smiles. "Panic room stays, check." He jots a note down next to his measurements, and I'm grateful he didn't push me to open up about why I want to keep it. Like June, he knows I've been through something, but he's respectful not to ask unless I offer up information.

Right now isn't that time.

As playful and flirty as he can be, Alex is a good person, and spending time with him has become one of my favorite things lately. I won't tell him that though, he doesn't need another thing to blow that ego of his up any bigger.

We move through the first floor with ease, Alex making notes and taking measurements as I ramble on about what I want each room to look like. I'm hopeful it will come to fruition, but the process still makes me nervous. Countless times I've had to refrain from asking June why she trusts me with this, too afraid she'll come to her senses and call it off.

I want to talk about it with Alex, I trust his input and I'm curious if he has an inkling why she allowed me to take on fixing up the house. When he got here an hour ago, he lugged in his tool box and a bagged lunch like he's still in grade school. Seeing him unwrap it now and set out a sandwich for each of us has me grinning like a school girl. He's adorable.

We're sitting crossed legged on the dining room floor, chatting about taking out the wall joining this room to the kitchen when I decide now is the time to ask. "Alex?" He looks up at me with a mouthful of ham and cheese, trying to nod but ultimately laughing when I burst out into laughter at the chipmunk look he's sporting. "I never know what to expect with you around," I joke as he swallows his heaping bite, wiping his hands on his worn jeans.

"A good time," he counters, and it makes me smile. "What did you want to ask?"

"Why do you think June asked me to fix up this house? I mean, it's been sitting here vacant for years, and you and your brother are more than capable of restoring it. So, why me?" My question hangs in the air as he ponders his response.

"Did she tell you we used to live here?" No. She did not, and now I have more questions about that slice of information than I do about why I'm the one restoring it. I shake my head and wait for him to continue, desperate for the knowledge of why they would willingly choose not to live in this beautiful manor.

"When we were kids, we grew up here with our parents. Mom was June's niece, so we spent a lot of time growing up here and eventually moved into the manor. My dad was a deadbeat, so he was never really around, always at the bars and cheating on our mom." My heart suddenly aches for the two little boys who had to grow up without a present father. It makes me miss my own parents, a lot more than I realized.

"Anyways, he was always getting into trouble at the bars, skipping out on bills, picking fights, that kind of stuff. Well, he messed with the wrong guy one too many times and instead of getting back at him, he took it out on our mom." My skin prickles with goosebumps, I get the idea I know where this story is headed and I have a sinking feeling I'll relate to it all too well.

"Probably thought she meant something to him, when in reality, he gave up on all of us long before." I feel tears welling up in my eyes, but I refuse to let them fall. I don't want to make this about me the first time Alex opens up. "I'm sure you can imagine the next part…" I knew his parents were no longer around, but I never for a second thought it was because of something this dark.

"Alex, I'm so sorry. I can't even begin to imagine what that must have been like for you both, at such a young age too."

"Yeah, well, I'm a few years younger than Stoker so I don't remember too much. But for him, it was a lot worse. He witnessed the assault, was the one to call for help." A gasp escapes me, and I quickly cover my mouth with a hand, hoping Alex keeps going while simultaneously wanting him to stop. "When the cops and rescue finally showed up, he barely spoke. It changed him, he was never the same after that night."

I resist the urge to ask, but I can't help it. "How old was he?" Alex stares at his hands for a few beats before slowly raising his eyes to meet mine.

"Nine."

The breath I was holding rushes out of me, picturing a little kid witnessing his mom being assaulted, and having to be the one to call for help because his brother was too young to understand. Over the years I've come to not be an affectionate person, Grant made me too afraid to even hug people, even if it was a woman. He never initiated affection, outside of sex that is, so I got used to not feeling seen.

The idea is so foreign at first, but seeing Alex, staring down at his hands as memories flood his brain, I move on instinct and lean across towards him, wrapping him in a hug. He startles at first, probably not expecting me to comfort him, especially since he's always the life of the party when I see him. But within seconds, he's hugging me back. Holding me with a firm embrace, like he didn't realize he needed a hug until this moment.

We stay like that for seconds or minutes, I can't really tell, until he mumbles a quiet thank you in my ear. Warmth radiates throughout my chest, and I'm happy I was here for him to open up to. I'm sure over the years he's had countless conversations about it, or maybe he hasn't, but sometimes telling a person who wasn't there to see it firsthand, makes it easier.

I know when I opened up to June about my own abusive relationship, I wasn't nearly as nervous as I was expecting I'd be. The words flowed from me with ease and she listened intently, only offering up a few words here and there if she felt like I needed encouragement.

The realization hits me now, as I hug Alex, that Abram might not have anyone to open up to either. He's not exactly a man of many words, and judging from the few interactions I've had with him, he's not the type to open up about his feelings. The longer I stay here the more of a mystery Abram becomes. With Alex, I'm able to see new pieces of him every time. Abram has layers, and each one is likely harder to uncover than the former.

I don't even think I've made it past one layer of who Abram Stoker is.

Alex pulls away from the hug first, but doesn't release me from his light hold. I think he's about to say something else when I feel his breath caress my face. I'm waiting for the warning bells to ring in my mind, telling me to run, this isn't safe and I need to get away. But they never come. As I stare at Alex, I don't feel the fear I've come accustomed to. His eyes bore into mine before they dip down to stare at my lips, then back up again.

I don't move, and I can hardly breathe as he slowly leans forward to brush his lips against mine. They're soft, and he's gentle with me. Another thing I wasn't sure I was expecting. His energy is always so high, I don't know how to handle the sweet and gentle side of him just yet. Pulling back slightly, he watches me for a reaction. "Is this okay?"

Is it? I don't feel threatened in any way, and if I didn't want him to kiss me I could have backed up and surely he would have gotten the message. I allowed him to kiss me, it was in my control and yet I didn't feel a zing or a rush. The kiss was nice, but it was missing something, and I'm not sure what. When I don't say anything right away, he pulls back farther, running his hands through his tousled hair. "I'm sorry, I should have asked first."

Despite the constant cover of clouds around here, Alex always seems to have a bronze glow to his skin, so I almost miss the blush that creeps across his face. He's actually apologizing to me, and that alone has words lodging in my throat. I don't want him to feel bad, or like he did something without my permission. But I also don't want to lead him on.

"Alex, how much did June tell you about me?" I ask as I toy with the hem of my shirt that is now covered in dust and dirt from cleaning.

"Uh, not too much. Just that you were in a tough spot and needed a place to rest your mind for a bit," he watches with rapt attention as I trace circles in my palm.

Of course she said it like that, she's empathetic to people and never alludes to anything more than what's necessary. "Somehow that doesn't surprise me." We both laugh, cause he too knows her, way better than I do.

"I feel like it's such a cliche thing to say *'its not you, it's me'*, but in this case, that's the truth. I don't want to get into the details, but I'm coming from kind of a shitty situation, and I don't think jumping into anything, whether that be serious or just for fun, is a good idea." He's watching me with curiosity, not contempt or anger, and it eases my mind that he isn't upset with me.

"I can't really give you anymore than friendship right now, I hope that's okay."

As if snapping out of a funk, he smiles at me with a nod of his head. "Perfectly okay, Isolde."

I don't deserve someone like Alex anyways. I'm too damaged to love anyone right now, especially when I can't even love myself just yet. Time heals all wounds, but no one ever tells you how much time.

ISOLDE

chapter four

Lithium • Evanescence

I need to find a job. A real one. Not that I haven't enjoyed fixing up the manor, but I can't keep spending June's money like this. When it comes to anything regarding the restoration, it's fine. Because I'm doing the work basically for a place to live and food to eat. But everything else, like clothes and everyday essentials, shouldn't be coming from her.

Last week, after the walk through with Alex, he and I have fallen into a good groove and work well together. I was worried that by rejecting his advances, it would be awkward around each other. But just as I should have expected, he went right back to his charming playful self.

After leaving the hardware store, I walk past some of the shops in town and notice a help wanted sign in the window of the only bar. The bar itself is an old one story brick building, with large windowpanes that flank a wooden front door. I did a little bartending in college, just before Grant and I became serious. Needless to say, that didn't last long. He was not okay with me working in an environment that opened me up to flirtatious men. I tried to fight it at first, but ultimately didn't see the point.

It might be nice to get back into it, and the tips would be a great way to make quick cash. When June and I sat down for dinner the other night, I mentioned my desire for finding a job to pay my way. She tried to brush it off and assure me I could get whatever I needed, but I gently informed her that finding a job *is* what I needed. That's all it took for her to understand, and see the hidden meaning in my eyes. I need to do this for myself, and she let me know she respects that.

Being the local socialite that she is, she did put a few feelers out there to see who was hiring but hadn't heard of anything yet. This job must have just become available. Checking my watch to see that they're open, I walk through the heavy oak door and march right up to the bar.

A woman, probably in her early thirties, is wiping down glasses at the counter when she raises a brow to me as I approach. Looking every bit as confident as I should feel, but don't. I can't let her see that though, or else she won't think I have what it takes for this job. "I saw the help wanted sign in the window." I try to make that seem like enough of an explanation, but she just continues her busy work without sparing me a glance. Tough broad.

I'm about to explain how badly I need this job, not caring if I sound a little desperate and probably pathetic, when she pipes up. "Got any experience bartending?"

"I do, actually. It's been a few years, but I'm sure a quick brush up on my skills is all I need." She looks hesitant as she looks me up and down. She has to be the owner. No way a regular employee would question me, they'd simply hand over an application and tell me to fill it out.

"Listen, I want this job. I bartended in college in a larger city. Not saying that the regular clientele here won't order something more than a beer or whiskey on the rocks, but I can do this job. Give me a chance to show you." There's the confidence I need, I knew I had it, I just needed to dig it up first.

She looks at me with an approving grin, and I think I've hooked her. Not sure I would be so quick to hire me, but I won't let her see that self conscious side of me. Not here. "You've got some fire in you, I can tell," she drops the rag she was using to dry the glasses, and holds out her right hand to shake mine. Gripping it with a firm hold, I smile and introduce myself. "Sasha. When can you start?"

Oh shit, this is happening. Okay. Keep it together, it's just a job. A job where I will be interacting with people everyday, not hiding behind a computer as I work from home because Grant didn't *trust* me to work in an actual office. Gulping a lungful of air, I shake my head to rid my mind of negative thoughts. "Tomorrow okay?"

Sasha seems pleased with that answer, maybe she expected me to say two weeks so I can quit whatever job I have, but that's not the case here. "Alright, tomorrow it is. Wear comfortable shoes, jeans are fine but you have to wear a black shirt. Meet me here around four." And with that she bustles in the back hefting the case of glasses with her as she goes. I found a job, all on my own, and I start tomorrow. Guess I need to go buy some new sneakers and a few black shirts.

I walk out of the bar with a warmth I haven't felt in years, and people look at me as they pass by, probably wondering why the new girl is walking around with a maniacal looking smile on her face. If I cared one bit, I would relax my face, but I don't.

An hour later, as I leave the store with a bag of new clothes to wear to work, I spot Abram leaving the arts and craft shop just two doors down. He doesn't see me at first, so I take the opportunity to watch him a little. Not in the creepy way, but in an exploratory way. At least that's what I'm telling myself. Bag in hand, he walks back to his bike and stuffs it into one of the saddlebags on the side before swinging one leg over and jump starting his bike.

I'm still standing on the curb when he lifts his head, covered by the black visor of his helmet, and stares right at me. My feet, which weren't moving anyways, plant firmly into the concrete and I become one with the sidewalk. Cutting the engine, he removes the helmet, and strides over to me like a man on a mission. I feel the air in my lungs rush to hide, leaving me literally breathless and slightly terrified. Is he like this with everyone?

"All alone, little bird?" His question catches me off guard, but not as much as the little nickname he's assigned me to. He leans against the brick of the building behind me, reaching into his pocket for a lighter. Igniting the end of his cigarette, he sucks in causing the smoke to billow out around him like a halo designed in hell.

"L-little bird? What is that suppose to mean?" We barely know each other, and have had like half a conversation since I moved here. I can't imagine he knows enough about me to feel inclined to give me a nickname.

With a shrug of his shoulders, he looks at me with a playful smirk, expressing more smoke around us. "Seems fitting." My body is buzzing from how close he is, practically bursting into flames from his masculine scent that I can't get enough of.

Still leaning against the building, he looks out ahead focusing on nothing particular when he asks, "how's the hand?" The hand? Oh, *my* hand, duh Isolde. He bandaged it up for me last week when I cut it open on broken pieces of a terracotta pot. I leave out the part where I was practically spying on him and that's why I cut my hand. It feels like an eternity has gone by since that one interaction, but I nod my head and assure him it's healing fine.

On a final inhale, he drops the cigarette butt, stubbing it out with his boot and wanders back to his bike with a slight smirk on his face, like I amuse him or something. I watch his movements like they're happening in slow motion, fuzzy from his words, or lack thereof, as he mounts his bike and kick starts it for the second time.

In a flash, he's racing down the street in the direction of his house. Having regained the feeling in my feet, and the rest of my limbs, I walk unsteadily back to my car, placing my shopping bags in the passenger seat. Alex is easy to read, upfront with his thoughts and overall optimistic in general. I'm quickly realizing how different the Stoker men are, and how quickly I want to know more about the man who seems to barely speak to me. That is if you don't count him bandaging my cut and calling me little bird.

The conversation from last week with Alex rings in my mind, reminding me of Abram's dark past. The thought of digging deeper into who he is, is slightly jarring. However, the alternative is even worse. I decide here and now, no matter what happens in the next few months, I can't leave this place without finding out who Abram Stoker truly is. Might be an impossible feat, but hey, a girls gotta try.

***

"I saw Abram leaving the craft store earlier this afternoon, does he have an interest in art that you know of?" June is busy rinsing dishes before loading them into the dishwasher. I cooked again tonight, and since neither of the guys are here, it was just her and I. I kind of liked it that way, especially after my weird run in with Abram today. If there was an awkward tension, I didn't want June or Alex picking up on it.

"He did as a boy, but I haven't seen him do anything in years. Makes me wonder what he was buying," she furrows her brows in thought, and I imagine her remembering the younger carefree little boy who loved arts and crafts before the dark reality of this world closed in on him stealing his light. Alex said he hasn't been the same since, but maybe he just hides those parts of himself now.

"It's not hard to miss that he's a man of few words, and Alex kind of opened up about their past a little. I had no idea, June, I'm so sorry."

"Oh dear, how could you know? I don't think most of the folks in town know what really happened. All speculations and gossip. Good people around here, but man they know how to yap like little chihuahuas." Her humor always makes me laugh, like nothing in life is too serious. The world needs more people like June.

"It's just," I pause, trying to figure out how I want to phrase my thoughts, "I don't want it to be difficult for either of them to work in that house. God, had I known, I probably wouldn't have even mentioned it in the first place."

June comes to sit down next to me at the table, drying her hands on a red and white checkered hand towel with little chipmunks on it. "Now listen, cause I know you and that brain of yours like to overthink things. What happened was tragic, yes, but that house wasn't at fault. Sure, it'll bring back some negative memories, especially for Stoker, but there's also plenty of good memories to hold on to."

"Plus, knowing that there could be even more good memories there, well, that's just a gift, now isn't it?" Every time I talk to June, I feel wiser. Like I can somehow absorb her words of wisdom and use them to help me be that way too. She's practical, but optimistic, almost like a combination of Alex and Abram. Except she has a better grasp on how to communicate with people without scaring them shitless.

"You're right. I just don't want to make things weird for Ab…well, for both of them." I curse myself for almost slipping up and voicing my concern for only Abram. Alex didn't allude to negative memories living there, just the main one being what happened to his mom. But he was too young to know or understand at the time. On the other hand, it doesn't mean he won't have new thoughts about it now as an adult. My head spins every time I think about either of the Stoker men, and not just because of how different they are.

June gets back up to finish the dishes, something that bothers me to see her do. Even though she informed me of the house rule early on, I still don't like watching her clean up just because I cooked. I'm going to find a way to break that mold, if only for her sake. The guys can continue with it the way they always have. That is, if they ever decide to join us again. "Why does everyone call Abram by his last name?" I wonder aloud, hoping I can understand him just a little better.

"He's been going by Stoker since he was younger, said he didn't like the name Abram anymore." That's all she says, and I have to wonder if it has anything to do with what happened between his parents. I don't want to speculate, but I also don't want to ask any follow up questions, not yet at least.

Deciding to call it a night early, I tell June I'm going for a walk before heading to bed. If she seemed nervous about me walking around on the property alone at night, she doesn't let on. Our conversation at dinner was great, and I told her all about the job I'm starting tomorrow. It took a few minutes of convincing her this was what I *wanted* to do, and not that I felt obligated in any way. Though that last part is only partly true.

Nights like tonight, I enjoy the peacefulness of Stehekin and the eerie way fog always seems suspended over the land like a thick blanket. It hangs around the trees and occupies so much of the open areas, you wouldn't know if you were about to walk off a cliff until you were falling.

There's a light drizzle, but I don't mind. As long as it doesn't start full out pouring, I think I'll manage.

When I first arrived, June showed me around the property, so I know my way around here a little bit. Of course, it's slightly different at night with no street lights and the moon just barely breaking through the dense cover of clouds. Checking that my phone has battery and service, I decide to walk down the wooded path that connects the houses together. If I follow it the way June originally showed me, I should pass the manor and Abram's place.

Alex lives in a one bedroom apartment in town, just down the street from the cafe. I never thought to ask why he doesn't live on the property too, but judging by the fact there only appears to be three houses, I'd say he just wanted something that was his. Abram is the oldest, so maybe he had first pick on houses, and for obvious reasons, decided not to live in the manor.

Surely Alex could have lived there, but that seems like quite a big undertaking for a younger guy. He told me once there's a four year age different between them, putting Alex around the same age as me and Abram just entering his thirties.

The path becomes a lot more narrow the longer I walk, and I start to wonder if this was a bad idea. Feeling the temperature drop significantly, I feel the first shiver wrack my slight frame. I can't escape the smell out here though, earthy and pine scented like Christmas. I try not to, but my mind wants to wander down memory lane and remember all the Christmases I spent with my family. I can't even remember the last time I saw them for a holiday.

Stopping to look at the map on my phone, I glance around to make sure I'm still where I think I am. But my earlier confidence quickly morphs into uncertainty when I realize everything around me looks the same as it did twenty minutes ago. Inhaling and exhaling a few times, I try to control my breathing. Freaking out won't do me any good, and at the very least I know I'm still on June's land.

A twig snaps somewhere behind me and I whirl around so fast I could have given myself whiplash. I strain my eyes against the darkness to see if I can make out where it came from, but I can't see anything through the fog. Okay, this is starting to feel like that horror movie I don't want to die in. Am I actually that naive girl who wanders around alone at night and gets murdered in the woods? Yes, I believe I am.

I turn and start walking faster than before, hopefully heading back in the direction I came from. A few more twigs and the rustling of leaves sounds from just a few feet behind me again, and now I'm panicking something is following me. I'm almost embarrassed to admit I'd be less scared if it was an animal. I've spent too much of my twenties being afraid day in and day out, I thought taking this walk on my own would force me out of my shell.

Stupid fucking idea.

Just as I'm about to break out in a sprint, my body stiffens as I catch a specific scent in the air. The breeze drags it over to me almost leisurely like it can predict my reaction. Everything around me seems to slow down, and I become hyperaware of my surroundings. Turning my body slightly to the left, I can see a red ember illuminating a cloud of smoke, before puffing out.

Achingly slow, Abram comes into view looking sexier than seems legal. He's wearing the leather jacket I saw him in the first time he pulled up in front of June's house, and his trademark leather boots with the top laces loose and hanging. As he emerges from the fog, with cigarette smoke circling him, I can't help but think he looks a lot like Damon from Vampire Diaries during the scene where he slaughters two campers in the woods.

I audibly gulp as his body moves closer to mine, slowly but with intent. If he didn't already know my heart is pumping practically out of my chest, and my blood pressure is likely through the roof, he's hoping it is. The way he looks at me, like I'm something to be caught is unnerving and a little exhilarating too.

"Do you always sneak up on people like a demon in the woods?" Now that the fear is gone, mostly, I let irritation take the wheel.

Puffing out a cloud of smoke, he lowers the cigarette to the ground, smearing the butt into the dirt. Littering isn't an attractive quality, I mentally remind myself. I need as many reasons to stay away from him as possible, and lately I'm finding it harder and harder to do that. Abram locks his eyes with mine before gradually taking in my whole frame. Like he's sizing up his kill, waiting for the right moment to pounce.

"When they're on my property, yeah," he snarls and I resist the urge to laugh, because last I checked, this was June's property. Though, come to think of it, how do I know if they don't share partial ownership? I never asked. There's a lot of things I've never asked.

"I just wanted some fresh air, that's all," I admit.

"Little far into the woods for some *fresh air*, don't you think?" The way he used air quotes reminds me of a teacher being condescending to a student, and it makes me want to force feed him a glue stick. "You don't know these woods like I do, and I can tell you, you're better off getting your fresh air in the backyard, not way out here."

He moves even closer, until my chest, rising rapidly, almost collides with his. "Wh-what are you doing?"

"You seem nervous. Is it these woods, or something else?" He lightly brushes a piece of hair behind my ear, trailing his fingers gingerly down my throat. I try and swallow down my nerves, but it does nothing. He knows he's making me nervous, and has known since our first encounter. This is the first time he's gotten so close to me, and definitely the most he's spoken to me.

"I-I'm not nervous. I'm c-cold, that's all."

He tsks, and I can feel his breath feather across my cheek as he moves to stand behind me. I know I should run, this situation demanding that I do, but a part of me wants to see what he'll do. The part of myself I buried so long ago, the adventurous side of me, still exists somewhere deep in the recesses of my mind. That girl is screaming to be set free, and a taste of this current predicament is baiting her out.

The larger part of me knows he can't be that bad or else June would never allow me to be near him. But the logical part is trying to remind me that I don't know her all that well either. I've been here almost a month, and there's so much I don't know about all of them. My gut has said since the beginning that they're good people, and I still believe that, so maybe that's why I'm allowing Abram to circle me like a shark in chum infested water.

"It's wrong to lie, did you know that?" he whispers, and goosebumps shoot all the way down my arms and legs.

"What, you're a mind reader or something?" I ask, trying to sound annoyed.

"Or something." Abram locks his fist around my ponytail, jerking my head back so I'm looking at the tops of the trees, and a gasp escapes me. I'm about to ask him what the fuck he's doing, when he whispers against me again.

"My mind is usually a quiet place, Isolde. But not since you showed up." Oh, god. "I don't usually waste my time on people, unless I need a quick fix, and even then I fill that need and send whatever woman deemed fit, on their way." I don't know where he's going with this, or why he's even telling me, but the grip on my hair is biting, and I have a feeling I shouldn't interrupt his little speech.

"Something about you bothers me, and I finally figured out what it is," his confession deflates my chest a little, and I snap at my inner monologue to shut the fuck up. Now is not the time to be turned on, or disappointed by his irritation with me, considering the position I'm in.

I find my voice, though I can't project it past a whisper, and try to turn my head to look at him as I speak. He allows it slightly, and I'm able to meet his eyes. "I've barely spoken to you. How could I possibly bother you?"

His laugh startles me, and the sound reverberating off the trees is jarring, almost maniacal. I'm trying really hard not to get too worked up, but his scent is invading all my senses, and my legs grow more and more wobbly as the seconds tick by.

"Little bird." There's that nickname again. I already asked him what the hell he meant by it the other day and he gave me nothing but a basic answer. *'It seems fitting'*. But why? He gains my attention again with a tug of my hair, and I look back at him as best I can, the position he has my neck in doesn't leave much room for free movement.

"*That*, is what bothers me. You look at me like you want to say something, and every time I think you will, you always shut down. Why is that?" What? Is he telling me the reason he looks at me the way he does is because I don't talk to him more and he wants me to? That seems like an odd thing to get worked up over, but I decide not to voice that right now.

"I thought you didn't like me, so I figured I should keep my mouth shut," he moves his hands to the base of my neck, testing the reaction of my skin there, before applying a small amount of pressure.

"You don't seem to have a problem chatting up my brother though, do you?" Holy shit, is he jealous? That has to be what this is about. I don't see why though, sure Alex is good looking and can probably bed any woman he wants, but one look from Abram and I was done for. Even if I wasn't ready to admit that considering my mental state upon my arrival.

I don't know what possesses me to poke the bear, but I do without thoughts of the consequences. "Jealous, are we?" Before the last word fully leaves my mouth, Abram is squeezing the base of my neck harder, and I choke at the sudden lack of oxygen.

"Funny. You'd like to think that's it, wouldn't you?" He spins my body so my chest is flush with his, and my eyes bug. "But I can see the way you look at me, even when you think I don't notice. *Especially* then. Something about me draws you in and either you *hate* that, or is *scares* you. But guess what?" he speaks so softly, almost tenderly as he hold my attention. "You can't escape me."

Blood rushes to my center, and something about this, while wrong, feels thrilling. He doesn't want to hurt me, not the way Grant always did. It's like he wants to *play* with me.

I glance around our surroundings, tall dark trees flood the area, blocking any moonlight from coming through. Even if I tried to run, he'd catch me before I could make it to the closest tree. Plus, like he said just a few minutes ago, he knows these woods. I catch sight of some wild berries, likely poisonous, and a thought occurs. If he wants a game, then that's what I'll give him.

The moment his hold on my neck lessens, I dance out of his space and walk over to them, lightly brushing my fingers across the dark pigment. I can feel his presence close behind, and the wind carries his scent over me like a blanket.

"I could eat these…then I wouldn't be around anymore to act as your play thing." A slight sadness engulfs me, reminding me that this has been a thought I've had more than once in my life. When things got really bad, taking my life seemed like the only option, and I contemplated it more often then I'll ever admit out loud. But now, I just want to partake in this twisted game Abram is playing.

He scoffs, actually scoffs, making me return my attention back to him. Asshole.

"Baby, I could just eat them too. Then I'd follow you in the afterlife and even there you wouldn't escape me until we figured out what this is," he threads his rough hands through the loose tendrils framing my face. I want to rear back and slap him, but the moisture building between my thighs says otherwise.

The nerve he has. I can't even tell him to fuck off, cause my threats mean nothing to him. If anything, they turn him on even more. This is a game to him, and I'm still trying to decide if I want to play along. The ache low in my belly, accompanied by the wetness gathering between my thighs is all the answer I need. I won't give in that easily though, he doesn't want me to submit, he wants a chase. Lucky for me, I ran track in high school, and even though I don't train like I used to, I think I can at least hold my own. For a few minutes anyway.

Abram gazes at me like he doesn't suspect I'll run, but he doesn't know me very well. His body is relaxed as he leans against a tree, pinning me with his light gray eyes, the same ones I'm ashamed to say have appeared in my dreams. I can't help the way I swim in them every time I see them, and when his gaze locks with mine, I feel like I'm drowning. The nonchalance with which he stands irritates me, though, so I take a minute to weigh my options.

"I feel like this is a game to you." He watches me, with no intention of answering my assumption. "Am I right? And remember, it's wrong to lie," I snicker, throwing his earlier words back at him. I don't miss the way he nods his head in approval as he glances at the ground. Using this as my moment, I take off in a sprint, happy I'm wearing my new sneakers to break them in for my first shift tomorrow.

Adrenaline is pumping through my veins as I try my best to head in the direction of the house. It didn't take him long to figure out my play, and I can hear his footsteps charging through the woods behind me. If I'm honest with myself, he absolutely could have caught me the second I took off. Which leads me to believe he really is about the game play. All he had to do was take a few easy strides and he would have had me.

Abram *let* me get a head start. He gets off on the chase, and I'm finding it hard to tell myself I don't. Even as my heart pumps wildly in my chest, it's exhilarating to feel the threat of him drawing closer. I know he won't hurt me, if he wanted to, he would have the moment he had his big hands wrapped around my throat.

The way his hands, with intricate tattoos and corded muscles, worked their way around the base of my throat gave me a rush of pleasure I've never experienced. When Grant had his hands around me in that way, it was terrifying, He would squeeze so hard, with both hands, until my face felt like it would pop from the pressure.

In my depressing trip down memory lane, I've allowed my pace to slow, and I can hear Abram just steps behind me, his steady breathing filling my ears, this asshole's not even winded. Forcing me legs to move faster, I push ahead as best I can until I feel a large hand wrap around my waist, pulling me to the ground with him as a scream escapes. We tumble through twigs and leaves until I'm on my back and he's hovering right above me. A rushed gasp escapes my lips as I grunt under the weight of him.

Abram doesn't take it easy on me, allowing me space to pull in a full breath, instead he keeps his full weight pressed into my front. The length of him digs into my inner thighs, causing my mouth to instantly go dry, and a grin slowly spreads across his beautiful face. From this vantage point, I can make out some of the intricate workings of his tattoos on the side of his neck. My fingers itch to reach out and touch them, but my arms are trapped beneath his knees on either side of me.

Pushing those thoughts aside, I stare up at him, waiting for his next play. It makes me feel like a walking target for abuse, like it must be me that attracts these kind of men into my orbit, as if they can easily take advantage of me. The idea makes me want to kick my way out of this, fight like hell since I never did before, even if a small part of me is enjoying the hunt. He's not going to hurt me, that much I can tell, but I can't say the same for him pushing my boundaries.

Frustrated with this position, I force some bravery from my lips, hoping he'll do something besides stare at me like a man possessed. "Well? What's your next move, *Abram?*" He watches my tongue dart out to wet my dry lips, feeling dehydrated from the impromptu run I just went on. "Because truthfully, I can't really tell if you're trying to scare me, or fuck me?" I don't know where this boldness comes from, but I go with it, running on mostly adrenaline at this point. I stare down at where our bodies are connected, where his erection presses into me.

Another minute goes by, him taking in as much of me as he can, watching me and enjoying the way I squirm beneath him. I never could have prepared for the words that would leave his lips, as he lifted himself up and headed back towards his house without sparing me another glance. Whatever this game is, he's all in, and the way his body hardened against mine screams he wants me to be all in too. "Both."

After a minute to collect myself, I stand and brush off the back of my pants, dirt and crumbled leaves fluttering back to the earth where they belong. I pay close attention to which direction he headed in, since I have no idea which way is out at this point. I don't even know how far we ran if I'm being honest. I just kept propelling myself forward, trying not to smack into a tree.

Careful to keep my distance, but also maintain sight of him so I don't get lost for a second time, I process his statement and the way he said it so matter of factly as if there isn't a doubt in his mind it'll happen. As June's house comes into view, all I can see is Abram's light gray eyes searing into me with a ferocity I didn't know existed. The way his voice brushed across my face, giving me the kind of chills that reached my toes. "I plan to sink so deep into you that you won't be able to tell where I end and you begin."

82

My head is screaming at me to rethink my previous thought about getting to know him better, steering clear of him seems like the smart thing to do. The guy is unhinged, clearly. But the way my whole body, still buzzing from his words and the feel of him pushed up against me, is shoving my brain aside and taking the lead. This might end really, *really* badly. Even as I slide under my covers, enjoying the feel of fresh sheets chilling my skin, I know how far I'm willing to go down this road. And if it ends bad, then so be it. God knows I've been down the wrong road before.

ISOLDE

chapter fuve

♫

STOKER

My legs are cold when I wake up. Which is weird, because I know I went to bed with my fuzzy pajama pants on. I'm known to slip my socks off in my sleep when my feet get hot, but I find it unlikely I completely removed my pants.

I notice my head next, and how it throbs painfully like a migraine or like I'm severely hungover. Both also unlikely since I only get migraines occasionally just before my period starts. I'm not due for another twelve days...

Sitting up slowly, noticing Grant isn't beside me, I try to recall the events of last night. We went to a charity event, and we were having a nice time until Grant saw me talking to a man and his wife. I know he's possessive and territorial at times, but surely he couldn't have been mad at me talking to someone who's married. Especially given said man's wife was a part of the conversation as well.

I knew he was upset with me, but he never dares show it in public. He simply sidled up to me, wrapping an arm tightly around my waist, and handed me a glass of champagne. Normally I don't drink much at these events, because he expressed long ago it's not lady like to get trashed during these high society outings. So it was only slightly odd he was permitting me another glass, considering I had one when we walked in.

Even being the light weight that I am, I would never get drunk off two glasses of champagne. Things aren't adding up, and waking up alone is making me feel like there's something really off.

Shuffling out of bed, I grab my pajama bottoms that are now at the foot of the bed, and slip them on. They were folded on top of the comforter, not smooshed underneath in the sheets like they should be if I somehow kicked them off in the middle of the night. My stomach rolls with dread as I slowly turn the knob of the bedroom door and look down the hallway.

Grant isn't sitting in his office, which is across the hall from our bedroom, and I don't hear any noise coming from the kitchen. Maybe he left for work early and all of this paranoia is in my head.

Deciding I'm being silly, and simply forgot I took my pajama pants off and have a migraine a week and a half early, I head to the kitchen to make some coffee.

Caffeine is always welcome, especially now.

Just as I breech the archway of the dining room, I catch Grant's silhouette sitting in the arm chair in the living room. My heart kicks into overdrive, nearly beating out of my chest, because my gut knows something is very, very off. Chancing pleasantries, I greet him good morning and offer to make us some coffee. When he says nothing, just continues staring out the window that overlooks the city skyline, I feel sweat begin to bead in my hairline.

"Grant? I-is everything alright?" I ask, only allowing the trembling to be held in my hands, not my voice. Still he says nothing. Simply turns his attention to me, a look of disgust painted in numerous shades of red on his face.

"You're something else, you know that Isolde?"

My head hurts as I try to ride through memories of last night. I know he wasn't happy I was talking to that man and his wife, but I can't remember much after that. If we had a fight, surely I'd remember it. Right?

I go to ask what happened, but close my mouth abruptly when he closes his eyes in frustration. His tell tale sign not to fuck with him, because he's barely holding it together. His temper has only worsened over the years, and I've grown terrified of the beast he unleashes far too often.

"Don't stand there, looking like a filthy whore, and tell me you don't remember last night." My limbs tighten as he stands from the chair and walks over to me. I wait with unease, watching his movements closely, until he's toe to toe with me. For several seconds he says nothing and does nothing. I almost wonder if I'm imagining his anger, when his fist connects harshly with my cheek.

My hands fly to the throbbing area on instinct, but before I can ease some of the pain, he grabs both hands, locking them between one of his. The other grips my pony tail so tight, I see stars behind my lids. Tears are threatening to spill, and without the use of my hands to wipe them away, they fall effortlessly as if they have no idea what they've just done.

Tears only make Grant more angry, feral almost. It's a sure sign of weakness, and though it's perfectly natural to cry when you've just been punched in the face, it's completely unacceptable in his eyes. "Fucking tears. Really, Isolde?"

My mouth is screaming to apologize, but my mind is quicker and keeps the words from tumbling free. Apologies have gotten me nowhere, so I don't see the use in trying now. I have to endure whatever it is he feels I deserve, and the impending doom of what that might be has me nearly vomiting all over the carpet.

With his fist still wound in my hair, he releases my hands and yanks me back down the hallway to our bedroom. That fear has formed itself into a heavy boulder, weighing me down somewhere between my throat and my stomach. Any hope of oxygen is cut off when he slams my body down onto the mattress.

I quickly try scrambling back, leaning my body against the headboard, as he pulls his shirt over his head and tosses it to the floor. Shit.

My body is trembling violently as he slowly crawls onto the mattress, grabbing my ankles and jerking my body forward so that I'm lying right beneath him. "Please." I beg in such a soft whisper, I don't think he even hears it. As soon as his fist slams into my face a second time, do I realize he absolutely heard me.

"You and I both know, begging will get you nowhere."

For the next fifteen minutes, I lay helplessly on the mattress while Grant assaults me, all while reprimanding me for my poor *behavior last night. Repeating over and over, I did this to myself. That girls who misbehave have to be taught a lesson.*

Once he's done, I lie there, staring blankly at the ceiling as he walks into the bathroom. The water in the shower starts, and I listen to the water hitting the tiles and pretend it's my tears. I'm not allowed to cry in front of him, so I live vicariously through other forms of water whenever I can. It brings me an odd sense of peace.

A few minutes go by and Grant reappears next to the bed. He drops a folded towel on my bare chest, he doesn't have to say anything, I already know the drill. But he always does anyways. "Go take a shower you filthy cunt." It's the same words every single time, and every single time, I do as I'm told.

It took me a while to realize he makes me shower after he rapes me so I can't sneak off to the hospital for a rape kit. It doesn't matter anyways, I never report him. Not after the first time I tried and wound up in the hospital. How sick is it that the man who put me there, showed up every day with flowers looking like the perfect boyfriend? Fooling all the nurses and doctors with the same charming smile that fooled me.

After I've showered and Grant has left for work, I pull up the rug in the spare bedroom. We only keep storage in here and we never have overnight guests, so we never made it into a guest room. Under the rug is a slim plank of wood that I wretched up one day and hid a journal in. Pulling it from the floor, I open it and look through all the dates I've written in here since the first assault happened two years ago. Grabbing the pen, I scribble in the date and mentally take notice that today marks his thirtieth assault. In two years I have been sexually assaulted thirty times. I quickly stuff the journal back in place, assure myself that the rug is put back perfectly and race down the hall to the bathroom to dry heave.

This is my life and I've allowed myself to get here. One day, just maybe, I can find a way out.

***

To say I'm nervous about my first shift at Pour Performer would be an understatement. I'm confident I can get the groove of the job down easily enough, and I've worked with POS systems before, too. It's not even the fear of mixing drinks, because like I said to Sasha, I get the sense people around here stick to beer and liquor on the rocks. No, none of that scares me in the slightest. But the idea of having to be a bartender *and* a conversationalist at the same time, is what has me breaking out in a nervous sweat.

Plus, last nights dream still lingers heavily in the forefront of my mind. No amount of coffee could wash it away this morning. It may have just been a dream, but it actually happened, and the fact that my mind is cruel enough to allow the pain to seep in and relive that nightmare, hurts a shit ton.

I try my best to shake it off and focus on my first shift. I know I can do this, and I don't have a psycho boyfriend here to keep watch over me, but still. When you spend six plus years avoiding eye contact with people, and staying glued to your abusers side at all times, it's not something one can easily break free of. But I'm trying, and that's what I keep chanting to myself in my head as I walk up to the door at five minutes to four. I wanted to be here early, and have been ready for over an hour already, so I took the leisurely way here since I couldn't keep pacing the floor at June's place.

Luckily she wasn't home to see me.

At exactly four o'clock, Sasha saunters over with her bag draped over her shoulder and a tumbler of what looks to be coffee. I offer her a smile and wait for her to unlock the door, following her inside as she flicks on lights. "Ready?"

The nerves in my belly swirl around like a tornado, but I nod my head and set my things down in the back next to hers. "Long night, so decided to caffeinate myself so I'm not as much of a bitch as I usually am," she chuckles at her joke and I offer a kind smile in return. I don't know Sasha well enough yet to know what kind of sense of humor she has.

I used to be practically fluent in sarcasm, but dropped that habit real quick when it didn't settle right between Grant and I. He used to say sarcasm was a poor excuse of disrespect and that I needed to know my place.

The more I think about him lately, and all the shit I tolerated, the angrier I get. Not even at him, but myself. For allowing it to go on as long as it did. I try not to be self deprecating, but honestly, it's fucking pathetic.

That's why I'm here, summoning my old college bartending skills and putting myself out there to work a job I would have been terrified of just a month ago. I can't kid myself, I am still terrified, but not in the same sense.

After a quick run down of the place, and showing me where everything is, Sasha brings me to the front of the bar to start setting up stations. Luckily, I remember this part too, though each bar differs from how they set up, it's a pretty basic concept. As we both busy ourselves getting ready to open, I watch Sasha as she moves with ease around the tight space.

I know she owns the bar, but I don't really know anything else about her. I'm hoping she's not going to be a shit boss, but the way she handles herself and how she's treated me so far, makes me feel like I'll be in good hands.

"Sasha?" I ask tentatively, still unsure how to have normal conversations without sweating out my palms and hairline. She regards me with a small nod before looking back at her task of slicing limes. "Can I ask where you got the name for the bar?"

She chuckles to herself for a second, and thinks about her response before she opens her mouth. I can say with certainty from the short time of knowing her, that her response is going to be sarcastic. It makes me look forward to hearing whatever her thoughts are at any given moment. People like Sasha, you never know what you're going to get.

"When I was younger I wanted to be a broadway star. Pretty obvious I didn't go that route," she gestures around the bar as if proving her point. "Figured out early on that I had no acting or singing abilities, so when I bought the bar I made the name an inside joke for myself."

"Over the years people have asked, but ninety-nine percent of the time, they just want me to pour their booze." I think about the pun for a moment, and can't help the smile that spreads across my face. Life is too serious and sometimes you have to find the fun in it, even as a business owner. Makes me wonder what kind of name I would have for my own business, that is if I can figure out what I want to do with my life first.

"My dad would love this place, especially the name. And he undoubtably would ask why you picked it. Guess he falls in the one percent." Just mentioning my dad has my heart sinking slightly. I wish I could find the courage to reach out to them, even if just to let them know I left Grant and that I'm okay.

I still don't think it would be wise to tell them where I am, not yet at least. But the longer I stay here, the more I come to like it. I can picture settling into my own place and having my parents come visit during the warmer months. They've always been active people, looking younger than their age, so I know we could find some really amazing hiking spots around here.

I'm lost in thoughts of them, so I miss when people start filing in to enjoy their happy hour. There's an odd beauty in bars. People from all walks of life come to this one place to forget about their troubles for a little while.

While I don't think it's smart to drink your life away, like some people do, there's nothing wrong with taking the edge off and enjoying a drink or two. Maybe even meet new people or have a conversation you never would have anywhere else.

Within thirty minutes, the place is packed. Music fills the space in between chatter and laughter, and honestly, it makes me smile like a maniac. I didn't exactly have time to get the swing of things before we got busy, but Sasha has been very patient with me. Once I pushed aside my nerves, because lets face it, we were too busy for me to focus on it anyways, I found my groove. I've mainly been waiting tables and replenishing drinks as Sasha stays rooted behind the bar, whipping out drinks like a machine. She's amazing to watch, and if Broadway wasn't her calling, I'd say she found her place here.

"How you doing, girl?" Sasha asks as she shakes a tumbler over her head, pouring the liquid over ice and sliding it to the gentleman on my left.

"Honestly, I feel great!" It's not even a lie, keeping busy like this has helped shut my mind off from other things. One in particular, my weird encounter with Abram. As much as I've tried to shove it aside, it's still hovering in the forefront of my mind.

"I gotta say, I was a little apprehensive at first. Thought maybe you'd be too sweet for this kind of place. But, you're holding your own, and that goes a long way with me."

Fuck, I am so not used to compliments, and right now I'm not sure how to respond. Sasha isn't a talkative woman by nature, preferring to nod in agreement or stay quiet all together. Kind of funny for a person who runs a business that literally guarantees talking to patrons. I take a page form her book, and nod my head with a soft smile before bustling back out to serve the tray of beers I'm holding.

There's a bell above the front door that jingles every time someone walks in. I haven't paid it much attention since people got here, but for some reason the second I hear the little bells jingle their song, I feel the hairs at the base of my neck rise.

Tingling down my spine, all too aware of whoever just walked in.

I'm afraid to look, because I know it's Abram, and I haven't seen him since our little encounter in the woods where he whispered against my ear how he plans to sink so far into me I guarantee I won't be able to walk for a week. A chill works its way over me, and I hate how affected I am by him and his dominating presence.

For someone who doesn't talk much, he commands a lot of attention. A proven point as he makes his way to the bar top and people turn their heads to stare.

Sasha, tough cookie that she is, addresses him with ease, already pouring some amber liquid over ice. "Stoker, been a while since you've come in. To what do I owe the pleasure?" Her sarcasm leaks through a little, and Abram just smirks, bringing the lowball glass to his lips and drinking a sample.

"Sasha, you know you serve the best whiskey in town."

With a shake of her head and an amused smile, I watch as she tips her head in accusation. "I serve the *only* whiskey in town, dumbass."

"That's why it's the best."

He starts to swivel on his stool, so I quickly grab my tray and head to the back and discard the empties. I feel his gaze on me the whole way, like embers dancing across my exposed flesh, singeing into me. I try to shake off the feel of his gray eyes, but the more I focus on something else, the more aware I become of *him*.

How does that make sense?

Having no choice but to face him, I head towards Sasha at the bar when her little bell dings, indicating a new order is ready to be brought out. I try so hard not to meet his eyes, but my self control is non existent at this point. "Isolde."

Goosebumps prickle my skin, and there's no way to hide my reaction to that voice of his, because I'm wearing short sleeves. Abram watches the little dots erupt all over my arms, and a knowing grin covers his face. I want to smack it off of him, turn on my heel and get back to work.

But Sasha is right next to me, and I don't think that would make the best impression on my first shift. So I go with unaffected cool, or at least, try to.

"Abram," I regard him with a tiny glance, afraid if I look too long I'll get lost in those eyes. The ones that burn me alive without even trying. His last name becomes more and more fitting each time I interact with him, and I hate him for it even more.

Still standing right next to me, Sasha glances up and looks between the two of us. A slow whistle leaving her lips as she pours a bottle of tequila over five shot glasses for the group of guys in the back. I wouldn't say they've been trouble since they got here, but they definitely don't have any manners to write home about.

"Well I'll be damned." Abram looks at her, shaking his head about to tell her something when she speaks up again. "You let her call you Abram?"

Wait, what?

"Leave it, Sasha," he doesn't make eye contact with me again, and now I'm genuinely curious about what I seem to be missing.

"Uh, isn't that his name?" The question leaves my mouth before I think better of it and I watch his reaction. Clenching his jaw tight, he keeps his gaze fixed on his glass. After a few labored seconds, Sasha pipes up again.

"He's gone by Stoker since he was a kid. Haven't heard anyone brave enough to call him by his first name in years." Grabbing the bucket beneath her station, Sasha heads to the back to get more ice.

I think back to the few times I've even addressed Abram, trying to remember if he gave any reaction to me using his first name, but I can't. I've always been so consumed by his presence that I hardly notice anything else.

The rest of my shift goes by quickly, minus the ruckus those five guys kicked up about an hour ago. Sasha had them not so politely escorted out, and I heaved a sigh of relief once they were gone. I wouldn't admit it to her, but I got a weird feeling about them.

Abram never left, just sat at the bar all night, nursing that glass of whiskey until it was so watered down, he gulped the rest in one shot. As much as I wish I wasn't, I was very aware of him the entire night. He volleyed between watching me intently, and ignoring me all together. At one point I chuckled to myself as the teenage version of me remembered the line in Twilight where Bella tells Edward his mood swings are giving her whiplash.

Very fitting, if you ask me.

By midnight, my feet ache from being on them for over eight hours and my wrist is sore from carrying around a tray all night. But my smile couldn't be kept off my face if I tried. Working hard tonight felt good, and the tips weighing down my apron don't hurt either. If I can work a shift like this even a few nights a week, I'd be able to save up for my own place in no time.

Sure, I'd miss living with June, and how close we've become. But I can't rely on her forever, and I think we both know that.

The bar is empty, and I don't miss how Abram is the last person to leave, and only because Sasha is practically shoving him out the door. A little part of me is hoping he only stayed as long as he did because I was here. But I quickly squash that thought when I remember he's been coming here for years.

"You did good," Sasha says like a proud mama bear as she locks the front door. I feel good, and hearing a compliment from her only improves my mood, despite how exhausted I am.

"Tomorrow you're gonna feel the effects of this shift, so take two days off and then come back. Sound good?" She brushes away her thick dark curls, and I'm suddenly envious of how striking she is. Looks to me like she's either superhuman, and the work from today doesn't deter her, or she's just used to working these shifts everyday.

A part of me wants to protest, knowing I can do this again even if I am sore, but I nod my head in agreement having the slight feeling I'll be thankful of this decision in the morning. Besides, this gives me more time to work on the manor in the meantime.

We wave goodnight, and I head over to my car across the street. It's dark out, aside from a few dimmed streetlights, and the soft glow of a cigarette floating in front of the dark figure leaning against my car is all I can see.

If I didn't suspect who it was, I'd probably run back to Sasha like a scared little kid. But the telltale ember burning mixed with his distinct scent of cedar and nicotine, has me relaxing only slightly. While I don't exactly feel safe with Abram, I also remind myself he could have hurt me by now. *Unless he's trying to earn your trust first.*

That snide voice always finds a way to stand out, and I shake my head slightly to rid myself of it. As I approach Abram, he doesn't look up. Focusing more on his boots than the fact that I just want to get in my car and go home.

"You're kind of blocking my door," I say, obviously.

After another ten seconds, I start to grow impatient and I'm about to tell him off when he looks up and our gazes meet, snuffing his cigarette out with his boot as he watches me.

"That's the third time I've seen you do that," I say, unable to hide my annoyance.

"And what is *that* you're referring to?"

"Dumping your discarded cigarette butt on the ground." I watch him for a reaction, and he doesn't give one, which irritates me even more.

"What's your point?" He finally asks.

"It's fucking unattractive to litter, that's the point," I manage to spit out, as if he actually cares what I find attractive or not.

Abram pushes his body away from my car, leaning in close enough I can practically taste the nicotine on his lips. I watch him watch me, wondering if he'll try something like he did in the woods. I'm always on guard when he's around now, equally loving and hating the way it makes my body feel. Nervous, but also alive in some fucked up way.

The street around us is completely empty, everyone gone home for the night to sleep off the buzz. I notice even Sasha's car has gone, and I feel the same unsureness I did the first time I was alone with Abram.

What feels like hours, but was probably a mere few seconds, goes by and Abram tucks a loose strand of hair behind my ear, lingering for a second as his hand grazes my lobe. His eyes burn into mine, and I wonder if he's holding back something he wants to say, but he just watches me with rapt attention. "Get home," he demands, with a bite in his tone, like his words are clipped for a reason I can't understand.

He makes no move to leave, watching me as confusion lines my features. "It gets dark around here, and I'm not talking about the sky." Tingles run down my spine, settling in the soles of my shoes.

Without another word, or even a glance, he strides away. I turn just in time to see him mount his bike before speeding off down the dark street. I rush to get in my car, suddenly feeling very unsettled with his statement. What the fuck did he mean by that?

***

Despite going to bed past one in the morning, I'm up and ready for the day. Feeling renewed after finding a job and doing well enough that Sasha praised me. My smile is present again as I think about how that felt to hear. I've gone so long without being complimented on anything, it feels weird and rewarding. A weird combination, and one I never want to go away.

June left early to open the cafe, so I miss her again this morning. We're basically programmed to only see one another at dinner, giving us the opportunity to catch up on the days events. Which usually results in me gushing over how excited I am with the progress in the manor.

Her and I decided it would be more fun to keep everything a secret until it's done. Once everything is ready, I'll surprise June with the reveal. I'd be lying if it didn't give me a little anxiety, but she keeps reassuring me I can do whatever I think is best with the space. She has no preference.

In some ways that makes the project more exciting, as well as daunting. I know she says she doesn't care what I do, but I also want her to love it. And not love it just because I did it and its given me some semblance of peace and independence, but because she truly loves the space.

Alex has been helping me with the renovations, while Abram mostly works at night when no one else is around. It bothers me sometimes that he doesn't feel like he can work in the house while we're there, but a lot of things about him bother me.

Maybe it's just because I don't fully understand him yet. Maybe I never will.

A comment Sasha made last night has been in the forefront of my mind since she said it. The fact that no one has been brave enough to call him by his first name, everyone just refers to him as Stoker. I want to know why that is, but it seems a little too soon to ask such a personal question.

Although, he kind of squashed that courtesy when he broke through my personal bubble and encased my body with his on the forrest floor. My skin flushes, and grows hot at the memory, like I can still feel his body melded into mine. I can still smell his hot breath feathering across my cheek as he whispered what he wants to do to me. I try to push it away, but it always comes back. Like a fucking boomerang. The sick truth is, I don't ever feel threatened by his words or his actions. He's never given me reason to believe he would actually hurt me the way I'm used to being hurt.

It's a thought that runs through my mind at all hours of the day. How I could possibly feel safe and scared, turned on and terrified all at the same time when I'm around him. I push the thoughts aside for now as I get ready to tackle the day.

I eat a quick breakfast, and head over to get started on today's renovations. Alex is supposed to meet me here after lunch to finish the clean up from taking out the wall between the kitchen and dining room. It already looks so much bigger and brighter in here, giving the space an open concept. As soon as he finishes up today, I can start painting. The thought makes me want to do a giddy little dance.

Without a second thought, I start dancing around the first floor, AirPods blaring in my ears as I listen to the Foo Fighters. The house smells like a mixture of cleaning supplies and paint, and maybe I'm high from the fumes but I swore I saw something move out of the corner of my eye.

I pull one AirPod out to listen more clearly, and ultimately decide I was probably spinning around too fast and thought I saw something. Putting the AirPods back in, I close my eyes and really let loose. I'm sure if anyone was here to see me, I'd be embarrassed, but there isn't, so I dance like my life depends on it.

I'm halfway through the next song when a firm hand grabs my arm, spinning me around. I don't know how loud I scream, but I can feel the sound ricochet inside my chest and I instinctively cover my eyes pretending there's nothing here to harm me. Suddenly, my headphones are ripped from my ears and a loud voice filters in, startling me more than when he grabbed my arm. I'm afraid to look, something tells me he's pissed by the way heat is rolling off his body in massive waves.

That same gravely voice I've heard in my dreams a few times lately, though I'll never admit that to anyone else, I can barely admit it to myself. "Look at me, Isolde." My eyes remain squeezed shut, and it feels like my heart is trying to leap frog out of my chest. The grip he has on my arm loosens a fraction, maybe hoping that will lessen my fear.

With slight irritation, he speaks again. "Please." Woah. I didn't know Abram had any manners, this is a new development. Before opening my eyes, I take a deep breath, inhaling as much of his scent as I can, cataloging it to memory in case we're never this close again. I will my heart rate to slow down too, but given the way my body reacts to his proximity and scent, it kicks into overdrive instead.

Slowly, I peak one eye open to find him staring down at me with a bored expression. His height towers over me, and his hair that's longer on top flops into his eyes slightly. He always smells so fucking good, and I've never liked cigarettes, so that's really saying something. Abram watches me open my other eye until I'm fully facing him, ready for him to raise hell.

When he doesn't say anything, just continues studying me, I smooth down my hair so my hands have something to do other than itching to reach out and touch him. I have a feeling that wouldn't go over too well. Though he seems to have no qualms about putting his hands on me whenever he sees fit.

"I was half expecting you to be mad," I admit as I try to turn away from him, but his voice always keeps me rooted where I am.

"Is that why it took you forever to open those eyes?" He asks. *Those eyes?* Do my eyes affect him the way his affect me? I think about it for a moment until I notice the annoyed look on his face again. He's losing patience with me, and I want nothing more than to tell him to fuck off. This is the moment in the movie where I'm about to throw him out because he messed up my groove. I'm sure Kuzco would approve.

"Your personality hasn't been the most forthcoming, so you'll have to forgive me for thinking you'd be irritated by my shrill screaming. Will your ears be okay?" I tease lightly, hoping he doesn't take it too seriously.

When he smirks just a little, I know I've got him. "What are you doing here anyways? I thought you didn't want to work around me." It can't be about Alex because they work together in construction on a daily basis.

"What makes you think I don't want to work around you?"

"The fact that you haven't been by the house *once* since I started restoring it a month ago. Either you hate the house, or me." I busy my hands by wiping down the baseboards in the dining room, hoping to distract myself from the fact that I brought up the possibility of him hating the house. I'm sure in some ways, he does.

I start imagining what color scheme I want for this space and I'm hoping to start painting in the next few days. I have a few color samples hanging on the wall since I'm finding it impossible to make a decision and stick with it.

I continue my work as Abram leans against the doorframe watching me. I can feel the tension, like he wants to say something again, but doesn't. Every time I'm around him I feel like he's constantly holding back his thoughts. I get the sense he doesn't extend the same courtesy to everyone else, so I try to take it as a positive.

"I think you and I both know I don't hate you, Isolde." The words hang in the air like the heavy fog outside. It's a simple sentence but I feel so much more from those few words, searching for the hidden meaning. I guess it's not an insane thought that he doesn't hate me. I certainly wouldn't mount a person I hate in the forrest, or hang out at their place of work until closing.

That one is still a mystery to me, though. Why bother hanging around just to inform me that it gets dark around here. That for *sure* had a hidden meaning, I just haven't figured out what it is. I'm constantly thrown around like clothes in a dryer when he talks to me. He watches me like he wants to kiss me or throttle me, and the scale isn't exactly tipping one way or the other just yet.

When he speaks, it's always in riddles or something, leaving me more confused and yearning to ask more questions knowing I won't get a straight answer. Several times I've had to resist the urge to beg him to play twenty questions with me, hoping I'll get *something* out of him.

It takes me a while to respond with my thoughts fighting for top priority. But when I turn around to face him, he's gone. Well that's rude.

I decide not to let it bother me and go back to what I was doing. This is the kind of thing that makes me crazy though, I think as I throw the rag down on the hardwood floors we finished sanding down and staining last week. Why does he have to be so aloof one moment, insanely intense the next, to disappearing without a word? If Bella thought Edwards mood swings were giving her whiplash, it's because she never met anyone like Abram Stoker.

***

By the time I push thoughts of Abram out of my mind, Alex has joined me to finish with the wall between the kitchen and dining room. When we're done and the sun is setting low behind the clouds and fog, I look around feeling immensely proud of what we've done in here so far.

When I first walked through those front doors, I hadn't been expecting what awaited me. I was hopeful, sure, but I really thought I was going to be walking into a moldy, ripped to the studs, *mess*. A surge of warmth rushed through me when I saw it's potential, and knowing I was going to be the one to bring it back to life oddly gave *me* life.

STOKER

I think I stumbled upon this town not only because it was fate meeting June, but because this house was calling to me. A soul mate doesn't have to be a person, maybe it's a place. And if that's true, then I might have finally found my home.

100

ISOLDE

chapter six

🎵

If We Being Real • Dark Academia & Brown Eyed Girl

STOKER

The next few weeks fly by as I continue working on the house and working several shifts a week at Pour Performer. Alex has become a staple in my life, alongside June. Who I still swear is my guardian angel. I've even seen Abram a few times, outside of working on the house and the fact that he shows up at every one of my shifts, sitting at a table nursing a whiskey on ice, until closing.

I tried telling him it was unnecessary, but something in his gaze told me not to push it. He was here for whatever reason made him sleep better at night. And even though I don't always feel entirely safe around him when I'm alone, it makes me feel better knowing he's here *if* I should need him.

Tonight, however, he's not here, and for reasons I can't place, I'm slightly disappointed. Every time the bell above the door jingled, I found myself searching the faces of who walked in. Each time it wasn't him made my heart sink a tiny bit more.

I lean against the brick of the building, letting the cold seep into my bones, as Sasha locks the door. It was packed tonight, being a Saturday, and I sweat through my shirt in the first hour. Thankfully it's black so no one could tell.

The group of guys who were here my first night, came back again, and unease crawled up my spine when they leered at me every time I dropped off their drinks. What's even worse is my car won't start. Fucking great.

Sasha already left, and I don't want to call her to come back and give me a ride. I also don't want to walk, especially this late and with hardly any streetlights. Words Abram spoke weeks earlier find their way to the forefront of my mind. *"It gets dark around here."* I try to fight the chill in my bones as I sit in my car, trying to figure out what my best option is, when headlights flash across my windshield, catching my attention. The car slows to a stop as it pulls up along my driver side window, and I feel that unease wash over me again as I hear the voices of the five guys who were at the bar earlier.

The driver of the car whistles at me, trying to get my attention, and my fingers instantly reach for the lock. At least if I keep the doors locked, they can't get to me right? That bitch voice in my head breaks through with a sneer, *they can always break the windows you idiot.* I really don't like it when my mind does that shit. Not helping! I want to yell back.

The guys have rolled down all their windows now, each of them trying to get my attention, knowing I'm actively ignoring them at this point. I really don't want to deal with this right now, and my body is starting to shake with nervous energy. Glancing down at my phone, I search for Alex's number when I see Abram's name pop up first. I don't remember him giving me his number though. He must have snuck it in there when I wasn't looking.

Normally, that would really piss me off. He has no right to go in my phone, but in this moment I'm thanking the heavens above Abram is the way he is. I type out a message quick, firing it off before I can change my mind.

Those rowdy guys from the bar on my first shift... they're outside my car right now. It won't start and I'm sorry to bother you, but... I need your help.

The text bubbles immediately appear, and I watch them as the guys voices grow more irritated with each second that I ignore them.

On my way.

I've never been so excited to see three words in all my life. I resist the urge to ask why he wasn't here in the first place, since he's been at every shift I've worked. Maybe he was with another woman, finally realizing he wasn't getting anywhere with me. The thought makes me sick, but not as sick as I feel watching the guy from the passenger seat open his door, and walk towards my car.

"Hey! Why won't you talk to us, you little bitch? Too good for us or somethin'?" His voice is slurring slightly, not as bad as he should be considering how much he's drank tonight, and I do know how much since I was the one delivering drink after drink for hours.

It only takes a second.

A blip.

A suspended moment frozen as I watch the hazy eyes of a man take in my fear and harness it as his own power. Power to make me cower and pull into my shell when we both know even that couldn't protect me.

I let my mind wander, imagining what his breath would smell like as he pressed himself up against my cheek. Holding me hostage with the scent of stale beer and a misplaced sense of privilege. It brings me back to all the times I *was* in exactly that position, with someone I trusted no less.

My nervous shakes are beginning to feel epileptic as I watch the guy come closer to my window, and just as I feel tears beginning to well in my eyes, the headlights of a motorcycle catch my eye. A breath of relief leaves me in a rush, making me lightheaded. Whenever I'm scared, I swear I can always smell rust. My therapist said it could be because of my trauma and all the blood I shed at the hands of Grant.

Blood has a metallic rust flavor, and I've come very accustomed to the taste of my own blood.

Abram hops off his bike, walking over to the guys with such grace and calmness, I almost wonder if he knows them and is about to send them on their way. The thought dissipates the second his fist connects with the guys nose who is standing next to my window. I scream as blood erupts on the glass, and I scramble back in my seat as Abram issues blow after to blow until the guy is a crumpled up bloody mess on the concrete.

Just as he turns towards the four other guys in the car, they speed off. Fucking pathetic. If the guy on the ground wasn't such a creep, I'd feel bad his friends just abandoned him in the street.

Without missing a beat, Abram grabs the neck of the guys jacket, and drags him back against a tree. He slumps to the side, passed out from both alcohol and a beating. As much as I wanted them to leave me alone, I didn't want Abram hurting anyone for me. My gut is unsettled as I watch him pull a cigarette from his leather jacket, lighting it and inhaling deep like it's his only source of calm right now.

He hasn't come over to me yet, as I sit huddled in the back seat of my car, still shaking like a leaf. I've never seen this side of him before, and I don't like it. I can't erase the image of his eyes, almost black with rage, as he grabbed the guy and smashed his face in. Maybe I should have called Alex after all. I doubt he would have gotten here as fast, but still.

Once he finishes his cigarette, he stubs it out with his boots and kicks it at the guy groaning against the tree. He'll be alright, I hope, but he'll have a nasty headache come morning. I just want to go home, snuggle under the covers and forget this ever happened.

I'm feeling a little like I overreacted, but due to my past I can't take any chances. I know I need to stop feeling like every man is out to harm me, but I can't help it. Those guys were rowdy and handsy all night, so I made an assumption when they pulled up next to me. Maybe I could have said hi, and told them I wasn't interested. Maybe they would have left.

Or maybe, they would have tak-... I smack my hands against my forehead, forcing that voice to stop before the words leak into my thoughts. I can't keep thinking like a victim. I need to be stronger than this, fucking hell.

The tap on my window startles me, and my heart leaps up to my throat before slowly settling down when I see Abram watching me. "Come on. I'll take you home." Judging by what I just witnessed, I don't know if I want him taking me home at this point.

I sit frozen in place, unable to exit my car when he knocks again. "Please, Isolde." Finally I lift my eyes to meet his, unsure if I'll find them black still, but my muscles relax when I see they're back to their light gray. Unlocking the door, I step out slowly, never taking my eyes off him.

"Ever ridden a motorcycle before?" His question catches me off guard, especially with how he said it with such ease. He just pummeled a guys face, and is acting like he could eat a stack of pancakes or something.

"N-no." What can I say? What makes any of what just happened normal enough that I can hop on this guys bike and allow him to drive me through heavily wooded dark winding roads?

He's watching me with that focus again, and I think he can see how freaked out I am. With slow, deliberate steps, he comes closer to me until I'm backed against my car. "Don't fear me, okay? It's all I ask." What? Everything he's done up until this point has filled me with nothing but fear, excitement, confusion and about a dozen other emotions.

"F-fear you? Abram, I barely know you! I shouldn't have called you. I should have known," he grabs my arm, forcing me to face him again.

"I am the *only* person you should have called. I told you it gets dark around here, and I may look like a monster to you right now because of all this," he gestures to the guy still slumped over covered in blood, before continuing. "But there are worse ones out there, and I guarantee, I'm the only one who knows how to take care of them."

The hold on my wrist isn't harsh, in fact its feather light as he traces lightly up and down my pulse point. It's a calming tactic, and it's working. He really doesn't want to hurt me. He wants to hurt *for* me, and those are two different things entirely. I should back away, create some space between us, but I can't. I feel my insides racing, blood pumping making my ears rings, and I'm all too aware of the finger brushing up against my skin so intimately.

Abram watches my eyes, only dropping them to my lips for a second when I lick them lightly. The air feels thick and I watch his resolve begin to fade, watching as he battles with what to do next. I don't know what comes over me, but in a split second decision, I make the decision for him. I stop overthinking and lean up on my tip toes to press my lips against his. They're soft and hard at the same time, like that's possible somehow, but only with him. He doesn't move at first, allowing me to sample him at a leisurely pace.

When I finally pull away, I feel the static and buzz of need dragging me closer to him. I've never experienced a kiss like that and maybe it's because of the situation, maybe it's something else. But all I want is to do it again and again and *again*. I want to drink in his flavor, savoring it and committing it to memory so I can experience it forever, if only in my mind.

Before I can move in to capture his lips for a second time, his hand is wrapping around my throat, pulling me towards him. Our lips clash in an aggressive need to taste each other. Give and take. His tongue pushes its way past my lips, dancing with my own and I groan into his mouth at the taste of him. Woodsy with a touch of mint.

Twining my arms around his neck I attempt to pull him closer. Afraid that if I think about what we're doing too clearly, I'll pull away and break this connection. I spend too much time overthinking and *way* too much time being scared. For once, I just want to be present.

Abram doesn't allow for anything else, keeping me so in the moment I truly don't know where he begins and I end, just like he said. Shit.

He's the first to break the kiss, and I whimper internally at the loss of his warmth. My eyes are still closed when I feel his thumb graze my lower lip, sending shivers down my back. "Look at me." He commands, and I'm helpless to the timbre of his voice. My eyelids flutter open until I'm looking up into his beautiful face, it should be illegal how good he looks.

"Let's go for a ride." I follow him on wobbly legs as he guides me to his bike. Concern for my car is a distant thought as I watch him swing a leg over the bike and hook a finger at me to join him. I'm about to climb behind him the he shakes his head no. "You're driving."

"W-what? No, I-I've never driven a motorcycle before. I doubt you want your bike mangled in a ditch by the end of the night."

"A. It is the end of the night," he says, holding up his watch to show me that it's well past midnight. "And B. You can do this, I'll help you." I don't know why he has so much faith in me when I have absolutely none in myself. This seems like an awful big gamble to take considering this bike is his main source of transportation.

I can see Abram eyeing me, watching me weigh my options, tapping his foot with impatience. "Isolde, you can do this. Trust me, okay?" I try really hard not to laugh in his face, because for whatever reason, he's being as sincere as he possibly can. But I'm not sure how I'm expected to trust him when history is giving me every reason not to. *He did just come pick your ass up and save you, just saying.*

That voice is often just a bitch, reminding me of things I already know and don't want to hear, but right now it's making sense. Heaving a sigh, I swing a leg over so I'm mounting the bike, leaning right up against Abram's chest. His muscled and warm chest, I might add. The smell of him encircles me and I breathe it in like it's my life source.

He places a spare helmet on me, but not before slipping one of his AirPods in my ear, placing the other in his own. I don't ask why, my mind too riddled with thoughts of us ending up in body bags by the time this little adventure is over.

Abram switches the key on and kickstarts the bike, making it vibrate beneath my seat, and I feel the adrenaline rush right to my chest. I've never even been on a motorcycle, Grant never would have allowed it and if he had found out I'd tried it, I never would have heard the end of my reckless behavior.

But he's not here, Abram is, and he's telling me I can do this. Assuring me I'm capable and that he has faith in me, even when I don't in myself. How can I pass up on this opportunity to branch out and try new things, even when they terrify me? I decided recently to quit being so scared, and life has given me a golden opportunity to test that new mindset.

Bringing my hands to the handlebars, Abram squeezes them over the clutch, and I feel like I might pass out. His breath tickles the spot beside my ear as he gently instructs me to slowly release the clutch when I'm ready.

A few deep breaths later, I release the clutch a millimeter at a time and I don't miss the way Abram chuckles behind me. He's probably been riding for years, and I'm thankful he doesn't appear to be annoyed by my snail pace progress.

My only instruction is to fully release the clutch, keep the bike straight and just drive. Abram increases the throttle slowly as we pick up speed, just as a song I've never heard filters through the one AirPod in my ear. The opening notes build behind the tiny speaker in my ear and I'm instantly transfixed. Giving my body over to the music as the thrum of Abram's bike vibrates beneath my thighs.

The wind is whipping at my face, causing my hair to swirl around us like a tornado. There's a light drizzle, and my body shivers from the cold but also from the excitement, and I don't think I've ever felt so alive.

With one hand, Abram wraps around my middle, pulling me flush against his chest, helping me relax. I'm trying to focus on the road but am far too aware of the way his body is making mine buzz with delight. He's barely touching me with that one hand, the other holding the gear shift, and my body is acting like his hands are everywhere.

I feel his breath on my lobe again, and smile instinctively, attempting to keep my eyes open and focused on the winding road ahead of us. "Keep your eyes on the road and focus, understand?" I am, I want to tell him, unsure of why he's asking me that, or was he telling me? Suddenly I feel the hand that was wrapped around my middle, slip beneath the hem of my shirt.

My breath lodges in my throat and I think I'm dreaming. He's not going to… touch me, is he? My breathing begins accelerating, faster than the bike at this point and I don't even know if I should tell him to stop, that this is crazy. One finger pushes past the buckle of my jeans and I swear I see stars, and he hasn't even touched me yet.

Just the idea of him touching me like this is making my heart thump erratically out of my chest, and he smiles against my cheek, knowing exactly what he's doing to me. "I bet you're already wet for me, aren't you?" I don't know, am I? This is the craziest thing I've ever done, and yet I don't want it to stop.

I can't answer him, trying so hard to maintain my focus, when a finger brushes along the lining of my underwear. I don't miss the growl of approval, even over the engine roaring beneath us, when his finger makes contact with that wet spot above my aching heat.

"I knew it," he declares triumphantly, and I don't know whether to be excited or horrified at the idea that I'm turned on by this situation. "You get off on the thrill, don't you little bird?" Without even mulling over his words, my head bobs up and down on instinct, confirming what he claimed he already knew.

"God, you probably taste even better than you feel right now," Abram growls in my ear again, barely holding back restraint, and I push my hips forward to connect with his finger. I don't even have to say the words, that action gives him all the consent he needs to slip a finger beneath the hem of my underwear, agonizingly slow, and run that same digit across my wet folds.

The feeling is electric, and I hold in a gasp, embarrassed at how much I'm enjoying this. "Don't be quiet, little bird. No one can hear you but me and the night sky. Tell us how much you love it, I want to hear you." Why does that make me feel worshiped in a way I've never felt? Abram adds a second finger, adjusting so that both are lined up at my entrance, and without warning, thrusts both inside me. I moan at the impact, feeling so full. He's barely done anything and already I could come undone.

'If We Bëing Real' flows through the AirPods in tune with the way my hips are now meeting Abrams skilled fingers, without even trying. I move on instinct, the soundtrack of the night mixing with the music is giving my entire being an out of body experience.

My cheeks flame red at the sounds I'm making over the music, the same sounds that are clearly driving Abram wild. I feel his erection press up against me, grinding into my back. I arch my back, pushing against his chest with each thrust of his fingers, feeling the waves already building, ready to crash. "You're filthy, aren't you baby? Loving the feel of my fingers fucking you while you keep us steady. Such a good girl," his praise cascades over me in waves, and I soak up every word. The honey of his praise mixed with the rough timbre of his voice is driving me mad, and I just want to lose myself to the moment, more than I already am.

Wind swirls around us like mother nature is dancing, the moon hanging high above us creating the only spotlight and the pavement beneath us acting like a stage. I moan in tune with the music and the way Abram skillfully plays with my clit as he slams two fingers in and out of me.

He quickens the tempo of his fingers, playing me like a damn piano and I'm so close. I don't even realize I'm moving my hips back and forth in time with his ministrations until I feel the bike wobble slightly. My eyes bug out and I try to focus on the road as much as I can, even though everything in me is screaming to shut my eyes and ride the high.

I can feel the wetness pooling between my thighs and Abram knows I'm close. Pressing the palm of his hand against my clit, while continuing his thrusts, I'm about to explode when I feel the bike abruptly stop. I panic, thinking I must have crashed us but Abram keeps going. "Let go, baby. Show me how beautiful you sound when you come with my fingers sheathed in your sweet cunt." Holy shit, the dirty talk adds to the heat building inside me, and I scream as the flood gates open, wave after wave of euphoric bliss taking over as I come.

Abram keeps his fingers inside me until I come down from the high, heated cheeks and pounding heart. Slowly, he pulls them from beneath my jeans and when I turn to look at him, he has this wicked glint in his eyes as he pushes both fingers into his mouth, sucking them clean of my arousal. If I thought I would die form embarrassment earlier, I surely will now.

I go to cover my face, when Abram stops me, taking my hands in one of his. He gently rubs a finger along my bottom lip, smearing what's left of my orgasm so I can taste myself. I've never done that before, and it feels like something that should gross me out, but as soon as the flavor erupts on my tongue, I gaze up at him. "You taste so good, little bird."

Jesus.

"Guess I found my new favorite dessert." My eyes are hooded, fogged with a lust filled bliss as I watch him get off the bike and scoot my butt back on the seat. Thank God. I don't think I could get us home in my post orgasmic haze. Starting the bike once again, Abram taps my arms so that I hold his waist.

We move much faster with him in control speeding down the unlit abandoned road. The trees whiz past me in a blur of black, only able to make out the patch of wet concrete in front of us. I squeeze Abram tightly, keeping my eyes closed at first, until he slows down a fraction. Hesitantly, I open my eyes to see the turn for the road to June's house, and I know we're almost back.

Feeling slightly disappointed the night is coming to an end, I try to work through how to say goodnight to him once I hop off his bike. Is tonight going to be something I regret in the morning? Not likely. But another thought has my stomach turning as he slows the bike to a stop in front of June's front porch. How many other women has he had on his bike like this? I try not to dwell on that, because everyone has a past and he doesn't need to explain himself to me. But I'd be lying if I didn't feel a twinge of jealousy at the thought of him doing this with anyone else.

As I climb off the seat, Abram pulls me back so that my front rests against his leg. I watch several emotions flicker across his face, excitement, regret maybe, and indifference. Maybe he's the one who will regret this in the morning. I'm about to tell him what happened was a mistake, giving him an easy out if he needs one, when he speaks.

"Don't look at me like that," he says as he watches me with hungry eyes. I try and switch my expression to a confused one.

"Like what?"

He rolls his eyes, brushing a hand through his hair that's longer on top, something I've really grown to love. "And don't play dumb, we both know you're not. You're looking at me like you're wishing I drove us to my place."

He could be a mind reader, or just really good at reading people. Something I'm still trying to work on. "I would have, just so you know. I would have brought you back to my place to see what you taste like as you come on my tongue first, then my cock. I want to see the look on your face as I drive into you to the hilt, slamming into parts of you so deep you didn't know they existed until I found them. But I'm heading out of town, so…I guess we'll just have to wait a little longer." I feel his finger lightly brush the shell of my ear, resulting in a crop of goosebumps.

My breathing is ragged, and my back is still pressed up against his chest where he's kept me firmly in place as he described the things he wants to do to me…*again*. He lets the last words hang in the air a moment and I realize I've lost all forms of communication the second he said *come* and *cock*.

"We don't know each other all that well yet, little bird. But I hope you didn't think I was going to say what I said the night I found you in the woods and not follow through with it. I plan on taking you many, *many* times, so don't even think about running while I'm away. Wherever you go, you know I'll find you."

Everything he keeps saying has my mind careening down the road that will take me far away from this man, knowing I damn well shouldn't entertain anything when it comes to him. But something deeper inside me, begging to be set free, is screaming to go for it. To follow that little voice bursting at the seams in the deep recesses of my mind to take that leap.

Abram Stoker is nothing like the men I've dated in the past, which already has a point in his favor. He's rugged and dark, rough around the edges and probably the insides as well. He's covered in tattoos and smokes a pack a day. He's everything my parents and society has warned me away from since I was old enough to find boys attractive. But the longer I look at him, the more I hear his deep voice vibrate through me, lighting up parts that have long been snuffed out, the more I realize he's not what I've ever wanted, but maybe he's exactly what I've always *needed.*

I went for the man I thought would be good for me, the man I *thought* I wanted, but he was only good on paper. And all it got me was a dozen hospital visits and a battered self deprecating view of myself. I can say with certainty, I don't know what I want to come from this *thing* with Abram, but more than anything, I know I don't want to walk away until I find out.

I swing one leg over the bike and twist so that I'm facing him once again. He lit a cigarette while I mentally went through the steps in my head of what I plan to do, and I watch the smoke frame his face the way fog hugs the trees. Every interaction with him has been initiated by him, and him *only.* As my hands shake, palms full of sweat, I make a decision that tells him everything he needs to know without uttering a word.

As he lifts the cigarette to his lips, about to inhale, I take the end from him and toss it to the ground, stubbing it out with my boot. As soon as he leaves I'll be picking it up to throw in the trash because I refuse to become someone who litters. Brows furrowing, he watches me as I lean up towards him, bracing my hands on the seat between our touching thighs. On a deep inhale, I breathe in his masculine scent, mouth watering at the thought of tasting him, and press my lips to his purposefully.

I start slow before slipping my tongue past his soft lips, opening for him so our tongues can dance, keeping time to the steady beat of my heart thumping in my chest against his. He groans against me as he grips my waist with forceful fingers, dragging me closer to him. Those same hands grip the underside of my thighs, pulling me up so my legs drape over his on the bike. Now straddling him, I weave my hands through his hair, tugging tightly to bring him as close as possible. My hips grind with his on instinct, and I let my body do the talking I'm unable to.

Thoughts flutter through my mind as his hands roam across my belly, just under the curve of my breasts. How long will he be gone? Where is he going? I want to ask so many things but can only seem to keep the conversation where it is. The wordless connection through our bodies that keeps bringing us back for more, it's not just him coming to me anymore. No, I want this with an undeniable force, a force so strong I try to match it with the bucking of my hips against his now rock hard length.

Disappointment lances through me when I feel Abram pull back slightly, nipping my bottom lip with his teeth before sliding me off his lap. The dance we were both willingly lost in, has come to an end as I watch his hooded eyes rake over every inch of me. "Such a vixen, little bird. And you don't even know it."

Abram stands and holds a large hand out to me, helping me off the bike next. My legs feel like jello as he guides me to the back door of June's house. "If I didn't have to leave right now, you know I wouldn't let you walk through that door without bruises on your neck and the remnants of my cum rolling down your thighs. But I do, so this will have to do for now."

"You're leaving right now?" I ask as I check my watch, the time reads almost two in the morning. I feel like it's only been minutes since he knocked that guy out and took me for a ride on his bike. My cheeks flush at the kind of ride he *really* took me on, and I feel Abram's fingers gently stroke the side of my face.

"Keep thinking what you're thinking," he instructs as he backs away slightly, turning towards his bike. I feel my body move towards him like a magnet, almost unable to resist the pull, but quickly right myself.

"For all you know I'm thinking I never want to see you again," I say to his back.

Abram barks out a laugh that echoes across the tress, and I try to hide the smile that threatens to give me away. "Baby, we're past all that now, don't you think?"

"I don't bug you anymore?" I carp.

Abram stops mid stride, turning his head to look at me over his broad shoulders. He closes the distance just as quickly and takes my face in his hands, making sure he holds my gaze. "You finally *see* me, don't you?" I want to ask what he means, I've always seen him haven't I? But then I remember what he told me on the street the other day, that he finally figured out why I bug him so much. He knew I was looking but never allowing myself to get too close. I never allowed him to see that I saw *him*, until tonight.

Tonight I took initiative, showed him what I wanted and how he made me feel. Instead of hiding away like I have for years. Finally, I took what I wanted. The way he's looking at me, like he knows what I'm thinking, that I realize what he's referring to, makes me feel strong. Praised in a way. The feeling is almost addicting, and I bite my bottom lip to keep from ruining the moment with all my questions and what if's. He's allowing me to be bold, take what I want without resistance and keep it without regret.

With his thumb, Abram pulls my lip from under the hold of my teeth. "Keep biting this lip and I'll have no choice but to bite it myself and feast on your blood."

Okay, Edward Cullen.

Leaving me with one last gentle kiss, Abram kick starts his bike and rides in the direction of his place. Gravel kicks up, raining around me in the darkness of night, only the red tail lights glowing across my still heaving chest and flushed cheeks.

I let myself in the back door quietly, so not to wake June. The house is dark and eerily quiet, matching the mood outside with heavy fog rolling through the yard. Just a sliver of moonlight casts a glow in the direction of where Abram left. I never asked any questions of where he was going and for how long. But knowing him, he'll show up when I least expect it. I need to be ready for that moment. Butterflies take flight in my belly and I smile despite my lingering fear of this man, he may not be what I ever *wanted* in a man, but Abram Stoker just might be what I *need*.

ISOLDE

chapter seven

♫

Exile • Taylor Swift ft. Bon Iver

Days turn into a week, then ten days, and still, I haven't seen Abram again. A small part of me began to worry something happened to him, but June would have alluded to that. The larger part of me worried he came to the realization he didn't want someone like me. That thought seemed far more plausible than something happening to him. Judging by the way he handled those guys, or the one more specifically, the night he came to my rescue. I'd be willing to bet he can hold his own no matter what he's up against.

I nibble on my lower lip, thinking about asking June where he went, but bite down harder to keep the words from stumbling out as she bustles around the kitchen humming. Her perfume floats around the room, doing a dance with her as she flits from task to task. The scent is comforting, like lilacs in spring.

Pushing my half eaten eggs around the plate I think about seeing Alex today at the manor to work on some electrical in the dining room. He's been so helpful, and especially so patient with me, as we work on each room one by one. I want to learn as much as I can from him while we're working on the house, and I blushed when he said I was like a human sponge soaking everything up with such ease.

I didn't inform him the fact that I second guess myself every step of the way and have only retained about twenty five percent of what he's taught me, I'd rather him feel pride in his teachings the way I felt pride in his praise for me.

I pick at the hangnail taking residence on my finger, lost in thought about asking Alex more about his brother. Asking him anything to do with Abram seems like a sore spot though, considering he made it known he was interested first and I politely declined. I really like spending time with Alex and getting to know him, but at the time he expressed interest felt too soon for me. Hell, it still feels too soon, but I digress. Things with Abram couldn't be planned I've come to realize. That's what I keep telling myself every time my mind brings me back to that night with him. I never would have thought things would go where they went, considering I didn't even think Abram had any interest. *Maybe he still doesn't? Maybe he's using you.*

That inner voice of mine loves to remind me that Abram is not the kind of man to be interested in me, tall and broad, and so, so strong its unnerving. He could easily snap me in half without breaking a sweat and the ink covering majority of his upper body adds an element of danger. Something I would easily run from considering my past, but oddly, it draws me in even more. I like to think he enjoyed that night too, that he wouldn't have slipped his fingers past my waistband and inside me while I drove us down a dark rode at night.

A chill works its way down my spine at the memory. The way the wind whipped around us like natures dance. I can still smell the scent of the forrest in the air, like an aphrodisiac. It's been over a week since that night, and it bothers me more than I care to admit that not only has Abram not returned home, but he hasn't once reached out. Not that he would, but my pride stings a little that he hasn't. *Silly girl.*

"All set, dear?" June says from beside me, causing me to jolt in my chair. She chuckles a little like she knew I was lost in thought and takes a small amount of enjoyment out of startling me.

"Y-yes, thank you," I say, the last word ending with a touch a sass, causing her chuckle to bloom into full laughter.

"Oh honey, you're too easy," she observes. "Having those two reckless boys around here for so many years, had me walkin' on eggshells in my own house. It's kind of fun to turn the games onto someone else for a change." Despite being the object of June's little games, I smile anyways. It's nice to see her happy, considering how much she's done for me. I'm about to tell her that, remind her once again I wouldn't be in the frame of mind I'm in if it weren't for her. She would just brush me off like she always does, and turn before I catch the subtle blush creeping across her cheeks.

As I go to open my mouth, my phone pings with a new text on the table. Reaching for it a little too quickly with a smile on my face, I realize how silly I must look getting excited at the prospect of a text from Abram.

That smile fades instantly when I see *Unknown Number.* Swiping it open my eyes scan the message causing all the blood from my face to drain.

It can't be.

It can't.

My hands begin shaking as I slowly read the words that I hoped would never find me again. Nightmares I've pushed aside, telling myself I'm finally safe. But that voice buried deep in the recesses of my brain always remind me that I'll never be safe. As long as he's still out there, I'll never be free.

Hello Princess.

Miss me?

I've missed you. I don't like the way you left without saying goodbye though, that wasn't very nice. Oh well, you can make it up to me. See you soon.

My hands are trembling so bad I drop the phone, startling June as it clatters to the table. If I could see my face I'm sure there wouldn't be an ounce of color left. All of it having ran off to hide, leaving me just a ghostly white. I feel like I've seen a ghost, or that I *am* the ghost. A breeze could sweep through the kitchen and whisk me away, like I was never even here.

That's what I should do. I should leave, keep running. I don't want to put these people in danger, and that's all I'll ever be, a walking target until he finds me. And like I've always known all along, he'll *never* stop looking.

"Isolde, dear? What's wrong?" June gently places a soft hand on my shoulder nearly causing me to fling myself from the chair. She must think her hands are made of hot coals the way I jumped back as if I was just burned. I feel like I can smell rust, like my insides are bleeding at just the idea of going back to Grant. I can't go back. I *won't*. But I can't stay here either. Fuck! Where am I going to go?

I'm pacing the kitchen, worrying the hell out June surely, but I still haven't addressed her question. I'm trying to slow my breathing so that it's not so erratic, when June steps in front of me, stealing my focus. She watches me as my wild eyes ping back and forth between her concerned ones. Slowly, she reaches out to touch my arm, attempting to stop my pacing. "Isolde…Honey, talk to me. What has you so spooked?"

My limbs go from feeling tingly with the electric buzz rushing through me to practically numb. All I can see is the bulging of June's eyes and her outstretched hand reaching for me as everything around me blurs and goes black. Her voice is muffled and sounds far away as the last thing I feel, and even comprehend, is my body slamming into the kitchen floor with a deafening smack.

120

STOKER

chapter eight

♫

The Search • NF

STOKER

This trip is taking far too long for my liking. Something I've never cared much about before. I do my work, keep to myself and focus on my art. Nothing else matters. Okay, June and my brother matter, but other than that I really don't have a fuck to give.

People around town always look at me like I'm a criminal, someone they should fear. The irony always makes me chuckle internally. God forbid anyone ever see Abram Stoker crack a genuine smile. It's been this way since I was nine years old. Speculation as to why I became so reserved has volleyed in circles, always coming back to the assault on my mother.

Sure, that has something to do with it, but it goes deeper than that. No one knew what it was like, how it felt to be present during something so heinous even a grown adult would cower away from. The memories are as vivid as they've always been, and I use that rage to harness my anger towards my target. I've been watching him for the better part of a week, waiting for the moment he slips up and I can act.

Usually assignments are quick, people too absorbed in their own fucked up delusional world, they don't see me coming until it's too late. I'll admit, there have been times I've feared of being caught in the act, but years on this job has given me the comfort of security. The people I get my assignments from know what they're doing, are highly skilled and heavily protected by law enforcement. They simply look the other way, just happy their jobs are made a little easier by men like me willing to get my hands dirty and take out the bad guys.

Cops are fine, but a bunch of wussies if you ask me. When faced with fear, it's easy to let it consume you. I harness it, use it to my advantage. Which is why I'm the best. Call me cocky, but I know my worth, and when it comes down to it, I'm the one everybody calls to take out the creeps that lurk all around us.

Some of them appear to be normal everyday people, it takes a keen eye to spot the monster just beneath the surface. To me, all their skin is translucent, I can see who they truly are. Find their singular tastes and use it as bait to lure the demon out, waiting to be slaughtered by none other than *me*.

I get a thrill at watching the light leave their eyes, knowing the disgusting horrors they've held. Horrors worse than having their dick sawed off and force-fed to them. I know what you're thinking, I'm equally as fucked up, that I won't try to hide. But I'm the fucked up type like Dexter, taking out the scum of the earth to better the lives of good people. I may have blood on my hands, but that blood is better than that of a child or an innocent woman.

When I got the call last week about this particular guy, I knew I had to go. As much as I wanted to stay and learn all the ways I could make Isolde Davies scream, duty called. Literally. I always get my information from the same guy, its better that way. The less I know, the better. Truthfully, I don't even know the name of the man I receive orders from. He simply calls, gives me the name and location of the target, and sends me on my way. I report back to him once it's "taken care of".

About an hour south of home, I lean against my bike outside a seedy looking bar waiting for Gregory Matthews to make his appearance. The man is more than a bit of a drunk, having allowed his life to crumble where it is, I suppose it makes sense to find solace in a bottle.

With a cigarette perched between my lips, I wait, rather impatiently, as he finally emerges from the thick rusted iron door of the bar. Figures he would stay until last call, making it that much more aggravating having to wait for him. I could easily have walked in, grab him by the neck and taken care of business within minutes. But per instructions, I'm not to draw too much attention to myself. One of these days I won't have it in me to stay so calm and reserved when it comes to these low life fuckers. What's life without a little show and tell?

An audience might be nice, and would undoubtably send a message. But, I digress. Can't go around eliminating people publicly, no matter how much they deserve it, without some kind of consequence. Law enforcement can only protect me so much, and drawing that much bad attention will only make me appear to be a monster. Don't get me wrong, I am, but I like to think of myself as a good kind of monster.

Watching as Gregory stumbles to his less than luxury Toyota, I stub out my cigarette with my boot. Before walking away I bend down to toss it in a nearby trashcan. That little vixen is getting in my head already, and I wish I could say I hate it.

Shaking her from my thoughts, needing to focus, I walk closely behind the man about to be erased from the earth. *Good riddance.* The voice in my head whispers, and I chuckle at my own mind. The sound escapes me and gently wraps around the man in front of me, causing him to spin around so we're facing each other. Without uttering a single word, I can smell the cheap gin on his breath, making me want to punch him for poor taste. If you're gonna drink your life away, might as well indulge in the good shit.

"Who the hell are you?" He asks with a slight slur. Not going to lie, kinda surprised he doesn't sound worse considering he drinks like a fucking fish. I don't respond immediately, preferring to make him uncomfortable with my quiet stance and piercing gaze. I need him to feel threatened, I want to be able to taste the fear leaking from his pores as I drive my fist into his jaw making him wonder what he did to cross me.

I wish I could tell him it's nothing personal, that we don't know each other and I'm simply carrying out orders. But that would be a fucking lie. Every single one of these scumbags that walks the earth assaulting and raping women and children has made it personal. Since what happened to my own mother, I vowed long ago to eliminate as many pieces of shit as possible. I take a great deal of pride and joy in what I'm about to do and I haven't even spoken a word to him yet. Whispering dark truths into their faces as I draw out their deaths is one of the best parts of this job. It makes me smile, and that has finally made the man in front of me step back warily. Despite his drunken state.

"Lissin man, I don't know you. Why don't you git out of my," his words are cut off by my fist slamming into his face. One down, and undetermined amount to go. "Tha fuck man!" He's holding his cheek as blood spills from his mouth, with a confused expression on his face. I love it when they bleed, makes my adrenaline spike all the sweeter. I wish they weren't all such fucking morons though, and realized why some random guy would come and beat them up. You rape people, this shouldn't be that surprising. The desire to yell that is overwhelming and I clench my fists tighter.

Giving him a second to process what's happening, I scuff my boots on the gravel, allowing the thrill to seep farther in as I gear up to punch him again. This time, he'll be on the ground. His eyes are closed, and I refuse to slam my fist into a mans face when he doesn't see it coming. That depletes the fun in my opinion.

I throw a second punch, this time to his eye socket. The shrill screech that leaves his lips has me grinning like a maniac. He blows out an unsettling smelling breath as he heaves forward to puke, narrowly missing my boots. That would have earned him ten more minutes of our little dance here because it no doubt would have taken me at least that long to wipe every trace from the worn leather. These boots have seen more than their fair share of torment over the years, and I know I'm due for a new pair, but what can I say, they're my favorite.

Gregory is losing his balance even more than when he first walked out here due to my punches mixing with his intoxicated state. Might be in his favor that he's such a sorry drunk, maybe he won't feel everything as vividly as the one's who don't indulge. Honestly though, most of them do. If they're needing to fill some void by assaulting women, I gulp down bile as the thought of these guys touching little kids makes me physically ill, then it makes sense they get drunk like this guy still throwing up at my feet.

I suppress an eye roll, because this is pathetic. Drunk or not, he should be able to hold his own better than this. The wind whips around us, kicking up gravel and dust from the parking lot with it and I smile down at my subject. I refuse to look at them as my 'victims', because they are not in the slightest. They are every bit the monster your parents worn you about. I watch him roll onto his back as I squat down to look him dead in the eyes. This is where the real fun begins, but I'll spare you the details.

Lets just say, this is where the pathetic life of Gregory Matthews ends. You're welcome.

***

The hotel rooms Ellis puts me up in are trash. He says it's better to go under the radar by staying in the slums than be out on display in nicer places. Easy for him to say. I bet he wouldn't feel quite the same if he had to watch a cockroach scurry across the floor under the bed. God only knows what else is under there. I resist the urge to check, knowing I won't like what I find.

Not much more can be said for the smell, either. The entire room reeks of cigarette smoke, vomit and cheap sex. I don't even dare touch the bed, not exactly the most welcoming with its brown duvet cover and yellow stained pillowcases. For all the shit I deal with and the men I take out for Ellis, the least he could do is set me up somewhere with clean linens and a continental breakfast for fucks sake.

But, I digress. What I'm doing may be dangerous work, but its all for the cause. If people like me don't take out people like poor old Gregory earlier this evening, then who else would? Ellis sure as fuck doesn't do it. He prefers to pay rough looking guys like me to handle the shady shit.

It used to bother me at first, the idea of taking another mans life. But after my first kill, after the adrenaline wore off I was left with this buzzing sensation, and I wanted to chase that feeling again and again. The feeling of power that with the flick of my wrist I could eliminate the bad guy, I prefer to take my time and cause them pain and suffering, but due to time constraints I have had to end a session earlier than my own choosing from time to time.

I may be seen as sick, like maybe I'm also one of the bad guys who enjoys torturing people and ending their sad pathetic lives. Perhaps I am sick. Truth be told, I don't have a single fuck to give. One look at Greg's face had me itching to end him. Knowing what he'd been doing, thinking he could cover it up with work and his drinking problem. Like I said, fucking pathetic.

A look at the old alarm clock sitting on an even older bedside table, has me groaning into my hands. I scrub them down my face internally wondering why I can't ever get a good night sleep. I've been this way as long as I can remember, but it gets worse after a job. My body can't come down from the adrenaline and relax like a normal fucking person. Then again, I'm not normal.

My black boots squeak slightly as I pace the brown stained carpeting in here, the only sound in this dim lit musty room. Was brown the only color option in this place? Fuck.

As much as I've distracted myself the last week, I can't keep my mind from wandering back to a petite little blonde who rode not only my motorcycle, but my hand as well. God, the feel of her warm skin writhing beneath me as the hum of my bike vibrated our bodies. Like an aphrodisiac I will never get enough of.

She's sweet and slightly reserved, I know I won't be able to push her too much too fast like I have with countless others, but I got a taste of her reckless side when she let me touch her. I didn't give her much choice in the matter, a fact I knew when I commanded her to drive. If she had really tried to object, she might have crashed us, an outcome I was all too willing to gamble with.

I wouldn't say I care about her, but there is something about her I can't quite understand. She makes me feral in ways I'm not used to. I'm the kind of guy to fuck a hole to fulfill momentary satisfaction from a woman before sending her on her way. If they feel used, then that's their fucking problem. But Isolde…Fuck, I don't know. I want to hurt her, to feel her fear skate down her body and watch her cry as I get off on the thrill of scaring her. Chase her through the woods, wondering when I'll eventually catch her. Because I will always catch her. The faster she runs, the more I can already feel my blood pumping in my chest leading straight to my dick. But the other part of me wants to know her, not just her body, and understand why she is the way she is.

From what my brother and June has said, she rolled into town with a look of pure terror, always glancing over her shoulder. The kind of person tries to hide with manners and a fake smile, only one of which she was able to convince anyone with. June said she took one look at the poor girl and knew she needed to do something. That woman, I heave a sigh as I think about the woman who practically raised Alex and me. Infuriating beyond all measures, but kind down to the marrow of her bones. I used to say her generosity would get her into trouble, but she would just click her tongue and wave me off.

The idea of getting hurt while helping someone always seemed worth the risk in her eyes. I never used to give it much thought until I started doing this work for Ellis. I came to terms with the consequences of this job long ago, knowing that if I got hurt or died on a mission, then at least I died knowing I was helping innocent people escape their abusers. Not a better way to go if you ask me. Well, maybe while getting my dick sucked, just as long as I finish first.

It's been a week since I've seen those eyes of hers, practically engraving the colors in my brain, memorizing each fleck. The clock still says two, but fuck it. I can't sleep and sure as fuck don't want to sleep in this room anyway. I fire off a quick text to Ellis, letting him know the job is done and I'm heading back home. If he has a problem with the room being paid for and not used, then maybe he should reconsider the places he expects me to stay. Motherfucker has more money than he thinks I realize, so he can eat the pennies it took to book this shit hole.

Bag securely in place, I flick my cigarette to the damp concrete and rev the engine. Smiling at the thrill it gives me, even after all these years. I refuse to ever drive a car again. Being on a bike is where I belong, and there's no one who will convince me otherwise. With that last thought, I ease onto the paved street, barely lit by dull streetlights and kick it into high gear with only one thing on my mind. Isolde.

ISOLDE

chapter nine

♫

Lose Control • Teddy Swims

I can't sleep again. Shocking, I know. I've never felt more safe than I do in June's home, but a part of me can't turn off the fear of always having to look over my shoulder to see if Grant is steps away from strangling me and dragging me back to hell.

After my little fainting spell this morning, June watched me like a hawk until I practically pushed her to go to bed. I know her routine by now and she's always in bed by nine, considering how early she starts her days. She means well and for that I'm so grateful, but I don't want June to feel like I'm some broken child that needs tending to all the time. If I want to see myself as a strong confident woman then I need to act like one.

Even if it takes me the rest of my life.

The night is clear for once, and the bright moon shines directly in my window making the covers glow under its light. A soft breeze filters in through the screen, erecting goosebumps all over, and I sigh at the content feeling of this moment. I've been working on pushing negative thoughts aside, making room for only the positive things right now. This past week since Abram has been gone, I've grown closer to Alex.

It's always so refreshing being around someone like him. His outlook on life in general is so positive its hard not to feel he same when he beams a megawatt smile just for living another day. I wish I could see the world the way he does, or be as confident in myself the way he is. Alex has a knack for showing his strong confident side without coming across like an arrogant asshole.

The same can't exactly be said for his older brother. The man with the eyes that have starred in every single dream this week. Some mornings I'd wake up, not even remembering my dream, but feeling the intense gaze of his dark eyes on me. Piercing through each layer of skin like a soft knife cuts butter.

Whenever I'm with Alex, I can practically tell what he's thinking with how expressive his eyes are. He's the kind of person to lay it all out and not shy away from anything. If I have a question, I can ask Alex and he'll answer with only honesty. Abram, however, always has a riddle attached to everything that leaves his mouth. The thought infuriates me at the same time it excites me.

If I were to pick a guy based off of what would be good for me down on paper, then no question, it would be Alex. But I don't feel pumping adrenaline rushing through my veins when I'm close to him. Our kiss a few weeks ago was nice, a completely satisfying kiss, but I didn't feel anything other than his lips are soft and he's not filling my mouth with saliva.

Abram kissed me one time and I felt the blood deep within me boiling at the simple touch. That can't be healthy, and yet I crave it more than I crave my next breath. I've spent years repressing everything, hiding my feelings and trying not to feel anything at all. The second I felt Abram's eyes on me, my body came to life again like it just spent the last six years in a coma.

My body is suddenly hot, even with the breeze wrapping itself around my flushed skin. It feels wrong to do this, especially in June's home, but its been a long time since I've felt this rush between my thighs. Not if you count the orgasm Abram brought me to last week while I drove his bike. Not something I ever saw myself brave enough to do. I didn't exactly have a say in the matter, but then again, I never told him no or tried to push his hand away.

As little as we know about the other, I feel like Abram knows just how far he can take me without breaching my boundary line.

Without too much thought, I slip my hand under my sleep shorts and gently rub circles over my clit. One thought about that mans light gray eyes has me close to the edge and I've barely done anything. Well, that and the handful of dreams I've had, I think as I feel the skin on my chest blush a deep red.

My fingers quickly become slick from my arousal, and I begin moving them faster over my sensitive flesh, happily chasing the release. I can't help but wish it was someone else's hands thrusting into my wet heat rather than my own.

With my eyes firmly shut and my back arching off the bed, I feel the rush of my orgasm coming closer and closer, and I know I need to be quiet so I don't scream June awake. I'd have to leave from embarrassment. With my free hand, I clamp it over my mouth just as my release crashes through me like a tidal wave. I buck my hips into my own hand, wrenching each wave of euphoria from myself.

As soon as I come down, heavily panting, I slide my hands out of my shorts, now glistening under the moonlight. As I rise from the bed to wash my hands, a crack of some branches sounds just outside my window. My body immediately freezes, and fear works it's way up from my toes settling in my chest. The rational side of me knows it's probably just an animal sniffing around for scraps. But the part of me still holding onto my trauma is paralyzed in fear.

When the wind flutters in once again, I catch the faint scent of cigarette smoke. My mind is playing tricks on me, that's all this is. I basically just got off to the view of my neighbors eyes and now I've gone insane thinking he's outside my window. I haven't heard a word from him in over a week, why on earth would he happen to be outside my window as I pleasured myself.

I'm just tired, I chant to myself.

Delusional won't look good on me if I can't get a proper nights sleep. I should pick up some melatonin next time I head to the store.

When I don't hear anything else, convinced it was only my tired brain, I turn to head to the bathroom once again. "That was beautiful to watch little bird," his husky voice sends delicious tingles all over my body, momentarily washing away my humiliation.

"I gotta say though, it's a shame you're going to waste all of that," Abram gestures to my still glistening fingers, making my skin blush even more than it already is. I stare down at my hand, unable to meet his gaze as it bores into my face. Searching for something he isn't going to find. I learned long ago to hide my emotions, knowing nothing good ever came from showing them.

"Come here." My body doesn't move, not even flinching as his voice reaches somewhere deep inside me. My mind registered the words, and my eyes meet his dark frame as it leans against my window. I watch him in fascination, the way he tilts his head to the side slightly, giving this entire scene an eerie vibe as he inhales a deep pull from his cigarette. I've always hated smoking and wouldn't be caught dead dating someone who as a smoker. But Abram has changed a lot of my former opinions it seems.

In such a short time, I've thrown away everything I thought I wanted in a man. Only to realize I settled for someone who was the farthest thing from that. Hitting a woman doesn't make you tough, if anything it makes them more weak. Unable to express themselves with words in a healthy way, they resort to physical forms of expression.

Not realizing I've been lost in my thoughts, Abram's voice rings through the haze, louder this time. "I said," another inhale of smoke then he's blowing it straight through the screen, settling on my covers. "Come *here*, Isolde."

Unlike the first time he asked, my legs slowly guide me towards the bed until my knees bump into the frame. I watch as he stubs the cigarette out, squishing it into the small patch of flowers June planted. I make a mental note to run out there first thing in the morning and remove it. I'm sure she's found hundreds of his discarded butts around the property, but this is a highly unlikely spot he would leave one. Right outside her house guests window.

Last thing I need is June thinking I'm some horny teenager letting boys climb through her window at all hours of the night. Makes me wonder if either Abram or Alex ever snuck girls in here.

Abram heaves a sigh before popping the screen on my window out of place, setting it on the ground against the house. Before I can say a single word, he's hefting a foot through the now open window, followed by the other until he's standing on the other side of the bed. I watch him with bated breaths, waiting to see what he plans to do, but as always I'm lost to his thoughts. He's always so intense, keeping a mask in place making it so hard to truly get a read on what he's thinking.

My body trembles slightly, still unsure of what to do. Without a word, Abram leans across the mattress and lightly lifts my hand up, watching me the entire time, before holding in front of his face like he's inspecting it. My breath hitches as he closes both eyes and lifts my fingers, still coated in my arousal, to his nose and inhales deeply. My entire body is scorched to the bone, feeling a mixture of embarrassment and desire.

One by one, he brings each finger to his lips sucking on them harshly until my knees wobble and my body threatens to discard me on the bed in front of him like

I'm his next meal. He groans against my two digits, and the goosebumps come back full force as I watch him lick my fingers clean. Why is this so hot? This has to be another dream, a much more intense one because it feels entirely too real. But there's no way Abram is standing here, in my room, licking my fingers after watching me come on them not five minutes ago.

At this realization, I relax a little enjoying the feel of attraction passing between us as if it's tangible. I want to give in to the fantasy and throw him down on the bed, but even dream me wouldn't be so bold. I did let him finger me on his bike though, another thing I would never consider doing.

Fuck it.

With a fistful of Abram's shirt, I pull hard enough to make him drop on the bed, both fingers still locked between his rough hand covered in tattoos. He rolls until his back is splayed across my linens, making sure to engrave his scent everywhere. I like the idea of falling asleep with him all around me.

When I don't move fast enough, Abram tugs on my hand until I drop down beside him on the bed. Before I can adjust, he grips me by the hips and lifts me up and over his muscular thighs. Yeah, this is definitely a dream. I've never had such a vivid dream like this, where I can feel every rigid muscle in his body. From his thighs up to his corded forearms and of course the abs I can see peeking through his black tee.

He smells like he always does, too. Like nature and cigarettes. Cedar wood with a touch of menthol, and it's quickly becoming my favorite scent.

Those gray eyes find mind, burning into me with what I can only decipher as desire. I don't think I've ever had a man look at me the way he is right now, and it's thanks to my own mind. If only I could catch him looking at me like this in real life, I'd melt into a puddle at his feet.

"Do you always allow men to climb through your window in the middle of the night, little bird?" He asks as his hands roam up and down my bare legs. Suddenly my sleep shorts and silk tank feel like a heavy parka keeping me way too warm. The room feels like an inferno as his feather light touches are blazing a trail of fire down my exposed skin.

I want to respond, but I don't ever remember much dialogue from my dreams, actions always speak louder than words, so I decide to talk with my body instead. Maybe it's time I keep a dream journal and right these things down the second I wake up. I want this version of me to be brave enough to go for it in real life, not just my fantasies.

With Abram's hands on my thighs, I grind my hips into his, moaning at the feel of his hard length notched right where I need it. I may have just gotten myself off, but that's nothing compared to the feel of him right now. Even through our clothes.

Before I can move a second time, he grips me around my throat hard enough to have my eyes ping open on a gasp. "Don't play with me," he says, his tone even more gravely than before. Oh, so only he can play games with *me*. I'm about to show him just how fun I can be.

With a smirk, I lace my fingers with his, loosening his hold as I do, and grind my aching center against his hard cock. Fuck, I knew he would be huge. Hopefully dream me can handle whatever he's packing under those worn jeans, because the feel of him right now has me suddenly feeling scared.

In two seconds flat, Abram has us flipped so I'm lying beneath him, fully at his mercy. Previous thoughts out the window. I'm gasping for air and hoping he isn't going to leave me begging, if he thinks I won't then he's got another thing coming. Hopefully both of us. I laugh to myself at my own little joke but when I look up into Abram's eyes, I see he isn't seeing the humor in this situation. "Do you think this is funny, little bird?"

I'm trying not to lose my shit and laugh hysterically, because quite honestly, he looks pissed, which oddly makes this all the more funny. "I-I'm sorry, I'm not laughing at you. This is just..," I can't help the giggles that slip free but cut off abruptly when Abram grips a hand around my throat and squeezes. Well, that feels pretty real. My eyes widen as his hands hold me steady, leaning in close enough I can practically taste the menthol.

"Tell me. What about my rock hard dick rubbing against that needy cunt of yours is funny?"

"I-I…I thought I was dreaming. Shit, I'm not, am I?" My eyes close as I place both hands over my face and for whatever reason I feel like I could cry. I acted on impulse thinking I was lost in an erotic dream when really, I was about to fuck my neighbor who probably would have let me if I didn't have a laughing fit.

Abram stares down between us where our bodies are joined, and his erection only seems to grow more, if that's even possible. When I feel his eyes on my face, he instructs me to open them. I can't. Even if I wanted to, I couldn't open my eyes and brave the look on his face right now. I've never in my entire life been as humiliated as I am in this moment.

There was that time my pants ripped at the mall when I was fifteen, and everyone saw my bright pink underwear with little bunnies all over them. I thought that was the low point of my humiliation scale. Turns out that was just the warm up for this exact moment.

What the fuck was I thinking? I tricked myself into thinking this was a dream, after not seeing or hearing from Abram in over a week I thought this was a made up fantasy. In reality, I taunted him with my orgasm soaked fingers and dry humped him like a teenager.

With my eyes still closed, I feel a strong finger lift my chin so that our faces are level with one another. "Isolde." He hardly calls me by my first name, usually preferring to call me little bird. He must know I've noticed, because as soon as it leaves his lips, my eyes are open, searching his. "If this is what you wanted, all you had to do was say so," his gaze is hooded, lips smirking as he hovers above me. I resist the urge to roll my eyes because I have a gut feeling that would result in me getting spanked.

Can't say I'm entirely opposed to that form of punishment.

Smacking his chest I roll out from under him, breaking the spell. I sit on the edge of my bed, with Abram back in his original position, this time with both hands behind his head. He's watching me. I don't need to turn around to know his eyes are tracing the curves of my back, I feel the tingle of his watchful stare racing up my spine

"Look, I don't usually act like that. I mean, it's not that I wouldn't, especially with you. I mean…shit." I slap a hand across my face, hoping the earth will open up and swallow me whole. "Oh my God, can you make me shut up already?"

With a fistful of my hair, Abram yanks me back and I land on his chest. I search his face for something, anything, when he pulls me forward to rest his lips against mine. He took my request literally and I don't hate it. As long as my mouth is occupied, I can't shove my foot in it again.

Attempting to deepen the kiss, I feel his tongue dance along the seam of my lips and I groan into his mouth as I open for him. The grip on my hair tightens, telling me he likes it too, I hope. Losing control with him would be catastrophic and I can't afford to do that so soon, not after my history of men. I don't have the best track record for good decisions in that regard.

He's the type of man a person could drown in. I may be a good swimmer, but I don't know how long I'd be able to hold my head above water when it comes to Abram Stoker.

****

Waking up a few hours later, I'm almost convinced I really did dream the entire thing with Abram. One look at my window and the dirt smudges from his boots reminds me that in fact it was entirely real.

As much as I wanted to take things further, all we did was kiss until he practically fell asleep in my bed. With what looked like extreme effort, he extricated himself from my room by climbing back out the window and heading to his cottage.

Its hard not to feel like a teenager when everything we did just a few hours ago is exactly what I did at sixteen. Sneaking a guy in through the window, dry humping a little before making out. Only thing missing was some *Trey Songz* buzzing from my stereo.

Counting my lucky stars, and hoping there's still a few left up there, I pull myself from bed and head to the kitchen. June is standing where she always is first thing in the morning, right in front of the coffee machine. Coffee always smells better when she makes it. I've tried numerous times to get it like hers, and every time I'm met with failure.

Bless her, she always compliments me, saying it tastes wonderful. But I've come to realize, she's just a real good liar.

Since I've been here, June has always made sure to be gentle with me, reminding me daily of my worth, helping me become a stronger version of myself. The thought sometimes stings my eyes, but I refuse to let the tears fall, even if they're happy ones. I just never thought I would meet someone like her, she reminds me a lot of my mom. Her kind and giving nature, and every time June does something to remind me of my mom, guilt creeps in a little more.

I've considered reaching out more times than I can count at this point, but every time I get close, something holds me back. I can't even put all the blame on Grant anymore. Enough time has passed, and I already got a new phone. So what the hell is holding me back?

"If you're gonna be thinking super loud over there, you might as well grab a mug and a chair, dear."

I giggle, not realizing I've been standing like a statue in the doorway. If June ever suspects I'm a head case, she doesn't let on, and for that I'm thankful. See, I know I am, but once others start to realize it, that's when I'll know I need actual help with my trauma. I'm perfectly happy living in denial for now.

"Sorry June, guess I just got lost in my thoughts, again," I admit the last part on a whisper, thus confirming something is on my mind. She watches me with wary eyes, the same eyes that have seen her fair share in life. Yet, she carries herself with such grace it's admirable.

"That, right there," she points a delicate finger at me before twirling it in a circle around my frame. "You do that all the time."

"Do-do what?" I stammer, fixing myself a cup of coffee to distract myself from her penetrating gaze.

"Honey, you don't need to say a word for me to know you're putting yourself down in that head of yours."

"How do you know I'm putting myself down?" I ask. "Maybe I'm just thinking real hard about what color to paint the dining room at the manor." The look she gives me, added with the pop of her hip tells me she smells bullshit.

"Bullshit," she says and we both laugh. "And no paint, that room deserves a tasteful wallpaper." Even when the mood is heavier because of my self deprecating thoughts, June finds a way to lighten it. Ever the peacemaker. "Now, sit down and tell me what's on your mind. We both know it'll make you feel better, so come on, out with it."

Her tone is gentle, like always. Even when she's being direct with me, it never comes off condescending or rude. Mug of coffee in hand, I lower myself into one of the creaking chairs at the kitchen table, pulling in a lungful of air as I do.

"I don't know. I guess I'm feeling guilty for how long I've been here and the fact that I haven't tried to contact my parents." The sting of tears comes again, only this time I'm unable to keep them from falling. They slide down my makeup free cheeks before pooling at my jawline and dripping onto my sleep shorts.

"We didn't talk much as it was before because of…well, just because. And now that I have a new phone and I feel like I'm in a safe enough place, I still can't dial the number. The same number they've had my entire life, the same number that's branded in my memory."

An overwhelming flood of emotions is brewing just beneath the surface and I'm afraid if I let even just one of them out, the rest will come flooding through in a monsoon of sadness. It's bad enough I've been living here, rent free, even if I am helping fix up the manor. Or the fact that June never once complains about having me here, got me in to see Dr. Lennox and stitch me up, and helped me get my new cellphone.

The pressure from all my thoughts is breeching the border of no return, and no amount of deep breaths can stop the flow once I let them out. June is watching me quietly, waiting for me to continue, but I feel the clog of guilt, sadness, fear and the feeling of being a burden lodging in my throat. One cough, and it'll all come tumbling out.

I'm about to choke it all down, chase it with a hefty sip of piping hot coffee when June places a soft, wrinkled hand over mine. "Isolde," her whisper soft voice soothing me in ways she doesn't even know, draws my attention up to her even gentler eyes. "Stop trying to put on a brave face everyday and allow yourself to grieve. You've been through a lot, and the only way you're going to begin to heal is if you let those feelings free."

"Every time you keep them hidden, they grow stronger, desperate to be let out, and eventually they'll find a way. It's healthier for you to gradually work up to healing, rather than be ambushed by a slew of emotions you were too stubborn to purge. Trust me, I know."

Her words register, slowly and one at a time. I haven't been allowing myself to fully feel the weight of my life the last six years. The way I froze out my parents, the way I ran from my problems and fear instead of facing them. And the way I'm attempting to push them down deeper, stacking issue after issue on top of everything else I've been carrying. The weight it too much, and it has been too much for far too long.

As if sensing the dam is about to break, June rises from her chair, pulling me to a stand with her, and wraps me in an all-consuming hug. The moment my hands clasp behind her back, every emotion bubbles to the surface and spills over the edge, threatening to wash me away. Just as I feel I might wash away, her grip on me tightens, rubbing gentle circles on my back. I inhale her soft scent of honeysuckles while I listen to her quiet shh's close to my ear, just able to make them out over my hysterical sobbing.

"There's no shame is being vulnerable, dear. Letting go of pain and guilt is part of healing, and if you're lucky, you'll have someone there to help shoulder the weight once you're finally ready."

***

After my impromptu morning therapy session with June, I showered and decided to put all of todays energy into the manor. I'm not ready to call my parents, as much as I miss hearing their voices. And I sure as fuck am not ready to dissect what happened in my bed last night with Abram. So I sent a text to Alex, asking if he was free this morning to help me make some decisions at the manor.

For you, anything.

That was his only response, and sometimes I feel guilty for relying on him so much. I hope he doesn't feel like I'm leading him on or messing with his feelings, because he's become a good friend the last few weeks. When I first arrived here, it was obvious Alex showed interest, but there was no way my head felt anywhere near ready to jump into that pool. Now I feel even worse, like I'm sneaking around with Abram behind his back.

As much as I wish I could say it's not like that, it quite literally has been. Every interaction I've had with Abram Stoker has been in private, away from the watchful eyes of Stehekin. The one exception was when Sasha heard me call him by his first name, her eyebrows rose so high they practically bumped fists with her hairline.

Doing my best to toss aside my guilt, I walk across the back lawn, freshly cut thanks to Alex, and unlock the front door of the manor. The smell of fresh paint, cleaning supplies and a touch a sawdust flit around me as I swing the door open. A stark difference to the first time I step foot inside this house, smelling strongly of dust and mold. The place was stagnant for so long, the smell can only be described as stale, a sad aroma of looniness, even if it is just a house.

The bones are good and always have been according to both Abram and Alex, as well as June. It's the history that makes this place feel run down. Knowing awful things took place within these walls made me feel like I was biting off more than I could chew in the beginning. But with each passing day, and every project I've tackled whether by myself or with the help of the guys, I've begun to feel a fresh start for this place.

I've resisted the urge to name it for weeks now, not feeling like I had any right to do so, and feeling slightly silly for wanting to in the first place. But as I glance around the first floor with it's newly open floor concept, fresh paint and a state of the art kitchen, that overwhelming urge is back. I thought about checking with June, but I know she'd just tell me to go for it. That I've been making decisions regarding the manor since she gave me the reigns and that it was ultimately my decision.

Something about that made me more nervous, like there would be an added pressure to pick the perfect name. I also thought about just naming it and keeping it to myself. Who needs to know? I doubt the guys would even care, and June wanted me to tackle this project with confidence, so maybe that's what I should do.

I mull it over a little more as I stare at the walls in the dining room. This room has been the hardest for me to revamp, never feeling like anything is good enough. Every other room, including the library and kitchen, which are two of the largest rooms, have felt like a piece of cake compared to the dining room.

Whenever I come in here, I feel a strong sense of something. Not quite dark, but not exactly cheerful either. Those feelings have made me want to keep this room completely different from the rest of the house. Each room has an amazing amount of natural light and new recessed lighting, which makes some of the darker painted rooms brighter during the day.

I also wanted each space to stay true to the roots of the home, matching the pointed arches and gables on the outside of the house. The only thing left to paint, aside from the dining room, is the exterior of the house. I've gone back and forth on whether to brighten it or keep it dark and ultimately decided it needs to be painted black, the way it originally was before it faded to a dull gray.

The same gray as Abram's eyes, a thought that has penetrated my concentration on more than one occasion.

I pace the bare room, running my fingers lightly against the unfinished walls. I just assumed I would paint in here, but after June said to use wallpaper I realized it was a no brainer. That's why I want Alex here today, to help me finalize which wallpaper works for the dining room as well as a few bathrooms and the pantry. Painting every room seemed boring, and putting wallpaper up in every room seemed like a headache. This is a happy medium.

A long whistle comes from the foyer and I round the corner to see Alex lifting his sunglasses atop his head. He looks around, taking in the first floor and the open concept I'm so happy we went with. Pride fills my chest when he meets me with a mile wide grin. "I'd love to take all the credit in here, but damn Isolde, this place looks amazing. You did good, babe."

"*We* did good," I correct him. Because the truth is, none of this would have been possible if not for all his help. Sure, Abram has been here too, but not the way Alex has. The long nights we've spent painting these rooms with mile long walls, laughing the whole way through as we scream sang the lyrics to *Alanis Morisette*. Or the daily trips to the hardware store for more supplies when I kept changing my mind.

Working on the manor has been a process, one I never imagined myself doing, but a healing one at that. Turns out June was right again, this was good for me and now I want to get my hands on more projects that bring me this kind of creative freedom. Not sure other people will be as open and willing to give a stranger the reins the way June has, but it can't hurt to at least try.

My next step is to take as many pictures in here as I can when everything is complete, a way to build a portfolio for if I really want to make this a serious job.

"It was mostly you, I just did the heavy lifting." I return his smile when he nudges my arm and we both take in the space. It makes me wonder what he's felt working in here as much as he has the last several weeks. Does he remember growing up in this house the way Abram does? Or are their experiences completely different because of what happened?

I watch him walk into the dining room, looking in every direction and skimming his fingers lightly along the wainscoting as if he's trying to touch a memory. "Alex?"

He doesn't turn around immediately, and suddenly I feel guilty that he ever joined me in fixing up the house. Was it too much to ask of them? I mean, technically June asked them to help because she saw the terrified look on my face when she said I should fix it up. I didn't know a hammer from a flathead when we started. But surely Alex, and Abram, would have turned it down if they didn't have the time or didn't feel up to it.

My mind is reeling with questions and guilt when Alex comes to stand next to me. He loosely intertwines our fingers together and a slight shiver runs down my spine at the intimate touch. We've become such good friends, I don't want any misunderstandings to ruin what we've built here, literally and figuratively.

He squeezes my hand once, twice, before letting go and shaking off the solemn look he just had on his face before facing me. "Sorry." Alex fixes his eyes on mine, looking into them deeper than I've ever noticed, the intensity making me a little nervous. We're standing so close to each other I can feel his breath fanning across my cheeks. Holding my gaze, he lifts a hand as if he's about to push the hair fallen from my ponytail behind my ear, but stops himself. "This place just amazes me sometimes, guess I needed a moment to take it all in and enjoy the moment with you."

Any response I may have come up with lodges in my throat. All I can do is smile up at him and turn around to examine the room for myself, something I've done a hundred times already. Nervous energy radiates around me, my hands twisting in front of me unsure of what to do or say. I won't deny there's an attraction there, I mean how could I not find him good looking? He looks a lot like Abram, but brighter in a way I guess. Where Abram is dark and brooding like a midnight sky full of clouds, Alex is sunshine in a cloudless blue sky. Total opposites.

But I also can't deny whatever it is I have going on with Abram. The intensity between us is almost tangible, I'm afraid of where it could go but even more afraid of not seeing it through. Trying to see if there's something there with Alex too would just get messy, and from what I just got out of, messy is the last thing I need.

Before I have any more time to think things over, I feel a strong hand on my elbow spin me around. I can't push away, I can't speak and I don't have enough time to stop what's about to happen before I once again feel Alex's lips on mine. It's more urgent this time, not as calculated and careful as the first time he kissed me. But I don't hear any warning bells going off around me, warning me that I'm in any kind of danger, because I know Alex wouldn't push me if I told him to stop.

His hand snakes around the back of my neck, holding my face to his as he deepens the kiss, taking this moment for whatever it is, as if he's afraid the spell will be broken and I'll pull away. A big part of me is yelling for me to stop this, that it's wrong and I already have something going with Abram. But what even are we doing? We've barely hooked up and then I didn't see him for over a week. It's not like I'm his girlfriend and I doubt he sees me that way anyways.

Unsure of how much time has passed, I take a moment to let myself feel the kiss on a deeper level. The way his lips softly brush mine, urgent but gentle at the same time. He tastes like a warm sunny day, citrus and sunshine, and my body finally relents, leaning into the taste and smell of him.

I feel him pull back, watching me, but I'm unable to open my eyes until I can process what I just let happen. I shouldn't feel guilty, and a part of me doesn't, but I still can't shake the feeling that we shouldn't have crossed this line. I can't process how I went from an abusive relationship, finally finding the courage to leave only to find myself in a weird triangle with two brothers. My life is starting to feel like an episode of Jerry Springer.

Opening my eyes, I stare at Alex as he rubs gentle circles on my cheeks with his thumbs, a shit eating grin on his face like he won the big prize at the county fair. "Am I interrupting something?"

That dark timbre runs through my veins like a shot of adrenaline, and I freeze to the spot. Terrified to move and see what expression is resting on his face right now. Alex doesn't even flinch, like he couldn't be bothered at all that we've just been caught in an intimate stance as he holds my face. Did Abram see us kiss? Oh God. I internally slap myself across the face, ready to crawl under a rock and never reemerge.

Abram's eyes go from Alex to me, then back again. I watch the tension build, his muscles flexing ever so slightly causing the veins in his forearms to protrude even more. "What's going on here?"

Alex chuckles, which only seems to irritate Abram more than he already appears. "I'm sure you saw enough to figure that part out, didn't you big brother?" Alex responds with too much arrogance for my liking, and suddenly I feel like I'm playing monkey in the middle with the two biggest kids in the schoolyard.

Nodding his head, Abram looks down with a smirk, rubbing his chin in thought. He takes a few steps toward us, boots thumping heavily on the newly sanded and stained wood floors. When he looks up again, his eyes sear into his brothers, a challenging glint in them. "What? You want to share her or something?"

Share me. What the fuck? Is he serious? His tone is sarcastic and if I wasn't mistaken, I'd say he sounds a little hurt. Which can't be right, because based on everything I know about him, he's not the kind of guy to get attached to some random girl.

They're in the middle of a stare off when I finally find my voice. "I'm not a fucking time share, you know. You can't just pass me on to the next guest when you're done."

Both men look at me, with entirely different expressions. Abram's nostrils flare, for reasons I'm not sure of and Alex just laughs like my anger amuses him to some degree. Not sure if I want to feel insulted and slap them both or just run and hide. Which has always been my go to move, run from the situation, defuse the situation and not make things worse. Don't egg them on in any way and crawl back into my little shell, the one that never offered much shelter anyways.

Fuck all of that with a capital F. If I want to work on myself and find my voice then I need to start using it when I feel it vibrating beneath the surface, begging to be set free.

I speak to Abram first, too afraid if I don't say what I'm feeling now, I'll chicken out. "Whatever that look is, wipe it the fuck off your face." Alex chuckles and I fix him with my rage next. "And you," I point a chipped fingernail in his face, causing him to drop the smirk. "Shut up, because you're no better than he is. I don't belong to either of you so I don't know what gives you the right to anything that was just said."

Alex goes to speak and I cut him off so abruptly I'm not sure I'm hearing myself right. "I'm not done. That is now the second time you've kissed me, and though I won't deny it was a good kiss, it doesn't give you any kind of claim." Abram clenches his fists tightly and I don't miss the subtle step of anger he takes towards his brother. Here I thought Alex might have bragged about our first kiss a few weeks ago, turns out Abram didn't even know about it. I don't have it in me to feel guilty about that right now, or ever. I've done nothing wrong.

"The two of you need to tone down whatever macho shit you have going on because I don't feel like being dragged along for a ride I didn't buy tickets for. And for the record, my romantic decisions aren't up to either of you."

Not giving them a second to defend or argue, I turn and head out the back door towards the woods. My pace quickens as I turn towards the path I took the first night Abram found me here. Despite everything I just said to the two of them, a small part of me is hoping he follows, and that truth bomb hurdles into me faster than a freight train.

I don't want to lead either of them on, and I certainly don't want to be responsible for hurting anyone. But I know where my feelings are, I'm just too irritated with the two of them to articulate how I feel. Judging by that kiss, Alex would gladly enter into something exclusive. But I don't think I can say the same for Abram. Which is another harsh reality I don't want to face.

Twenty minutes later I've picked up my pace to a light jog and have circled the back half of the property, heading back to June's place. I never saw Abram on the trail, or even Alex for that matter. Knowing him he would have wanted to talk me down and apologize, promising to just get back to work on the house. Just as I'm about to breech the clearing where the forest meets the backyard, I hear twigs snapping accompanied by that distinct smell of cigarettes I've grown drawn too.

He might try to act like he doesn't care and nothing affects him, but the truth is, I've gotten under Abram Stoker's skin, and I'm ready to peel back all the layers.

ISOLDE

chapter ten

Do I Wanna Know • The Arctic Monkeys

"Damn, they're even more intense than I realized," Hailey says as she sips on her mug of beer. "Here I was thinking it was just Stoker who got like that."

I heft a glass rack onto the bar top and beginning sliding them back into their slots above and below the bar. Hailey has been coming in here on the nights she has off, but only when I'm working. She insisted I stop calling her Dr. Lennox and ever since we've become pretty good friends. About time I found someone my age to hang out with, as much as I've loved living with June.

"I mean, technically that's true. Alex is intense in his own way but when he's up against his brother he looks like a fluffy golden retriever." We both laugh, but I feel the sadness laced in my voice. I haven't talked to either of them in two days, not since I stormed out of the manor like a fifteen year old who got her feelings hurt. I just couldn't stand there and feel like a pawn in whatever game they were playing. Actually, it was more of a rivalry, which in my opinion is worse.

I've seen countless stories where a girl gets a ton of attention from several guys, making her feel special and desired only to find out those guys made a bet on who could get her first. I refuse to be one of those stories people tell twenty years from now.

I can feel Hailey's eye on me, but I pretend I don't and keep busying myself with restocking the bar. It's only a Wednesday, so we aren't as full as we would be on a Friday or Saturday. The money might be less, but sometimes I prefer nights like these. When it's quieter and people like Hailey or June sit at the bar to keep my company.

Nothing like getting paid to do something fun and talk with friends at the same time. It makes me miss the college days when I did this carefree. Before Grant swept in and took away every single thing I loved and was good at, making me feel like I had to depend on him for everything.

"I gotta be honest, Isolde. I don't like you working those shifts at the bar so often," Grant strokes my cheek lovingly as he stares into my eyes with what I can only assume is concern. I melt at his touch, loving how protective he is of me, wishing I could bottle up this feeling forever. "I worry about you so much," he kisses the tip of my nose, making my heart flutter erratically in my chest.

Before I have a chance to say anything, he speaks up again, with a little more bite to his tone. "I think you should quit your job, work from home or do something else. I would feel much better knowing I can keep a close eye on you."

A soft warning bell begins to ring in my mind, but I brush it off, positive I'm being too sensitive. "Grant, come on. I have to work, and the money is too good to pass up right now. I promise, I'm safe working there. You don't have to worry." I give him a quick kiss and start to head to the bathroom to shower when I feel his presence looming behind me.

I don't have a chance to turn around before I feel his strong hand squeeze the back of my neck and spins me so fast I almost lose my balance and fall on my ass. His tight grip holds me up as his eyes bore into mine with a sinister look I've never seen him make.

"I said, quit your job." I break out in goosebumps, suddenly unsure of what he might do or say if I don't comply. A part of me wants to tell him to fuck off and that he isn't going to become some crazy boyfriend who controls my life. But my brain is quickly chanting fight or flight, leaning heavily towards the latter, and right now I just want to defuse the situation I've landed myself in.

Swallowing audibly, I nod my head and offer a weak smile. Grant obviously finds this acceptable, smiling his megawatt smile in return and kissing me sweetly. "I knew you'd understand, baby."

Only after I lock myself in the bathroom, letting the room fill with steam from the scalding hot shower, do I sit on the floor of the tub hugging my knees and allow the tears to fall.

"Hey," Hailey's soft voice pulls me back to the present. "Are you okay? Your face went kinda blank for a minute there."

My head quickly snaps in her direction, righting the haunted look on my face I smile reassuringly. "Oh, totally fine. Sorry, I tend to zone out every now and again." It's not a complete lie, I do space out often, but I know I'm being dishonest with her. I don't want to build a friendship on lies, but June is the only person who knows the extent of my abuse. And she used a damn good method to get it out of me.

Right now, while I'm working is hardly the time to dredge up my past with someone I'm still getting to know. Sure, she's a doctor and no doubt adheres to the HIPAA laws, but there is a lot to unpack from my history. I'm not sure I want to go down that dark road again with her or anyone else right now. *Especially the guys.*

I try to brush off those internal thoughts, focusing back on the job at hand, but they never stray too far from the forefront. I can feel the words right there, like word vomit, so often it literally makes me ill. Probably why I caved and told June as much as I did. But I know she would never betray my trust, especially since she told me some harrowing stories of her own. Her and I are kindred souls, something that has been proven the more time I spend in this town.

Glancing around to make sure there aren't any patrons watching, I whisper to Hailey. "Girl, check out the scar." Slowly, I lift the hem of my shirt to show off the slim scar that begins right about the button of my jeans and ends a few inches above my belly button. She did an impeccable job with the stitches, and because of that the scar is hardly noticeable to someone who didn't know what happened.

I felt ashamed of it at first, embarrassed by what someone might think if they saw it. Now, I'm proud of it, wearing it like a badge of survival. I made it out of there alive, and that's not something that happens to everyone in a situation similar to mine. I'm grateful I took the opportunity I had and ran, because if I hadn't…I shiver at the thought. That was almost two months ago, who knows what else Grant could have done in that time. As it is, this cut was the biggest and deepest he's ever gone.

Most days towards the end I felt half dead, pretty sure I'd be actually dead and six feet beneath the ground if I'd stayed another day.

With a sly smirk, Hailey tips her glass before taking a long pull. "What can I say without sounding arrogant and conceited?"

"Are you kidding? Brag! You and June literally saved my life, I don't know how I'll ever be able to repay either of you." I mean that with everything in me. I don't know what would have happened if I didn't stumble upon this town and get the help they so generously offered. My wound was bad, as much as I tried to play it off like I was okay, I knew better. If June hadn't brought me to Hailey to get it cleaned and stitched, it no doubt would have gotten infected.

Laughing, she shakes her head a little shyly, "you know that's not my style. I didn't get into this field for bragging rights, it just feels good to help people."

"That's what makes you one of the best," I wink before refilling her beer. "This one is on the house."

After making the rounds a few times to what little people are in here, Sasha and I close up for the night. Even on a slower night, I'm so grateful for this job. For the people that come in and treat me like one of them, not some random girl who showed up one day looking for handouts. I know that's not how June sees it, but sometimes it's how I've felt.

Probably why I've spent so much time making sure the manor is perfect. I want her to be proud of our hard work, and maybe even rent it out to earn some extra cash. Knowing her, she'll way me off, but it can't hurt to mention.

"This has been a good fit for you, girlie." A compliment from Sasha is few and far between, even if I know she sees how hard I work. So I take it with a smile trying not to look too much like an over excited kid about to chow down on a bucket of candy.

"Thank you, truly. Not just for the compliment, which I'll gladly accept," I tease with a flip of my pony tail. "But because this job has been amazing, and I'm thankful you took a shot on me."

Lighting a cigarette and putting it between her lips, she just shrugs. "If you had sucked, I would have just kicked your ass to the curb. So, thanks for not sucking." We both laugh as I tell her goodnight and that I'll see her for my shift Friday.

I'm going through my to-do-list for tomorrow since I have the day off when I see a lone headlight moving in the direction of my car. Last time I saw his bike coming towards me he was on his way to rescue me from a bunch of drunken idiots. My skin heats at the memory of what transpired shortly after, but right now I'm still a little pissed at him and Alex. I don't want to be volleyed between them like a toy, and I feel like I made that pretty clear.

If my body could speak, it would be laughing at me for just thinking that. My mind may want to smack them both, but my body and wetness pooling between my thighs at the sight of him tells me otherwise. Traitorous hormones.

Pretending I don't see him, I stroll across the street to my parked car with my head held high. I won't let him see me slip, and I can't afford to fall into this trap with him. I have too much going on as it is, I don't need to be in some weird triangle with him and his brother. No matter how hot it sounds. *Jesus, Isolde, get it together*. I snarl at myself.

As I climb into the front seat of my car I hear Abram idling next to me. His eyes bore into the side of my face, and I feel the inferno igniting me, threatening to swallow me whole. I'm trying so hard to look distracted, but his presence is not so easily ignored. Just as I'm about to give up the fight, his knuckles rapt loudly on my window, startling me to my bones.

Making quick work of starting my car so I can roll down the window, I try to hide the sudden tremble in my hands. "Trying to give me a heart attack, asshole?" I yell just as the window lowers all the way down, allowing his intoxicating scent to invade the cab of my car. I couldn't help the reaction to him if I tried, and I have tried so hard.

The bastard just chuckles, fucking *chuckles*, like my irritation with him is comical. I can't tell what facial expression he wears with the helmet on, but I feel as though I can picture exactly what look he's giving me. The one that has my panties threatening to melt under the heat of his gaze.

"Do I amuse you, *Stoker*?" I never call him by his last name, and he's never seemed bothered by me calling him Abram. Pretty sure I'm the only one who calls him that, based on what Sasha said a few weeks ago. He never seemed perturbed by it so I kept it that way.

With a subtle nod, he removes his helmet, placing it on the handlebar of his bike before looking directly at me. His eyes are fierce, almost angry, as he sits quietly and unmoving staring into my soul. I squirm in my seat, uncomfortable with the sudden change in him and questioning what I said to make his mood change.

"Little bird, to everyone else I am Stoker." He dismounts the bike, leaving it a few feet from my car in the middle of the road. With each step he takes closer to my open window, I feel both fear of the unknown and hot desperation. His wild side scares me as much as it excites me, in ways I've never known.

Without warning, he firmly grips my chin between his rough tattooed hands, holding my face hostage so I have nowhere to look except his enchanting eyes. "Make no mistake, to you I am Abram, nothing else. Understand?" Before I can nod or whisper my understanding, my brain is quickly searching for the warning bells and red flags, but I find none. He's controlling, yes, and intense, double yes. But I don't feel threatened and I can't figure out why.

Abram Stoker is a complicated man, and I've only just scratched the surface of what lies beneath. But the way he's looking at me, still clutching my aching chin in his hand, makes me wonder if he enjoys me calling him by his first name. Where it irritates him with everyone else, it doesn't seem to when I do it. So many layers.

I stare back into his eyes with the same intensity, blinking once before nodding my head what little I can to acknowledge I understand. He releases me and smirks as I rub a soothing hand over the spot he just had in his grip, weirdly already missing the warmth of his touch. "Good girl."

Without another word, he revs his bike back to life, slips on his helmet and rides off in the direction of June's property. I want to say I'm still mad, that I didn't even have a chance to tell him off again but I can't bring myself to care. That issue seems long gone and unimportant all of a sudden. In some ways I've been telling myself I'm more mad with Alex for kissing me again when I thought I made it clear I wasn't ready.

It's a hock of shit anyways, considering what I've already done with Abram. Maybe they've talked about it and that's why Alex felt like he could make a move again. My head hurts too much after a long shift to try and direct what may or may not being going on with the two of them. And honestly, I don't have it in me to be mad about it right now. If anything, I'm tricking myself into feeling flattered.

That's the feeling I focus on as I finally pull away from the curb in the dark night and head in the same direction Abram went just moments before. I may not know where my life is headed right now, but I know what I want to do while I figure it out.

STOKER

chapter eleven

♫

Daylight • David Kushner

STOKER

It's been a while since I've worked in my studio. Between work for Ellis lately and my annoyingly ever consuming thoughts of the dark haired beauty next door, it's long overdue. No one knows about my little side hobby, and I like it that way. I don't need people looking at me any other way than they already do. My exterior is hard and I want them to think the same for my interior.

It's not that I'm a bad guy per se. I take out the bad guys, and happily, I might add. But I'm not a white knight either. You won't find me riding in to save a damsel in distress. *Even though you basically already have.* Shoving the thought aside I remind myself it's better to keep people in the dark about majority of my life and interests. Less likely to disappoint them when they don't have high expectations to begin with. I've left that up to my brother, Alex, instead. The golden retriever of a human being with his happy demeanor and carefree spirit.

As a kid I'm sure I was a lot like him, but life has hardened me in ways I don't see softening now or ever. Some things can't be erased, and while I had to witness a lot of shit I wish I could eradicate from my mind, at least it was me who took the brunt of it and not my brother.

We may be polar opposites in so many ways, and his goofy attitude irritates the fucking shit out of me most days, but he's still my brother and there's nothing I wouldn't do to protect that aura about him. With that said, I don't like him around Isolde.

Women have held little to no interest to me over the years, preferring to sink into them for a night, get my fill and then forget all about them. Barely making note of their first name, let alone the prospect of ever seeing them again. That's primarily why I don't sleep with women from around here. I prefer to get my fix with a random stranger on the road, not giving a single fuck if we ever meet again.

This last trip was the first one in a long time I didn't seek out that release, and as much as I tried convincing myself it's because the dance is getting old, I knew better. Without any reasonable ideas, other than Isolde being a complete knockout, it doesn't make sense why I'm so drawn to her.

Her eyes pull me in, like deep pools of sorrow she tries to hide but can't. So many times I've bit my tongue to keep from asking her what ghosts she's hiding, and more importantly, which ones she's running from. No one just shows up in a town like this with nothing but the clothes on their back if they're not running from something. Whatever it is, it terrifies her. I saw it the night I showed up to take care of those asshole drunks.

I've also resisted the urge to ask Aunt June about her, because that woman can get even a priest to admit his sins. She knows the right way to talk to a person, making them feeling instantly at ease until they can't help themselves. I have zero doubts June knows everything that's happened to Isolde, and it's driving me wild not knowing.

If I ask her she'll look at me, the way she does when she knows what you're thinking without you having to utter a single word. I hated it as a teenager, she read Alex and I like an open book no matter how under wraps we tried to keep our feelings.

My thoughts about Isolde give way for a moment as I open the doors to my studio. Really it's just a small shed behind my house that I keep locked at all times, even when I'm inside. My aunt and brother have never outwardly tried to breech my privacy, but one can never be too careful. Especially with the way Isolde wanders the property. She's curious, which I can't blame her for considering how beautiful this property is, but it makes me uneasy sometimes.

Not just for the fact that she could stumble upon this work space and if I ever forget to lock it, there's nothing stopping her from peeking inside. A small part of me wants to show her, but I also kind of like that not a single soul knows about it.

After my mom was killed, Alex and I both saw a therapist. I refused for almost a year until I saw how much it was helping Alex. I finally caved and went, dragging my feet the whole way. As much as I hated the idea of therapy, I just wanted to feel something again. I was so numb to everything and the weight of that was slowly and painfully killing me.

After the first few sessions, the therapist recommended I find a hobby that would keep my mind and hands busy. She listed a few ideas off and for whatever reason, pottery piqued my interest. I went home and looked up what I would need to get started, too afraid to ask to take classes. I preferred the idea of self teaching, so that's what I did.

It's not technically true that no one knows about it, because I frequent the art supply store often, but the owner doesn't ask any questions and I've never offered up what I do either. It took a few years before I was able to acquire a wheel and a kiln, but once I did I became obsessed. I spent most of my teenage years locked away in this studio spinning the wheel and making anything and everything.

One of my best kept secrets is that majority of the pottery June has in her house was made by me. I always told her they were handmade gifts, but never that I was the one who made them for her. I've wanted to and almost have a few times, but something about keeping the secret is more appealing. One day, maybe.

***

After overhearing Alex on the phone earlier, with whom I could only guess was Isolde judging by the way he was smiling like an asshole - he's at the manor. She has work tonight though, so I know it'll just be him working there. Time for a friendly chat with my little brother.

I have to admit, with all the work that's been done around here, mainly due to Isolde's keen eye for design, this place looks better than ever. With the help of Alex and I in the construction and electrical areas, I guess we've made a decent team. Not that I'll say that to him, kid's already got a big head.

I make my way through the arched front door, painted a soft periwinkle blue color, which at first I thought was insane because the rest of the exterior is black. Also seemed insane. But seeing it all come together, it really looks amazing. The light blue against the dark black house adds a lightness I never would have thought of. This house has been a dark memory for as long as I can remember, Isolde might just be the light that's been missing.

Maybe Alex and I should consider hiring her on as a design consultant. Jesus, what the fuck is with me? I barely know the girl and already I'm thinking of hiring her to be a part of the business my brother and I started. I need to just fuck her out of my system and move on, that's all this feeling is.

The house smells like citrus cleaning products and it's a welcoming scent since it only ever smelled of dust and depression, another thing Isolde was able to eradicate from this place. The floors that were sanded and refinished have been swept clean and there's already a few runners in the hallway leading to the dining room where I find Alex.

Alex said he and Isolde pulled an all nighter to get the wallpaper hung so we could finish up the electrical in here. She wants to hang vintage candle sconces on the walls between each window giving it an old fashion look. Her words, not mine.

Looks like he's about half way done, so I grab my electric screwdriver and head to the wall opposite him and begin working. Neither of us says much for a while, even though the tension in the room is thick. I know he has shit on his mind just like he knows I have some on my own. I guess it's no longer a secret that we both want Isolde. The difference between him and I is he's likely to wine and dine a girl whereas I'm likely to fuck her into oblivion until her legs are wobbly and she doesn't remember her own name because she was too busy screaming mine.

But, something about Isolde is different, and I don't know why yet. I intend to find out though, and I won't let my baby brother get in the way of that. Even if that means we have to share her.

"Just say whatever is on your mind, Stoker. Your thoughts are loud as fuck right now and it's distracting."

I chuckle to myself, not allowing any sound to come out because I don't need my brother of all people to think I'm softening. "Way to beat around the bush, brother."

"Oh, fuck off. We both know you're gonna say and do whatever you want anyways, might as well get on with it."

"Isolde." That's all I say, letting the weight of her name hang in the space between us. He knows that's why I'm here. He also knows I trust him to do the electrical himself and because of that there's no reason for me to be here.

Alex sighs, dropping the screws in his hand on the ladder beside him. "I figured that's why you wanted to come here. I never need your help with this shit."

Growing up, all we had was each other. It's not difficult to read the other and that's worked well for us in the past. And lucky for Alex, I never dated around here so he had his choice of any woman in town if that's what he wanted. Makes me wonder what his thoughts are on me being interested in the one woman in town he also wants.

"I know you want her. As secretive as you can be, you're doing a shit job of hiding your interest in her." Taking his backwards ball cap off, he runs a hand through the floppy strands before returning the hat to the same spot. "Thing is…"

"You want her, too," I say, cutting him off.

The silence stretches on as we stand in the dining room staring at each other. Every time I want to say something, I can't find the right words. I don't want to fight with my brother over a girl, but I don't know that I can share her either. Inhaling a few deep breaths, taking in a lungful of lemon disinfectant with each one, I watch a lightbulb flicker over Alex's head.

"Listen, last time we tried talking about Isolde right in front of her, she got pissed and wanted nothing to do with either of us."

"Pretty sure she still doesn't," I scoff.

"Because we didn't include her in the conversation. Girls like that don't want to be ignored."

"Girls like what?" I ask, unable to keep the curiosity at bay.

Alex looks at me as slow smile spreads across that stupid face of his. Fuck, I want to punch him so bad sometimes. Arrogant son of a bitch, I think as I roll my eyes. He knows something, and he just realized that I am not in on whatever it is.

"Huh," he laughs to himself making me grind my teeth together in irritation. "Here I thought you had gotten closer to her than I had. Guess I was wrong, brother." Yep, I'm gonna pummel him in two seconds. I take a step forward, ready to react on my inner caveman when he holds his hand up to stop me.

"Chill bro, I don't know much. Just that she's been through some rough shit. June knows a lot more, I think, but you know her. That woman is a damn vault, and if Isolde led on that she doesn't want anyone knowing, then June won't speak a word of it. We both know that much."

He's right. My aunt is an incredible woman, loyal almost to a fault. She'd go to jail for someone before spilling any of their secrets. "Then what are you suggesting?" His beating around the bush is not worth it right now, I'll just go find Isolde myself and make her talk to me.

"She has the reigns here, and she's in charge. As much as we both hate to take a backseat, I think we need to. When it comes to this at least."

Fucking idiot might be right, and I hate that. Placing both hands on my hips, I puff out a breath as I think about what she might have gone through. Whatever happened to Isolde before coming here shook her up bad, and maybe for once she needs to feel in control.

"Whether she wants one of us or both of us, it has to be up to her and in her time. All you and I can do is talk about what it might mean if she wants one of us or both of us."

Christ, Alex and I haven't shared a woman since high school, and it was much different. None of those girls meant jack shit to me, so I really didn't care of they chose him. Can't say I ever blamed any of them when all I cared about was what they would sound like as I drove my cock into their tight cunts. It never lasted long and I'd just move on to the next piece of ass without a care in the world. It's not like that anymore, and fuck, I cannot for the life of me understand why.

"Have you thought about it?" I ask, almost afraid of his answer.

"Yeah, a little," he scrubs the back of his head, and I know right here and now it's been on his mind longer than I thought. I didn't even think Alex knew there was something going on between her and I. Maybe he's right, I haven't been hiding my interest as well as I think I am.

"It's different though," he says matter of factly and I don't have it in me to brush him off and deny it. So I say nothing, which is all the confirmation he needs.

With a heavy sigh, Alex drops his head to his chest in thought while I wait. "Alright, I don't think we should do or say anything until she does. For all we know she hates us both and we do all this talking for nothing. It's clear though we both want her though, and I don't intend on backing off."

"Neither do I," I agree gruffly.

Standing straight, Alex walks over to me and stops inches away with his right hand held out. "May the best man win." I wish he didn't make it seem like a competition, that never ends well for him and I. But if Isolde is the prize, then I'll stop at nothing to get what I want.

With a smirk, I place my hand in his and give it a firm shake. I love my brother, and aside from June, there aren't too many people I care about anymore. And as much as we've always had each other's back, I've never wanted to see him fail the way I do now. May the best man win. I grin at his choice words and squeeze his hand a little tighter.

"I intend to."

ISOLDE

chapter twelve

♫

My Love is Like Wo • Mya

With a tray under my arm, a pocket full of tips and a smile on my face, I make my way behind the bar to fill another large order. I couldn't have predicted how much I would love this job, considering how nervous I was when I first started, but it's been a life saver in it's own way. Coming here is a way to escape reality for a few hours, something I've grown addicted to.

When I'm working here or at the manor, I feel a sense of belonging and peace. Something I haven't experienced in such a long time I feared it was gone permanently. Add all of that to how much I've grown to love June and making friends with Hailey and Sasha, I finally feel happy. I keep waiting to wake up from this blissful dream to face the reality of the living hell I've been stuck in for six years, but it never happens.

If this all ends up being a dream, then I never want to wake up.

"Look at you smiling like a little kid," Sasha says over her shoulder as she makes a drink in the shaker before straining it over fresh ice. I've never seen someone so effortlessly mix a cocktail, it's almost mesmerizing.

"I'm…I don't know, I'm just happy," I laugh with a shrug of my shoulders. It feels foreign to say out loud but cathartic in a way too. I don't want to voice it too much and ruin the chance of this all being temporary, which is why I've preferred keeping it inside. To hold on to it tighter, I guess.

Sasha lines the freshly made drinks on a tray for me to take over to the table in the corner and winks at me. "Happy looks good on you. Now, get these drinks out so you can infect the room with your happiness and make us some damn good tips tonight. Yeah?"

"You got it, boss," I salute her and take off with the drinks to deliver to the group of woman laughing their hearts out. As I make my way to their table I catch a glimpse of the phone screen they're all staring at and drooling over. I laugh to myself, because I hope to someday find a group of women I can sit at a bar with and ogle pictures of young hot guys with. As I set down the last drink I get a closer look at who they're checking out and I almost choke on my next breath.

There on the phone screen is a picture of Abram and Alex glistening with sweat and no shirts on as they work to rebuild a house. It looks like a newspaper clipping and suddenly I have the urge to find out who took these photos and if there's more. "I would love to lick the sweat right off those abs," one of the women says chuckling loudly with her friend. You and me both, sister.

"Isolde, dear, come take a look at this," the woman in her late forties with red hair, I think her name is Sandra, says. Little does she know, I've already gotten an eyeful of that picture.

"These Stoker men, aren't they somethin' else?"

I pretend to look at the photo as though it's not already been stored in my brain for later use, and nod my head in agreement. What am I supposed to say? *Yeah I'd lick their abs all night, at the same time...* Woah. Where did that thought come from? Right now I'm not talking to either of them because I need to figure out what their game is and if I even want to play, and suddenly I'm silently fantasizing about having both Stoker men. I need some air.

Before I can give them an answer, their eyes bug out and they all go still. I feel a presence behind me, radiating heat all the way down my spine. Fuck, I hate that he gets this type of reaction out of me. Just my body, I remind myself, because anything else is more than I can handle.

"Now that *is* a good picture, thank you Sandra." Her name is Sandra, I knew it! There's ten women sitting here, I wasn't likely going to remember each of their names. Wait, that was Alex who just spoke. I spin around to face him and stumble backwards slightly before righting myself when I realize both Stoker men are now watching me.

When they stand side by side like this something happens to my insides. I get all flustered and my knees feel weak. I'm such a girl, I chastise myself.

"Gentlemen," I say with a slight tremor in my voice. "There's a table by the window or you can sit at the bar. Your choice." Without giving them an option to respond, I skirt around them and head behind the safety of the bar. I don't think it would stop either of them from talking to me, but at least I can try.

Sure enough, they take two stools at the bar right at the end in front of my station. *Great.* Sometimes I feel like a walking magnet drawing in unwanted attention. *But you like it, and you know it.* I wish I could slap that voice right out of my mind without looking like a head case. But I know it's right, and that's what pisses me off.

"What can I get you?"

Alex places a hand over his heart, trying to be playful like usual, but it's not going to work this time. I don't want to be a conquest for these men, and if they think I'll fold that easily, then they've got another thing coming. If I manifest these thoughts enough they're likely to come to fruition, right?

"Isolde, why the cold shoulder babe?" Is he serious? Alex is flirty and overall kind, but he's delusional if he thinks I'm going to just forget how they talked about me without acknowledging my thoughts the other day.

"Alex, we both know you're smarter than whatever it is you're doing right now. So, cut the bullshit and order a drink. Or leave," I say with a fake smile. "Either choice is fine by me."

Sasha chose that moment to join me behind the bar and whistles as she walks up beside me. "Damn boys, what did you do to piss off Miss Sunshine here? She's been in an amazing mood all night," before Alex can open that mouth of his again, the same mouth that gave me a toe curling kiss just two days ago, Sasha holds up a hand. "I don't actually care. But if you're gonna sour her mood, then get out."

Jesus, I love this woman even more now. She's a ride or die if I've ever met one. I already knew I'd want her by my side in a bar fight cause Sasha is a tough broad, but now I want her around to shoo away anyone who threatens to dampen my good mood.

"Aw, come on Sash, you wouldn't kick us out, would you?" Alex makes a fake puppy dog face and I feel Sasha's urge to punch him come off in waves. I almost want to run in back and grab my phone to document it.

"No, but I'll punch you right now if you call me *Sash* again."

"Fair enough," he says holding up his hands in surrender.

While they continue their playful banter, I chance a look at Abram and find him paying them no attention. His gray eyes are fixed on me, blazing into mine with such intensity all previous thoughts of falling at their feet goes out the window. I don't want to be that girl anymore, the one who goes along with whatever the man wants. It's time I learn to stand up for myself. No matter how bad I might want him to take me home and have his way with me.

I busy myself with pouring a drink for Abram, not bothering to ask because I know what he likes. Something I probably shouldn't have done when I notice the look on his face when I place the whiskey in front of him. With a smirk, Abram wraps his fingers around the rock glass, gently brushing mine. Unable to look away, I watch as he lifts the glass to his lips and takes a sip. "You remembered my drink of choice," he says matter of factly. "I'm flattered."

"It's not complicated," I retort before heading back on the floor to check on my other patrons. Maybe I'm being too harsh with them both, it's not like we're in a relationship and we haven't known each other more than a couple of months. I should get to know them both and then decide if I even want to get involved with with either of them.

Feeling my mood shift back to a happier one, I go back to face them and let them know my thoughts about whatever the hell is going on with us three.

Sasha is making drinks at her station, so I know she won't be listening in. She gets so in the zone when she's working, it's admirable. Except for the times when I need her assistance and she's too consumed to hear me.

At work isn't the ideal place to have a conversation like this, but I don't know if I trust myself to be alone with them just yet.

They turn on their stools to face me as I approach the bar top. "I'm not usually an uptight bitch," I start and Alex almost chokes on his beer, clearly not having expected me to start that way. "What I mean is, there is clearly something going on with…us," I gesture between the three of us and don't miss the way Abram smirks ever so slightly. "And…I don't know what to do about it exactly."

STOKER

"What do you want to do?" Abram asks, taking another sip of whiskey.

Does he realize he just asked me a loaded question? If I answer honestly they might be disgusted with me for wanting to sample both of them, which I've only come around to the idea of myself. But if I say I only want one of them then I could risk losing the other. Not exactly something I feel ready to make a decision on right now. My mind and my heart have never been in sync with each other, which in past experience hasn't gotten me into a lot of trouble. Literally and figuratively.

Hesitantly, I meet their gazes, both still fixed on me waiting for my reply. If only Sasha needed me for something, pulling me away from this situation that has both my cheeks flushing and underwear dampening. How I managed to fall into this trap I'll never know, but maybe it's time I stop fighting the attraction and take what I want for a change. I've never been in control when it comes to my romantic life.

"Babe, the wait is killing me. Tell us what you want and we'll do whatever you say," Alex's voice has lost it's fire just a touch, replaced with a hint of pleading. I almost enjoy making them squirm like this. Who am I kidding? I love it. I feel powerful and in charge, and that's a feeling I could get used to.

Decision made, I slide my tray under my arm and grab my notepad off the bar top. It might be the sound of Mya singing her heart out to *'My Love is Like Wo'* giving me a semblance of courage, focusing on that instead of the loud thumping in my chest. Both men watch me walk around the side of the bar to stand between them, eyes never leaving my body. I feel a rush skate up my spine, igniting a feeling I thought was long ago snuffed out. "I've got work to do," I contemplate leaving them hanging before adding, "meet me here at closing."

And with that, I stalk off to continue my shift. Feeling their eyes on my ass the whole way and adding a little sway just for them. I don't know where this side of me has been buried, but it's about time I picked up the shovel and dug it out.

***

Sasha closes and locks the front door before saying goodnight and heads to her car across the street. My earlier confidence has dissipated slightly as I spot both Abram and Alex leaning against my car under a lone streetlight. From this distance they appear intimidating and if I didn't know them I'd run in the opposite direction. Abram is covered in tattoos, some even working their way up his neck to where his head is shaved on the sides. And while I find the cigarette between his lips sexy as hell, it also makes this scene slightly unnerving.

Alex doesn't have nearly as many tattoos, but his build is almost as big as Abrams and the look he's giving me as I slowly make my way over to them is like a lion ready to feast on it's prey. Underneath his sunshine exterior there might just be a beast waiting to emerge.

Coming to a stop in front of them, I feel my inner walls closing in around me, attempting to protect me from failure. I've spent so much time in the previous years fearing that I'm destined to fail, never wanting to allow anyone to see deeper than the facade I put on. My outside voice is foreign to my inside voice, and the way I spoke to the guys earlier tonight has that inner voice frantically searching for an escape route.

I don't know if I'm capable of doing this with them. Even if the details are still unknown.

"Do you always surround yourself with walls, little bird?" Abram's voice, a deep tone that has my toes curling in my shoes, penetrates the darkness and I glance up to lock eyes with him. How does he always see right into my soul? He's a mind reader, like my own personal Edward Cullen.

"Yes," I breath. Unable to say anything else.

"Why is that?" Alex asks, and suddenly I feel dizzy hearing both of their husky voices circling me in a haze of desire.

"Because…U-up until the two of you, no one else deserved to see what was behind them. And no one ever bothered to try," I end on a whisper, embarrassment threatening to take over as my cheeks heat with shame. The words spill out of my mouth before my mind has a chance to stop and think about what I'm doing. I'll be mad about it later because the look on their faces was worth the risk.

Feeling the shift in the mood, I wait with bated breaths and hope one of them says something. If the tension keeps building I'll start to babble nervously and kill the mood entirely. Dropping his cigarette to the ground, Abram squishes it under his black boot and takes two large steps towards me. His scent overwhelms me in the most delicious way. Always the same, woody with that hint of mint mixed in, but never any less intoxicating.

Instinct has me backing up slightly, but Abram snakes an arm around my waist and pulls me flush against his chest. With no time to react, his other hand goes to my neck and he's fusing our lips together in a hungry embrace. I worry Alex might feel uncomfortable watching us make out in front of him, but the moment Abram pushes his tongue in my mouth to dance with mine I forget we're not alone standing in the street.

It's so easy to lose myself in his touch and taste. Abram Stoker is a walking aphrodisiac.

When he finally pulls away, a gust of much needed air fills my lungs, and I silently pray they don't want to do this. The unknown of what they expect of me is almost too much, my mind racing to the speed of my hands shaking. On the other hand I want to rip the bandaid off and get past the first time before I have a heart attack.

It feels like an eternity has gone by since Abram's lips left mine, but it's probably been a matter of seconds. Still, my nerves are at an all time high and I'm nervously waiting for one of them to say something in hopes I don't accidentally put my foot in my mouth.

"I-I've never done something like…this," I gesture between the three of us and gulp audibly, eliciting a chuckle form Alex. "I'm not sure wh-what I'm supposed to do…or say." If only I could make my voice not sound squeaky like a prepubescent teenager as I silently pray one of them would just throw me a rope and take the lead. If they're waiting for me to do that then we'll be here all night.

"Well, if I'm being honest I was hoping for a little taste of what you so confidently said earlier. What about you brother?"

"Couldn't agree more."

My eyes ping pong between the two and as much as I hate to think it, its feels like we're back in that game I said I didn't want to play. So much of me is screaming to go home and not entertain the two men in front of me, knowing it's not likely to end well. While the other part of me, buried deep down with desires I've never shared with a single soul, begs to be set free. To grab this opportunity and run with it as far as I can. Broken heart be damned.

"This isn't a game."

"No one said it was, little bird. You hold the reigns here, we're just along for the ride."

My gaze flicks to Alex as he nods his head in agreement, allowing me to feel slightly better about the situation. I know he's interested in me but I also know he isn't trying to hurt me. I turned him down once already and he was just as kind as ever.

I can't imagine either of them would go to this much trouble for someone like me if they weren't genuinely curious about getting to know my body and hopefully more importantly, me as a person. It's probably safe to say it's the former, but I'm trying to better my self deprecating mindset.

"Listen babe, this doesn't have to be an all in one night kind of thing. Let's just get to know you individually and if a situation arises then we'll cross it when it comes. Sound good?" Alex is the voice of reason. The kind soul who wants to protect and put a smile on the faces of people he cares about. One glance at Abram tells me he's stripping me down with his eyes, wanting to devour my entire being, inside and out. It's frightening in a sexy kind of way and I don't know what corrupt shit this town is conjuring and pumping into the air to make me think this way.

For whatever reason, be it curiosity or the need to learn the dark hidden parts of myself, I agree. So, why does it feel like I've signed a contract with the sea witch? d

STOKER

chapter thirteen

🎵

Bodies • Drowning Pool

Lately it feels like every time I make some kind of progress with Isolde, I'm called away on another job. I guess there really is no rest for the wicked. However, it does feel busier than usual. Either that or Ellis is in a shitty mood and wants to bring me down with him.

Every so often he goes off the rails in a way. I've never actually met him in person, just email correspondence and phone calls or texts, but after years of working for him I've come to recognize the signs. He used to say it was personal, not that I ever asked, I don't give a flying fuck what he does during his off time. Only if it affects my job. He may be the one who assigns them to me, but I don't need his distractions.

There was one time that stood out, a couple of months ago, he was calling me like crazy and I had half a mind to block his number. Can't imagine that would have ended well. Anyways, he was practically manic, talking a mile a minute while simultaneously making no sense at all. Only reason I remember the time so vividly, not the actual purpose of his call, was because I had a chick bouncing up and down on my dick in my sleazy hotel room as he yammered on.

I was a little surprised she willingly came into the room when I invited her, if I were her I probably would have left. Ellis just loves to set me up in the cheapest rooms with no amenities, as if it would kill him to at least book a Hilton for fucks sake.

Whatever set him off that time, I got a two week vacation out of it. When he called me for my next assignment he was back to his usual straight forward self. Always the down to business guy, explaining my assignment before emailing my room info. Majority of the jobs have been semi local, most of them just a few hours away with the occasional flight. I decline those when I'm able. I don't like flying to begin with and something about having to rely on a flight to get me home makes me uneasy.

The risk with this work is too high, which is why I prefer to take my bike. Even if that means a four hour ride where my asscheeks ache and my thighs burn like I've been clenching them together for too long.

That's where I'm at right now, three hours East of home about to pull up to the location Ellis sent me. A nice house in a cul-de-sac with two brand new Mercedes in the driveway. My target is a high profile lawyer, self proclaimed family man and husband of the year. Little does his botox loving wife know, he fucks other women and occasionally a teenager. I'm going to enjoy this one.

As always, whenever I'm sent on a job to take someone out that has a family, I confirm with Ellis the kids won't be home. Sometimes I feel bad at the prospect of the wife finding the husband, but they should know what kind of person they're married too. In situations like this, I like to leave a present behind, just a little keepsake if you will.

Usually a file filled with photos of their significant other in the act, sometimes I even include an untraceable flash drive with videos and audio. If only I could be a fly on the wall when they watch what their loving husbands spent years doing behind their back.

Fucking classic.

It always ends the same, the grieving wife plays her part at the funeral, distraught over the death of her husband but ultimately wides up fucking the pool boy or gardener and moves on with her life.

The thing about couples like that, they're just actors in their own lives. None of them really care about the other, if they did they wouldn't be fucking around in the first place. I'm all for getting my dick wet, but not with prostitutes and underage girls.

The house is dark as I pull up, a lone front light casting a glow on their expansive front porch. A beautiful house like this is wasted on stupid people like Daniel McGreevy. Even his last name sounds stupid. I'll enjoy this one. I think I say that ninety-nine percent of the time, but each new kill brings about a wave of unmatched euphoria. At first, taking someones life took time to adjust to, I puked right after each one in the beginning. But now, I find it peaceful because I hold the power to end the lives of despicable people who should never have existed in the first place.

Ending them is doing the rest of humanity a favor, and I take a lot of enjoyment in my part of the deal. Even when they beg for their life, blood pouring from every surface of their body, as if I could save them at that point, I just smile at them. Feeling just like the maniac I know I am deep down.

My bike is safely parked around the corner and I take the backyards of Daniel's neighbors, careful to avoid cameras, until I reach his back door. Rich people often leave at least one door unlocked, feeling like God's creations and that no harm will come to them. My eyes roll so hard I feel my irises touch my brain at the thought.

I luck out on my first try, feeling the doorknob turn with ease as I let myself in through the mudroom at the back of their expansive home. Sometimes I wonder if the surviving spouse keeps living in the house I murder their loved one in, or if they sell. For me it would be the latter.

Thankfully the McGreevy's don't have any pets, I hate to injure an innocent animal, but if I have to incapacitate them for a short time to get the job done, then so be it.

Making my way down the corridor to the master suite, I run through my game plan. Ellis provides me with floor plans ahead of time so I'm not walking around blindly looking for the target and accidentally bumping into someone getting a glass of water in the middle of the night. Apparently that exact scenario happened to a guy a few years back and ever since then, Ellis and his guys take extra precaution.

It's just past midnight, which means Daniel has reached rem sleep by now. I love pulling them from whatever bullshit they dream about and scaring the shit out of them. Sometimes literally.

Seeing two still forms lying in bed, I curse to myself. I was hoping the wife was out of town since she often is, looks like I need to adjust my plan slightly. I never make my kills quick, wanting these low life's to feel every second of pain I inflict while reminding them of the vile crimes they've committed. I always hope they think about it, even a little. Like maybe if they didn't give into these desires, disgusting as they may be, then they wouldn't have wound up tied to a chair in a musty basement with nails in their eyeballs.

I silently chuckle when I remember the time I hammered nails into a guys eyes because he liked watching little girls on the playground. Fucking prick deserved worse than what I gave him but he still cried like a baby as a blood and drool dripped off his chin.

Since the wife is here I have to make quick work of getting Daniel out of bed with minimal noise and movement., not exactly my favorite way to remove a man from his bed. I prefer dragging him out with rusty pliers attached to his toes as he lands on a blanket of broken glass. My imagination knows no bounds, hence why I'm the best.

After pouring over the blueprints creating a plan for execution, I noticed they have a sound proof room in their basement. I'm hoping to find a bunch of instruments down there and not a creepy dungeon used for the vile things this man is interested in. Unfortunately I've seen my fair share of those.

I'm rewarded with the former as I open the door and find a drum kit, a few amps and some pretty sweet acoustic guitars hung on the wall. If only Daniel took more interest in playing music than raping women I wouldn't be about to rip the flesh from his hands so he can never touch an innocent woman again. Lucky for me I brought a potato peeler to do exactly that.

As much as I enjoy dragging out the pain for my benefit, not theirs, I want to get this one done with. The cleanup is much more extensive when I let loose and since the wife is still upstairs I want to create as little disturbance as possible.

Once my tools are set up, I connect my phone to my pocket bluetooth and set the scene with some music. Even though the room is soundproof, it's rather small and Daniel's screams will piss me off more if I don't have something else to focus on. *'Bodies' by Drowning Pool* echoes in the space, and I chuckle at the subtle innuendo at what's to come.

With zero fucks, I drag Daniel into the room by his ears before tying him to a chair. After pulling him from his bed in a half asleep daze, I blindfolded him and gently escorted him downstairs. I wanted him to think this was some kind of kinky role play his wife was surprising him with before darkly whispering in his ear, *"we're going to have so much fun."*

His body went rigid at the timbre of my voice and I silently absorbed his newfound fear just as I kicked him to the ground and yanked him in the room. Now that I'm all set up, music on full blast reminding myself - and hopefully Daniel - that bodies will indeed be hitting the floor tonight.

Using my pocket knife, I slide the blade under the fabric of his blindfold to cut it away from his face. A small trickle of blood rolls down the tip of his nose landing on his silk pajama bottoms. What kind of man wears silk fucking pajamas to bed?

Daniel looks around frantically before his eyes settle on me in a mix of confusion and terror. "What the fuck?" He asks stupidly as he pulls on his restraints. For someone who's suppose to be a high profile lawyer, he sure looks stupid right now. "Who are you? Why are you in my house?"

Rolling my eyes, I pull a cigarette from behind my ear, light it up and inhale deeply. For some reason, despite the situation we're in, these guys get really fired up when I smoke in their house. "Really? That's the question you want an answer to?"

"Well, I.."

"Let me stop you there, Daniel. I expected more from you if I'm being honest." Inhaling another puff, I slowly begin circling him in his chair. "I read all about you and you're one of the top lawyers at your firm. I was expecting something more… articulate from you."

Stopping in front of him, I blow a puff of smoke in his face causing him to swear and turn his head away from me. With a firm grip, I grab his chin and straighten his face so that he's looking directly at me. "I'm disappointed."

He scoffs. Fucking *scoffs*, as if he's trying to muster some kind of bravado. Not going to work when I already saw the blood drain from his face as he realized I wasn't his wife being kinky.

I don't give him a chance to say anything, not wanting to hear whatever sewage he'll spill anyways. To ensure I have his full attention I slap him across the face hard enough to leave a handprint. It's nice not having to worry about wearing gloves or covering my tracks. Ellis always sends in a team to clean up the mess, disposing of the body with such precise detail it'll look as if nothing askew happened in here.

"Cut the tough guy shit, we both know you don't have any balls and even if you did they'd probably be found in a nice little display case on your wife's vanity. Usually I take much enjoyment out of ending someone as pathetic as you, but tonight I'm feeling impatient." His eyes widen as my words sink in one at a time and now I know I have his attention.

There's something beneficial for the ones who die in their own home. A subtle comfort of knowing there's a chance someone will hear and come save them. Unfortunately for him, I injected his wife with a sedative to keep her in a peaceful slumber. As if he can read my mind, Daniel leans around me towards the door as if willing his wife to walk in.

"Oh, yeah she's not going to save you. I gave her a little something to keep her happy in dreamland, completely unaware of the horrors you're about to face," I offer a sinister smile for emphasis, enjoying the way he's looking at me like I'm a maniac. I am. "But, like I said, I'll make it quick. Not because you deserve any mercy, but because I'd like to sleep in my own bed tonight and not some rancid hotel room."

Daniel just watches me, sweat beading in his receding hairline as reality keeps seeping in more and more. "Surely you understand, right?" I slap his shoulder like we're buddies, enjoying the game I'm playing with him and making a mental note to do this more often. The feeling reminds me of when Mom used to tell us not to play with our food. We always ate it, but sometimes it was fun to play with it first.

"I wanted to keep it a surprise, but maybe you'd like to hear the things I plan to do to you. Mix things up a little," I chuckle darkly and pull a screwdriver from my back pocket. Twirling it between my fingers I watch Daniel with a wide grin on my face. I should really bring some mirrors next time so I can see how deranged I look. I could place them around the room, it'll feel like a funhouse. I fucking loved those as a kid.

Catching myself in my thoughts again, I focus back on the present and hand the screwdriver to Daniel. He looks at it with a puzzled expression and I swear I can hear my eyes rolling. "First," I say, pointing at the screwdriver. "You're going to take that screwdriver and jam it into your own leg." His eyes practically bulge out of their sockets as he shakes his head frantically.

"Y-you, I-I can't do that. What the fuck is wrong with you?" He's screeching now, and even the music doesn't hide the annoying pitch of his voice.

"Well, to be fair, so many things. But tonight isn't about me, Daniel. Tonight is all about you, buddy," I slap a hand on his shoulder like we're old pals. "So, you're gonna jam that into your leg right now, or I'll take it and jam it into your precious jewels there," I point at his groin hoping my point is crystal clear.

As if he wasn't already white as ghost, Daniel turns an even lighter shade of white as reality has fully sunk in. He's not getting out of this, help is not coming and tonight he will die. So exciting! Yeah, I'm fucked up. But who isn't?

"The choice is yours, but just know if you don't do it yourself, I'll be taking over. Got it?" He still doesn't move, I don't even think he's blinked in the last two minutes, so without warning I grab the screwdriver from him and bring it down harshly on his inner thigh. Purposely missing to drag it out a little. I didn't say I would make it painless, just that I wasn't going to drag it out for hours on end.

The moment the tip connects with the meaty flesh of his inner thigh, his face goes a deep shade of red as he holds his breath. I see the moment the vessels in his face almost pop and he releases the air he was holding on a scream. Daniel McGreevy could be featured in a remix of this song with how well his howling voice mixes with the song. "Beautiful," I say as I watch his cream colored silk pajamas turn a deep shade of crimson.

After an hour of torturing Daniel on and off, stabbing him in places to cause enough pain and bleeding but not enough to kill him, I decide I'm bored. Final moments are in motion as I pull a folder from my bag. The room reeks of rust and sweat and since we're in a basement there's no ventilation and I'm starting to feel nauseous.

You'd think the blood and guts would take me out, but nope, it's the smell of someone else's blood and sweat that does it to me. Don't get me stared on the smell urine, I gag just thinking about it.

Only needing to pull one photo from the folder, I slap it on Daniel's lap and wait for the reaction I know won't come. They never feel guilt or remorse. Someone capable of raping a young girl repeatedly just to ultimately leave them to die, doesn't posses such emotions.

People like Daniel look at their victims like trophies, like something to be proud of. It makes me sick to my fucking stomach and the sooner I end him the better.

The second a slight smile stretches across his face my fist connects with his nose. Just as I suspected, he feels a sense of pride, maybe even power over his crimes. Fucking scumbag. Where's all that power now, asshole? I want to scream in his face, but what could would that do?

"As much as I've enjoyed my time with you, Mr. McGreevy, more than I thought I would," I say with mock thoughtfulness. "I have a feeling I'll enjoy watching what little light is left of you fade to nothing."

Eyes still on his victim, I pull a hunting knife from the table where the rest of my bloody tools lie, ready to be cleaned and used on the next lowlife Ellis sends me to. With one swift movement I cut open his throat and watch as the blood paints his body, and ugly fucking pajamas, a beautiful crimson. He gurgles a few times, hands fisting the crumpled picture of the fifteen year old girl he raped, and slouches to the side as his last breath whooshes out of him like even it feels relief to be away from this monster.

Daniel died with his eyes on that fifteen year old girl he raped and killed a few months ago. I sincerely wish she could find him in the afterlife to torment him herself, but angels go to heaven and demons like this get to burn behind the gates of hell. One more tick on my sheet of kills and one less monster that gets to roam free.

Sometimes I wonder where I'll end up in the afterlife.

ISOLDE

chapter fourteen

♫

"If we're going to restore the patio, then we need to do a supply run," Alex says as he hops out of his truck. I texted him not even half an hour ago with an idea to fix up the patio that looks out onto the woods along June's property. It also has a perfect line of sight to Abram's house, but I dismissed that as the main reason I wanted to take on this project.

June has so much land, and while she's maintained the areas around her house, planting flowers and keeping up with the yard work, I really think she would enjoy seeing her entire property at it's best.

Back before my life went off the rails to say the least, I used to love gardening. It felt peaceful to connect with the earth and find ways to improve it's beauty. Something I can see myself enjoying again here.

Whenever I think about my time here I try to push the negative thoughts aside. I don't know how long I can stay, or even how long I'm welcome. June would probably slap me if she heard me speak such words aloud, but I don't want to be an imposition. As much as she's assured me I'm not.

"Lucky for you, I wrote a list of everything I think I'll need to make this space useful and beautiful again." Smiling, I hand Alex a folded sheet of paper and don't miss the way his fingers linger a little before he takes the list.

"It's a bit of a drive. Want to take a ride with me?"

"Oh…" I try to think of a reason it might not be a good idea, but nothing comes to mind. My face feels hot, and I smile shyly at Alex hoping he can read my mind. I don't want him thinking I don't want to spend time with him. I just don't know how to do any of this with either of them.

"You know you want to. Plus, I'm less likely to pick the wrong tile if you're there to get exactly what you're envisioning."

Shit. He's got me there. As good as Alex is at his job, paying attention to minor details does not come easy to him the way it does for Abram.

Alex looks at me with pouty lips and puppy dog eyes, and I couldn't stifle the laugh that bubbles up if I tried. He really is like a golden retriever majority of the time. I have yet to see a serious side to Alex. "Fine. But I get to pick the music on the way there."

With a knowing grin, Alex opens the passenger door to his truck, gesturing for me to climb in. I catch his sweet scent as I use the handlebar above the door to lift myself into the seat. He always smells like sunshine, like hot days on the beach covered in coconut sunscreen.

He rounds the front of the truck, hops in and starts it up. Without permission, I reach for his phone in the center console as he drives us down the dirt road away from the manor. His hand grips mine and I drop the phone as if it burned me, waiting for him to yell for touching his phone.

I should have known better to ask again, I'm such an idiot. "I-I'm sorry, Alex. I should have made sure it was okay to pick the music. H-here you go," I hand his phone to him with shaky hands and wait for the anger to burst out of him.

With eyes closed and shoulders bunched up to my ears, I wait. His voice meets me in a soft caress, "Baby, hey, look at me."

Making sure to take a few deep breaths first, I slowly open my eyes to see his concerned face watching me with caution. "I was just going to say no Taylor Swift, that's all."

Now I feel like an ever bigger fool. Again the damaged girl flings herself to the surface ensuring I look as pathetic as I feel. "You can take my phone anytime you want, play any music you like, aside from the former request, I assure you I have nothing to hide."

"Th-that's not what I meant. I…I'm sorry, some things are still a little tough for me. I feel silly," I say on a whisper, hoping he'll drop it like he usually does. If this happened in front of Abram he would have demanded to know what just happened. Alex can usually tell I'm uncomfortable and unable to talk about my past.

"It's not silly, Isolde," he pauses as he reaches a hand across the console and interlaces our fingers. "If you want to talk about it, I'm all ears. If not, well then that's okay too. Just know that you can and it won't leave this truck."

"Have you ever heard anything by Taylor Swift?" I ask, although I'm pretty sure I already know the answer. Alex looks at me and I know I caught him off guard a little considering how serious I just was.

"Never mind," I laugh nervously. "Well, there's a line in one of her songs that has always stuck with me. *'Time won't fly, it's like I'm paralyzed by it - I'd like to be my old self again, but I'm still trying to find it."*

Alex is quiet for a few beats, and I twist the sleeve of my shirt in my hands nervously. Every time I try to open up it feels like an elephant is sitting on my chest. Like I can't breathe and the thought of talking about the things I've been through could actually kill me. "Anyways," I blurt out, desperate to fill the silence. "That's kind of been my mantra for so long now I don't remember a time where I felt, *normal."*

I didn't even realize we've been driving until I look out the window and see the town blurring by us as Alex heads towards the interstate. "Please say something, I feel like I just shoved my foot in my mouth."

Alex laughs lightly, "truthfully I want to say something inspiring or helpful, but really all I can think about is hearing this song now." We both bust out laughing despite the awkward tension filling the cab. Not wanting the weirdness to carry on, or worse, risk Alex asking more questions, I put on *'All Too Well'* by Taylor Swift.

As soon as the song starts I feel goosebumps break out across my bare arms. I quickly brush it off, convincing myself it's just the wind coming in the open windows with the smell of the forrest around us. I can smell rust too, somewhere off in the distance but growing stronger the faster we drive. Soon, it's as if the rust is inside the cab of Alex's truck and I find it difficult to breathe through my nose.

Alex sits beside me unaware of my impending panic attack, tapping the steering wheel as he bobs his head to a song by a woman he not minutes ago banned me from playing. Taking advantage of his preoccupied mind, I try to work through my panic attack with the breathing techniques I learned in therapy.

After several rounds of breathing, the panic in my chest hasn't let up. If anything, it's worse. The thick smell of rust permeates the entire truck now, and I hold my breath to keep it from seeping in and infecting me with it's poison. I steer my brain to think about something else, *anything* else, hoping I can keep my mind from spiraling down the dark road of my past and careening off a cliff.

I feel the darkness start to take over and I know there's nothing I can do. As hard as I try to keep my thoughts at bay, they always find a way in. I close my eyes, pretending to enjoy the music as the first flashback takes root, replaying like an old black and white horror film.

I feel the slap of his hand like a hot brand across my cheek. Each time he does it, I feel the sting worse than the time before. My skin so raw and tender from the previous blow it almost feels like I'm bleeding. Maybe I am.

"Will you ever learn, Isolde? I swear it's like you want *me to get mad at you. You must like the punishment, you sick freak."*

I wish I could laugh or even scoff in his face at such an insane accusation. Why on earth would someone enjoy this kind of punishment? And by insane punishment, I mean the fact that I am tied to a chair in our dining room, completely naked I might add, as Grant slaps me across the face. Oh, and apparently I'm *the sick freak.*

If past punishments have taught me anything, this is just the appetizer. So if I want him to take it easy on me I need to stay completely still and refrain from showing any weakness or pain. As much as my body is buzzing from anger and fear, my eyes begging to let the tears building behind them fall, I must remain calm.

I wish I could fight back, do something to defend myself, but there's no point. Even if I wanted to take self defense classes, Grant would know. He controls all of our finances, including the personal account I set up before we even met. He says as the man it's his job to handle our accounts and what we use our money for.

I have to check with him to buy a goddamn coffee for fucks sake.

"Tell me why you touched my phone without my permission?"

Even when I give him the truth, he doesn't believe me, all women are liars according to him. Takes one to know one, I suppose. Another slap stings my cheek, catching me off guard because I stupidly took my eyes off him. "Tell me!"

I flinch at his tone, knowing this will only get worse if I don't say something. "I-I thought it was mine," I say weakly, knowing he isn't going to like that response even though it's exactly what happened. Our phones were both on the counter, and I walked into the kitchen to grab mine when I picked up his by mistake.

Before I could set it down right where I found it, Grant walked around the corner and saw me fumble with it before picking up my own. To him it looked suspicious, like I was trying to go through it behind his back. When really, I just grabbed the wrong one and panicked he would think I was trying to snoop. I should have just handed it to him and walked away.

Wouldn't have worked, I think to myself. I know him all too well by now. That knowledge is both a blessing and a curse, right now being the latter. Everyday I fight the feeling that I'm cursed for some reason, that I'm being punished for something I did in a past life to attract this kind of malicious person.

Grant walks into the kitchen, opening and shutting drawers before rounding the corner once more, holding a silver piece of metal that glints under the chandelier above me. I gulp audibly, knowing what's about to happen, and try to fidget in my chair. As if that'll do anything, I'm fucking tied to it.

As soon as the first slice opens up my once untainted porcelain skin, I smell the rust. The sickening scent of blood filling the room making me want to vomit. I've always hated blood, the smell it, the sight of it, even the taste. That's another story for another day.

My head begins to feel heavy, swaying under the weight of my brain running in circles attempting to figure out how to escape this. There is no safety for me as long as the man in front of me, wielding a knife to my breast, has me in his clutches.

I feel myself fading out as my body shuts down from adrenaline and the last thing I remember is the thick smell of blood as I pass out, still tied to a fucking dinner chair.

"Earth to Isolde," Alex's voice cuts through the haze, *'All Too Well'* still playing in the background, softer now. Was the song on repeat? I wonder to myself, hoping Alex buys my excuse of zoning out.

"It's played three times in a row," he looks at me with slight confusion. Shit. "At first I thought you played it again to see if I would like it more the second time around, which I will neither confirm or deny at this time, when it played for a third time I knew something was up."

God, this is utterly mortifying. Why can't I keep my emotions locked up for even short amounts of time? It's like they come on faster than I have time to process lately. I remind myself it's just from the trauma I've been through, but a small voice deep in the recesses of my mind knows it's because of the text I got from him a few weeks ago.

It's been radio silent since that one message, which puts me on edge more. He's planning something and it's unnerving to say the least. I'm not sure if I should run again or stay and fight against him. I don't want to put Alex and Abram at risk by leading him here, or worse, leading him to June.

I don't think he would hurt her necessarily, but if it meant getting me to come with him I expect he'll stop at no cost.

"Isolde," Alex says again, firmly this time. Not like he's annoyed with me, but more like the quiet tension is too much for him to bare any longer. "Baby, I need you to talk to me," he says calmly this time. Alex knows I'm not okay, not because June told him anything but because half the time we're together it's written all over my face. *'Worst Way' by Riley Green* plays softly in the background as I collect my thoughts the best I can.

I'm jumpy, always looking over my shoulder, scream at loud noises that normally wouldn't make a mouse flinch and a few times I saw him eyeing the scars on my body. Grant was usually careful to keep most of the bigger ones hidden, hence the fact that he cut up my abdomen with a knife just before I wound up here. But a few are visible depending on what I'm wearing.

I've always been able to brush him off, assuring him it's nothing but an old scratch, but this time it feels like he has no plans on letting it go.

"I'm sorry, I feel like you guys have been walking on eggshells around me because it's evident I've been through some shit. I just…I don't know how to talk about it," I sigh into my hands knowing I need to let it out. My therapist used to tell me holding things in that hurt you aren't only hurting you but the ones around you. How can someone help if you're not willing to let them in?

I used to roll my eyes at that, because the last time I truly let someone in they abused me for six years. I kept that comment to myself back then and for some reason it's been harder and harder to get that one sentence out.

"Listen, I don't want to push you. But it's obvious something is going on and I want to help. When you're ready, I'll help you," his voice is sincere, and full of empathy like he gets it. I'm sure it hasn't been easy watching his older brother struggle from his own trauma. And from what I've seen, he's a lot like me when it comes to letting people in.

I'm about to tell him okay, that I'll try, when we pull into the gravel lot to the supply store. And when I say store, I mean massive warehouse. The place looks like an Amazon facility with how big it is in scale and the amount of trucks parked along the side. Now I understand why Alex didn't want to do this alone.

Cutting the engine, Alex hops out of the truck, a wave of his sunshine scent floating past me, mixed with his cedar scent, warming my insides. He rounds the front, coming over to open my door for me. Before I hop down alongside him, I catch his blue gaze and hold it for a few seconds. "I'll try," I say in a hushed tone as if all the people in the lot will hear me and know exactly what I'm referring to. They don't, but my paranoia gets the best of me sometimes.

Smiling softly, Alex laces our fingers together and walks us to the front of the building and through the doors. For the next two hours we aimlessly peruse the facility picking out everything we need to finish the manor, including the perfect tile Alex admits he never would have selected had I not been here.

We're carefree, enjoying this time alone and leaving the heaviness of the car ride where it belongs, back in the truck. I know I need to open up to him, and

Abram, especially considering how close we've grown these last few weeks. They both deserve to know what they're getting into with me, I'd never forgive myself if something happened to either of them knowing I could have stopped it if I just told them.

As we make our way to the front of the store to cash out, that's when I hear it. The heavy rain and hail pummeling the side of the building and cars parked outside. Deep inside the store we never heard anything, too busy caught up in our casual conversation to notice.

A group of guys linger by the entrance door waiting out the storm, hoping it'll pass quickly, just as our phones go off with a storm warning alert.

"Shit," Alex grumbles as he watches the radar on his screen. This is not a passing storm by the looks of it, and since we're a ways out from home, I'm not sure it's safe to drive in this kind of weather.

Mr. Optimistic next to me doesn't even exude his normal chipper behavior, just looks at me with a soft expression mixed with unease. "Normally I would just drive through this if I was by myself, but since I have you with me…" He lets his statement hang in the air a moment, and I feel the anxiety dripping from his lips. He cares. Something about that does weird things to my insides, making me want to melt into a puddle at his feet.

"Well, there goes that idea anyways." I'm about to ask what idea he meant when he turns his phone so I can see what he's shaking his head at. Oh.

"The road back to the interstate is closed due to flooding. There's literally only one way back to town, and that is it." Alex runs his hands down his face, scratching at the little stubble he's grown in, before placing both hands on his hips.

Not knowing what to do, I nibble on my thumbnail in thought when an idea comes to mind. "It might seem dramatic, but maybe we could find a place to stay for the night."

Alex faces me, eyes boring into mine with a hint of mischief causing my cheeks to redden. "Ms. Davies, are you trying to shack up with me for the night?" He asks playfully.

Shoving his shoulder and walking closer to the entrance I mumble back at him, "got any better ideas?"

Knowing he doesn't, I look up the closest lodging to us and put it in the maps. Two miles down the road is a small motel, nothing special but it'll do until the storm passes. Showing him my phone, he nods and we race to the truck as fast as possible. He beats me by a few strides and insists on opening my door and hoisting me up as he gets pummeled by hail. "Stop being a gentleman and get in the truck you idiot!" I yell over the howling wind surrounding us.

As soon as he's in the safety of the truck, he looks over at me with rain pouring off his hair and down his face in rivulets. We stare at each other for a minute before we both burst into fits of laughter. "You called me an idiot!" Alex yells through his laughing, holding onto his side like the act is causing him physical pain.

"I thought you were about to buckle me in too! You were getting hit by hail, it was either that or smack you," I say as my own laughter is wheezing out of me, understanding now why Alex is holding his ribs. As soon as we come down a little, I lean back in my seat resting my head on the head rest and glance over at Alex again. His face is lit up like a happy kid on Christmas morning, always so excited for a new day.

"I haven't laughed like that in so long, it feels good," I admit, my eyes still locked on his. Alex smiles at me again before breaking the connection and starting the truck. I almost forgot we were in the middle of a severe storm watch with how much our laughter drowned out everything else.

Putting my phone in the cupholder so Alex can see the directions to the motel, he backs out slowly and heads two miles down the road until the quaint place comes into view. I'm sure when it's nice out this place looks charming, but right now with the weather and flowers flying all around, it looks more like The Bates Motel. It's just one night, I remind myself confidently. There's nothing to be afraid of.

Those thoughts rush out of my head when I see Alex watching me with an expression that has my insides on fire. I bite my lip but remain silent, unsure of what to do next. This is all so foreign to me and I'm still trying to understand my attraction to both men. *Brothers*, I remind myself. God, this is so messy already.

Waiting in the truck while Alex books us a room, I shift uncomfortably in the seat. What if there's only one bed? What if I accidentally grope him in his sleep? Chuckling to myself, I realize he'd probably encourage that when he comes running back with a room key in hand.

As soon as we unlock the door, my worst fear comes to life, there is in fact only one bed. Great. I'm not worried about Alex necessarily, considering he's already reassured me on numerous occasions he's not the type to push. If I tell him I don't want anything to happen between us he'll respect that.

I'm worried about me, and what lines I might cross. My self restraint hasn't exactly been stellar lately, and the last thing I want to do is send mixed signals to Alex or hurt him and Abram. We've never really discussed what this all means between the three of us. There's still so much gray area and it makes me uneasy.

"I would have gotten us a room with two beds, but of course they're booked," Alex admits sheepishly as he rubs a hand down the back of his neck. It's adorable in a way, seeing him flustered even a little. I know he didn't plan this and feels bad he might make me uncomfortable, but we didn't have any other options so we just have to make the best of this situation.

"It's okay," I whisper, looking down at my drenched clothes sticking to me and highlighting my nipples that are currently ready to rip through my thin t-shirt. "I'm more concerned about not having dry clothes to change into," I laugh nervously.

"Yeah," Alex agrees before perking up. "Hey! The guy said there's a laundry room attached to the motel at the end of the other hall. Plus, he sells sweats in the main office. I'll go buy us something warm to put on while you shower, then we can throw our wet stuff in the dryer for tomorrow. Deal?"

Smiling brightly, I nod my agreement as Alex leaves once again to retrieve us something warm and dry. My skin is pebbled with goosebumps and I try like hell to peel my wet clothes from my body when I hear the door open again, "forgot my wallet," he announces. My arms are stuck mid-air with my shirt over my face, revealing my black lace bra underneath.

Sighing with defeat, I slump forward slightly, feeling embarrassed beyond measure and ask Alex to help me. I feel his warm hands lightly grasp my shirt and tug until it comes up and over my head. As much as I can tell it's killing him, he doesn't let his eyes wander lower to where I'm exposed, he keeps them locked firmly on mine.

Something about that makes this more intimate than if he just checked out my rack. I lick my lips, afraid if I break contact one of us will pull away. In this moment I'm not so sure I want to pull away.

Alex watches my tongue dart out to wet my suddenly parched lips and winces like he's in pain. "Baby, this is killing me. *You're* killing me," he says turning around abruptly, being the one to break the spell. I should hurry off to the bathroom and take my shower like I intended. But a brave part of me comes forward, pushing aside my fears currently occupying front row.

Alex doesn't move, just continues standing with his back to me and head hanging low, chin to chest. Before I lose my nerve, I reach a trembling hand towards him, touching his soaked back lightly, trailing my fingers through the muscles rippling underneath his shirt until I reach the hem and tug on it.

Achingly slow, Alex turns around as my fingers skim beneath the hem of his dark gray t-shirt feeling even more muscles beneath. He's holding back, I can see it in how stiff his posture is. He's unsure, like me, with how far we should take this.

I watch him closely as I begin lifting the shirt off of him, the way he did for me not a minute ago. Reaching behind him with one hand, he pulls the sopping material over his head, discarding it on the floor with mine.

My breathing is heavier as I take in his toned form. I've seen him without a shirt on plenty of times, but that was when we were working. Sure, I may have salivated over how attractive and in shape he is, but when Alex is in the zone it's hard to pull him out. His work means that much to him, even if he comes off playful ninety-nine percent of the time.

When I make no other move, Alex pushes the wet hair lining the side of my face back behind my ears, letting his fingers trace the outline of my eyes, nose and lips. I open my mouth on a gasp as his thumb grazes my full bottom lip, enjoying the tingling sensation it brings. I clench my thighs together, to relieve some pressure but all is does is draw his attention more.

With a growl, he grabs my hip with his free hand, pulling me closer to him allowing me to breathe in his fresh scent mixing with the rain. It's intoxicating and I hate to think that whatever soap products are in the bathroom will wash it away. Holding me against him I can feel his length hardening against my stomach, my body trembling in response.

"Alex," I manage to whisper. He nods his head as one hand still grips my hip while the other toys with the hair hanging loosely by my breasts. "I know, I-I know I said I wanted to feel this out," I gulp audibly, hearing how shaky my voice is from the sudden lust filling my lungs. "Take things slow, but…"

Before another word leaves my lips, Alex hoists me up around his waist, holding my ass as he walks us to the bathroom. Setting me down on the counter he watches for my reaction, silently wondering if he can take control. I want him to so badly, because I have no idea what to do in this moment and I need someone to lead the way that isn't me.

With deft fingers, Alex slowly undoes the button on my jeans, eyes never leaving mine, patiently waiting for me to stop him or keep going. Biting my bottom lip I nod slowly, giving him full permission to keep going. "Words, baby, I need to hear you say it."

"Yes," I voice confidently just before Alex lifts me up and rips my soaked jeans from my body, leaving me in nothing but the black lace cheeky underwear that matches my bra. I reach behind me to undo the clasp when his hands stall mine.

"Let me," he growls in a sultry voice that has liquid heat rushing between my thighs. I've never had someone take their time with me, simply enjoy the way my skin feels beneath their touch. I feel drunk from the way his fingers caress my skin, the way his voice rumbles across my body leaving goosebumps in their wake.

As soon as my bra falls from my shoulders, Alex swats it out of the way and steps back to admire me. "God, you're so fucking beautiful Isolde."

When he says those words, I actually feel them. It doesn't sound like something he's saying just to get me to have sex with him, he says it like he truly means every word and I bask in the praise.

Leaving me on the counter next to the sink, Alex reaches in to start the shower. When steam begins filling the small room I watch as he unbuttons his jeans, sliding them down his muscular thighs. My mouth goes dry instantly as I take in the bulge beneath his black briefs. Fucking hell, these men are built.

Sensing my sudden nerves, Alex comes back to stand in front of me again, rubbing his hands in a comforting way up and down my thighs. "Hey," he whispers, tipping my chin up to look in his eyes. "Let's just shower, okay? We don't have to do anything."

I think back to a time when I said no to having sex with Grant, how it always ended in me giving in and having sex whether I wanted to or not. I was never allowed the luxury to tell him no or that I wasn't in the mood. He took what he wanted when he wanted and I just had to deal with it somehow.

Right now I have a near naked man standing in front of me telling me we don't have to do anything if I'm not comfortable. A gush of heat rushes to my center, the one in my chest, as I realize how caring Alex is. I never want to lose sight of the light that emanates from this man, he makes me want to search for warmer days.

Hooking my legs around his backside, I pull him into me, gasping as his hard cock rubs the sensitive spot right between my thighs. Not understanding the words about to come out of my own mouth, I push my hips further into him sighing at the contact. "What if I want to?"

As if that's all he was waiting for, he lifts me up and pulls me into the steaming shower with him, both still wearing our underwear. His mouth meets mine in a heated frenzy as we explore each other with not only our hands but our tongues as they dance a routine you'd think was choreographed. He tastes like warm summer days, and I melt into him fully.

Our bodies mesh together effortlessly, my front pressed firmly into his enjoying the feeling of the light hair on his chest rubbing against my hard nipples. The contact is almost too much as hot water cascades down our joined bodies, steam billowing out around us.

Fireworks explode above me as one of his hands travels down my backside, cupping me from behind. He works the material of my underwear to the side and plunges a finger deep into my aching wet heat. I moan at the invasion, grinding my body against his hand like a silent prayer to keep going.

He's still holding me up around his waist as a second finger joins the first and begins working in and out of me in perfect synchronization. My body is wedged between his hard chest and the hard tile of the shower wall, an exquisite contrast of hot and cold causing my body to erupt in more goosebumps.

I feel that sweet sensation building deep in my core as I buck my hips against his hand harder, edging me closer and closer as his palm presses firmly against my clit. Biting my bottom lip to stifle the impending orgasm, I feel Alex yank it free with his teeth. "No way, baby. I want to hear you scream for me."

Holy shit, why is that such a turn on?

A few more urgent pumps of his fingers and I feel my inner walls clenching around him as the first waves of my orgasm take over. I'm falling blindly to the euphoria, moaning and writing in his hold as my orgasm peaks. Without any thought to who might hear us or the embarrassment that might come after, I scream out his name as I ride the final waves of pleasure.

When I come down, literally and figuratively, as Alex sets me on my feet in the shower, I feel my face flush a deep crimson and suddenly feel scared to face him. His gentle touch finds me, lifting my face up to his to see him smiling. "That was incredible. The way you let go for me, just," he sighs in contentment which is surprising since I haven't even done anything physical for him yet. "Fuck."

My blush fades slightly, feeling his words and their meaning soak into my soul. He always means what he says, and it's becoming a turn on for me. I love when a man isn't afraid to express their thoughts and desires. Alex is never afraid of looking foolish in front of other people, he's always candid and unapologetically himself. I could take some lessons in that.

Holding on to my bravery, I start to sink to my knees in the shower, ready to return the favor when he stops me. "What are you doing?" He asks with furrowed brows.

"Oh. I just thought…You don't like receiving?" I ask, suddenly confused myself. What guy doesn't want to get his dick sucked?

He chuckles lightly, watching me with admiration, making any previous doubts scurry down the drain with the water. "Oh, I do, believe me. But I don't want you to reciprocate just because I did that for you." Is he for real? I really thought I was expected to get on my knees for him. Hell, usually I had to do Grant first and never got much back in return. Each moment I spend with Alex reminds me more and more what kind of shitty one way relationship I'd been stuck in for *years*.

"Listen, whatever past relationship you had before is exactly that, the past. I don't ever want you to feel like you need to do something for me just because I did it for you first. I mean, I won't say no if you simply have to have me," we both laugh at his joke during a serious moment, always ready to lighten any mood. "But that's not why I did that."

"So why did you?" I ask the question before thinking it through, not knowing if I want the truth.

"Because I had to feel you. To know what you feel like as you come undone for me. To listen to the way you sound as I bring you to the edge, keeping you there just long enough to feel you explode on my fingers as you scream my name."

Woah.

"Well, at least I hoped that's what would happen. Luck has it, you exceeded any and all previous fantasies." I love how he said fantasies, not expectations. Like he wasn't expecting me to respond a certain way to him. Truly everything with him is effortless in a way I'm still not accustomed to. Whether I ever get there or not is to be determined.

Feeling the water run cold, Alex shuts off the faucet and grabs two white plush towels that smell like clean linen for us. We still don't have any dry clothes but getting dressed is the last thing on my mind. I just came and already I'm dying for another hit.

I've been scared to get myself back into intimate situations because everything in previous years has been centered around pain and non-consent. I just want to let myself go and feel good for the first time in a very long time. Alex gave me that, and now I want more.

Facing the bed, Alex wraps the towel around his waist and shakes off the droplets of water clinging to the ends of his hair. He starts talking about heading over to the office to buy some sweatshirts and pants when I slowly make my way around him, without my towel, and crawl onto the bed. His movements halt as he sees me sit back against the pillows, arms resting on top of them at my sides.

I'm really putting myself out there, fully exposed to him in a way I dint think I would be comfortable with. But the gaze in his blue eyes and low growl of approval has me wanting to surrender to this feeling indefinitely. I think I may have a praise kink. I could watch the way Alex reacts to my body any day.

With one swift maneuver, Alex drops the towel, exposing himself and all his ripped glory to me. I didn't get the best look in the shower since he was too busy taking care of my needs. Seeing him up close, the sheer size of him has me wondering where all that is going to fit.

Noticing my unease and the way my eyes bugged out of my head, Alex crawls up the bed until he's seated in front of me. Grabbing both knees he gently opens them wider for him to nestle himself between my thighs. I can practically feel my arousal seeping out of me with the way his eyes devour my most private parts.

"Fuck, you're soaked already." Licking his lips, he reaches down with soft fingers to run them through my wet folds. "We'll go slow, okay?"

I feel the weird need to cry, moisture building behind my eyes. But not because I'm sad or scared, because this man is making sure to go slow and take his time with me. He's making sure I'm okay and comfortable with everything he does and it's such a foreign feeling for me that I accidentally let a tear slip down my cheek.

Alex catches it, licking it off his finger before caressing my cheeks in a soothing motion. He waits patiently as I find my words. "I'm sorry, this probably looks so bad. I'm just…no one has ever thought about my feelings this way. I've never been…" I trail off, unsure of how to finish my thought.

"Cared for," he says confidently like he knew those were the words I was searching for. Too afraid to admit it's the raw truth. I nod and he holds my eyes captive with his stern and serious stare. "I would *never* hurt you, Isolde. We're taking this at your pace, okay?"

Another few tears slip past before I'm able to hold them at bay and I swear I could kiss this man for eternity and not get tired. I can't believe I almost held myself back from this person. Someone who cares deeply about the people in his life, showering them with love perfectly tailored to their needs, not his own.

Right now he knows what I need, and instead of making me feel foolish or rushed, he's patient and kind.

Sitting up I wrap a hand around his neck and pull him into me so I can kiss him. It starts off slow and passionate, my way of thanking him for his respect and the way he's letting me take control. As we deepen the kiss I feel the tingles between my legs at the closeness of his growing erection. It's going to hurt for sure, he's practically twice the size of Grant, but I want to feel every inch stretching me in exquisite agony.

With pleasure there sometimes is pain, and this is the kind of pain I'm ready to experience.

He slides both hands under my ass, pulling me down flat on the bed as he hovers just above me. Trailing kisses down my neck and breasts, biting playfully at my nipples that are practically begging for attention. Alex takes his time worshipping my body while at the same time rushing to have me. Like he wants to go slow and savor the moment but can't control himself long enough to do so.

After caressing and kissing both breasts, he looks up at me with undeniable lust taking over every surface of his features. "Are you sure?" He asks again before reaching for his discarded wallet on the nightstand. Assuming he's retrieving a condom, I nod my head nervously but with excitement as well. I want to do this.

He looks at me again, with a smirk and I know he wants to *hear* my consent. No, he needs it and I could cry again for that. Alex knows I've been through trauma and he wants to make sure my voice is heard. That is the sexiest fucking thing *ever*. If only more men took notes out of Alex's guidebook.

"Yes, Alex. Please, I want this."

Holding himself above me with one hand, he rips the condom open with his teeth before sheathing himself with it. I feel him adjust above me but keep my eyes closed, breathing steadily through my nose. You'd think I was a virgin for how nervous I am right now.

"Baby, open your eyes. Keep them on me, understand?"

I open my eyes, staring into his like the deep pools they are, getting lost in their depths. We both look down to where our bodies are almost joined in the most intimate way possible, and watch as Alex slowly pushes into me. I try to close my eyes again but Alex grips my chin firmly, tilting my face up so I keep focused on him. On this connection we're forming. "Good girl," he growls against my ear sending shivers down my spine as he thrusts in a little further.

"Almost there, baby," he says into my ear again, trailing kisses down my neck before nibbling the sensitive skin there. Fuck. He's not even all the way in? I don't know how much more I can take, but as he encourages me and praises me for how well I'm doing, I know I can get there. I can open myself up to him in not just one way.

"Fuck, yes. You feel so good sweet girl. I can feel you gripping my cock so tight." Another thing I could get used to, this sexy talk during sex. Just something else I never got to experience in my past relationship. I could smack that man for how little he did to make me enjoy sex, instead he made me feel like it was a chore. Or a duty.

As soon as he's all the way in, pushing to the hilt, my body relaxes a little. Allowing my muscles to loosen slightly, I welcome him in and revel in the feel of him sliding in and out of me with ease. I can feel how slick my walls are, arousal practically pooling on the sheets beneath us, but I don't care. I need more.

I grip his shoulders tightly, using them as leverage to grind myself against him harder hoping he understands what I need. I feel an overwhelming sense to dominate but I'm too scared to take over. "Do whatever you want, baby. Show me how you take control."

We're so in tune with each other he can read my thoughts without having to speak them. With his words of encouragement, I buck my hips into his so I have space to flip us. Alex rolls onto his back with ease when he realizes my intent, grabbing my hips as I place both knees on either side to straddle him.

Immediately finding my rhythm against him, I start riding him like I was always meant to. Each rub of my pelvis against him hits that spot that has me rolling my eyes back into my head in delicious bliss. Alex grips my hips hard as I continue moving against him with more enthusiasm, groaning in his own pleasure as I work him in and out of me.

Bracing both hands on his chest, I lift up leaving just the tip of him at my entrance before slowly sliding him back in. I repeat this over and over again, picking up speed each time until we're both sweating and moaning against each other. I can feel my release building in my core ready to throw me over the edge of pleasure. I chase it, needing to reach the destination more than my next breath, seeing the look on Alex's face match mine.

"Fuck, you ride me so good, sweet girl." He reaches up to tweak one of my nipples between his finger and thumb while the other lowers to my clit. Rubbing and twisting both in sync I work myself harder on his shaft as I feel the first wave of my orgasm take over, making me scream out in pleasure.

"Yes, just like that. Keep going, baby."

"Oh God, Alex it's too much. I can't…I can't stop," I scream louder as one orgasm flows into another, my body tensing as I fall forward onto Alex's chest unable to slow my breathing as the waves slowly dissipate. My body is tingling all over and yet I've never felt more alive.

Alex flips me onto my stomach, grabbing me by the hips and lifting my ass in the air. I feel him line himself up once again and thrust back in with much more force than the first time. He's pumping in and out of me with such vigor all I can do is hold the bed frame with shaky hands as he plows into me in search of his own release.

I feel him lose control as his movements become choppy, his moans louder as he leans forward to bite the base of my neck. I throw my head back to give him better access as he stills, spilling himself into me on a groan.

I'm spent. My body collapses back to the bed as Alex pulls out of me and rolls to my side. We're both breathing heavily, enjoying this calm moment after letting ourselves get lost in each other. The funny thing is that by losing myself in the moment I seem to have found a small part of me that was missing for so long.

Sweat lines my forehead and I'm thinking I'm going to need another shower when Alex faces me after discarding the condom in the trashcan next to the bed. "I guess I need to take you shopping for tiles more often," he chuckles and I can't help but smile as I swat his arm playfully.

"I think we needed that," I say feeling his eyes on my face. "I know I did."

"Baby, I've been wanting to see what you felt like since I saw you in the diner that first day," he confesses. "But I knew you needed time and I wasn't going to push you into something you didn't want. But judging by that," he looks down to where our bodies were just joined together, smirking, "I'd say you've thought about it more than once, too."

He's right. I have thought a lot about this with him and with Abram. For a while there I felt like my connection with Abram was stronger but only sexually. This bond has been building with Alex since the beginning, something like this was bound to happen. I just don't know what it means moving forward and what Abram will think.

"Yeah I won't lie I've thought about it, but I've also thought about…" I let the words hang in the air as I close my eyes, hoping I don't kill the mood we're still coming down from.

"Stoker, I know baby. We told you, we're not going to make you choose."

"I don't understand why though? I never thought either of you would be okay with something like this. Me not knowing what I want or what to do ninety-nine percent of the time. It's frustrating for me so I can only imagine how it makes the two of you feel."

"Well, that's for him and I to decide. The truth is neither of us was willing to give you up, so if that meant us both having you then so be it. He's my brother, a pain in the ass obviously, but I don't want to see him hurt."

I think over his words, chewing on my bottom lip as his words sink in. It's true, I didn't ask either of them to do this, it was their idea from the beginning. And if they didn't want to share me then I would have been forced to choose, something I'm still not sure I would have been able to do. I need both of them in my life for different reasons.

Alex is safe and comforting, always providing me with the warmth I'm missing on those cold days where I feel lost. He brings me out of my shell and out into the light to be grateful for each day and just live.

Whereas Abram is the darkness I need, the darkness I crave. I'm still learning to accept my past and be okay with the darker parts of myself, desires I'm not sure how to express yet. Abram shows me that I can embrace those sides of myself without losing my light.

He makes me see the deepest darkest parts of myself I didn't even know existed, or the parts I was too afraid to allow to the surface. And Alex reminds me of the good things in life.

They are my sun and my moon. Each morning the lightness comes out, brushing away the darkness until it's turn to come out again. As soon as the sun has warmed the earth the moon shines at night to keep the balance. Alex and Abram are my balance, the thing I needed all this time but couldn't find until I made the decision to leave.

The thought of losing either of them at this point would be the end of one side of me, the lightness or the darkness. I need them both to feel alive and if I lost one of them I'd feel like I lost them both. I couldn't stand to lose them, not now. It's time I open up and tell them who they're getting involved with. I want to give them both the opportunity to walk away in case my baggage is too much weight to bear.

When we get back home we'll discuss everything and then I'll know for sure where I stand with them both. Focusing on the present, I face Alex and show him just how much I need him in my life, the only way I can right now.

STOKER

chapter sixteen

♫

My Sacrifice • Creed

After my impromptu night with Alex - which was amazing I might add - it feels good to be back home and working. Hailey isn't on call this weekend so she came by to keep me company at the bar. Since I've been here I've come to truly enjoy working at Pour Performer, not just the work but the people too.

My mind stays busy as I brush up on my bartending skills and it allows me an opportunity to get to know more people in town. Besides June and Hailey, I haven't made many other friends. Not because I don't want to, simply because I don't even know how to make friends anymore. It's not like being in grade school and realizing the kid next to you has the same juice box automatically making you best friends.

My parents always told me, when it comes to friends it's quality over quantity. I've never forgotten that and lead with it every time I meet someone new.

June is honestly my guardian angel and with Hailey it was effortless. She helped me in a time I truly needed it, with the help of June, and we just clicked off the bat. I smile at her as I mix another drink while she nurses her cold beer.

"What were you up to this past weekend?" She says casually enough, but my cheeks blush a deep red as if thinking she already knows something.

I wish I could hide my reactions better, but I clearly don't have much of a poker face. Trying to brush off the comment, I tell her I did some work on the manor, hoping she takes that as an honest answer. But of course, she doesn't. She's a doctor so she's trained to pay attention to the minor details.

"Hold up, what was that face you made?"

"What face?" I ask feigning disinterest. I refuse to even turn around and face her right now, giving me away even more than my red face and lack of eye contact.

"Girl, I know we haven't known each other all that long, but I'd like to think we're friends. And as your friend, who stitched you up and saved you from infection, I might add, I demand you tell me what you're trying to hide!"

Shit, she's good. I turn around slowly to face her, face still ripe as a tomato I'm sure, and set the glass I was obsessively cleaning down on the bar top. "I-I don't really know how to talk about it? Does that make sense?" That's at least the truth. How am I supposed to explain to someone that I'm technically in a relationship with two guys, who happen to be brothers? I can practically taste the impending judgement. Not from Hailey so much, but I'm sure there are people around here who will have some comments.

"Oookay," she drawls, stressing the O as she eyes me. "Can I guess?"

"You can try, I guess," I shrug, hoping there's no way in hell she'd come close to guessing what's actually going on between me and the Stoker brothers.

Clapping her hands together, she wiggles on her stool with excitement. "Okay, I can figure this out," she confidently says before sipping a big gulp of beer.

She's quiet for a few minutes, brows furrowed with a pensive look overtaking her normally soft features. Hailey is a classically beautiful person, with super fair skin and a dusting of freckles on the bridge of her nose. She has the most insane green eyes I've ever seen. Dark rims with light hues of green and gold in the middle making her freckles more pronounced. Her hair is shoulder length and auburn red, something I'm insanely jealous of. It's mostly straight with a little wave throughout as if she curls it each day.

It could be because I've gotten to know her a little more the last few weeks, but everything about her screams kind. She definitely got into the right field of work, the world needs more doctors like Hailey Lennox. If only I had been so lucky to have a few nice ones like her along the way.

"I got it," she says triumphantly and I scoff at her assuming she's going to be dead wrong.

"Let's hear it."

"You said you were working on the manor, correct?"

Shit, she's got her detective face on. "Yes…"

"Well, last week you told me you only had some tiling left to do and that you had to go to a special store to get it since the hardware store in town has like two options." Hailey smiles at me knowingly and I just hang my head, ready to get this over with. "Should I continue?"

"By all means, Nancy Drew," I gesture my hands towards her, letting her know she has the floor.

"Right. So, since you're new here that would mean you don't know where that special store is, even though you could use google maps if you wanted to. But since I know your history a little, I know you opt not to use your phone as much as possible. That would mean you'd need some help getting there, which leaves two options."

I can feel sweat beading on my forehead the longer she talks. I knew she was observant, but this is otherworldly.

"My first guess would be Stoker, because well, I've seen the heat between you two and you sizzle when you're near each other. But I saw him leaving the craft store on Saturday, which coincidentally was when you were gone."

"Oh my god, are you like the town detective or something?" I ask with surprise and suspicion.

"Not quite, I'm just really observant," she says acknowledging my earlier thoughts.

"No kidding."

"I'm gonna ignore you and continue now, cause I'm on a roll." We both laugh, and knowing now she has no intentions of judging me, I relax a little, enjoying her storytelling abilities.

"Those men are the only two who have been helping you with the house, so it was Alex who went with you to the giant warehouse an hour away. Oh, and Saturday was also the day we got that nasty storm, and June said you never came home that night." Taking one last gulp of her beer, she slams the glass down victoriously like she just won the damn Olympics.

Shit! I forgot she owns the damn medical practice in town and likely checks in with Hailey on the regular. A tiny little comment like that struck a root in this detectives mind and she ran with it, evidently. I roll my eyes in mock frustration. She's good, damn good. I make a mental note to check with her anytime I need her people watching skills.

"Now I can't say for sure I know the details past that, but I'm guessing you stayed the night with Alex since you got caught in a storm and didn't come home. The part I'm fuzzy on is where."

I watch her, mouth slightly agape and eyes blinking rapidly. I wouldn't be able to deny any of it now that she's seen the expression on my face. "You have a gift," is all I manage.

Pumping a fist into the hair, she hollers excitedly and demands another beer. I give her this one on the house because frankly I'm thoroughly impressed and slightly terrified of this woman. I don't ever want to be on her bad side knowing what she's capable of finding out having not spoken to either Alex or I before this moment.

"Please tell me you had sex," she says a little too loudly and I swat at her to keep her voice down. "Honey please, majority of the people in here are well on their way to being buzzed or they simply don't care. Spill it."

I look around and realize she's right. Most of the nearby patrons are men, and they're far more interested in the contents of their glasses than what chit chat Hailey and I have going on over here. It's slow on Sunday's around here anyways.

"That man's entire body was sculpted by the Gods, and designed by Leonardo da Vinci himself." Hailey says on a sigh, stars in her eyes. I should feel threatened but I don't because she's only speaking the truth. I'm sure she has similar thoughts about Abram, and who could blame her?

"Not all of him," I say with a coy smile before taking a long pull of my own IPA. Sasha always allows me to have at least one drink while I'm working. Usually I don't bother because I don't care to drink too much anyways, but with Hailey it's nice to have a beer occasionally.

I can feel her eyes on me, impatiently waiting for me to expand on that not so subtle comment. "Are you really going to leave me hanging here? If we were texting that's like you leaving me on read."

I raise both hands up in mock surrender, "I'm just saying, certain *parts* of him may have been sculpted by the devil himself." Hailey slaps her legs, trying to stifle the squeal ready to erupt out of her like a damn volcano. I knew that her and I would click from the moment I met her - it's been refreshing to finally have a girlfriend again.

"Ugh, I want to be jealous because I've been in a dry spell for far too long, but truly I'm just happy for you. This is probably the happiest I've seen you - genuinely - since you got here."

I can't help the smile that stretches across my face. Alex brings a lightness to my life, and I was so blinded by trauma and fear I almost didn't allow myself to enjoy all the sunshine he exudes. Just as I'm about to dish on more details of my weekend, like how we ended up in a motel room to begin with, the bell above the entrance door dings.

Unable to help my body's reaction, I feel his presence before I hear his voice. The way it reaches into my chest, gripping parts of my soul and digging them out to take with him as souvenirs. All the hair on my exposed arms stand to attention, as if saluting the man before us.

"Dr. Lennox," Abram says in his deep voice, making even an esteemed doctor like her blush. She barely gets out a greeting before he takes a seat and stations himself right across from me at the bar.

The thing about brightness with Alex couldn't be any different than the toe curling darkness Abram brings. Whenever he's near me I can feel my body's response, the way my mind surrenders to any previous caution. Willing and ready to take on whatever he throws my way. Abram brings out a hidden side of myself I didn't even know existed until I showed up in this town.

Memories of our first encounter when he fingered me to oblivion on his motorcycle rings in my mind like a sirens song. I'm transfixed by everything about him. The way his gray eyes pierce mine, holding me captive with their steely chains. Or how his hair, longer on top, always seems to drape across his forehead lightly falling in his eyes.

Just the scent of him has me clenching my thighs together, wondering what it would feel like to have his body covering mine. To have his scent of woods and menthol covering my body like an invisible blanket.

His hot gaze tears me away from my fantasies, leaving behind a deep blush that indicates I was thinking about him. Smug bastard knows it too, the way he smirks at me with that knowing look. "My usual," he gestures to the row of bottles behind me.

Making quick work, I grab a glass, pouring two fingers of whiskey into it before setting it down with slightly shaky hands in front of him. "Nervous, little bird?"

"No. Why would I be nervous?" I cock my head to the side, trying to play tough but knowing he sees right through me. He always does. As if confirming my thoughts, he chuckles to himself before taking a small sample of his drink.

Hailey sits there, eyes pinging back and forth between the two of us, mouth agape, and I can only imagine what's going through her head. Purposefully plopping a glass mug on the counter loudly, I pull her from whatever trance she was in. The same one I'm usually in when I'm around him, I'm sure.

Righting herself, hoping Abram didn't notice, she hops off her stool and lays down a few bills to pay for her drinks. "I'm gonna head out," she throws her arm over her shoulder, jerking her thumb towards the door. I want to tell her to stay. That its almost closing and I don't know if I trust myself to be alone with Abram, but she's already backing away holding her hand up to her ear indicating I call her.

Can't wait for her to Nancy Drew the rest of this situation and expect details on *both* men.

Inwardly groaning, I shove my face into my hands with my back turned to Abram. I don't want him thinking he has any kind of affect on me, but he does and we both know it. I just need to finish my shift, close up and head home without stripping this man in the parking lot.

A part of me feels guilty about what happened with Alex, while the other part of me wants to kick that shit under the bed and indulge in the man before me. They outwardly expressed I can have them both and they're okay with it. So why do I still feel like I'm doing something wrong? *Because in the past you weren't even able to look at another male without getting backhanded for it later.*

Memories of my past flood in faster than I can process, and I quickly busy myself counting out tips to split with Sasha as a distraction. Abram's eyes never leave mine, I can feel them on me everywhere I go in this tiny bar. He doesn't say much, shocking, but his energy says more than any words could anyways.

He has this way of making me feel so many things without opening his mouth. I wonder if he's silent in bed too? Jesus Christ, Isolde. Where the hell did that come from? I feel heat rush to my face at my sexually intrusive thoughts and catch Abram looking at me with a tilt to his head. Him and Hailey would be great detectives together with the way they observe every little detail.

"Why are you looking at me like that?" I ask with a little bite to my tone.

As usual, he doesn't say anything, just sips his drink eyeing me over the rim of his glass. Always playing games, this one, I huff to myself.

"I was just wondering what you must have been thinking about to make your face that red," he declares, pointing at my reddened cheeks.

I knew he would catch that. No amount of makeup could hide my blush and the idea of caking my face with foundation makes me physically itchy.

Feeling bold, because apparently I can be that version of myself around this man, I blurt out the first thing that comes to mind. "I was wondering if you're just as quiet in bed as you are right now." I shrug my shoulders hoping to appear unfazed. When really my heart is ready to burst out of my chest with the way it's rapidly beating. I don't know why he makes me so nervous, but its an involuntary reaction at this point.

I turn around but not before I catch the slight smirk Abram lets slip past his cool demeanor. Judging by how he handled those drunk guys a few weeks back, how he let me drive his motorcycle without batting an eye and how he behaves in general, it's like nothing gets under his skin.

His personality is impenetrable, and something deep inside me wants to find one thing that might break through his rough exterior. I've held myself back from so many things, always afraid of what Grant would do and how he might react. For once in my life I feel brave, being around Abram allows me to dive into the daring side of myself and I think I'm going to like what I find there.

I forgot he never responded when almost ten minutes go by, his drink is empty and he's standing from the bar stool. Slipping into his leather jacket, he watches me with dark eyes, the light gray gone only to be replaced by a dark gray that almost appears black in this lighting. "I guess you'll have to see for yourself."

Abram walks out the front door with the same ease he did coming in - never looking back - and I stand behind the bar watching the empty space he occupied like his essence is still present. It feels like he leaves behind a new fragment of himself each time I see him. Maybe one of these days I'll have enough pieces to put together the mysterious masterpiece that is Abram Stoker.

***

As much as I've loved working here, I love closing for the night even more. Pocket full of tips with a mile wide smile on my face. Which is exactly how I leave tonight. After waving bye to Sasha I head for my car when something catches my eye. A girl around my age is facing the street where I parked my car talking to a tall man in dark clothing. I don't want to eavesdrop, but given my history, I'm always on high alert.

What if she's feeling trapped? They're in the opening of the alley next to Pour Performer and he's blocking her exit. The man is talking quietly, too soft for me to hear his voice but the look on her face doesn't send off warning bells. Feeling like I'm overstepping a private conversation, I begin to turn back to my car when the man faces the street.

My eyes lock on his momentarily, but he doesn't see me. All the air rushes out of my lungs as I duck behind my car, watching Abram escort this woman to her car, hugging her before helping her in and shutting the door. He said he wasn't dating anyone but that clearly looks like someone he knows well. I know I shouldn't because we never established anything formal, but I feel like I got punched in the gut.

I feel bad enough entertaining both Alex and Abram but I thought it was obvious there was no one else for me. It feels childish that I didn't clarify the same thing with both of them. What if Alex is sleeping with other women and I was just another notch on his belt?

No. I can't do this to myself, I can't let myself be defined by another man, *men.* Shaking my head I try to shake off the impending tears. I don't even know what I'm about to fucking cry, it's not like they owe me anything and I haven't exactly told them much about myself for god's sake. I've been here for months and I've skillfully avoided letting them into my dark past.

I'm a fucking hypocrite.

Wiping the traitorous tear that slips free, I open my car door and start it up. I just want to go home and sleep off this stupid feeling that's taken root. I left the bar feeling happy and hopeful, and now I just feel emotionally drained.

Pulling away from the curb I catch Abram watching me as he strides toward my car. I don't have it in me to have this discussion right now and truthfully I'm feeling dumb for believing he would want someone like me to begin with. Ignoring his advances, I cut left and speed down the road void of streetlights to June's. One of these days I'll have my own space to call home. A place I can escape to and not have to worry about putting on a happy face to ward off questions I don't want to answer.

A few minutes down the road I see the lone spotlight from his bike, cursing under my breath, I turn up the radio hoping I can ignore his presence gaining closely behind me. *'Boom' by P. O. D.* is flowing through the speakers and I can't help but feed into the intensity of the song. Blasting the volume I press on the gas and take my chances on outrunning him.

Am I being childish? Probably. Do I give a shit right now? Not one fucking bit.

I pick up speed even more, knowing he can easily match it and floor it down the dirt road to June's property. I haven't seen much of her the last few days since we have opposite schedules and now I feel bad I might accidentally wake her up with my reckless driving.

Throwing it in park, I try to leap from the car and make it to the door before Abram catches me but as always, wishful thinking. He's on me before my second foot even hits the gravel. My chest is heaving, completely out of breath from adrenaline whereas Abram looks like he just spent an hour bathing in the sun. Always the calm, cool and collective Abram. "What the hell was that?" He asks with a threatening bite to his voice.

"Nothing, I'm just tired," I snap back. I'm good and worked up now, that drive having done nothing to calm my irrational irritation.

I try to walk around him but he grabs my arm, spinning me to face him. "If you don't want me to throw you over my knee and spank your ass raw I suggest you tell me what the hell your problem is."

These stupid fucking tears are trying to make another appearance and no matter how hard I'm trying to keep them from falling, they do anyways. I'm not even sad or upset, I'm more angry with myself right now and I can't help the way those emotions are trying to exit my body. "I'm so fucking sick of crying!" I yell.

Abram watches the few tears slide down my cheeks, grabbing each one that falls with his thumb and licking away the salty wetness. "Then stop crying."

"Oh gee, thanks! It must be that *easy*." I throw my arms in the air, knowing how ridiculous I look, exactly like a spoiled child.

"It is," he counters. I wish I could get away with slapping him. I'd end up bent over his knee like he threatened. I don't understand why that doesn't have me running in the house and locking all the doors. And why are my insides on fire and my underwear soaked from the excitement of that one threat?

His voice is so soft though, like he didn't intend to irritate me with those two tiny words. He's attempting to sound calm, maybe his way of distracting me from my emotions that have taken a dive off the deep end. His scent is calming too, if that even makes sense. I breathe him in steadily and enjoy the way his familiar smell soothes my aching insides. I'm being irrational, emotional and over the top and I wish I could explain to him why I'm feeling all those things without sounding like an adolescent teen.

My thoughts are all over the place between what I saw tonight and how I feel about both Stoker men and what it means for us moving forward. I don't even know if Abram knows I slept with his brother. For all I know sleeping with me is some kind of competition between them and Alex already rubbed it in that he won. I don't see him that way, but I didn't think Abram was talking to other women either, so what the hell do I know.

"I don't need you to protect me, Abram." I don't know what compels me to say that, or why I feel its relevant in this moment. But the way he went from agitated with me to soothing has me wondering if maybe he's not as rough as he appears.

"Maybe not. I mean, you've made it this far on your own," he tugs my ponytail until my eyes are looking up into his, searching, waiting. "But, maybe I want to. Maybe for once you can allow yourself to feel safe. As foreign as that may be for you."

My brows arch high, surprise taking over my face. I don't know how to respond to that. I want to just ask who the woman was but I get the feeling we're past that at the moment, this feels deeper and more important.

"I don't always do the right thing, but protecting you seems to be the only thing that feels right."

I watch him with fascination as he runs a hand through the loose hair on top, smelling his shampoo as it lightly washes over me. He shows the world his tough exterior when underneath is someone softer, maybe not all of him, but parts. I want to feel those soft parts of him, understand why he keeps them so well hidden.

"Who was the woman I saw you with?" The question tumbles from my mouth before I have a chance to swallow the words and I'm afraid it'll piss him off. I finally see a softer side to him and I blow it by asking something that's none of my business.

Instead of looking annoyed or angry like I expected, he laughs. Fucking *laughs*. "I should have just spanked you," he murmurs darkly. *I kind of wish you would.*

"If you have no plans to answer me, I'd like to go inside now. Like I said, I'm tired." A part of me knew he wasn't going to let me do that, but the firm grip on my arm tells me I also won't be going to bed anytime soon. Spinning me around so that my nose practically crashes into the side of my car, I feel him breathe me in like a fresh bouquet of flowers.

"You're practically edible. Did you know that?"

"Well, I've never tried to eat myself, so I guess I wouldn't know," I respond dryly.

His rough hands, covered in a dozen tattoos, wrap around my neck pulling me closer. I feel his hot breath on my cheek as he leans in to brush his lips against the shell of my ear. I gasp and shudder against him, feeling the lick of his tongue as it dances down the slope of my neck and back up again. "Funny," he murmurs, "I haven't stopped thinking about peeling those jeans off of you all night and tasting your sweet cunt."

Oh fuck, my legs might actually give out if he keeps talking like this. Where Alex is sweet and respectful, Abram pushes me to my limits, I just hope he doesn't take me past them before I'm ready.

"I already know how tight you are, the way you squeezed around my fingers that night. I want to see if you do the same to my tongue, then my cock."

I feel my heart rate accelerate, sweat beading in my hairline at his words. Grant never went down on me, something he found to be disgusting, so it always made me wonder if maybe it was me he just didn't want to do it with. It basically gave me a complex and now I'm scared to even have Abram's face near that part of me.

I'm feeling the sudden urge to bolt, like maybe I'm not as ready for this kind of relationship like I thought I was. The energy between us crackles like the embers in a fire and if I'm not careful I'm going to end up burned. I still don't trust myself entirely and as much as I want to let go and give myself over to what we could be, something still holds me back.

I can't even tell if it's because of my past trauma with relationships or the fact that I haven't told Alex or Abram about said relationship. The worry that follows me might as well be visible the way I wear it like a heavy jacket. I can never seem to shut my mind off for more than a few hours at a time and the stress of that is killing me.

"I want to show you something, little bird." His voice cuts through the haze in my mind and temporarily shuts off all other worries in my brain. Like a magic switch only he has access to. With hooded eyes I look up to see him watching me again, always watching like he's studying me. It makes me feel equally uneasy and desired in some way.

"Okay," I whisper. I don't think I could tell him no even if I wanted to. He has me in a lust filled trance and I keep forgetting I was just upset not ten minutes ago. He didn't even answer my question about the woman I saw him with outside the bar.

Again, I know I have no right to ask things that aren't my business, but the other side of me feels like I deserve to know if I'm going to continue giving him pieces of myself.

We walk away from June's towards his house that lines the woods. I see the opening of the path I ran out of the night he found me lost back there. I remember feeling uneasy with him that close to me, never being able to tell what his intentions were, a part of me still can't. His parting words come back like a freight train, smacking into me with a need so strong I could just drop my pants right here. *I plan to sink so deep into you that you won't be able to tell where I end and you begin.*

***

I've only been inside Abram's house one time. The day he helped bandage my hand when I was sort of spying on him and cut it on a broken terracotta pot. I never confessed that was the reason I was bleeding, too consumed by his presence and the fact that he was helping me. Probably wouldn't paint me in the best light if I admitted it now, so I keep my mouth closed.

"Want something to drink?" He asks from the fridge, and I nod a little too eagerly. I'm way too nervous, so hopefully a cold drink will calm my nerves some.

Abram's space is warm and welcoming compared to his rough exterior. It might just be the mostly black wardrobe or the fact that he's nearly covered in tattoos, but there's a darkness that's buried deeper. Something I equally want to uncover and am afraid of. I'm willing to take whatever parts he'll give me, knowing I won't get the answers from anyone else.

Alex and June know his past, but neither of them can tell me what it was like not having gone through it themselves. Maybe this is why I was drawn to him initially, despite our first few interactions. It's as if my damaged soul could recognize another and want to understand what made them that way. I've wanted to open up about myself so many times, but each time I feel myself close to spilling everything, something holds me back.

Blame it on cowardliness or fear, whatever the reason, it's never felt right. I want them to get to know me for this version of myself, not the broken version that rolled into town with nothing but her car, the clothes on her back and numerous hidden scars. If Alex noticed my scar the other day, which lets be honest, he had to of. He didn't say anything about it, I never even noticed him looking at it.

I jump when Abram places a glass with ice and a clear liquid in front of me, sensing my hesitation he quirks a brow. "Just water, little bird."

Whispering a thank you, I take a large sip, hoping the cold liquid will soothe the aching heat building like an inferno in my chest. Why am I here? He said he wanted to show me something, but that could have been a distraction to keep me from hyper focusing on my anger. I still have so many questions I want to ask him, ones that have nothing to do with tonight.

I swallow them down, pushing everything else aside, things that can wait, as I focus on the way Abram stalks towards me, a smoldering look in his eyes. If he's seeing other women I definitely want to know, because I don't plan on being one of many. But no matter how hard my brain is screaming to ask these questions, my body and racing heart just don't want to listen.

Still in just the outfit I wore to work tonight, Abram eyes the thin straps of my black tank top, toying with the material between his finger and thumb. His touch brushes against my exposed skin, causing goosebumps to flood every inch as I shudder under his gaze. He's always so intense, and the earlier question I blurted out comes to the forefront of my mind once more.

"Still in that naughty mind of yours, I see." A flare of satisfaction lights up his face as he realizes he's right. "Such a vixen, little bird." With a slip of his fingers, one side of my tank top falls off my shoulder, hanging on for dear life as Abram slowly lowers the other one.

I clench my fists at my sides, unsure what to do with my hands, as my chest rises and falls faster with each second that passes. I'm waiting for him to do something but he's just watching me, taking in every inch of my body and I'm not even naked yet. *Woah, I'm getting ahead of myself.*

"You're stunning, Isolde," he murmurs in a low and serious tone. His voice always sets my heart racing, my ears tricking me that the sound alone is a trance I can't help but fall into.

Abram's jaw clenches as his eyes bore into mine, practically eating me alive, as he lifts me up from under my thighs and places me on his kitchen island. I was perfectly fine sitting on the stool, but I don't dare say a word. I hold my breath as Abram leans closer to kiss my collarbone and up my neck.

My body involuntarily shivers against his touch, his lips like magic as they dance along my skin. "So soft, so sweet," he murmurs even lower, his voice laced with dark desire. As scared as I've been to go further with him, I know my time of waiting is up. An earthquake could threaten us and I don't know if I'd notice the ground shaking beneath us.

He licks his lips as he reaches for the button on my jeans. Without thinking, I place a hand on his. To stop him or keep him going, I'm not entirely sure. I'm still nervous beyond comprehension and at this point I might pass out before he even touches me.

Confusion lines his features, and I don't even know what to tell him. Should I be honest and just say my ex never did this? I don't want to bring up sexual experiences with other men, I'd be pissed if he did that, but it feels relevant in the moment. "You don't have to…you know," I say like an inexperienced teenager.

Embarrassment takes over and I feel my blush go past my cheeks and cover my neck and chest. This is humiliating and I'm making it worse but stumbling over my words. "Have to?" He asks with a tilt to his head. I really don't know what to do right now, and judging by the way he's looking at me, he can tell.

"Relax, baby," he says soothingly as he coaxes me out of my jeans. I'm left sitting on his countertop in just my tank top and underwear, feeling the cool bite of the marble against my bare thighs.

"I..I'm trying," I try to say confidently but I probably sound scared. I need to just get this off my chest, maybe then he'll understand and cut me some slack. "It's just, my ex, he…he never really liked to do this. So I didn't want you to feel obligated or anything." I sound like an idiot, and the jerk just smiles at me like I'm a little kid. I need a bucket of water to dunk my heated cheeks in, pronto.

"Obligated?" He snorts. "I have been dying to taste this cunt, so if you don't lie back and shut up I'm just going to do it anyways."

He wants to go down on me? I thought guys didn't even like doing it, kind of like most girls don't like to suck dick. Maybe I have things all wrong because I actually want to taste Abram's cock filling my mouth until he's all the way down my throat and I can hardly breathe. Now *that,* is not something I normally think about. This is what I've come to realize, I am someone totally different around Abram. I'm learning things about myself I didn't know existed and it's both exhilarating and terrifying.

"If you're done overthinking this, I'd like to proceed," he says annoyingly like I really am keeping him from his snack.

"I'm sorry, I just felt like I should say something so you didn't feel," I'm cut off when Abram stands before me pressing against my chest until I'm forced to lean back on my elbows.

"Lie the fuck down or I'll spank you until you're begging me to lick your cunt."

So bossy, I say to myself. No chance I'll voice that out loud or he really will spank me raw. I might just let him one of these days to see if I enjoy it.

Taking a much needed deep breath, I lie back all the way until my bare back touches the cold surface, wincing until it warms from my touch. Relaxing as much as possible, I close my eyes as I feel Abram slowly peel my underwear down my legs, past my knees and off my ankles. I open my eyes just as he stuff them into his pocket. "Are you…keeping those?" I ask in bewilderment.

His response doesn't come with words, just a hooded gaze as he lowers his mouth to run his tongue up the length of my slit. Oh, *fuck*, that feels amazing. Abram doesn't even give me a chance to wrap my mind around what he's doing before his tongue plunges into me at the same time two fingers do. I arch my back in response, squeezing my thighs around his head, holding him hostage in my grip. I'm not sure he can even breathe.

His grip is stronger than mine, pulling my legs wider apart with both hands on my thighs. He goes on ravaging me as a relentless string of moans slip from my mouth in euphoric bliss. Instinctively, I wrap my legs around his neck again and arch up to meet his strokes. If Abram wasn't enjoying himself, I wouldn't even be able to tell. His own groans of pleasure meet my ears and I feel them pink from the heat of his gaze as he watches me watching him.

A part of me wants to feel embarrassed and look away from his intense stare, but I can't make my eyes close or look away. His light gray eyes hold me captive, ensuring I stay with him in the moment as my orgasm builds in increasing waves. After what feels like only minutes, I start to feel the pressure build inside me, like a damn flooding the gates just waiting to finally push through.

Pulling back to look at me, I stare at my arousal on Abram's face, glistening under the muted lighting above us. The rest of his open concept space is dark, the only light above the kitchen island I'm currently spread out over. As if we're on stage under a spotlight. "You taste like my new favorite meal, I could feast on this cunt for the rest of my days."

I can't respond, not that I would know what to say anyway, when he mouth is back on me. Licking and sucking like his life depends on me reaching orgasm. His teeth graze the sensitive bundle of nerves making me scream out his name. His resounding growl tells me he enjoys it when I yell for him, and I can't help the pleas that fall from my mouth as he hooks a finger deep inside me. "Please Abram, *more.*"

I feel his mouth falter for a second as he chuckles darkly, but that doesn't deter him for long. He's pushing me closer and closer to that finish line, like a coach guiding their teammates to victory. I've never thought of an orgasm as such a thing until now. I never enjoyed sex until I met these men so willing to give me the kind of pleasure I didn't know was attainable.

My core tightens as my back nearly bows off the counter and I feel the first intense wave of pleasure rip through me. My release flooding my mind and body as I come violently on Abram's tongue and fingers. "Fuck, Abram!" I yell so loud my own ears are ringing and I send up a silent prayer that June's house is a far enough distance away she wouldn't be able to hear her nephew going down on her housemate.

That would make our next dinner night awkward.

Breathing heavily, I try to lift up on my elbows to look at Abram like the God he actually is. I once called him a demon of the woods, but now I'm second guessing that name. I watch in fascination as he licks my arousal off his face and fingers, the way someone would after finishing a sticky wings.

"Now that is something I could get used to," he says in that deep tone of his.

"Me too," I agree easily.

"You almost kept me from enjoying my feast, little bird." Abram reaches behind him to pull his black t shirt over his head, tossing it down on the counter next to me. He loosens his belt next and I feel all the blood in my body rush to my center. My face goes crimson at the sight of him, covered in tattoos like a work of art on display for my own private viewing. "Ready for phase two?"

"Ph-phase two?" I ask with a nervous tremble. I still can't breathe properly after the high I just reached and he chuckles darkly as he leans his body over mine. Gripping a strong hand firmly around my throat, he pulls me closer.

"You came on my tongue, little bird. My cock is ready for it's turn, now."

Oh shit. I can see his length painfully straining against his jeans and I can't help the gasp that passes my lips as he pulls the biggest dick I have ever seen out. If there was a section in the *Guinness World Records* book on dick size, Abram would undoubtably hold the title. How is it even humanly possible for two brothers to be blessed with the bodies of Gods?

Is he going to fuck me right here on the counter? I don't even think I would protest which is strange in itself. I'm a sex in the bed kind of girl, anywhere else was strictly forbidden. Ridiculous even. I hate how much I've missed out on just by being with the wrong person for so long. But judging by the way Abram is staring at me like a prize at the county fair, I have a feeling I won't be able to walk right tomorrow.

Sinking into a chair at the kitchen island, Abram uses his index finger to indicate I come closer. Without hesitation, I hop from the counter and nervously stand in front of him. He's going to have to guide me if he wants me to do certain things, I am way out of my element right now.

Eyes never leaving mine, voice dark and laced with undeniable desire, he tells me exactly what to do and I breathe a sigh of relief at the instructions. "Undo my jeans and take them off."

I lower to my knees before him and with slightly shaking fingers pull his jeans down his muscle clad thighs until they pool at his feet. Once I discard them on the floor next to where I'm kneeling I lick my lips in anticipation of what to do next. I've never been a dominant person, especially in the bedroom, being submissive is where I thrive. "These too," he says avariciously.

Digging my fingers into the waistband of his briefs, I slowly pull them down, repeating the same process I did with his jeans. As his cock springs free from all confinements I nervously stare at his length which is even larger than before if that's possible. I truthfully don't know how he's going to fit inside me. Mouth included.

Sensing my nerves, Abram pulls me in to lay a chaste kiss on my lips. "Turn around," he orders and I do as I'm told. I sit before him with my ass resting against my calves as he threads my long dark hair through his fingers. At first I'm unsure if he's simply playing with it to soothe my racing heart, but quickly realize his intent as I feel the strands weaving through one another.

Abram makes quick work of braiding my hair until its in one long braid down the center of my back. Kind of an odd thing to do with his cock in my face not two minutes ago, but then again everything with him is different than what I'm used to. Just as he finishes I feel his hand wrap around the braid giving it a firm tug.

"Perfect," he sighs against my neck, caressing my pulse point with soft fingers. "Face me and take this cock like the good girl I know you are."

His voice is firm but not threatening with the way he's commanding me and I feel my desire pooling between my thighs. I could easily tell him to fuck off, that he can't tell me what to do but I want to feel his length slide into my hot mouth and down my throat. I don't know where this side of me is coming from, but I'm hoping like hell Abram can keep drawing it out of the deep recesses it's been hiding.

Holding his thickness, I slowly lick the soft veins running its length before taking the head into my mouth. Instinctively, Abram fists his hand around the braid, drawing me closer to the base of his shaft with each tug. Remembering to breathe steadily through my nose, I attempt taking him to the back of my throat. "Fuck, baby. Keep going."

Yup, I definitely have a praise kink. I pull back slightly, bobbing my head up and down as saliva gathers around my mouth and drips down his length. Lowering my mouth to the base once more, I feel him grow even bigger in my throat as I take all of him in. I feel the tears welling in my eyes fall down my cheeks, splashing against Abram's thighs, but I continue.

Lifting his hips up lightly, his thrusts meet my mouth in perfect synchronization causing me to gag around him. With my braid still in hand, he lifts me up to standing and pins me against the kitchen island. My head is delirious from lack of oxygen and my legs wobble from the desire leaking down my legs. "Was that okay?" I ask with less confidence than intended, suddenly feeling nervous it wasn't up to his standards.

"Unless you wanted me to come down that pretty little throat of yours and not your pussy, I had to stop." Oh. I'm taking that as a compliment. Abram snatches my throat in his strong grip, halting my triumphant smile. "Let's see how well your dripping cunt can take me."

I want to tell him I don't think he will fit, but I thought the same thing about fitting him in my mouth. Yes, I struggled slightly, but I still managed. Maybe I need to give myself more credit when it comes to this. I may not have had the best experiences in my past, but I'm not a virgin either. Abram makes me feel bold and stronger than I see myself, a very foreign feeling. Instead of getting in my head like I always do, I let instinct take the front seat and go with bold.

"Then stop talking and fuck me."

Abram's eyes widen at my impulsive words and now I'm feeling less bold, wanting to slip into hiding so he can't berate me for talking back to him. I would have been slapped several times by now if I said something so offhand to Grant.

I'm about to apologize when he captures my lips in a bruising embrace, biting my lower lip as his hands hold my throat captive. A deep moan fills the void around us and I honestly can't tell who it came from. "There's my little vixen," he moans his words into my mouth and my knees almost give out.

With swift and steady hands, Abram lifts me under my thighs and drags us back towards the chair he was just seated in. Placing my legs on either side of him, I straddle his thighs with his cock just inches above where I need him. "Please Abram," I whimper, not caring how needy I sound. I do need him, in more ways than one and I'm tired of pretending I don't.

"Are you gonna beg for me, little bird?"

"I'll get back on my knees and plead if I have to."

Satisfaction roll through him as he smirks his approval. "You don't even need to with the way your pussy weeps for me, but God do I love it when you beg."

"*Please*," I say again, hoping it's enough.

Abram clicks his tongue in disproval and I feel my chest deflate. Why is he making this harder than it needs to be? "Tell me what you need, baby. I want to hear your words."

Jesus, he's really going to make me articulate exactly what I want him to do. My boldness from before sparks to mind and the way he responded to my words. I know what he needs just as much as he knows exactly what I need right now. Instead of pushing us both to our breaking points, I tell him just what he wants to hear.

"I want you to fuck me so hard I won't be able to tell where I end and you begin."

Recognition flashes across his face as he remembers when he said those words to me in the woods not too long ago. The same night I swore I was going to stay away from him, yet here we are. I feel a desperation take over as he lines his cock up to my entrance, sweat beading in his hairline as the restraint not to slam into me begins to crack. I'm shaking like a leaf in anticipation, barely holding on myself, when I feel the tip push into me in achingly slow.

"Jesus Christ, Isolde. You're so fucking tight," he grunts as another inch slides through my slick wet heat.

My body is trying desperately to accommodate him, but the burn from him stretching me has me lifting up and off of him. Before I can gather myself, Abram grabs my shoulders and slams all of my body weight back down onto him, impaling me on his hard as stone cock.

I cry out at the intrusion, feeling more pain mixed with pleasure as he gyrates his hips into me. The burning is still present but the more I relax my muscles the more I begin to enjoy the mixture of pleasure and pain. It's euphoric the way every nerve ending lights up against his touch, his taste and the way he smells. Like my body has no choice but to submit.

A few years that have welled in my eyes begin to fall, not making it to the cliff of my chin and falling off before Abram licks them up the side of my face. "Your tears are mine, little bird."

I'm not sure what he means by that but I can't focus on the meaning while his cock is thrusting in and out of me at a speed I didn't know was possible. His length touches my back walls causing me to clench around him and moan my approval. Each time he shifts me forward slightly I can feel the head of his cock rub against a spot somewhere deep inside me I've never felt.

"Oh *God*," I scream into the crook of his neck as he continues slamming into me. Whatever that spot is I never want him to stop reaching it. I can feel my release crashing into me like a tsunami ready to detonate my entire body. I'm not sure I'm ready for the intense pleasure it's sure to bring me and as if reading my mind, Abram slows down a touch.

"Don't call out to him, little bird. Every time I hear you yell out, it better be my name you're screaming, understand?" To emphasize his point Abram smacks my ass so hard I know there's a handprint outlined on my bare cheek.

"Ahh!" I scream in response, earning me another slap to the other cheek this time.

"I can do this all night, baby." Another slap.

"Fuck! Abram!" I clench around him harder than before as the sting of his slaps bring a weird mix of anger and arousal to the forefront. Only times I've ever been slapped was out of anger and for actual punishment. Abram is pushing me but not more than I can take, he's edging the line without crossing it. "Happy now, maniac?"

His laughter fills my ears like a pitch black orchestra of darkness. Scaring me just enough that I tread lightly, but not too dark that I can't see my way out. This dance with Abram is like being back in those woods with him. Feeling his presence looming around the corner, watching me like a deranged stalker but never taking what doesn't belong to him. He pushed me back then and I wanted so badly to pull back, to not allow him access to my fragile heart.

If anything, he's showing me just how strong my heart and head actually are. That I'm not some fragile, broken girl on the run from her abusive ex. I have a voice and desires that I've kept hidden, rooted to the deepest depths of my being. Abram could sense them from the very beginning, even when I still hadn't noticed them within myself.

It was Abram who reached deep into my being, finding the dark strings tethered to my heart and yanking on them until they breeched the surface. Now that I can see them, dangling in front of me unused, do I feel the boldness to be who I want to be.

I don't taste the fear in my mouth the way blood leaves a metallic tang. I don't look over my shoulder for the dark shadows lurking behind me at night, ready to expose themselves as my worst nightmares. I no longer see every face I pass during the day as the one that's haunted me for six years.

With Abram I see a stronger version of myself, not shrouded entirely in darkness, but a darker part of myself coming forward to blend in with the lighter parts of me. That's why I've felt an indisputable draw to both Stoker men, why they *both* bring forth the parts of me that have been buried far too long.

Alex is my softness, my comfort and sunshine, the one who's there to hold me up when I'm low. Abram toys with the edge of my moral compass, making me want to branch out to new experiences without reservations and without regret. I need them both to unveil this person that's been locked away in a cage most of my life.

As my orgasm crashes into me with a force like something supernatural, I tighten my hold on Abram's broad shoulders as he buries his head into my neck. Peppering kisses up and down my collarbone before sinking his teeth into the tender flesh.

"Abram!" I cry out, tears burning my eyes at the pain that's mixing with the high of my orgasm that still has me in it's clutches. I feel the hot liquid pooling between my collarbone and breast as it drips down my bare chest. The sight of blood usually makes me queasy, having seen too much of my own for my liking. I can almost taste it as if it's spilling out of my mouth the way it is down my chest and rolling off my nipples.

Before it paints any more of my porcelain skin, Abram lashes his tongue out and licks my breast clean, toying with the nipple as he coats it in my blood. I want to feel disgusted, or maybe even angry that he drew blood from me, but it's erotic in a strange way. The way his eyes dance with mine, never missing a beat as his tongue massages my nipple before moving up to lick the wound he inflicted.

My blood must be an aphrodisiac for him, because as soon as it invades his mouth I feel his length harden even more, his movements become less fluid and the head of his cock swells inside me as the first jets of his cum decorate my insides. Fuck, we didn't even use protection! I'm on birth control, but still, that was fucking dumb.

"What the fuck was that?" I ask in an agitated tone I only partially feel. "Are you a vampire or something?" How could I have missed the signs? I read about this shit, how the woman never believes in mythical beings until one day she's ravaged by Dracula himself.

Abram chuckles against my sensitive skin, "your blood is my holy water, little bird."

"Pretty sure there already is holy water, Abram."

"Yeah but it doesn't work on demons like me." Well, that answers that I suppose.

"We didn't use protection," I admit, hoping it doesn't freak him out the way it's freaking me out right now. I'm barely holding together my anxiety and if he does the same then we'll just be a mess of idiots who forgot to use a condom.

I hold my breath and wait for an answer, an explanation, anything. But he just watches me with lustful eyes, not having come down from his own high. "Earth to Stoker," I say, waving my hand in front of his face.

He grabs it and fixes me with a deadly stare. "Do not call me that, little bird. I am Stoker to everyone else, but *you*." I don't have the energy to unravel whatever that means, so I leave it. It did what I intended it to do though, it got his attention.

"I'm not fucking anyone else, so what's the point. I assume you're on birth control, am I right?" I nod my head in agreement. "And the only other person you're fucking is my brother, also correct I assume." My face floods with heat and the embarrassment I know I shouldn't feel but do nonetheless.

"Judging by how pussy whipped that man is for you, I'd say he's not getting his dick wet by anyone else either." I'm not sure how to respond, but honestly that kind of fixed the problem I was having in my head. The complex I gave myself thinking they were just sleeping with me for fun and still getting their fill elsewhere as well.

"You look relieved," he says nonchalantly as his dick is still hard inside me. How can he still be hard after that? I can feel his cum leaking out of me and pooling between us in his lap.

"Yeah," I pause, searching for the words I want to use. "I wasn't sure how to have a conversation with either of you about our…situation, so that kind of helped in a way."

With that smoldering look of his, he lifts me off of him, and the gush of liquid that follows has me going even more red. Holding me bridal style, he walks us past the living room into his bedroom to where the bathroom is. "Lets clean this up," he says, eyes focused on the blood stained teeth marks he left on me. I'm ashamed to admit I kind of enjoyed it, the idea that pain can be mixed with pleasure and not only be pain.

After cleaning the cut and placing a small bandage so no one asks questions later, rightfully presuming June will say something, Abram draws us a bath. By the time we exit and I'm drying off, it's well past two in the morning. My body is satiated but exhausted as I try to put my clothes back on. Most of them are still strew about the kitchen island form earlier.

"Drop the jeans, Isolde," Abram scolds behind me. I drop them on reflex and lift my hands up in surrender like I'm under arrest. "Let's get you to bed."

I don't have the energy to argue with him, too tired to stand properly. I was tired before but the warm bath with his chest at my back holding me up, made me extra sleepy. The last thing I remember before falling into a deep sleep, is the feeling of soft sheets on my bare skin and the warmth of a hard body covered in tattoos engulfing me in his arms.

ISOLDE

chapter seventeen

♫

Broken • Seether ft. Amy Lee

"Why are you trusting me with this?" I ask as I nervously wring my hands in front of the long t-shirt Abram gave me. At least it's warmer in here - the chill from outside had goosebumps dotting my skin faster than my mind had to feel the cold.

He leans down to adjust the clay on the wheel before giving me a devilish smirk. "Who said I trust you, little bird?"

"The fact that you're allowing me to use a piece of machinery that obviously means a shit ton to you," I gesture around the room for emphasis. "Oh, and also a probably insanely expensive piece of equipment."

When he doesn't respond with anything but a slight head shake, I stand back quietly as I admire him working. He moves around the room with such ease which is a feat in itself considering how cramped it is in here. Never mind him working alone in here but now I'm just awkwardly standing here unsure of where to go. I try to move so I'm not in his way, but every time he brushes past me he gives me a squeeze of reassurance. Like he can tell I'm nervous to be in his personal space.

I'm trying to work on that - feeling like I can belong somewhere - but it's hard. For so long I walked on eggshells, never feeling like anywhere was safe to let my guard down. But the last few months of getting to know both Stoker brothers has given me a slight confidence I didn't think I was capable of.

Don't get me wrong, I still have a shit ton to work on - but it's a start.

I can tell Abram's studio means a lot to him so the idea of bumping into even the smallest piece of art makes my stomach roll with instant unease. I would never be able to look him in the eyes again if I broke something of importance to him. That realization slams into me like a freight train - realizing I truly care about him, and the things that make him who he is.

I can feel the racing thrum of my heartbeat under the thin t-shirt that smells deliciously like Abram - a scent so uniquely him I want to have a bottle of it made up so I can always have it. I don't even care if that sounds weird.

"I can feel those beautiful eyes on me," he says with a firm tone laced with something I can only describe as desire. He turns to face me just as he finishes his setup. "It's distracting."

"Well you would know all about that, wouldn't you?" I snort.

Abram sighs against the side of my neck, his hands blazing a trail down my sides before resting on my hips. His voice, like a deep timbre of need, echoes around me and I feel flutters deep in my belly from the affect. "One of these days little bird, that mouth is going to get you in a heap of trouble."

I shiver at the promise in his tone, almost wanting to push my luck and see where it takes me. I want the beast in Abram to emerge - to show his true self to me so that I can accept all of him the way he seems to have accepted me.

The parts he knows about, that is.

Baby steps, I remind myself. This is him trying - and I realize I need to do the same. I not only want both of them to understand the darker parts of me, but I feel like they need to. After I received another text from Grant a few days ago, it became very clear he isn't going to just give up finding me. I can't begin to imagine what that will mean for Alex and Abram if he does. They're both good, hard working men and the thought that Grant might hurt one of them, or both…It's too much.

"Hey," Abram says gently in my ear, bringing me back to the present. "Where did you go just then?"

How do I answer that? It's not as simple as laying everything out in front of him. Or is it?

I'm about to open my mouth when I feel his rough hands guiding me towards the stool set up in front of the wheel. I watch him take a seat - his wide strong legs opening for me to sit in his lap. I watch the movement as I feel his eyes trained on me. Waiting for me to join him.

As if in a trance, I walk over to him before slowly lowering my body onto his. He guides me so that my back is against his chest while he holds both hands in his.

With both hands, he reaches under his thighs and lifts the chair up a few times until my knees are touching the wheel. I've never worked with clay or pottery before, and this scene feels a lot like Patrick Swayze and Demi Moore in Ghost.

A muscle in his leg jerks as he presses down on the pedal and the wheel begins moving. Knowing I've never done this, he goes slow at first. Guiding my hands around the wet clay and allowing me to work into it.

It's cold and almost sticky in a weird way - but the clay is smooth and molds easily enough. A few minutes in and I feel like I find a rhythm when Abram starts whispering filthy things in my ear. The things he wants to do to me, the ways he plans to use his fingers, tongue and cock on all areas of my body.

Suddenly all the work we've accomplished in the last five minutes is squashed beneath my tight fisted trembling hands. I can feel the flush moving from my cheeks down to my chest as my heartbeats pick up speed. Words I want to speak get caught in my throat - unable to voice my disappointment that we ruined what we started. But as soon as one of his clay covered hands wanders up to the base of my throat, I forget about everything entirely.

The tiny room we're in blurs until nothing is recognizable. And I can hardly smell the mustiness either. The only sense that is lit up like a damn Christmas tree is the way his fingers feel against my exposed skin. All I have on is the t-shirt he gave me, and suddenly I want to feel his hands on every piece of my body. Clay covered hands or not.

"What are you thinking, little bird?" His voice rumbles through my chest, vibrating with need just like my needy body wants him. No, *needs* him. This obsession with him touching me will turn unhealthy I fear, but another problem for another day if you ask me.

"I-I can't think straight at all when you're doing…*that*," I release a breath on a whisper moan as his fingers toy with one of my earlobes. I don't know why they've always been sensitive and at this moment I don't care. It sends tingles down my spine until my toes are curling against the concrete floor.

Abram hums against my throat, "mmm, and what exactly am I doing?"

He's toying with me. The asshole knows how easy it is to rile me up and he's testing me to see how quickly I fall into his trap. Too bad for him I have more self restraint than he thinks. At least that's what I'm telling myself so I don't spin around and mount him here and now.

"Distracting me, *Mr. Stoker*," I growl in response as my hands move back to the wheel in attempt to fix the piece we started. The hand around my neck tightens and I feel his hard on pressed into my back. He told me never to call him anything other than Abram, that he's Stoker to everyone else apart from me. I can't help but feel the buzz of excitement that calling him by his last name might get me into trouble.

I've been dying to see the wild side of him unleashed. A side of him he can't hold back because of his need for me. I want to feel cherished and *wanted* in such a way. His eyes always give him away though, the way they smolder and burn through me straight to a part of my soul I never knew existed. I can practically taste how badly he wants to let go and have me the way he wants me. Abram Stoker has a way of bulldozing through all of my previously and carefully built walls, I just wish I had to the guts to do the same.

"What did I say about calling me that?" He grinds out the words in a controlled irritation as I do my best to stifle the laughter desperate to burst out of me. I know if I so much as chuckle he will have me flipped and pinned to the floor in a matter of seconds. Why does the thought of that turn me on? I'm starting to wonder if there's something wrong with me.

Note to self: ask Hailey if there's a therapist around she recommends.

"Here I thought the *Mr*. Added an air of sophistication."

Suddenly the wheel stops moving, and Abram pushes the chair back, removing his hands from where they were just gripping my throat. He doesn't say anything, but his eyes are always more expressive than any words ever could be. I look over my shoulder and see his finger move. With one digit, covered in clay, he motions for me to come closer. I move on instinct until I'm right against him, but unsure of what he wants me to do now.

Ten seconds ago I was prepared to push him and see how much it takes to break him - just a little. Now I'm following his movements like a damn moth to a flame.

His face is calm, almost unnervingly so, and even his scent envelops all my senses - like the smell of him becomes a part of me, working its way down to the deepest parts of me and resting there like it was meant to all along. My body relaxes in his hold, recognizing comfort from his touch, the warmth of his hands and the intoxicating smell that is only him.

The moment feels tender as I allow my guard to come down a little. I feel the change a millisecond before he moves - like the air around us gets supercharged and there's static radiating off of him and bouncing against each piece of artwork in this tiny space.

Abram has me lifting off his lap and spun around so that my thighs are straddling his defined abs before I can even process my next breath. As soon as his ass hits the chair once more, one his his beautifully tattooed hands is back around my throat.

My eyes bug at the tightness and I try to gulp against his firm hold but he doesn't budge. Maybe I shouldn't have pushed him - maybe it was utterly moronic of me to test a side of him I know nothing about. Nevertheless, here we are. I can feel my chest tighten from lack of oxygen and my eyes begin watering without my consent.

Abram tilts his head to the side slightly, fascination decorating his features while delight dances in his eyes. I've always known he was a little unhinged - I mean can we not remember the night in the woods where he pinned me to the forest floor beneath him? But something about the way he's watching me now is different.

Like he's in control but barely. The very idea of hurting me is not an option - that much I can tell by the way he handles me with care. But as I look deeper into his beautiful blues, I see the beast itching to come out. Inching forward just a little until Abram allows that side of him to be freed from it's confines.

I'm so close to what I set out to do a few minutes ago. I may not be prepared for what he will inevitably unleash - but I feel some kind of absolution I've never felt before.

My soul knows that he will bring me to the edge over and over again, breeching those high built walls of mine, but also knowing that he won't cross them. Not unless I give him full approval to.

Indecision mixes with excitement and I can feel the hesitation in him, we both need this though. He needs to show me the sides of him he's held back for however long just like I need to trust him with the broken parts of me he doesn't know exist.

I can't allow my fear for another man to keep me from experiencing exhilarating things with someone who I know I can trust. Call me naive or just plain stupid - but Abram Stoker is not like Grant. The ways that Abram has hurt me is a far cry from the ways Grant tormented me for years. And even if he doesn't know about any of that, I need to show him I am not my past - just like he is not his.

We both have darkness in us - abused from life's cruel circumstances. The darkness does not define us though - the ways in which we choose to live *after* the darkness tried to pull us under is where we thrive.

"This delicate neck of yours," he whispers against my face. Sending the loose hairs around my face on a journey of their own.

"What about it?" I ask, confidently hiding the tremble in my voice.

"You called me a vampire earlier tonight, when I was fucking you so hard your eyes rolled back into your skull."

When I don't say anything in response, he licks a trail from my earlobe down the base of my throat. I shiver in his hold, wanting him to keep going but also afraid of where this is going to end up.

"When my cock is buried deep in that hot, wet cunt of yours, I think about sinking my teeth into the soft skin right here." His teeth nip at my neck lightly before he bears down a little harder. I wait for the telltale alarm bells to go off, but there's nothing but adrenaline and arousal coursing through my veins. I like seeing the controlled side of him play with the unhinged part of him - like *Dr. Jekyll and Mr. Hyde.* The two dominant sides of Abram want to come out at the same time - and fuck, do I want to see it.

"I can feel you soaking through those tiny panties of yours," he groans against me before sinking back in. His hard cock rubs up into me at the same time as his teeth break skin in my neck.

Feeling my body tense, a scream ready to burst out of me at the odd sensation, Abram releases me and begins licking the wound. Gently rubbing his tongue over the raw flesh and placing soft kisses around the sore area.

The quick change from pain to pleasure has my head spinning and before I can say another word, he does it again.

This time I can't help the scream that comes barreling out of me. "It fucking turns you on, doesn't it little bird?"

How am I supposed to answer that? The screams should tell him it hurts, but the way my pussy is grinding against his thick cock says otherwise. I always knew I was fucked up, but I assumed it was from abuse and the torture I went through at the hands of someone who should have loved me. Now I'm not so sure what to think.

Using one hand to hold me in place, Abram lifts up slightly. I don't even know what he's doing as pain and an odd kind of euphoria pumps through me at an alarming rate. All I can hear is my heavy breathing and the loud thumping in my chest. I'm not even able to open my eyes - too afraid to see blood dripping off Abram's chin like an actual scene out of Dracula.

A matter of seconds pass before I feel a hand reach beneath my legs, eyes pinging open, I watch as my once perfect black thong falls to the floor in shredded pieces. The moment my eyes land on the discarded fabric, Abrams cock thrusts into me with so much force my screams might be heard all the way to June's house.

"The taste of you sets me on fire," he grunts as his thrusts go deeper. "Like a literal inferno takes over and fuck, I couldn't handle not being inside you for a second longer." His voice is desperate, the way my body meets his thrusts has me feeling the same way. The way I come alive for him is like a drug I could never find anywhere else and would gladly overdose on him.

"Sometimes I wish you were a virgin. So I could know what it feels like to have your blood soaking my cock as I take your purity away with each pump into this tight pussy."

A moan slips free, mixing with the cries of pain I'm unable to hide. Tears are flowing down my cheeks and soaking into the t-shirt but I don't care. All I care about is the way the tip of cock keeps hitting that spot that has me rolling my eyes back and seeing stars. "It hurts, so bad," I cry out. Wanting him to stop but praying to God he doesn't. "Please, don't stop."

"Yes, baby. You fucking love taking my cock like a good girl, don't you?"

I nod my head up and down over and over again as blood rolls down my neck and between my breasts. I watch Abrams eyes track the trickle of blood before he rips the shirt away from my body the same way he did with my underwear.

My body heats with a feeling I can't identify. Lust? Embarrassment? Maybe a mixture of both as he licks a line up my sternum, cleaning away any evidence of blood with his tongue. "Fuck, you're strangling my cock so tight, little bird. Want to come all over it?"

"Yes!" I scream as the orgasm rushes to the surface without warning. Crashing into me, out of me and all over us both with a force stronger than anything I've ever experienced. I can feel my cum leaking out of me and sliding down Abram's cock as he pumps into me faster than before. I feel his length harden even more as he buries his face into the blood soaked crook of my neck, letting out a string of curse words, just as the proof of his orgasm mixes with mine. Painting my insides with our joined release.

***

We may have knocked over a few pieces of pottery - to my horror - but Abram brushed me off and said it was fine. More specifically, he said it was worth it and he would happily trash the place if we could do a repeat.

My cheeks heat with the idea of doing that again. I can't decide if I loved it, hated it or hate the fact that I loved it. I'm a complicated mess.

Abram's eyes are on me, I can feel the intensity of them searing into the side of my face, but I refuse to meet his gaze. It's always piercing, always electrifying and if I look now then we for sure will have a repeat of what just transpired not long ago.

"Isolde." His voice is gentle but there's that touch of sternness in it. The voice he reserves for times he wants answers. No beating around the bush and definitely no brushing him off. I've learned the hard way that results in him spanking my ass raw. Another thing I never thought I would enjoy and somehow I do.

"I already know what you're going to say," I mumble into his shoulder with my eyes closed. We stayed the way we were after our impromptu fuck sesh - but Abram reluctantly stuffed his dick back in his pants. By some miracle he had a sweatshirt in here so I'm fortunate enough to be covered up. I didn't even think about what I would wear back to the house when he shredded my underwear and his shirt.

"You think you do," he counters.

"Fine, I know what you're going to ask. I'm just not sure I'm ready to elaborate on it fully."

The room grows quiet for several minutes. Just the steady beat of crickets chirping outside penetrating the small room we're holed up in. I'm not sure I could ever work in here knowing there's only one exit and no windows. I would have felt claustrophobic had it not been for the thick and hard distraction being driven into me to help keep me calm.

I don't do well with small spaces - fair enough considering the shit Grant did in the past. Two words: locked closet.

"You and I both know I'm going to ask it anyways, might as well rip off the bandaid."

Fucking prick. Sometimes I want to throat punch him for the shit he spews. If I couldn't feel the warmth beneath his touch and the sweat dotting his hairline then I'd assume he was a robot - unfeeling and uncaring.

Heaving a sigh and suppressing an eye roll, I give in and let him ask his fucking question. One I don't know how to process sometimes myself let alone answer for someone else.

"Where did you go earlier?"

I know what he's referring to. Not a place I literally went to but a place I escaped to in my mind - something he clearly noticed. I need to work on my facial expressions, and probably my reactions as well. I'm too much of an open book when I don't mean to be and not enough of one when I should be.

"Listen, I want you to cut the shit. If I sound like an asshole I don't mean to, but I think we're past the point of acting like we're not getting to know one another. I've let you be as closed off as you see fit for a while now. And though I'm not one to talk, I think it's pretty obvious you're running from something."

He probably meant it hypothetically. There's no way he actually knows I'm quite literally running from something, *someone*, but hearing the words leave his mouth still sends goosebumps scattering across my skin the way rain scatters on a windshield. I feel the blood drain from my face, leaving behind a white mask of fear.

Abram tightens his hold around me when he sees my change in demeanor. I know I haven't done the best job mastering my poker face, and even though June never alluded to anything - the guys know I have some dark secrets.

It feels wrong to have this conversation without Alex present, though. I've kept them both in the dark for months now and if I'm going to finally let them in then I need to let them in together. This is not the kind of conversation I want to have more than twice. I wish I only had to have it once but considering June has known everything since I moved here, twice it is.

"Can you call Alex?" I ask with a tremor in my voice. I take a few much needed deep breaths before locking eyes with him. When they land on his blues I don't find any resentment or jealousy - instead, I see patience. Something I never thought I find on Abram Stoker's face.

"I only want to have this conversation once if that's okay."

Nothing needed to be said after that. Abram helped me off his lap before turning off the machinery and all the lights. We exited the studio in silence and I stood close to him, absorbing as much of his body heat as possible, while he locked up.

He held my hand as we made our way back to his house and sat me down on the couch wrapped in blankets while he started a pot of coffee.

My eyes vacantly watched the room around me as the sun began streaming in through the windows, casting a warm glow around the open floor plan. In my peripheral vision I could see Abram working in the kitchen as he pulled out the fixings for bacon and eggs. I also heard soft rumblings on the phone to who I could only assume was Alex.

By the time breakfast is done, Alex is walking through the door and shoveling pieces of bacon in his mouth like a caveman. My mind and body feel numb and I don't have it in me to laugh the way I normally would when catching Alex in one of his goofy moods. Abram must not have said why he wanted him here - probably for the better.

As soon as his eyes find me on the couch however, they turn from light and carefree to confused and concerned in half a second. I wish I didn't have to do this. I wish I didn't have to drudge up my past and spill my darkest secrets. It was hard enough telling June, but woman to woman made it easier in a way. That and she assured me she had been through some rough shit of her own.

Trying my best to keep my emotions at bay, I breathe in deeply as I prepare myself to tell them *everything*. Six years is a lot to unpack on a person, and I have to unpack it all for two. There's a possibility that once I tell them the truth they won't want anything to do with me. I'm too far in at this point to even consider that as an option, though. My heart is already more than halfway to being in love with these men - my darkness and my light.

I promised myself when this all began that for their safety I would tell them about Grant. They deserve to know what kind of woman they're getting involved with - and if its too much for either of them, or worse - both - then I'll pick up and leave. No questions asked.

I owe them both that courtesy if nothing else.

Tears prick my eyes at the thought of leaving. June has practically become family. The woman literally saved my life in more ways than one. But since the manor is basically done, and I'm more of a financial drain here than I'd like to admit - if they wanted out then I would give them that. After everything the three of them have done for me in just a few short months - I owe them not just gratitude, but respect above all else.

My body is sweating, my nerves are completely shot, and a slight tremor is shaking my whole frame as Abram and Alex make their way into the living room. Two sets of eyes on me.

When they both take a seat on the sectional couch beside me, I fight the urge to burst into tears. I can do this. Closing my eyes, I find the strength I once had and harness it as I let the words come tumbling out like word vomit. Not stopping once to let them speak or ask questions. Too afraid I won't be able to finish. I lay everything out in front of them - like my own personal trauma platter.

Focusing only on my hands as I speak, I let the words flow and hope to God they can stomach the details of my tattered past.

ISOLDE

chapter eighteen

In the Shadows You'll Hear My Voice

• KIRRA47

A steady beeping sound comes from the room to my left - a person being monitored and kept alive by machines. If they're lucky, someone they love and care about is beside them, maybe holding their hand and offering comforting words. I'm not sure what happened to them, causing them to wind up here - but I know what happened to me.

And right now all the brain capacity I have is only capable of thinking about tonight.

The way his hands landed on me over and over again with a loud smacking sound that ricocheted off the walls. The way my sobs seemed to sync up with the loud yelling accompanied by the sting of each blow. Or worse, the way my mind went blank, my body went still and my eyes never closed - just staring up ahead at the ceiling fan rotating in slow motion.

I never thought I'd wind up in a hospital like this, waiting for a rape kit, no less. Especially not after being with a person I love so truly, so entirely that the idea he would ever hurt me never crossed my mind. That was dumb, clearly.

Grant has spent the last two years treating me like a princess - like the most precious thing in his life. I never thought I would find a man who loved me the way Grant loves me, the way he takes care of me and makes sure I have everything I could ever want. Including the top floor apartment in the most sought after building in the city.

I used to look up at that very building, wondering what it would be like to live there. Now that I have it, I wish I could set the goddamn building on fire and watch it fall to ashes on the ground. Nothing but a distant memory of future hope - a future I no longer want anything to do with.

We moved in three days ago. Three days. *Nothing could have prepared me for what would happen just three days after moving into my dream apartment. Three days after everything in the last two years has been nothing but perfect. Three days after Grant told me he couldn't wait to marry me.*

Marry me!

In that moment, the joy that emanated off us both was practically tangible. We made love that night in our new home and made promises I never had any intention of turning back on.

I've never gotten any red flag moments that I was in danger with him - or that I could be at any moment. He's treated me with care - as if I was a delicate flower he was hellbent on protecting. Little did I know the only thing I needed protecting from - was him.

The kind nurse who brought me back here is walking through the curtain once again, only this time the look on her face isn't soft and gentle - she's wearing an uncertain look that has the hair on the back of my neck rising.

"Ms. Davies?"

"Is everything okay?" I ask quickly, unable to hide my unease as she moves farther into the room. I hear footsteps behind her and assume its a doctor coming in to explain the results of the rape kit to me.

I was wrong. So, so wrong.

"Isolde!" Grant yells in fake concern. Moving swiftly to my bedside and grabbing my bruised knuckles from my initial attempt to fight him off. I gave up quickly when I realized all my efforts were futile. He was going to rape me and there was nothing I could do but accept my fate and pray it was over quick.

"Oh sweetheart, I'm so glad you're okay!" Fuck, his voice makes my teeth grind in irritation. How dare he come in here and ask me if I'm okay when he's the one who put me here?

"Ms. Davies, is this man a welcome guest?" The nurse with the kind eyes asks with a glare over her shoulder at Grant. Before she or I can say anything else though, Grant fixes her with the most sinister look I've ever seen a person make.

"Of course, it's okay. I'm her fiancé. Why the fuck would it not be okay for me to come and check on her wellbeing after what she's been through?"

I resist the urge to snort at that statement. I never noticed what a fucking prick he could be until this very moment. Sure, there have been some signs, but this is the first I'm seeing it directed at someone with such candor.

"My apologies sir, I just wanted to make sure my patient was okay with the intrusion."

Damn, if this were any other kind of situation I would beg her to be my friend. She's the kind of person I need in my corner.

The awkward stare off makes my palms sweat - I've never been good with confrontation - and soon the nurse gives in and begins heading back to her station.

"Press the button if you need anything." And with that, she leaves me alone with the monster I gave my heart to so willingly two years ago.

After being discharged from the hospital - with the reassurance my rape kit was to be thrown out - Grant brings me home. That night was the beginning of a four year trip to hell. A trip I never wanted to go on and tried everything to escape. Four and a half years later and I still feel like I'm running.

***

It's been two weeks since I told the guys everything. Two weeks that they have both doted on me and treated me like a fucking porcelain doll. As much as I appreciate the concern - I want things to go back to normal. Because I swear to God, if one of them doesn't fuck me to within an inch of my life, I might actually lose my fucking mind.

Which is exactly why I devised the plan I hope to execute, without a misstep, tonight. I've spent the last few days while Abram was away on a job studying the woods behind the property. Every night I walk back here, memorizing the trails and even the parts off the trail not as easily found.

I've gotten lost countless times and since I get no service this far out, I've taken screenshots of the area on my phone to look back at for guidance. Let me tell you, that has come in handy more times than I care to admit when I got lost out here in the dark. Given everything I've told Alex and Abram, they'd probably both strangle me themselves for being out here alone at night.

One thing I know for certain though, is how much Abram loves a chase.

That's why I am standing at the opening of the trail that connects the back of June's yard to the woods. I sent a text about five minutes ago that I desperately needed Abram's help and to come right away. Knowing how on edge they've been with my past experiences - they've been taking my safety way more seriously.

As soon as I see the lone headlight coming down the dirt road, I hit send on the message I already had typed out to Abram. Without a second glance back, I take off running at a full sprint into the dark woods. Adrenaline and a distinct kind of excitement pumping through my veins. The initial idea of letting Abram hunt me gave me hives and made my body break out in a nervous sweat.

I felt like I was hunted for years by Grant, and not in a fun way. This is a way to rectify that fear - by letting Abram hunt and chase me for *fun*.

As soon as I hear the engine of Abram's bike cut off, I smile triumphantly to myself - feeling a sense of accomplishment I could easily become addicted to. Sure, he might be mad but something tells me the excitement will outweigh his momentary irritation with my antics.

Even with my massive head start, I can hear his thunderous steps gaining on me. My fight or flight instincts kick in a little even as I remind myself I planned this whole thing out and can stop it at any time. At least, I hope I can. It never crossed my mind to come up with a safe word to stop everything if it becomes too much.

Oh well, too late to dwell on it now.

I push myself harder, propelling myself to move faster than before as I fly through the woods. Branches snap beneath my feet as leaves brush past me in my attempt to outrun him. If I can get far enough away, then I can hide and lead him in a different direction.

I'm still a little fuzzy with the trails back here, but I'm confident I can keep it close to the property line without having to go too far. The idea of not only getting lost in here but losing Abram in the process is giving me an impending anxiety attack, one I quickly brush off as I feel my feet pounding into the dirt.

My chest is heaving as each precious breath I pull in makes me acutely aware how out of shape I am. I'm fit, but not running through the woods being chased by an unhinged man who likes to drink my blood. Yeah…I may not have thought this fully through.

Fuck that voice that always finds a way to creep in and make me doubt myself. That voice started with Grant and it ends here and now. I can fucking do this and I plan on showing him just how strong I am. That my past experiences and tragedies do not define the woman I am now.

I'm fucking scared out of my mind. My heart is pumping at an alarming rate, my palms are dripping sweat to match the beads forming in my hairline, and I desperately need a jug of water to chug. But I refuse to stop. I refuse to stop pushing farther and farther until I find that sense of satisfaction and accomplishment I'm so desperate to have. I want Abrams eyes on mine as he plunges his cock so far into me with words of praise and awe.

Feeling like I've put enough distance between us, I crouch down behind a bush and work on settling my racing heart and erratic breathing. I need to rest if I plan on continuing this little manhunt I started. I never thought about what would happen if he didn't catch me - quite frankly that thought was ridiculous though. There's no way he won't find me - and when he does, I know exactly what I'm hoping he does.

My leggings grow damp as desire pools between my legs. I opted to forgo underwear - something I know will drive Abram wild - but now I'm thinking that wasn't too smart as my own arousal glides down my slick thighs. He's always boasted about being able to smell when I'm turned on - let's put that theory to the test.

With quiet ease, I rise to my feet and scan the dark woods, listening closely for any sign Abram is near.

When I convince myself the noises I keep hearing are just the sounds of the forrest, I take off running back in the direction I came from. A few minutes in and I start to feel pride that I outsmarted him - that I was able to deter him and shake off his attempt at finding me. As soon as I allowed that feeling to sink in and take root was when I fucked myself.

A strong tattooed arm reaches out from behind a tree, grabbing around my waist with little effort, and dragging me to the ground in less time than it takes to blink. My back meets the cold hard ground and a groan escapes my lips as I close my eyes and hide my face from my captor.

A powerful heat radiates off his body - whether from anger or desire, I can't tell just yet. Probably a mixture of both in this moment.

"And just what the *fuck* do you think you're doing, little bird?"

Judging by the tone of his voice, I'm gonna say anger has taken the front seat. Good. I want him to let go of this careful and sweet side of him that has been at the forefront for the better part of two weeks. I want the old Stoker back. And if I have to stoop to that level, I will.

With a few controlled breaths, I match his look of indignation before answering his question. "Whatever I want."

His eyebrows furrow a little as he watches me, presumably waiting for me to laugh and say I'm just kidding. Well, he'll be waiting all night if that's what he expects. Tonight I plan on pushing his buttons, crossing some lines and seeing how far we can push our boundaries. I'm still scared shitless to provoke him - but I've made it this far.

With a humorless chuckle he looks back down at me, "oh, is that so? And what exactly is it you want?"

Yes. This is what I've been waiting for! Him to give in and see that I'm capable of stepping outside my comfort zone. Lately it's felt like I need to walk around with a sign around my neck that screams *'I am not the things I've been through!'* For some reason it feels like people look at me and see a scared little girl. It's time I brave this newfound side of myself and take what I want.

"What do I want?" I snicker at him, ready to see the beast let loose. "I want you to chase me through these woods, Abram. I've been studying them for nearly two weeks now and though I may not know them like you do, I think I can at least give you a run for your money."

"I mean, I kind of already did," I smirk in response. Abram has a hand firmly gripped around my throat as I wiggle beneath him, rubbing myself against the bulge in his jeans. Hoping for any kind of contact. "If you catch me," I begin to say when he abruptly cuts me off.

"*When* I catch you, little bird." Cocky bastard, I resist the urge to say.

"Fine, *when* you catch me, you can do whatever you want with me." I watch him carefully, waiting patiently for him to back down and say this isn't a good idea. I'm praying he doesn't let me down - Alex, yes. He's the sunshine in my life, the happy golden retriever who only wants to see me happy. Not Abram, though. Abram has a darkness in him - one I'm convinced matches mine.

It's time we stop fucking playing nice and open up these desires of ours until our chests ooze with the darkness bubbling just beneath the surface. I don't want to be afraid anymore. I don't want to hide anymore. I don't want to be what Grant tried to mold me into. I want to be the version of myself I feel deep inside - and I want Abram to help pull it out with his own darkness. Tethering his to mine until we twine together as one.

The silence stretches in an uncomfortable way and I feel like he's about to tell me we shouldn't act out this fucked up fantasy of mine. I see the glimmer in his eye though - the same one he had the first time he had me pinned to this very forrest floor - and I know I've won.

Even if he catches up to me in ten seconds flat, the very idea that he's willing to entertain this means I've won. And I can't help the Cheshire Cat grin that spreads across my face.

"Run, little bird."

Without any hesitation, I'm on my feet and running farther into the woods -

farther than I explored on my own these last ten days. I feel confident in my direction knowing that Abram is chasing me so even if I got lost, I'd have him to lead me out.

The earth smells more potent out here, musty in a refreshing kind of way as I pass a river to my right that leads back behind the manor. The running water smells crisp and clean and I have to resist stopping to take a much needed drink. I didn't exactly think about hydration when I planned out this manhunt.

Deciding to follow the water - knowing it leads back to the manor - I run along side it, careful not to get too close so I don't accidentally slip in. The temperature is dropping around here and colder weather works it's way into the forecast. I want to have fun, not catch pneumonia.

Allowing myself to appreciate the serenity out here, my guard drops slightly and I feel like if this were a movie the whole crowd would be screaming at me to pay attention. I'm the fucking idiot who wouldn't last five minutes in a slasher film.

In that moment Abram catches me.

Half of me is thrashing like a wild animal, terrified of what I've allowed myself to get into. While the other half of me is giggling like a schoolgirl - excitement seeping out of my pores.

Both of his large hands come around my body - holding on tightly like a fucking koala bear in a tree. One hand is firmly gripped around my throat - my favorite, and he knows it. I've missed it the last couple weeks. He's been so gentle with me and it's made me want to scream in frustration, *just choke me already!* The other hand roughly pulls at my leggings, reaching in to cup my bare pussy.

I don't miss the look of satisfaction when he finds out I went commando for our little adventure. An evil glint lights his face in the next second, and I gulp audibly at the look he's giving me.

"You paraded around these woods with no underwear on? What if some other creep was out here waiting for you?"

I wish I could laugh, but he's holding my throat so tight I'm surprised I'm able to breathe at all. Straining to speak against his hand, he loosens it slightly to allow a few words free. "The only creep in these woods is *you*."

Without warning, Abram thrusts two fingers deep inside me, rubbing them roughly until my body is practically bucking against him. He brings me to the edge so fast I feel like I might pass out from the pleasure. Just as the first wave of my orgasm begins to ripple in my core, Abram withdraws his fingers and I groan in protest.

I'm about to tell him off when those two fingers are shoved in my mouth, roughly massaging into my tongue so I'm unable to escape the taste of my own arousal. I have to say, it's not that bad. I've never loved the idea of tasting myself but I kind of see why Alex and Abram are so hellbent on eating me out. I taste good.

I moan against his fingers and I feel the length of his cock push against my exposed pussy. He may have ripped my leggings, but I don't even care - I'll buy more. "You like tasting yourself on my fingers, don't you baby?"

Eyes wide, I watch him as I nod my head up and down. "Now you understand why I can never get enough of this cunt," both fingers push back inside before a third joins the movements. My eyes roll back again as my body arches into Abram's touch. "This cunt is mine, do you understand me?"

I can't speak, euphoria pulsing just beneath the surface as my orgasm, the first of hopefully many crashes into me. I let out a scream of pleasure, giving the night sky a chance to experience my release with me. Wave after wave comes until I feel it slowly subside.

My chest is rising and falling so fast and for whatever reason, I want to egg him on even more. Make him take everything he wants from me. Do I have a death wish? Not exactly - maybe I'm just a masochist. "Need I remind you," I pause, waiting for those blue eyes to meet mine. "Your brother had me first."

I'm playing with fire, but this is the game Stoker and I play. He wipes his hand roughly across his face before smiling down at me with that same evil glint from before. He pulls me flush against him as he growls in my ear sending shivers down my spine - effortlessly reaching the tips of my toes. "I intend to be your last."

With swift, quick movements, Abram has his jeans pulled down and cock in hand before thrusting into me all the way to the hilt. I cry out at the welcome invasion as my walls immediately tighten around him. Setting a slow but rough pace, I feel Abram watching me until our eyes meet. "Brother or not," he murmurs against my cheek, licking a stray tear that has fallen without me realizing, "if he touches you again his head will be severed in your honor."

The beast is unleashed as Abram fucks me savagely on the ground. I feel twigs and rocks biting into my thighs and back, blood dripping from the cuts on my hands and elbows all while Abram punishes me with his cock.

If this is the way I die, then I'll gladly go as long as I can come again.

Feeling another orgasm blooming in my core, I wrap around him with my arms and legs until I'm able to buck us forward. Abram allows me to take control and falls back onto his back so that I'm straddling him. My turn to take the lead.

I set a rapid pace as I race to the finish line - needing to come more than my next breath. My pussy grinds against Abram without abandon, without embarrassment as I take what I need. "Yes baby, fucking bounce on my cock. Let the forrest hear how beautiful are as you come all over us both."

"Fuck, Abram. I'm gonna, I'm gonna come…" My release hits us both and I feel Abrams cum filling me up to the brim as he comes with me. Both of us moaning into the other as his hands hold wherever he can reach and I continue bouncing on him until cum is leaking out of me and spilling down my bare legs.

Abram sucks one of my bleeding hands into his mouth and I swear his dick is already getting hard again. I don't know how someone can have the stamina this man does, but I would happily keep going. If I plan on walking out of these woods instead of being carried though, we better make it back to the house at least.

"You really do like the taste of my blood, don't you?" I ask as my body stays straddled around his waist.

"Baby, I love the taste of *you.*"

STOKER

chapter nineteen

♫

One Step Closer • Linkin Park

STOKER

This is the first job since being with Isolde. Hell, the first job in a while, actually. Ellis has been weirdly quiet lately - either using someone else for assignments, or it's just been quiet. Either way, I'm back on another lonely highway making my way out of town to fulfill a job I'm liking less and less lately.

It might be that I hate these long drives, hours on end driving empty roads until reaching my target. It might be because I can never fly to my assignments - too much of a risk being caught. Or it might be because the last few weeks my bed has been occupied by a bombshell with dark brown hair and eyes that see into my very soul. What soul I have left, that is.

Each time I've had to leave in the past it was a welcome break. Getting the job done, seeing a hefty amount of money shoveled into my bank account and fucking a random stranger until I felt satiated enough to go home. Rinse and repeat.

For years that setup has worked beautifully in my favor - except the seedy hotels Ellis always puts me up in. I've always wanted to ask him why, but it never seems worth it. He's a man of few words - if any at all - and I've never actually met him.

Some might wonder how I could possibly work for someone, doing this kind of work when I've never even seen their face. Well, to be honest I didn't give a shit at the time. My life felt out of control after my mom died - this job was a welcome distraction. A way to let my anger out without repercussions. Plus, I got paid.

As I edge closer to my destination, I notice a car parked in the driveway that shouldn't be there. It doesn't belong to one of the owners and no one else is supposed to be home. Ellis always gives me a full rundown of the area - cars, guest houses, etc. I even get blueprints to the home sometimes to ensure easy access without being caught. I study them like a school exam the days leading up to familiarize myself with the layout and any blind spots around the property.

My body is tense as I approach the black sedan with my concealed gun under my jacket - ready to draw it if needed. It takes a lot to rattle me, but having been on the job as long as I have seeing an unforeseen vehicle is slightly alarming.

A tall man with light brown hair and sharp features steps out of the car with ease. He's dressed in what looks to be a stupidly expensive suit and the ugliest fucking loafers I've ever seen. I kind of want to take him out just for looking like an entitled prick. Knowing I could take him if it comes to that, I exit my car as well.

The man smiles at me like we're old friends and opens his arms in a welcoming gesture that has me clenching my fists. Something about him is giving me a weird feeling of unease. "Always on time Mr. Stoker, how prompt."

His voice sounds oddly familiar, but I know I've never seen him. I want to ask who he is but my mouth stays clamped shut and he comes a little closer - close enough to smell his expensive, disgusting cologne. He watches me watch him, and that spine-chilling smile grows larger, giving off Pennywise vibes.

Why the fuck is he looking at me like he knows me? I have not the slightest idea who would be at this exact location at the exact time I'm supposed to take out… Fuck! I know who it is but it seems very strange he would be here right now when he never shows up to a job.

"Ellis?" I ask. Wanting to sound confident in my response but hearing the question in the air is agitating to say the least. I don't like being caught off guard and this interaction shoots to the top of the list for me.

"I always knew you were the best," he steeples his fingers in front of his unbuttoned blazer, an air of authority around him. Whenever we'e spoken on the phone - the few times he's called me instead of sending a text from some burner - he always sounded…normal. Now he almost seems a little unhinged.

And I would know what unhinged sounds like.

"Why are you here?" I'm unable to hold back asking that question any longer. The thoughts of why and how running around in my mind too fast for my liking.

"Oh, that," he chuckles like he forgot his grocery list at home. "The job has been completed by another colleague. I just wanted to meet you in person and figured luring you out on a job was the only way. I mean, you tempt a person with a lot of money and they'll do just about anything. Am I right?"

Fuck, he's a cocky dickhead. How could I have missed that?

"Okay, but that doesn't explain why you're here. Why not just meet me somewhere closer to home? Why make me drive five fucking hours for an impromptu meet up?" I'm trying to hide my irritation and judging by the flinch in his eyebrow, I'm doing a shit job at it. At the end of the day, no matter how harrowing his presence is, he's still my boss.

A crack chips in his bubbly, but fake, demeanor. Ellis has always been all business and I would much prefer he skip the asinine pleasantries and get to the real reason he dragged me out here.

"Isolde Davies."

I feel some of the blood drain from my face but quickly correct my features to look unfazed. I'm hoping it was quick enough for Ellis to miss, but judging by the way he's watching me so intently, I'd say he caught it.

"What about her?"

"I hear she's taken up residence in your podunk town. How quaint," he spits out with another fake smile. "Before you ask me why I'm inquiring about a seemingly waste of space nobody," he continues on and my teeth crack beneath my closed mouth at the way he's speaking about her.

"It is my job to find the women who have been brutalized, tortured and mistreated by another, and bring them peace. Which is where you always come in, my protégée."

Wow, I have never wanted to knock someone teeth in so completely until this moment. And I kill rapists for God's sake.

"Ms. Davies has been through a terrible ordeal, you see. Something I have no doubt you are aware of. I wish to see for myself that she gets the care she so desperately deserves."

"Ellis, not to be crass, but why the fuck do you care about some dumb chick? Sure, she's got a nice rack, but so do a ton of other women." My fingernails dig into my palms at the way I'm degrading my little bird. She deserves to be spoken highly of, not brought down to a low level of the nothing Ellis claims her to be.

"Because that is my job!" He roars into the dark night sky. His cool and collected facade is cracking with each passing minute and it's driving me mad that I can't figure out why.

Deciding I would rather end this conversation sooner rather than later - especially since my assignment was already completed - I direct us back to safer ground. "My apologies, sir. I was merely curious is all."

Ellis straightens his jacket, smoothing down wrinkles that aren't there and I think I've contained the beast a little. "I will gladly keep tabs on her and report back to you if anything seems off."

"Much appreciated," he says flatly. The sharp tone may be gone, but that fire still blazes just slightly in his eyes. A slow simmer that has the ability to rage again if I misspeak a second time. Carefully choosing my next words, hoping to extricate myself for this fucked up meeting, I step closer to my freak show of a boss and extend a hand.

Ellis takes it in his smaller one and shakes firmly. I nod my head in silent agreement and make my way back to my car, subtly trying to wipe the unpleasant feeling from my hands when his voice reaches me.

"I'll be seeing you again, Mr. Stoker." And with that he ducks his head into the open door of his flashy Mercedes Benz before speeding off.

I have five hours to drive home and ponder why coming all this way to meet me and ask about Isolde was so fucking important. When I spoke about her poorly, rage lit up his eyes. If I had to guess, I'd say Ellis is related to Isolde somehow and doesn't care too much for the way her ex, Grant, treated her all those years.

If that's the case then I will happily flip every rock and knock on every goddamn door to find the man who hurt her for fucking *years*. All he had to do was say that. So why do I still have an unsettling feeling about the man I have worked for, done countless dangerous jobs for and called my boss all these years?

ISOLDE

chapter twenty

♪

Young and Beautiful

• Lana Del Ray

"To what do I owe the pleasure, dear?" June asks from her seat at the kitchen table. We haven't been able to spend much time together lately - which is my fault - and I feel terrible about it. June became the mother I was missing - another thing that's on me - and I owe her so much for allowing me to stay here.

In fact, every time I try to thank her or I bring up how she literally saved my life, she just brushes me off like all she did was loan me some sugar. A true martyr.

"June, are we really going to play this game again?" I ask with a playful huff. She always brushes off compliments but a part of me is beginning to wonder if she loves to hear them, just doesn't know how to accept them. Something I am all too familiar with.

"Well then, a thank you is all that's needed I suppose," she chuckles before taking a sip of the fresh tea I brought over in one of the teapots Abram made her. I smile every time I see a piece of his artwork in her home, and she doesn't even know he made them all for her.

Taking a sip of my own peppermint tea - seemed appropriate with the cold weather coming in - I narrow my gaze at her until I know she feels it boring into the side of her face.

I shouldn't be nervous, but I am, I can't help it. June gave me a huge responsibility in fixing up the manor, and while I'm so grateful, it would kill me if I let her down, even a little. Alex has reassured me over and over again that she's going to love it, but I have to see for myself.

"Out with it, dear," she laughs around the brim of her cup, eyeing me like I was her just moments ago. "I can tell you want to say something, so spit it out so I can enjoy this wonderful tea you made."

I laugh with her, enjoying the playful banter she always dishes out knowing it's just for fun. June doesn't have a mean bone in her body.

Twisting my hands in my lap, keeping my eyes trained on the movements, I try to figure out how to tell her the house is done. A part of why I'm afraid is I'm not sure what comes next. Sure, I've been working at the bar and saving up, but not enough to move out. I wouldn't dream of encroaching on either Alex or Abrams space - even if they did insist - because everything between the three of us is still so new. That and Abram distinctly said he would chop his brothers head off if he touched me again.

So, there's that.

"June…the manor is done." The words settle in the space between us, heavy and weightless at the same time. Like a lead balloon has been lifted off my chest but only to be replaced by a mask stifling my breathing. She could tell me to move out now. She could easily say I've completed what she asked of me and it's time to find a place of my own. A part of me knows she wouldn't because of how amazing she's been so far - but still, a small part of me worries.

"That's wonderful, Isolde! Oh gosh, I can't wait to see it restored to it's former beauty but with a Ms. Davies twist on it." She gushes for several beats before catching the look on my face I'm trying so hard to mask.

"Why do you look upset, dear?" Her once beaming smile and excited tone turn warm and comforting, like her soft hand that's now holding mine in a reassuring grip.

"I don't know," I sniffle, mad that any emotion is seeping out. "I guess I just don't know what happens from here. I-I promised to fix up the house in exchange for a place to stay, and I've been so grateful June, I hope you know that."

"Oh I know, honey. You tell me at least fifty times a day," she says with a playful eye roll.

When I don't continue, recognition flashes across her face and before I know it she's scrambling to her feet, pulling me along with her. "My darling Isolde, I hope you didn't think that because you finished the house I would simply kick you to the curb. Did you?"

"No. I mean, maybe a little I guess," I reply sheepishly. "Not that I think you would do something so abrupt like that, but I guess I just assumed since I finished… you'd maybe want me to find a place of my own. I wouldn't blame you, after all."

June scoffs, shaking her head like she's just heard the most ridiculous thing and it makes me smirk a little. Sometimes she can be so theatric, it makes me love her even more.

"Well, that would be a pretty shitty thing to do, wouldn't it?"

We both laugh at her use of a curse word - they're few and far between in her vocabulary - as she turns me to face her fully. Both hands hold mine as she watches me with careful eyes. "Isolde, I gave you that project so you would find some motivation, feel a sense of purpose. I wanted you to find that confidence buried inside you that some man tried to strip you of. Something he wasn't able to succeed in if you ask me."

A few more tears slide down my cheek and I swat at the traitorous liquid causing June to grin. "Sweetheart, I wanted you to fix up the manor and make it something you would love and be proud of so *you* could live there."

Her confession hits me like a bomb and my body goes still as stone as her words sink in. "What?" I whisper, almost to myself, but she hears me.

"No one has lived there in years, and yes it may have a sordid past, but that doesn't mean it can't have a hopeful future. You and that house are one in the same if you ask me. All you needed was something good to bring you out of the darkness. That manor is meant for you, Isolde."

Tears well in my eyes, falling down my face like Niagara Falls as I hug June and thank her repeatedly. I can't believe this woman who is so full of love and compassion exists and is one of the most important people in my life.

"Now, quit all this crying and show me the damn house! I've been dying to take a peak but wanted to wait for you to be done and surprise me."

Wiping my eyes, I beam at her, thrilled that I can finally show her around. Show her all the hard work not only myself has put in, but Abram and Alex as well.

***

June loved the manor - just as much as I hoped she would. Even more with the way she gushed over the wallpaper in the dining room - her idea - and the tiniest details throughout the house. She especially loved what we did with the basement. Gone is the creepy, musty basement that I was once too afraid to step foot in alone. Now it's a completely renovated recreational room with an open floor plan, equipped with an entertainment center and plenty of room for a pool table.

As promised, the panic room indeed stayed in place and something about having it there makes me feel more at ease. Even more now that I know I get to occupy this home and call it my own - something I'm still not over the shock of.

Goosebumps line my arms as I stare at the small room made to keep out the monsters of my nightmares, and I feel a pang of guilt I haven't told the guys everything about Grant. I got another text message last night, and this one scared me more than all the rest. It made me feel like he's closing in on me - like he's close enough to smell my fear. Something the sick asshole gets off on.

Not the way Abram enjoys my fear - that's entirely different because all I have to do is tell him to stop and he will. That's exactly why he gave me a safe word - so that we both knew my limits and not to cross them. He's been patient with me in more aspects than one, Alex too. I honestly don't know how they can share me the way they have been and not want to rip the other's head off in jealousy.

I know I wouldn't be able to handle sharing either of them with another woman - call me selfish, but it would kill me.

Aside from the one threat Abram made about severing his own brothers head, things have been oddly calm. Which is exactly why that text last night through me off balance. I began moving what little belongings I have into the manor and started shopping for furniture. The house is huge and surely I don't need all that space, but it feels good to put my energy into something good rather than obsessing over the maniac still coming for me.

My screen lights up as I unlock it and stare at the simple, yet haunting, message from Grant.

I promised you a long time ago, I would never let you go. I'm not leaving until I uphold that promise, Princess.

My body shakes with silent trembles as I feel the threat settle deep in my bones. No matter how much I busy myself, I can't shake the feeling that he's closer than I feared. Why the hell else would he say he's not leaving until upholding his promise? My head keeps screaming at me to tell the guys, that they deserve to know and maybe can help somehow. But my heart - the stupid organ that's in love with both of them - wants to sneak away in the quiet dark night and draw Grant away from this peaceful place.

I can't even fathom him hurting either of them, or June. It makes my stomach roll with unease and my eyes sting with unshed tears.

A car door shuts outside, causing me to jump up from the little bench I've been dwelling on. Alex said he was going to meet me here to take a look around to help with measurements for furniture - but that little message plays on a loop in my mind, making me frightened of every little sound.

"Baby! Are you here?" Alex yells from the foyer, helping my heart settle a little as I ascend the stairs and meet his smiling face. The same face that brings a warmth and a lightness to every day I'm around him.

"Hey," I greet him with a somber voice, one I quickly try to eradicate before he notices. "Ready to help me pick out furniture?" I say with fake excitement, something he thankfully sees right through. As much as I love Alex, he's easier to distract whereas Abram won't let the tiniest thing slide - always seeing deep into my mind as if he can read it like his favorite novel.

"I was thinking we should start with a new bed…" I watch Alex's eyes roam over my curves, assessing and appreciating my body in ways I've grown to love and even welcome. He slowly draws them up, settling at the apex of my thighs as I rub them together under his hooded gaze.

It's almost embarrassing how quickly he can get me turned on.

"Alex," I warn. Though I'm not sure I want him to stop his perusal. The feel of his eyes devouring my body is similar to the way his fingers dance over my skin, caressing the most sensitive parts of me.

"Mmm, I think I want to play a little game of hide and seek. What do you think, baby?"

"H-hide and seek? There's not even any furniture in here yet!" I balk even though I really do want to play. The way his mind seems to be working has me hoping this little game won't really be about hiding as much as seeking.

Before any words leave his mouth, I take off in a sprint, racing up the stairs and clutching the newly polished banister in hopes I don't accidentally fall. Before I reach the top landing, I hear his heavy footsteps close behind me as he takes the stairs two at a time. Shit, I should have done that.

I'm already losing ground so I quickly throw open one of the upstairs bedroom doors and slam it shut, locking it in place just as Alex tries to push it open. Racing to the other side of the room I go to close the door with the adjoining bathroom, but I'm not fast enough. Alex slowly makes his way into the room, eyes searing into mine as he shuts the bathroom door behind him.

I shuffle backwards as he stalks towards me with a fire in his eyes, until my back hits the wall. I didn't realize as I raced up here that I automatically came into the master bedroom - a large room with a massive walk in closet. I don't have a ton of clothes to utilize the space, but over time I hope to change that.

"Well, well," Alex clicks his tongue as he glances around the sparse room. "Looks like my plan worked after all."

"I didn't even get a chance to hide, you asshole," I roll my eyes playfully, knowing what the gesture does to him.

"Babygirl, did you just roll those beautiful eyes of yours at me?"

Gulping audibly, I look around for something to slow him down, something to distract him with, but there's literally nothing in here. "That won't work, you know."

"And what exactly are you referring to?" I ask with growing excitement.

"There's nothing in here that could distract me from those pouty lips I want to shove my cock through. Or those piercing eyes I want on me as I thrust into you so hard, June will be able to hear what I'm doing to you."

Jesus, why does the sound of that turn me on and melt my insides into a puddle of desire?

I love messing with him, because he can actually take it without letting words get under his skin. Taking a hesitant small step towards him, I watch his eyes flare slightly as I close the distance between us. "That's if you can," I challenge.

A quirk blur, and I'm pressed back into the wall I just vacated as Alex pushes his front against mine - crushing my body into the newly painted midnight blue walls. I wanted an edgy vibe for the bedroom and this color felt perfect.

Laughing against my cheek, Alex plays with the strands of hair that have fallen out of my ponytail. "You and I both know how loud I can make you scream. Isn't that right, baby?"

Desire pools between my thighs and no amount of pressure relieves the building ache in my core. I would never have been able to choose between the two of them - I needed the darkness and the light to find my way out of the hole I'd been living in.

"Say it," he commands as one finger lightly traces the space between my breasts before settling at the button on my jeans.

Nibbling my lip, I watch him closely but refuse to say anything. I love to watch the desire build in him, waiting for it to blow over the top until he can't take it anymore and has me the way he wants. Alex has always been the caretaker, more gentle and considerate of my feelings. But all these weeks with them both, I've come to realize I crave the darker side sometimes. The way Abram has pushed me almost past my limits but never too far where I fear I won't be able to handle it.

There's a side of Alex that wants that too - I can sense it in the way he hold back sometimes - but he allows the fear of hurting me keep him from taking it. If I'm able to work past my fears, then I want him to as well.

"I will…under one condition," I finally say. "No holding back."

His eyes ping back and forth between mine, looking for any indication I might be joking. He won't find anything, though. If he wants me as bad as he says, then I want him to have me the way he craves. "Isolde," he whispers. Tiny fragments of that timidness deep inside coming to the surface. I want to free him of that feeling, assure him I can handle whatever he gives me.

I'm not sure he knows what Abram has already taken - I prefer to keep our private interactions just that, private. I also don't want to make it some kind of competition, they've allowed me to have them both and I can only hope they both treat me the way they would if they were my only.

"Please," I breathe against the hand still holding my cheek in a loving caress.

Eyes never leaving mine, I watch the dam inside him break and can't help the victorious feeling that washes over me. The hold he has on my face turns branding as he slides it to the base of my neck and tilts my head up, ripping at loose tendrils of hair.

"I've never felt comfortable enough with a woman to show this side of me. I…" his voice trails off and I don't want him to shut down now that I've gotten him to open up a little. I've never felt unsafe with Alex, and I want him to trust me as much as I trust him. To trust that I know he will stop if it becomes too much.

"Show me," I plead.

Brows furrowed slightly, he grips my neck even tighter and I feel the prickle of pain at the base of my neck. "Fuck," he curses before slamming me into the wall and lifting my legs around his waist. His mouth finds mine in a heated frenzy, and he bites down on my tongue as I slip it past his lips.

Groaning into him, I push my pelvis against his hard body, seeking the friction I so desperately need as his hands squeeze the flesh of my hips. "Alex, please," I manage to get out before he bites into my tongue again, tasting the tang of blood on both of us.

"Shh, you don't get to make the calls right now baby. You wanted this," he growls into my ear as a free hand reaches into my shirt and past my bra to pinch a already hard nipple between his pointer and thumb. Alex swallows my cries of pleasure before pulling back to look me in the eyes. "I'm going to take whatever I want from this greedy little cunt."

My nails dig into his back, ripping tiny holes through the cotton of his shirt as a hot need rips through me. Alex works the button of my jeans open as I yank his shirt over his head. I don't know how he manages to hold me up while pulling the material over his head with one hand, but it's my new favorite thing.

His voice caresses my ear in feather light softness as he lowers me to the floor, but his words are sharp and dangerous as he works my jeans down my thighs. "Take them off," his voice is demanding as he stands there staring at me with his hands on his exposed hips. "Slowly."

I do as I'm told, enjoying the hungry look on his face as I reveal my white cotton thong. A barely there scrap of material that's wet with evidence of what he does to me. His hungry gaze turns practically feral once he notices the wet fabric on display for him - solidifying my need for his touch.

"Go stand next to that window," he points a finger to the front window - the one that looks over the front yard of the property towards June's house and the dirt driveway leading to the manor. There are no blinds or curtains on the window and a part of me feels nervous I'm about to be on full display.

Anyone could come down the road and see me standing here hold naked and fully aroused, but I do as I'm told nonetheless.

"Good girl, now loose the shirt."

Hesitating only for a moment, I remove my gray long sleeve shirt until I'm left standing in my thong and matching white bralette. A spark of approval ignites Alex's eyes and I revel in the unspoken compliment. Every time he looks at me like this it's as if his eyes are saying all the things his words can't convey. It's addictive.

"Perfection," he hums in a low sultry voice. "Now, face the window and place your hands on the windowsill."

Turning away from his heated stare, I can still feel the intensity of it on my backside as he slides up to me and grips both asscheeks in his hands. "Has anyone been here before?" I know what he's asking but a part of me doesn't know the real truth. I've never willingly done that, but Grant used to drug and rape me so I honestly don't know.

My lack of response has him stiffening slightly because he knows my past and he knows the likelihood of me doing anal was because someone took without asking. His fingers toy with the hem of my thong, sliding towards the cleft of my ass and I can't help the way my body tightens at his soft touch.

"Relax baby, I won't take anything you don't want to voluntarily give me. I just want to make you feel good, desired."

He always does. Doesn't he know that by now? I want to tell him how cherished, how wanted he makes me feel just by looking at me. But I miss the chance when a finger lazily circles the opening to my back hole just as another reaches into my underwear and sinks into me.

My back arches into him as I let myself go to the sensation of both fingers toying with me in ways I've never experienced. The touch behind me in foreign, almost uncomfortable while the one in front is making my knees tremble. The mixture of both is making my head dizzy and a deeper part of me doesn't want him to stop.

"Breathe through your nose and relax. Let me in," he murmurs. I do my best to relax, focusing more on the finger in my pussy rather than the one probing the opening of my ass as he slides a second one in the front. I move towards the feeling, needing more just as a single digit slips past the opening of my back hole and begins massaging my insides slowly. "That's it, good girl."

"Fuck, it feels weird, but also kind of good," I confess. Unsure of how to explain the sensations he's drawing out of me.

"I'll always make you feel good, baby. If it gets to be too much, let me know. Understand?"

I nod my head in agreement as I feel the finger slowly pull out of me. Alex keeps fingering me with one hand as I hear the buckle of his belt and jeans hit the floor in unison. The head of his cock lines up at my wet center and he replaces two fingers with his shaft, pushing into me with a slow agonizing pace.

Pushing my ass towards him, I feel his light chest hair tickle my back as he wraps an arm around my chest, pulling me closer. My bralette is ripped away from my boobs and my hard peaks pebble against the cool glass causing a soft whimper to leave my lips. God, I hope June isn't home right now because I would never be able to face her again if she saw what was happening.

"No one can see us, baby. Stop worrying." Did I walk right into a family of mind readers? I don't know how they can always tell what I'm thinking before I even say it - I must be that predictable.

"I don't even care anymore, just keep going."

Alex pumps into me, *hard,* and I cry out in bliss. As one hand holds my hips steady while he thrusts into me from behind, I feel a finger press into my backside again. Not as nervous as a few minutes ago, I relax at his touch and arch into his finger, seeking the unfamiliar sensation. It slips inside a little easier than before and I gasp at the intrusion.

The feeling of being so full overwhelms me and I feel an orgasm building quickly. Alex matches the thrust of his finger with his cock as he takes what he wants from me, giving me just as much pleasure in return. He taps the side of my thigh, "lift this leg up, place it on the windowsill."

As soon as I lift my leg I feel the shift in the angle, throwing my head back against Alex's shoulder and moaning to the empty room. Our pants and moans of pleasure echo around the space as the glass fogs up in front of my face from my heavy breathing.

"Your gripping me so tight, fucking hell," he grunts from behind me, never missing a beat as his thrusts pick up speed once more. "I can't wait to sink my cock into this tight hole of yours, claiming all of you."

The building pressure in my core comes to a head as I feel the first waves of my orgasm crash into me. It's intensity is almost too much and I scream loud enough to startle the birds in the tree across from us. Alex keeps moaning words of encouragement and pleasure beside me as he races towards his own finish.

Ripples of desire keep coming as the orgasm stretches on and on. I hardly notice when Alex pulls out of me abruptly, replacing his finger with the head of his cock. I'm about to say no when I feel him spit against my ass, rubbing himself up and down the slit of my ass. He won't hurt me, I know he won't. I chant that to myself as I focus on the orgasm slowly subsiding rather than the sharp stretching feeling behind me.

Alex pushes two fingers into me, thrusting hard and fast drawing another orgasm out of me as his cock pushes into the tight opening of my ass. It hurts but the feel of his fingers massaging my clit and the way my nipples keep rubbing against the cool glass eases the discomfort.

"Almost there," he mumbles into my shoulder, biting the exposed flesh like it's helping him not ram into me the way I know he's dying to. Each muscle relaxes as he slowly glides in farther and farther and I feel my body give itself over to the pleasure, rather than focusing on the tightness.

"Fuck me, please. I can take it," I reassure him knowing his control is slipping. I can practically feel it radiating against my back as he pushes into me a little more, achingly slow.

"I don't want to hurt you, baby," he confesses.

Giving him the only encouragement I know how, I push my butt backwards as hard as I can until all of him is sheathed inside me. I've never felt as full as I do now, and there's something deliciously erotic about the way this feels. "I want this, Alex. Please, don't hold back anymore. I trust you."

His muscles rippled beneath me, next to me and all around me as he pulls out and thrusts back in so hard I feel my bones rattle. My cries of pain mix with my moans of pleasure, beads of perspiration dotting my hairline as Alex fucks my ass with unrelenting force.

I can't even begin to explain why I like the feeling as much as I do, the way I crave the pain to make me feel less guilty about enjoying the pleasure. But Alex gives into the desire, the need to fill me as he pumps into me over and over again, drawing out yet another orgasm.

I feel my body give out as a strangled scream hits the window, only being held up by the hand Alex has wrapped around my middle. We both go still as his own release crashes into him, leaving behind the evidence of how hard he came. His cum is leaking out of me and down my legs, and I don't have it in me to feel embarrassed anymore.

I'm standing naked in the window with sweat, cum and probably some blood sliding down my body with zero remorse or regrets. I'm sick of feeling bad for the pleasure I allow my body to enjoy. I've never experienced love like this and it's time I take what I want too.

"Shit baby, are you okay?" The soft, sweet Alex comes back to the forefront and the concern in his voice has me wanting to cry. Not tears of sadness but tears of gratitude. It's overwhelming to say the least and I can't help the tears once they've started to fall.

Turning me around to face him, I see the way his eyes goes wide with panic as he takes in my tears. "Fuck, I'm so sorry baby. I shouldn't have gone that far, I should have stopped." He starts reaching for parts of me that might be hurt, gently caressing my skin and peppering me with sweet kisses.

Covering his mouth with my hand, I shake my head to stop his panicked rambling. "I'm okay. You didn't hurt me, I promise. I just…" I don't know how else to explain to him how I feel in this moment. How to express how truly cared for he makes me feel.

"I've never been cared for the way you and Abram care for me, sometimes it's overwhelming," I begin. "In a good way," I add when he looks pained at the word overwhelming like it's a bad thing.

"You let go just now. You trusted me enough to show this side of you, and I…I love you, Alex."

His eyes look glassy as he searches my face for any regret I might feel at allowing that confession to slip free. But all I feel is relief. Offering him a small smile, I sense the hesitation melt away as his eyes hold mine with deep concentration. "About time you caught up babygirl. I love you too."

Sometimes it really is as simple as that.

STOKER

chapter twenty-one

♫

So Called Life • Three Days Grace

This job feels different. Every other job I've been assigned has been far enough away from home I don't have to worry about looking over my shoulder for someone I know recognizing me. But ever since I met Ellis in person, the way he obsessed over Isolde, things have felt...*off.*

I was tempted to ask her about him, see if maybe she knew him from back home. But I didn't want to worry her about something seemingly insignificant. While his delivery was unnerving, the sentiment behind his words was positive at least. I think.

His entire job is to find and protect women from abusive relationships. That's why he has me - the man he sends out to kill off the scum of the earth, wiping out as many as he can find. I was easily on board with his mission when I first encountered him, and this is why.

The guy may look like a complete tool - dressing like a pompous rich guy and smelling like a teenager from an Abercrombie & Fitch campaign - but his purpose has never wavered.

Hence why I am here, outside Pour Performer ready to take out yet another piece of shit walking around freely when he should be six feet under. Six feet isn't far enough if you ask me. I'd happily dig holes deeper to ensure their trip to hell is as close as possible.

This is the only assignment, since completing my first, that I feel the nervous tremor in my bones. Not because I'm afraid to kill - in all honesty I get a high from it. But because of where I am. Ellis has always respected my need to complete jobs far from home. So why is it different now?

Something feels wrong about this whole thing, but I can't fight him on it. I'm under contract and not completing an assignment means I don't receive my bonus. I know that sounds fucked, because at the end of the day the money isn't why I do this work, but I'd be lying if I said it didn't help.

All I was given was a name, where to find the guy and to report to Ellis once it's done. Not something new.

I get this prickly feeling at the base of my neck like someone is watching me, keeping me on high alert more than before. If Ellis is close by and watching then maybe this is a test of some sort. Not sure why the fuck I need to be tested when I've proven my loyalty time and time again, but whatever.

Isolde isn't working tonight, thankfully, so I don't have to worry about her coming out and finding me murdering a lowlife rapist. I'm not entirely sure how that conversation would go if I'm being honest. Something like, *"hey little bird, I want to be transparent with you and let you know what I do for work..."*

I can picture the look of horror now as if she's standing in front of me. She would undoubtably be terrified of me and that's the last thing I need. I'll do anything to protect her at this point - I'm so far in she doesn't even realize it. I act like nothing gets to me, when in reality everything concerning her has me on edge and ready to take out an entire town to prove my love and devotion.

I'm aware that's not healthy, but nothing in my life is. Not for a very long time.

I witnessed my mother's murder and did nothing to stop it. Sure, I was only a kid, but standing there and watching the life drain from her eyes changed the very fabric of my soul. I refuse to allow such a thing to occur a second time. If that means I continue getting my hands dirty to protect the ones who can't protect themselves, then so be it.

My target emerges from the bar, staggering in the street towards his beat up car. He's not a local, no one I've seen before, and I thank whatever deity above for that.

It's already dark out, the streets only dimly lit by flickering streetlights that never got fixed. An ominous fog floats over the damp concrete, setting the scene for what's to come. I want this one to be quick - not feeling the rush of excitement I usually do at the prospect of killing. I'm unsettled enough as it is, I don't want to risk drawing this out and getting caught by my kindergarten teacher for fucks sake.

You better believe she still lives here.

With uneasy steps, he fumbles with his keys as he makes his way to a beat up rusted car parked on the street. Drawing in a drag from my cigarette, I flip the lighter in my hand over and over. A nervous habit I used to brush off, never wanting to appear fazed. But everything about this job makes me uneasy.

I follow the man's footsteps around the side of the bar where his car is parked and take in the way he tries to open the lock with what appears to be a house key. Something I've grown to love is taking out the ones who use the bottom of a bottle to solve their problems. They're always so far gone I can catch them as easily as a moth to a flame.

Occasionally it takes the fun out of the hunt - getting to chase down the clear minded ones who practically ooze fear from their pores is a high I'll never get enough of.

"Hey buddy, need some help there?" I offer in a seemingly kind gesture. One he gobbles up with unknowing pleasure. That'll be the last of it for him, so I allow him to indulge.

"Yeah, th-thanks man," he leans his left shoulder against the side of the front door. "These ke-keys won't work." His swaying has paused due to the way his body uses his car as support so I take this opportunity to grab the back of his neck and slam it onto the hood. The resounding thunk echoes in the air around us, muting all other noises as his shrill shrieking pierces my ears.

I fucking hate it when they yell. Pisses me off more than when my neighbor's dog growing up would bark first thing in the morning. Pretty sure the little fucker thought of itself as a rooster.

Using one hand, I slap a firm grip over his mouth, dragging his flailing body against my own. He smells like cheap whiskey and stale cigarettes. No wonder he had to rape his coworker - no one would willingly get close to the disgusting man before me.

"You're going to listen now, got it?" I ask quietly, not giving him air to breathe let alone respond. "You've done some fucked up things, am I right?"

The man hesitates, not wanting to give too much without realizing I already know his darkest secrets. After a two second pause, my grip over his mouth and nose tightening, he nods once.

"Good boy, cooperating is only going to speed this process along faster. Not that it benefits you in the end, but I'd really like to finish this unpleasant meeting as quickly as possible."

His shit brown eyes widen in fear, realization of impending pain seeping into his clogged pores. Years of not taking care of oneself and getting away with rape will dirty a person from the inside of their lifeless soul to each wrinkled crater on their face. And he has many.

"I'll be honest with you, I usually enjoy the hell out of myself knowing I get to personally rid the planet of creeps like you. But tonight, I'm feeling impatient and I'd prefer to spend my evening fucking my girl so far into the mattress she won't be able to move tomorrow morning."

Someone walking by wouldn't miss the way his muscles tighten slightly at the mere mention of sex. He really is grotesque in all the ways one can be. The man is about to be wiped off the face of the earth, nothing left behind but his lifeless rotting body. Creating a stench for everyone nearby to recognize the piece of shit that he always was and was able to hide until death beckoned for him. Hope he rots in hell with the rest of the assholes I've had the delightful pleasure of taking out.

Pulling a knife from my jacket, I hold the blunt side of the blade up to his throat. "Any last words?" He begins bucking himself wildly, hoping to break free of my iron clad grip on his face and body. I'll give it to him, he has some fight in him. A lot of them are too far gone to recognize their impending demise - this guy lit a fire under his own ass to prevent the sharp slide of my knife cutting open his throat so he can bleed out all his demons onto the sidewalk.

Too bad for him that won't be happening. Growing tired of the fight already, I quickly slash a cut through his throat before allowing his body to drop to the wet ground and crumple into the pathetic ball that he is. His gurgles are soft as the blood pours out of him in quick succession, guaranteeing a quick retreat from this mess and an early night home with my girl.

Lighting up a new cigarette, I wait another minute before firing off the text signaling the cleanup crew to come in and handle the mess. Business like this is straightforward since most of the targets don't have anyone in their lives that would care about them when they ultimately go missing.

Such a shame.

As soon as I'm about to round the building and head back to my bike I catch the sight of beautiful hazel eyes, wide in horror gazing between me and the man dead at my feet. My heart thumps wildly in my chest as I watch my little bird slowly back away, eyes never leaving mine. Shit.

Without thinking I might scare her even further, I run towards her and watch as she trips over herself before sprinting down the street to where her car is. She wasn't supposed to be here tonight! I knew something felt off the moment I got this assignment and knowing I couldn't exactly turn it down, I went through with it anyways - risks be damned.

This was not the kind of risk worth taking though. I never got a chance to explain to her what I do and why it's actually important work aside from the killing part.

I can practically taste her terror as she runs in front of me, the fear mixing with the delicate scent of her soft skin and the lavender aroma that always has me feeling weak. Like a little kid again ready to give her my whole lunch if she asks me.

Trying to calm my racing heart, I yell out to her as if she might turn around and give me a chance to explain. "Isolde, stop!" Nope. She keeps running like she's been secretly training for a marathon I didn't know about.

Her past comes into focus as I imagine her running from her abusive ex. Desperately trying to outrun the monster that he is knowing what he's capable of doing when he catches her. Bile rises in my throat at the thought of him hurting her. I promised myself I would never let anything like that hurt her again and here I am chasing her down in the street like the maniac I know I am deep down.

If I have to tie her down and make her listen, then I will. Consequences be damned.

"Baby, stop. You know I'll catch you eventually." Her steps falter just before she reaches her car. Her movements seizing completely as she drags in shaky breaths. One after another, attempting to calm herself down in the face of someone she likely sees as another monster.

Straightening her shoulders, I watch her reign in whatever confidence she can find and turn to face me. A look of terror mixed with defiance shining back at me. I want to bend her over this car and fuck her fast and hard while she listens to me explain what she just saw.

Probably won't go over well, so I give her the time to speak first.

"Wh-what the fuck was that?"

I resist the urge to say she knows what the fuck she just saw, figuring an attitude won't bode well for me. Her eyes rake over me like she's trying to understand how she missed something so monumental about me. How I could possibly be the man she thought I was and also be capable of taking another's life. I know this is my moment to get it all out - the way she did that day she told Alex and I about her ex. She let her guard down and allowed us into a darker part of herself.

She might not like it but that's what I have to do here and now. Knowing I might not ever get the chance to again - she's a flight risk as it is.

"My job," I respond dryly. Letting the first portion soak into her mind.

"Y-you, murder people for a living?! Jesus, Stoker! How am I supposed to accept something like that when you present it so simply? You're not reciting a fucking grocery list!"

My teeth grind together when she says the name I hate to hear fall from those delectable lips. I've told her multiple times I allow only one person to call me Abram, and whenever she uses the name everyone else does, it feels like she's minimizing the bond we've built.

"Don't, little bird. We've talked about this before," I warn.

"Oh, fuck you! I think we're past the name part for the time being. Why don't you start explaining why I just witnessed you murder a man in fucking public for Christ's sake!"

She's too emotional, too worked up right now. Nothing I say is going to get through but I'm also aware she won't willingly go anywhere with me to talk. Not with the way her breathing has picked up again. The sweat lining her hairline isn't helping either. She'll send herself into cardiac arrest before sitting down to talk about everything.

So, I do the only thing I can think of to distract her - I kiss her. Enjoying the way her sweet taste calms my black soul. Praying to whatever God there is that this won't be the last time I have her like this. Her body tries to pull away, but the hand gripped around her neck holding her to me won't allow such nonsense.

Within seconds her body melts into mine, recognizing the comfort of my touch like a second skin. Using the distraction of her body's reaction to mine, I deepen the kiss. Holding her body hostage against my own like a human cage unwilling to release her from my confines. She doesn't realize not only does my body have her in my chokehold, but my heart as well.

Love has never been something I thought enough about to even consider feeling. A useless emotion in every way if you ask me. But this woman has pulled things out of me and breathed life into my heartless mind in more ways than one. She couldn't possibly understand the way I would level cities for her - take out any monster from her past and future just to keep her safe. It's frightening the way I would die for her and she has no fucking idea.

Breaking the spell, she pushes against me hard enough to have me stumbling backwards. The gravel shuffles beneath my feet as I steady myself. Seems my little bird was using my need to feel her as a distraction of her own. She creates more distance as her eyes ping back and forth across my face and tight gripped fists by my sides. A look of horror passes over her and I realize she actually thinks I might hurt her to keep her quiet.

"Wipe that look off your face, little bird."

"What look?" She whispers in response.

"The one you're wearing like a neon red sign of fear and questioning. I would never," I pause, taking a slow step closer to her with quiet ease. "*Never*, hurt you."

Before biting her lower lip, I watch it tremble slightly, waiting to see which emotions will win out over her racing mind.

"Hurt *for* you, yes. I would take out every single person who so much as looked at you the wrong way. But don't ever fear me, baby. I told you that when we first met - it's the only thing I ask."

"Do you remember my response, Abram?"

I do, I remember her telling me she doesn't even know me. That she couldn't possibly trust me without knowing anything about me. That isn't the case anymore - Isolde knows me better than anyone else ever has. Or has ever tried to.

"You do know me, little bird," I remind her.

"No I don't! I thought I did, I thought…I thought you were dark around the edges, sure - but not a monster who kills people in the dark of night."

I want to slap her ass so hard for that comment, knowing I am a monster but only one for her and people who have dark pasts like her. Not the kind of monster she's making me out to be. Not the kind of monster like her lunatic ex who got off on hurting and raping her.

"You hurt people, Stoker!" There's that name again. I'm about to throw her over my knee and teach her a goddamn lesson, prying eyes be damned. I already killed a man outside her place of work and the clean up crew hasn't even come by yet.

"I've seen it, and I can't unsee what just happened. That's not," she heaves a breath, trying to gain a semblance of composure in this fucked up situation. "That's not something I can get behind."

I inch closer to her, wincing at the way she backs up slightly, matching my steps one for one. Gripping her throat, I tip her head back to ensure her eyes are on me. She's putting on a bravery act, one I can see right through like a freshly wiped window. Doesn't she know how well I know her by now? That I've studied her facial expressions enough to understand what she's feeling before it fully registers in her own mind.

"I do hurt people, Isolde." I love the way her eyes flicker with hurt when I don't use her nickname. Hurts, doesn't it baby? "It's literally my fucking job, and I'll continue to do so because someone has to."

"But you know what, little bird?" I lean into her, holding her hazel eyes captive, making sure I have her full attention. "You're capable of hurting people too."

Those same eyes bug out of their sockets slightly before she rights her face, another wave of anger taking over. "I would never do something like that!" She shrieks as she points to the street where the dead body stills lies. Thankfully he's not under a street light.

"Tell me something," I say before she has a chance to respond to my previous statement. "If someone needed help, needed saving in some way, would you help?"

The wheels in her brain start turning, processing each word as I speak. Without too much thought, she nods her head and I hold back the grin threatening to emerge at her compliance. I've got her.

"If someone was coming after them, and you knew the only way you could help was to eliminate them entirely, would you pull that trigger or let them run for the rest of their life? Always looking around the corner, always checking over their shoulder and wondering if their own personal demon was lurking in the darkness just waiting to strike."

Her eyes close for a moment, reopening with tears that spill down her flushed cheeks. The pain engraved on her face causes me physical pain. I know it hurt to hear it that way, knowing I was describing her current life. She's always checking over her shoulder, looking for the man that nearly broke her as if we don't all notice. She thinks no one can see her inner struggle when she hides behind a smile and false pleasantries.

I've seen her do it at work as well - acting like everything is fine, interacting with customers and coworkers. But as soon as she turns her back, the worry is there. She can never fully hide it - no amount of concealer can erase the demons of her past. And as much as I've tried to ensure her safety in this town with me, and even my brother, I can't take it all away knowing the sick bastard is still out there looking for her.

Inching closer to her, I pull her lithe body flush against my chest. Feeling like the beast holding onto Belle like she's the most precious thing in his world. Within seconds her body relaxes into my touch - tears staining my shirt. I'll hold all of her tears if it means her mind can be lighter.

"You don't get it," she sobs against my chest. My heart breaks a little more each time I feel the tremors rack her body. "You don't know what it's like to feel haunted by a past you have no control over."

She doesn't know the full story about my mother, unless Alex or June filled in the blanks. We're more alike than she realizes and she needs to understand she's not alone in this. That we're here for her even if she feels like she's fighting her demons alone.

"Yeah, I do fucking get it little bird." Pulling her back, I fix her with a stare, making sure she sees how much I get it. "Everyone has walls, and if you can't tear them down then you find the right fucking equipment and fight your way through them, over them, whatever it fucking takes."

Eyes I could get lost in, swim in for days on end without growing weary, lock onto mine. I can feel the pain in those eyes like it's palpable. Like her pain is now somehow my own, a pain I can feel restricting my breathing in an invisible way. "It's not always that simple," she sighs.

"Yeah, baby, it really is."

I'm not sure we've made any progress here. If this was just another way to distract me so she can bolt again. But the way she searches my face - like she's looking for answers - has me feeling a confidence I probably shouldn't that she'll at least hear me out.

My entire existence has been devoted to taking out the men who have hurt and abused women, knowing they weren't going to get caught for it. Whether it be a lowlife nobody that lives in the gutter, or a high profile lawyer who comes across like Prince Charming in public. If she allows me to explain what she saw, she might understand why I wasn't just murdering some man in the street. I was taking out the monster that a tired girl is sick of looking around every corner for.

I may have killed him, but by that action alone I've given that young girl a chance to live again. To delight in the freedom that was ruthlessly taken from her at such a young age. I've given her hope that lightness can come from even the darkest depths.

All I need to accomplish now is gaining back the trust of the only woman I've ever once considered presenting my black heart to. Hoping I can convince her to accept my warped form of love.

ISOLDE

chapter twenty-two

Iris • Goo Goo Dolls

In the last few years, everything in my life has felt like a fight. A fight to get away from my abusive boyfriend. A fight to find myself again after years of hiding inside the shelf of the person I once was. Now I feel like I'm fighting my instincts to turn and run from this town that just an hour ago felt like my slice of solace.

I can't get the look of the man Abram killed out of my mind. The way his eyes lost what little light was left in them. His body, crumpled to the cold concrete beneath him as Abram stood above him like this was any ordinary day for him. I could practically smell the rust of his blood seeping across the street and into my veins like an infection I'll never be able to get rid of.

Seeing him take another person's life is forever branded in my mind like the kind of tattoo you regret getting and even if you cover it up you know what still lingers underneath. The idea makes me want to vomit everywhere and hide away in the panic room I'm so thankful we kept at the manor.

Reluctantly, I agreed to come back to Abram's place with him so he could better explain his job, even if I don't totally believe that's what he was doing. Because of my past, I'm questioning every little thing, even when my heart tells me to trust this man before me. He's never given me any reason to believe he would do the things Grant used to do. But still, that voice I tried to bury comes to the forefront, reminding me that not every man is good but they're not all bad.

My brain hurts as I try to wrap my mind around everything I've witnessed tonight. The way Abram looked horror struck when he realized I witnessed his crime - and not the kind of look like he thought I would rat him out. The kind of look like he might *lose* me.

The idea has crossed my mind. I could easily trick him into thinking everything is okay to give myself enough time to leave. But a life on the run is already exhausting from one guy - I really don't want to be running from two. Everything I've learned about Abram thus far is proof that he too would not stop until he had me again.

Something deep inside me burns at the thought - but not in the way I've always feared Grant finding me. Like a forbidden desire lighting me up from the inside and burning it's way to the surface until I'm hot and panting for another touch. A branding of his own, pulling me into his depths of lust and longing. I must be sick, like him, if this is how I'm feeling in the face of the man I know I'm in love with but also witnessed him commit murder.

If I thought I needed therapy before, I definitely need it now.

"Your silence is killing me," Abram says, startling me from my wild thoughts. I don't know what he expects me to say. There's no way I can make him understand that none of this is okay. None of what he did is normal or even legal for that matter. My parents raised me to know the difference from right and wrong - which is why it killed me to cut them out all these years. One of the biggest things they taught me I completely ignored. I knew what Grant was doing was wrong but I was too far in at that point.

Even when I tried to leave he found me and beat me to within an inch of my life. The fact that I actually made it out this time was miracle enough.

"What do you want me to say, Abram?" I ask with tired eyes and a voice that sounds foreign even to me.

His sharp intake of breath has me watching with wary eyes, half expecting him to brush this all under the rug while the other half wants to hear him out. "I need you to at least let me explain and then I'll let you decide for yourself what you think is best for you. If you want to walk away," he pauses and my heart skips a few beats, not even wanting to entertain that idea but knowing I likely will. Depends on what he says I guess. "I'll let you go, if that's what you want."

Tears spring to my eyes, every emotion running through my body bouncing around inside me, unsure of what to do and where to go. My tears escaping is the only way I can let any of my emotions show without crashing out and tearing the place apart. Cathartic as that may be.

My chest pounds loudly under my sweatshirt, and I know Abram can hear it. He might even be able to feel the rumble of the couch beneath us as my body silently shakes. I know he said he wants me to trust him, and not to be afraid - but that seems kind of moot in this moment.

Nodding my head slightly, I inhale a breath, holding it, and wait for him to explain everything.

"A few years ago I found a job posting, something unconventional and definitely illegal. My interest was piqued immediately - something I was ashamed to admit… at first."

Whatever demons Abram has had to fight in his life has brought him to this moment. A moment of truth laced with calmness as well as nerves. I can sense the emotions he's feeling exuding from his body like an invisible force. Coming to the surface and resting over him like a thick blanket of armor.

"I spoke with a man, who is now my boss, on the phone, and he filled me in on what was expected of me. As soon as I hung up the phone I narrowly made it to the bathroom to throw up. The idea of taking someone's life seemed inconceivable to me at the time."

Trying to picture a younger Abram having such an intense conversation at just the mere idea of killing, has my body shaking in disgust and curiosity. What could possess a person to hire a hitman to murder in cold blood? And how could Abram willingly agree having never met this man? So many questions run through my mind, rapidly fighting the other to be spoken into existence first. My mouth can't keep up with the thoughts consuming me, so I keep it shut for now. Hoping he continues.

"Turns out, the job wasn't about being hired to be a hitman. I was being hired to kill a serial rapist. Someone the cops had been after but weren't putting enough effort into finding. My boss found him easily and sent me to take care of him, for lack of better term."

"He gave me the opportunity to back out, but said I was only allowed that one time or else he would move on and find someone able to get the job done. I've been working for him ever since."

The silence drags on for several minutes as I take in each word. Dissecting everything he said and breaking down the meaning of it all in hopes it will help me understand better. The thoughts that were running wild inside my mind have tripled in the last five minutes and I now have more questions than I can process.

In quiet moments when I'm feeling homesick and missing my parents, I yearn to reach out to them. Just to hear their voices and tell them how much I miss them and how much I truly love them. This is one of those moments. Wishing I could collapse in the arms of my mom and cry until my eyes are puffy and have run dry. To listen to my dad use reassuring words to soothe me as he rubs little circles on my back like when I was little.

Instead of the warm and loving embrace of my parents, I'm sitting across from the man who ignites a fire inside me - one I fear may burn me alive.

Finding my voice, I begin asking some of the questions I hope he can answer - give me some sort of clarity as to who I've been giving my mind and body to. "How long?"

"Four years," he answers without pause.

"If you were so unsure in the beginning you could even do this, what made you stick with it?" This is one of the questions I'm scared to hear the answer to, not knowing what kind of dark response I'm going to get. Might as well get the hard ones out of the way.

"When I made my first kill," he begins, interlocking his fingers in front of him as he leans on his knees across from me. "I was terrified of what it would do to me mentally. After watching my mother get murdered, I didn't think I would be capable of doing that to someone else. The thing is, my mother was a good person and didn't deserve what came for her."

I feel the tears building as I listen to Abram talk about his mom for the first time with me. I've wanted to ask before, but his rough exterior and gruff responses majority of the time held me back.

"But the men that I'm sent after are vile human beings. People who shouldn't be allowed to walk freely knowing the things they've done to innocent women and children."

Bile rises in my throat at the mention of kids being tortured and raped. In a dark way I kind of understand the desire to make someone that evil pay for their crimes.

"In an odd way, it felt like I was avenging her by taking out the kind of men who took her from us. The kind of men who came in and attacked my mom like it was just another night to them. Raping and abusing her for hours before finally putting her out of her misery. I only saw the last part, but I knew enough of what she went through in the weeks following."

A question comes to mind, and I don't even know why I feel inclined to ask it. Something about this moment has me wondering if my suspicions have been right all these months. "Why don't you allow anyone to call you Abram? Why only me?"

His eyes grow heavy, a sadness taking over the lines creasing around his irises. The kind of sadness that runs deep to the very marrow of our bones. A kind of sadness I've become all too familiar with. "She was the last one to call me by my first name. When she died…I couldn't stand the thought of anyone else calling me that. I threw tantrums whenever someone tried. After a while everyone in town knew to only address me as Stoker. It was easier that way, less personal," his voice tapers out to a soft whisper and in this moment I want to hug him until his demons fade away into nothing but vapor.

"When I met you..," he watches me, waiting for something I can't describe. "You were the first person who made me feel like I could be Abram again. Not this brooding guy with dark energy and a tainted past. But Abram, the little boy who loved his mothers cooking and singing songs with her in the kitchen as she made us breakfast."

The tears that started to build are falling down my cheeks in streams as I listen to him describe what it was like to have the mother he did. Before she was cruelly ripped away from him and Alex. "June did her best, and I truly do love her for that, but nothing she did could even come close to that feeling my mom gave me. Seeing you and realizing we were cut from similar cloths when it came to trauma, I knew I could be myself, *fully*."

"I'm sorry about what you saw tonight, I really am. I was hoping you would never have to find out about what I do, or at least have the time to explain it to you the way you deserved to hear it. I'm especially sorry that you have to hear the gruesome details I'm about to share with you, but it feels necessary."

Gulping audibly, I wait patiently for him to continue. Heart hammering away in my chest. "I take great enjoyment from ending their miserable lives. If that makes me a sick and horrible person, then so be it. I'm already well on my way to hell so might as well feed the flames while I'm at it. My mother was brutally murdered right before my eyes and when the opportunity presented itself to take revenge on like minded people, I jumped at it. I'm the best at what I do because for me it's personal."

As crazy as all of this is, I feel deep in my gut he's telling the truth and that I can trust him. What that says about me, I don't know. But I can confidently say if my life was in jeopardy, Abram Stoker would do all he could to pull me from the depths of hell. Even if that meant sacrificing himself to the flames in the process.

"The choice is yours, baby. I would never expect you to just be okay with all of this because you're a good person to your core. But just know this, there isn't a place on earth I wouldn't travel if it meant keeping you safe. I may not be the best guy, but I'll always be the best at protecting what's mine."

"Is that why you took an interest in me right after we met?" The question tumbles out of my mouth before I have a second to think it through. I'm not sure I want to know the answer. If he says yes, then I'll feel like everything we've built was based on a lie - that he only wanted me because of some sick form of protection.

"No," he responds quickly, squashing my previous thoughts and easing my anxiety.

We sit quietly again, side by side watching the flames in the fire pit across from us. The heat from the hearth warming my chilled skin from everything that transpired tonight. I bask in the glow, hoping it can mask the feeling of confusion taking root in my belly. Even though I trust Abram, I'm still a little shook up. The information he's laid in front of me would be a lot for anyone to digest, and that's after watching a man die not fifty feet away from me.

The room smells like him, manly like the deep woods with that touch of mint around the edges. Inhaling a deep breath of everything that is him, I face him - knees touching. The simple touch sends electricity through me and even with everything I've learned, I love this man. Broken soul and damaged past.

"Can a play a song for you?" His question startles me even though his voice is a soft whisper. I nod my head and watch as he reaches around the leather couch for an acoustic guitar. I didn't even know he played having never seen the guitar or heard him play. Suddenly I'm completely focused on his hands as they lightly trill up and down the delicate strings. Soft notes float into the air around us, my eyes shut against the calming lullaby until the notes form a song I instantly know.

I can hear the words in my head as if my parents were right here in the room with us. My dad playing the guitar while my mom sang quietly next to me, lulling me to sleep. Blackbird is my favorite song by the Beatles, something I've never shared with anyone.

Abram plays with a skill that must have taken years to master. It's fascinating to watch someone play an instrument with such ease considering I myself never learned anything.

When I was little I used to watch my parents sing together while Dad played the guitar. We had a small piano in the living room and sometimes my mom would join him and play softly beside him. Never did they try to outplay the other, never once in competition. It was as if they were in their own little world, enjoying the way the notes coursed through them and throughout the room. Filling it with love and a kind of warmth so few are lucky to witness.

This moment has me feeling some of those same feelings I did as a kid. Warm, like the musical notes are hugging me in their melodic embrace. A gentle sigh leaves me with ease as I allow the sound of Abram playing to soothe my racing mind. All the things I've had to take in tonight put on the back burner just so I can enjoy right now.

I have many more questions, things I feel I'm entitled to know at this point considering Abram told me what he does for a living and I witnessed it firsthand. I don't want to be an accessory to whatever fucked up shit he's involved in, but another part of me does. Knowing I love him enough to protect the broken parts of his soul fixes something in my own chipped soul.

We heal each other in unconventional ways that would feel wrong with any other person but him. The way I willingly loose myself in him should scare me when in reality it makes me want to free fall into him more. My battered heart was lying half lifeless for years until he jump started it with a rough exterior that contradicts his protective interior.

The way I love Alex is different yet similar in it's own way. He's the softness I need to get through each day - the sunshine warming all the dark parts of me I keep hidden from the rest of the world. He knows how to find the deeper parts of us both, bringing them to the light and showing me I don't need to feel embarrassed by it, that it's okay to feed the darkness.

I want to be wherever they are.

"I take it you know this song," Abram says, pulling me from past and present memories. Nodding my head, I watch him as he watches me. Playing the notes with ease, eyes never leaving mine. This can't be one of those songs he's just learned, given how well he can play it now. It makes me wonder if there's meaning behind it for him the way there is for me. I don't bother to ask, knowing if it was something he cared to share with me, he would.

Choosing to stay in the moment with him, I watch his fingers dance over the strings, listening to the way his skilled fingers fill the room with his talent while his eyes never leave mine. I can feel the heat of them burning through me, searching for the parts of me I try to keep hidden. He can always see past it though. Abram has a way of uncovering parts of myself I didn't know existed, pulling them out of me and carrying them when they become too heavy.

I wish I could do the same for him but I don't know how to when I feel like I don't know enough about his past to help him reach the future he wants. If he even wants one. The type of work Abram is involved with comes with it's own risks - ones I'm sure he's aware of. My stomach churns at the thought of him getting caught. Locked away in a cell just for doing what the police couldn't. Finding men who get off on torturing women and taking something from them they can't ever get back. Even if some of them do survive their attackers, they won't ever be the same again.

I can say from experience what I went through with Grant changed something in me. A rewiring of my brain chemistry that's now hardwired so far into my being I wouldn't know how to cut it out without severing my lifeline in the process. I would bleed out from the attempt. Which is why I haven't done more to heal myself, knowing it's pointless with how deep the trauma is. Grant is like a parasite I can never extricate from my body or mind - I've never had the strength to rid myself of him completely.

When the music slowly fades, I feel the shift in the room. The somber tone from moments ago is filled with that unavoidable tension. I wish we could forget it all happened and just move on. But it's not like we can pretend it was just a bad day and hope for something better tomorrow.

"Isolde," his voice is low, the rumble of it sending tingles down my spine as my body reacts to him on instinct. He moves in closer to me, running his hands along the back of the couch until they rest near the base of my neck. I feel tendrils of hair moving lightly as he toys with the loose strands. "I need to know what you want to do."

His words work their way through me, cycling around in circles until I have a grasp on them and can let the meaning sink in. What does he want me to do? Say all of this is okay, that I support his life choices despite being in love with him? I ran away from a life surrounding fear and abuse. And while this may not be aimed at me, I still feel a part of it. Can I trust myself and him to fall even farther into the pits of the unknown with someone I still know little to nothing about?

"I-I wasn't expecting this type of relationship, Abram."

"And what kind of relationship is that, little bird?" He's quick to respond, an answer ready for anything I might throw at him. Like he's thought about what this moment might be like and prepared for it ahead of time like a test.

Breathing deeply, I lean into the soft touch of his fingers as he plays with my hair. "The kind where shit always hits the fan, to put it bluntly. Sometimes I don't know how to weather your moods as it is. This just adds another layer of fucked up to the cake of chaos."

He laughs lightly, his breath feathering across my cheek as his body inches closer again. I can't help my body's reaction to his close proximity, having a mind of it's own, and a soft gasp escapes my lips when I feel his other hand run up my bare thigh.

I should not be turned on considering the events of this evening, yet here I am melting into a puddle of lust.

In a hushed tone, he whispers against my ear, licking the lobe lightly before nipping it. "Baby, I *am* the fucking storm. Don't doubt that you have what it takes to survive, it's time that you believe that. I'm not some Prince Charming, Isolde. But I'll be here to help you see your strength if that's what it takes."

A humorless laugh escapes me at how he can go from seeming like the darkness itself, to ensuring I feel the strength he knows I posses. "So, what? You're the villain then?" I ask, unable to get the image of him taking another life out of my mind. There's still dried blood on his clothes and knuckles that he hasn't seemed to notice.

"I prefer Dark Knight. I'm not the bad guy baby, I can promise you that. But you're not some damsel in distress that needs me to ride in on my white horse, either." There's a long pause as Abram ponders something unknown to me. The way his brows dip with concentration has me watching him with rapt attention. Taking in the details of his chiseled features. The way his hair, longer on top, falls forward into his eyes occasionally - giving him even more of that bad boy look he already wears so well. He's absolutely striking.

Looking at him used to be a little unnerving for me. Not because of how insanely beautiful he is, but because of the feelings that stirred deep within me when I looked at him too long. I used to avoid him at all costs just to try and escape the intensity of his presence. Having given up on that long ago, I allow myself to study him now. Appreciate all he is despite the horrors I know he's capable of.

"It's important you know I wouldn't hurt you. *Ever*. If anything, you're the one who might end up hurting me."

Confusion consumes me as I mull over his words. I know I would never be capable of hurting him, or anyone else for that matter. The words in my head tumble out of me before I have a chance to keep them inside where they belong. "You're not capable of getting hurt, Abram. You do the hurting."

I don't miss the way he flinches slightly, like my words might actually impact him in some way. The idea seems ridiculous but I need to remind myself that he isn't a bad person - he's just been through some bad shit - and he's never given me reason to believe he would do anything to cause me actual pain.

He tips my chin up so that I'm looking directly into his haunting light gray eyes. "See, that's where you're wrong, little bird. I am capable of getting hurt, and it's you who holds all that power in these delicate hands of yours." Holding my hands in his, he rubs gentle circles on them, lulling me into a state of ease despite his words. "The day you're no longer mine is the day I'm in ruins."

Warmth unfolds in my chest at the way he looks at me and the way his words seep into the deepest parts of my tattered soul. We are one in the same in a lot of ways. I may not understand how he can murder someone with no remorse, and continue to work for a man he's never met. But I can understand his need to remove all the monsters in this world that still haunt their victims in ways I can relate to all too well.

If you asked what part of me came to the conclusion I feel in my gut, I wouldn't have a direct answer. I can't articulate what I feel for Abram and why I'm willing to lay my heart on the line for someone who stalks and murders the bad guys in the dark of night like some vigilante or Dexter. But I do. I know that in the face of everything, Abram has my heart and there's nothing I can do to try and take it back. He may not know that I love him and I know I'm not ready to say it. But the way he looks at me, with soft eyes he only reserves for me, I can trust his words and work to get past everything else.

I can only hope that by putting my trust in another man it doesn't turn around to bite me in the ass and threaten to destroy all the work I've done to strengthen myself. This version of me is not the strongest, but I'm not weak. It's time I stop closing in on myself like a turtle hiding from the world in it's shell. I'm ready to face my life and fight for it.

***

After the other night I realized I needed to *actually* learn to fight for my life. Given the deranged man that's still on the hunt for me, I need to learn to defend myself in case my two knights in shining armor aren't around.

It took a little arm twisting, but with some encouragement I was able to convince Abram to teach me how to fight. As I lay on the forest floor, heaving in breath after breath, I may have underestimated how hard he was going to be on me. Not that I want him to take it easy, but this isn't what I was expecting.

"Get up," he orders from above me. His broad frame blocking out the sunlight streaming in through the trees. I resist the urge to roll my eyes at him, or better, kick a foot out and knock him to the ground. I don't need to guess what that will get me. "Every time you get knocked down, you need to jump up ten times faster. You're just giving your attacker an easy out by lying here."

Grunting as I rise and brush the dirt from my leggings, I look up at him with an unpleasant expression making him smirk in amusement. Not going to lie, I'm reconsidering the kicking him down bit. "It's not like I haven't been trying, Stoker!" I yell in his face, knowing how much he hates when I call him that. If he wants me to fight, then I'll give him a fucking fight. He's been working me like this for days. My muscles are strained and sore, my head is a mess of movements and training tactics I still don't fully understand, and I need a fucking drink.

"Watch it," he scolds, turning away from me to get into position again. I was kind of hoping for more of a fight, maybe a distraction is needed for both of us right now. Not giving me a second to breathe or live out the fantasy that was working it's way to the forefront of my mind, Abram cuts into my thought process again. "Tell me again. What are the five A's of self defense?"

I fucking hate when he quizzes me like a child. I want this particular lesson to be over though, so I appease him with a fake as fuck smile and recite the response he wants to hear. "Awareness, alertness, avoidance, anticipation and action." Smiling triumphantly, I notice his face hasn't changed. No hint of approval, no job well done, nothing. I'm disappointed because over the last few months I've kind of developed a praise kink and was hoping for more of a reaction.

"Get that naughty head of yours out of the gutter and fucking focus, Isolde. No one is going to take it easy on you, least of all me. How can I know for sure you're able to defend yourself if you can't stop thinking with your cunt?"

My mouth hangs open in surprise. He reads me so well its almost annoying at this point. I wish I could be more secretive with my desires and thoughts, but evidently, I'm an open fucking book. "It's not my fault when you're standing there looking like that," I yell, holding my open palm out to him, "when I look like a sunburnt tomato!"

I catch the smirk before he's able to hide it, and a flare of satisfaction rolls through me. I can still get to him even if he's unable to admit it right now.

We've been going at this for nearly two hours. Sweat is pouring down my face and back, I can feel it pooling between my ass cheeks. I'm tired and sore and all I want to do is take a hot shower and wash away the realization that I'm not strong enough to take on the monsters of my past. I feel tears breech my open eyes so I slam them shut before even one has a chance to escape. I've gotten better at controlling my emotions, but I'm not perfect. Feeling inadequate is not something I enjoy, and as much as I want to quit, I know I have to keep trying.

Still, that voice inside me makes her voice known at the worst of times. Reminding me that I'm nothing but a weak, scared little girl who had to run away from her problems rather than face them head on. Sighing in defeat, I drop my arms to my sides and admit my poisonous thoughts to my teacher. "I'm not strong enough, Abram." I feel my heart crack open at my admission and hope like hell Abram doesn't break me down a little more in light of my confession. Braving a chance to look at him I catch him eyeing me with a gaze that could bring me to my knees with ease. His hard eyes, dark as stone not moments ago, have softened to that light gray I love so much. His body, though still strong and rippling with muscles for days, has relaxed into a normal posture rather than the rigid stance of a drill sergeant.

"You are," he assures me. I can still feel that sliver of doubt laced within my veins, pumping into my heart attempting to make me believe I'm not enough. But his words register inch by inch, icing out the doubt and hesitation I harbor within my walls. "You *are* strong enough," he says again, driving his point home as he wraps a fist around my ponytail and pulls my lips flush against his. The action makes me realize when his words aren't enough, then his actions will prove what words cannot. That with his guidance I can find the strength he knows I have inside me.

Dragging my body into his, he pulls me against a tree, hidden from the walking paths within the woods. We stay there for what feels like hours as I give my body over to him even more than I have already. Never getting enough of the way his lips eat me alive, his fingers exploring my body without the need of a roadmap because each line, each curve is like the backroads to his favorite place. He holds me like my body is the only home he's ever needed, all I have to do is open my legs - baring my body and heart to him - welcoming him home.

I guess lessons are done for the day, I grin to myself.

ISOLDE

chapter twenty-three

♫

Little Girl Gone • CHINCHILLA

"A team effort today, huh?" I ask as I take in both men standing before me. It should be illegal how insanely attractive they both look right now. With the woods at my back and the Stoker men at my front, I feel my chest tighten with excitement and anticipation.

As part of my training, Abram thought it would be smart to educate me on the woods a little more. Our fun little hide and seek game didn't do much for me in the long run. While I held my own and was able to outsmart him at least once, Abram caught me with ease and showed me just how much can be done in the hidden parts where no one can hear me scream. Both of them still know this forest better than anyone. Having grown up running around back here its not a surprise they could find me blindfolded if they had to.

With both hands firmly planted on his hips, Alex laughs from where he stands across from me. "We just thought it might benefit you to learn the ways around here with a little more pressure at your back," he speaks casually though his eyes hint at a certain kind of fire burning inside. I know the feeling as liquid heat radiates in my core sending a throbbing sensation between my thighs. I can't even try and pretend this stuff doesn't turn me on anymore, Abram has already informed me he can smell my arousal when he's close enough.

The first time I heard that, heat flamed my cheeks at the embarrassment I felt. Now, all I feel is excitement that he knows my body well enough and gets turned on just at the thought of touching me, tasting me.

"Plus," Abram interjects with his own thoughts, "it's more fun."

I scoff at his choice of words, "maybe for you." I roll my eyes for dramatic effect, knowing that Abram at least won't do what he really wants with me while his bother is present. No. He'll save that special punishment for later - which further adds to the wetness pooling just below my waistband. The form of punishment he supplies me with is nothing like what I'm used to. Being beaten for someone else's pleasure isn't at all fun and surely doesn't have my panties dampening at the thought. However, when one of the Stoker men deem me fit for a little disciplining, they take me to the edge repeatedly without ever dragging me over that line.

The invisible line they both acknowledge when it comes to anything sexual. If they feel my hesitation in the slightest, they both pull back. Never wanting to push too far outside my comfort zone but also toeing the line so I can learn what I can and cannot handle. It's liberating most of the time, even if I cry from the overwhelming nature of it sometimes.

"We always make things fun for you, don't we baby?" Alex teases lightly while bouncing up on his toes like he's preparing to run a marathon. Abram whacks the back of his head and I chuckle at the look he gives him. "What the fuck was that for?"

"You two gutter brains need to knock it off and take shit seriously," Abram responds dryly. He can act like this doesn't rev his engine but I'm beginning to know him all too well, just like he knows the inner workings of my brain.

Rubbing the spot Abram just hit, Alex shakes his head, feigning innocence like he isn't completely aware of what he's doing. "I wasn't referring to anything dirty, you creepy old man. I was just stating to our sweet Isolde here, that we always have fun together. It's not my fault you think with your head," he looks pointedly down at Abrams groin area, showcasing his point without words.

"Stop looking at my dick, and I'm not that much older than you, boy."

I laugh, taking in their playful sibling rivalry, knowing it's nothing serious. Sometimes I wonder what they were like together as kids. June always talks about how they caused a ruckus wherever they went, but Abram has been different since his mom died. So was it before or after that? I hate to think about him as a young boy becoming so closed off that he couldn't play freely like the child he should have been. His innocence taken away from him at such a young age, being confused about why he felt the way he did and saw the things he was forced to witness.

Then add in the fact that Alex wasn't their to see the gruesome murder of their mother. Sure, he knows the story but it's different hearing it versus living it. I imagine Abram felt some kind of jealousy at the carefree spirit Alex was able to keep as a child and into his adult years.

If only I could go back in time and save him from his pain, I would.

Checking that his laces are tight, Alex rises to full height again, choosing to ignore the verbal jabs from his brother. "Shall we lay the ground rules?"

"What ground rules?" Abram quickly interrogates. "There are no rules when you're being chased by a maniac, the sooner she realizes that, the better."

Gulping audibly, I realize just what hell I may have gotten myself into by agreeing to test this out. Not only am I supposed to dodge *two* of them, but also learn my way around these woods as if every corner doesn't look exactly the same.

"Here's the rules, run like your life depends on it and imagine the worst person in your past is chasing you. Got it?" The playful Abram is long gone. Replaced by the tall and serious man before me, not taking my safety lightly at all. My eyes still wince at the way he so easily mentions the man that still haunts my dreams and waking hours, knowing that I literally am still doing just that. But I choose to brush it off and use it as motivation to outsmart both guys.

I don't miss the way Alex eyes him, though. His protectiveness stems differently than Abram's, causing me to smile.

"Five minutes, little bird. That's the only courtesy we're granting you."

Nodding my head, I give them both one last look before turning on my heels and taking off into the woods. The last time I did this with just Abram it was more for fun, allowing us both the excitement of the chase knowing what would happen once he caught me. This time feels far more significant, like my participation and willingness to be serious is crucial to the success of getting any from my alleged *'attacker'*.

A deep rooted part of me knows something like this is coming, and better to be prepared than struck into stillness as overwhelming shock takes over. I don't want to face Grant again and freeze up because I'm unsure of how to fight back. Between my lessons in self defense with Abram and this little game of hide and seek with both guys, I feel more confident than I have in years.

Picking up speed, I put my new running sneakers to the test as I dodge tree branches and mud puddles. My heart rate accelerating quickly as I resist the urge to glance behind me and see if they're already catching up. Pretty sure its only been two minutes, but I never expect them to play fair. Well, not Abram at least.

I need to treat this test like a real life situation, use my head and devise a plan on how to escape before they even get a chance to smell the sweat forming in my hairline.

Stopping for a moment, I take in my surroundings, awareness at the forefront as I listen for any sounds out of place. Heavy breathing from the guys chasing me, twigs cracking in the distance or an unnatural silence that doesn't fit when hidden deep in the forest. Alertness goes hand in hand with awareness, knowing I need to keep a clear head but also be on guard for anything.

Anticipating an attack, I keep my body ready. Hands raised as I look around the trees for a color out of place. Abram is in all black, as usual, whereas Alex went with heather grey. This time of year, the trees are changing. Bringing to life pops of warm colors, ranging from deep red to soft brown. Almost getting lost in the beauty of mother nature, I sprint back into action, hoping to outrun them a little longer and avoid getting caught.

Memories of Abram finding me and tackling me to the ground the last time we ran through these very woods has my insides on fire for another touch. The way he let himself go in my presence, allowing his baser instincts to take over and have me in the most animalistic way. A small, selfish part of me desires for them both to find me and have me at the same time. Embarrassment for having such a thought hinders my alertness and I'm caught off guard when a plastic pellet hits the back of my calf.

Not able to help the scream that erupts from deep in my throat, I crumble to the ground as pain radiates through my leg. Fucking hell, when Abram said there were no rules, I never imagined he would bring physical pain to the test as well as mental paranoia.

"The next shot won't be in such a soft place, little bird." I hear him yell out from behind a tree somewhere. He's giving me the opportunity to run again, something I'm familiar with. I've always been good at pushing my pain aside in times of flight, and I refuse to let the fear and soreness deter me now.

Alex's voice wraps around me from not too far off, his caring nature always ever-present. "Did you really feel the need to shoot her with a fucking BB gun?"

"The next fucker might have an actual gun, dickhead. She needs to feed into the fear."

Feed into the fear. I've always pushed it aside, or simply ran from it. Never feeding into it the way I should. Allowing myself to become one with the very thing I've done my best to avoid for years. Pulling myself from the ground, leaves and dirt falling from my leggings, I take off in a spring as heat radiates through the sore spot on the back of my leg.

Tears build behind my eyes, and I use that as motivation to push harder. Harnessing my fear, even though I know it's only Alex and Abram, I allow it to take over as my only instinct in hopes to get out of this situation only partly scathed. I knew Abram was unhinged, in more ways than one, but shooting at me with a fucking BB gun is a new low, even for him.

It's his warped way of pushing me, showing me that no one else is going to take it easy on me. But fuck, did it hurt. The sadistic side of him that loves my blood, is battling his urges to pull me to the ground and drag me behind a tree so he can fuck me senseless. Whereas the softer side knows he'll take me home later to clean me up and tend to my wounds. Like Dr. Jekyll and Mr. Hyde, Abram Stoker has two sides that he battles with mentally.

As soon as I feel like I've ran far enough ahead of them, I crouch down behind a boulder beside an enormous pine tree. The scenery around here is breathtaking - nothing like being in the city. Having been here for several months, I still find myself admiring everything this town has to offer. I never anticipated living in an area like this, so far off the grid. But now I can't imagine ever living anywhere else. The only thing that would make it perfect is if my parents were here.

Nestled against the large rock, I inspect the cut on the back of my calf. Blood rolls down the back of my leg, seeping into my socks and pants. I'm surprised the impact didn't cut a whole through my new leggings, I would have made him buy me several new pairs if that had been the case.

I needed a few minutes to catch my breath if they expected me to keep this up, but as soon as I feel my breathing even out, I hear the rustling of leaves again. Jesus, they never give up. I've held my own through all their training tactics, but I think I'm done for the day. I'm ready for a soothing bubble bath and a fucking foot rub. These new sneakers are great and all, but definitely not worn in enough to be running around the woods like a crazed maniac is chasing me. I giggle to myself knowing in fact there is a maniac on the loose chasing me with a goddamn BB gun.

Standing from my spot hidden behind the trees, I come forward with hands raised. "I surrender you guys." Looking around, I don't see any signs of them. Everything surrounding me is greenery with touches of reds and orange mixed in due to the changing of the season. I can't spot Abram's all black silhouette and definitely not Alex's goofy chuckle that always has me laughing.

The same sound I heard just a moment ago is back though, and I spin around in search of where it's coming from. When I'm met with an eerie silence once more, I feel the hair on the back of my neck stand to attention. Something feels off, but I know it has to be all in my head. They're probably messing with me to ensure I keep my guard up, knowing I had just begun to let it drop. I feel safe in these woods with them - but now I'm feeling unsure.

Feeding into the fear, I take off running again. This time in the direction of where I left the guys. I hope I'm just being paranoid, but nothing says fear like the idea that your worst monster, the demon of your living nightmares, is out here searching for you. As my breathing escalates into a growing panic, I try to calm my nerves, reminding myself he doesn't know where I am. Sure, I've gotten text messages here and there with classic Grant threats, but he *can't* know where I am physically.

I run like he's chasing me. I run like the bleeding cut in my leg is nonexistent, acting like I can't feel it at all. I run, focusing only on the way my heart beats erratically in my chest, matching the labored pants of my breaths hitting the air. I run, knowing I won't stop until I collapse or I'm taken to the ground and have to fight for my life. I run and I run until I hit what feels like a brick wall.

Pain explodes in my face, immediately putting me off balance as I sway to the sensation now buzzing in my head. Soft hands encase the sides of my face and I feel my body being gently laid down, but I can't open my eyes to see who the hands belong to. Muffled voices flow in and out of my ears, but not a single word makes it through the haze. All I can focus on is the swarm of bees causing chaos in my mind as my head fights like hell to regain some awareness.

The voices grow more panicked the longer I lay in a pile of leaves and twigs, unmoving and terrified of opening my eyes. More than one set of hands is inspecting all areas of my body, lifting limbs while gently consoling me, telling me how good I did. I'm suddenly struck with the realization there's two voices, not just one. My fear takes a backseat and embarrassment winds it's way to the forefront.

Peeking one eye open, I look up to find Abram and Alex both leaning over me, matching looks of unease on their faces. I must look insane right now - lying on the ground covered in dirt, with tears streaming down my face. This is one of those moments I wish I could hide forever, crawl into my imaginary shell and shut out the world along with all my problems.

"Baby, what happened? Are you okay?" Alex's voice is strained, like it hurts him to see me in such a panic. I have the sudden urge to run my hands through his soft hair and reassure him I'm always fine when he's near.

Glancing at Abram, his brows are pinched and if I didn't know him yet I'd say he looked pissed. Maybe he is. There's still so much I don't know about him. Eyes ping ponging between the two of them, I focus on Abram, wanting to face the brunt of his disappointment first. "I-I'm sorry, I thought there was…" my voice sounds weak and scared. The sound of it hitting a nerve somewhere deep inside me that doesn't want to admit I'm still not as strong as I like to pretend I am.

"What the fuck happened out there?" Abram asks with a bite to his tone. Yeah, he's mad alright.

"Stoker, chill bro," Alex begins to chastise but shuts up real quick when Abram turns that glare of his on his brother. I can tell he wants to say more, but decides against it as they both wait for me to explain why I freaked out.

"You ran face first into my chest, and no matter how many times I tried to call to you it was like you couldn't hear or see me, Isolde." His use of my name always makes me more alert, he doesn't use it often so whenever he does I feel like I need to pay closer attention to his words. "What were you running from?"

"I…" Words evade me as I try to understand what I was actually running from. I heard the rustle of leaves and knew they were close, but that little voice warned me it wasn't them. It had to of been though, because no one else comes into these woods. It's private property and given the way this town is, no one would disrespect June by coming onto her property without permission. "I heard you guys behind me but couldn't spot either of you. I guess I panicked, and I just…ran."

They exchange a look before abruptly standing and scanning the area around us. I watch them from the ground, unsure of why they're paranoid all of a sudden. The fear I felt earlier comes back at warp speed, and not the fun kind of fear that came out when we started this training. The kind of fear that they know something is off and they don't want to alarm me. Too late. Warning bells sound off in my brain and I jump to my feet to stand between them, despite the pain still throbbing in my leg.

"Wh-what is it? You guys have that look on your face and I'm not sure if I should feed into the fear or succumb to it with the way you're looking around."

Not answering my question, Abram scoops me into his arms and starts walking back towards the manor. I wish they didn't treat me like a child the way they are right now. I want to know what has them spooked because I'm still in that same state of paranoia. It doesn't help that every two seconds Alex peers behind us as if the boogeyman is right there.

"Seriously guys, what the fuck? I know I came in hot but I just assumed I let to fear overtake my other instincts. Tell me what's going on!" I shriek and as soon as the words leave my mouth, Abram plasters a firm hand over my mouth and nose, effectively silencing me as he fixes me with dark gray eyes.

"Shut the fuck up, little bird," Abram demands and my body shakes at the tone of voice he's using. "I swear to God I will withhold air from you until you pass out. We need to go."

That's all he says and when I look to Alex for any kind of help, he just looks away quickly before studying the area around us again. If this is part of the training, it would have been nice if I was let in on it beforehand. I never know what to expect with them and I know that's part of the lesson, but this feels too extreme. Especially after Abram shot me.

Within minutes we're back in front of the manor, June's car parked in her driveway next to her house. Everything seems normal as I take in our surroundings. Abram doesn't put me down though, just walks us into the house while Alex runs over to chat with June. "Abram?"

"That wasn't us in the woods behind you." His words are definitive, leaving no room for argument and certainly no indication in his eyes that he's kidding. This was not part of the training and suddenly the realization that it could have been anyone, including my psycho ex boyfriend, is too much.

"B-but, who could it h-have been?" I ask, unable to hold the question in. Feeling the weight of it wanting to burst through my chest as my teeth chatter.

"I don't know. Which is why I told you to close that beautiful mouth of yours," he remarks.

I smirk at him, "or you would have done it for me, right?"

"Baby, the sooner you realize I will do whatever it takes to keep you safe, the easier it will be for all of us."

"Okay, but it could have just been someone in town, right? I mean I know this is private property, but surely June allows friends to hunt back here."

"No," he says abruptly. "There is no hunting back here and everyone stays off the property for respect of June."

Respect for June? I feel like I have more questions than I did five minutes ago, and none of them are getting answered. "Why would hunting back here disrespect June?" I ask, unable to take the secrets any longer.

I'm not prepared for his answer though, assuming he isn't going to tell me anything. "Her husband was shot and killed out here, years ago."

My brain rattles in my head, bouncing around like it's trying to shake the information from its confines. June told me her husband was the town doctor, that he owned the clinic for years, but that he died a while back. I had just met her so I never asked any questions on how he died because I didn't know her well enough. Even now, it seemed like an odd and insensitive thing to just ask out of the blue. *'No hunting back here', everyone stays off the property'.*

A gasp escapes me as a tear glides down my face. "Someone shot him while hunting, didn't they?"

"Yes," he replies immediately. "It was an accident, but one June was never willing to risk happening again. The property is private and hunting is banned for exactly that reason. She lost her husband because some fucking idiot didn't wait long enough to make sure it was a deer they were aiming at, not a person."

June has always been an upbeat person, happy to live each day. She's been there for me since day one and I didn't even know the worst day of her life occurred right behind her house. How she managed to keep living here is a mystery to me. But I guess in some ways it keeps her closer to him. Knowing that his soul might still wander around these woods in hopes to be close to her.

"I'm so sorry, Abram. I had no idea," I murmur against him. My hands find their way around his muscled back, stopping when they're both wrapped around his front. Pulling him into me, I lean my head between his shoulders, letting the silent tears soak his shirt. June raised these boys the best she could after they lost their parents, now to find out their uncle was killed in a freak accident shortly after is too much for anyone. No wonder being here has been a mix of emotions for Abram. So much has happened, things that can never be erased. It's no wonder he ended up the way he did.

With one hand, he squeezes my arms, a quiet thank you just between the two of us. We stand together like this quietly for a few minutes, enjoying the warmth of each other when he finally speaks. "So, to answer your question, I don't know who was following you. But whoever it was, shouldn't have been there."

The finality of his words has a shiver working its way up my spine. Dread settles in the pit of my stomach and I hate to admit it, but I have a feeling the only one stupid enough to trespass on someones private property is the same someone I've tried convincing myself wasn't closing in on me. It's true what they say, even when you run from your monsters, they somehow always find you.

***

"What the fuck do you mean, he's been texting you?" Abram snarls from the window where he's paused his pacing, his face red with rage. After Alex went to check on June, he came back to the manor and I told them about the texts I've been getting from Grant. The guilt gnawed at me as it was, feeling bad that I didn't let them know what was going on. One look at their faces tells me I should be feeling more than guilt.

It's not like I didn't trust them with the information, I just didn't want to pop the little bubble we'd been blissfully living in. I fear it may have been naive…Okay, it was for sure naive of me to think I could keep this a secret knowing Grant was going to make an appearance at some point. The thing is, while I know he's dangerous and reckless, I never pegged him for someone capable of doing real harm. The way Abram does, for the greater good, I remind myself.

"I was kind of hoping he would just go away when he realized I wasn't texting him back. I even tried blocking the number, but he'd just text on a new one." Fiddling with the sleeve of my sweatshirt, I watch them both look at me like I have a sign plastered across my chest screaming, *world's biggest moron*. "Look, you don't have to say it. I know I'm an idiot, but I didn't want to burden you guys with any of this."

My words are abruptly cut off when Abram slams his fist into the wall, knocking down a few pictures in the process. Flinching, I back away without realizing it, the action catching Abram's attention. His eyes soften a tad, but not much as he levels me with a gaze that surpasses rage. "Isolde, you're not an idiot," Alex chimes in causing Abram to inflict his rage on him for a second, releasing me of the harsh glare for a moment. "Fuck off, Stoker. Don't look at me like I'm some little kid and you don't have the patience to discipline me right now. She made a mistake but instead of looking like that," he waves an arm towards Abram with the way he's standing, ready for battle, "let's find a solution."

Alex, always the peacemaker between the two - where he is good at defusing an escalating situation, Abram is ready to light the place up in flames. To hell with casualties.

They stare at each other neither willing to back down from their feelings on the situation. If I wasn't scared shit right now, I'd be entirely too turned on by the image before me. Abram breaks first, rubbing a hand over his face, pinching his thumb and pointer over the bridge of his nose. "Fuck," he mutters. Abram is an act first, ask questions later kind of guy. Something I'm used to obviously, but not something I'm trying to revisit. While I appreciate his concern for this growing issue, I think he realizes I'm not the main problem here, Grant is.

He walks over to me, the energy in his eyes matching the stride in his steps. Whole body radiating with unresolved fury as he tries to get a handle on what's happening and what he can do to fix it. The muscles under his shirt ripple as his body shakes, differently than my own. While I'm shaking in fear of the unknown, he's shaking with a rage he's failing to reign in completely. "I'm not like my brother over there," he throws a thumb over his shoulder at Alex. In the last thirty seconds, he's made his way to the kitchen and is currently stuffing his face with leftovers from the fridge.

We both look at him. Me suppressing a laugh that wants to bubble out of me as he looks at us like he doesn't get what's so funny, and Abram looking as annoyed as ever. "What?" He says with a mouthful of cheese. "I get hungry when I'm anxious."

Abram grabs my shoulders, forcing me to look at him as my laughter towards Alex lodges in my throat. "Sometimes I'm gonna say the wrong thing, and probably hurt your feelings. But I don't give a fuck if I make you cry or if I have to yell some common sense into you when it comes to your safety. You want me to open up to you and tell you things about myself? Then you have to fucking trust me with the big things too, little bird."

A few tears slide down my cheeks, and I can't be bothered to wipe them away as I stare into Abram's gray eyes. They've softened a bit, which helps me relax in the face of his anger towards my carelessness. I didn't even think to say anything about the texts, truly wanting it all to just go away. Now I'm flat out terrified to show them what was delivered to the manor this morning. Before I met them in the woods, I found a package addressed to me, on the front steps. There was no return address, no name from the sender - and no postage. Just a small box with my name scribbled on top.

Whoever sent this, dropped it off on their own - and that has me more jittery than a caffeine addicted businessman. I was more focused on our impending training session with both guys, that I tossed it on the entryway table Abram made for me and left.

Minutes have passed and I haven't responded to what Abram just said. Honestly, I don't even remember what words fell from his lips. My body is completely still as the chills take over my body, goosebumps dancing across my skin under my clothes.

Alex makes his way back over to us, standing tall next to his brother. His hand reaches out to touch my arm and without warning, I flinch away from his touch. Hurt skates over his features and I shake myself out of the daze. "I-I'm sorry, I just remembered something."

They follow me to the entryway and flank my sides as I stare at the unopened box resting before us. A seemingly harmless package, but I'm not so naive to think it's a cute gift from my parents who have no idea where I am. He's found me. And now not only am I in danger again, but the people who mean the most to me - aside from my parents - are at risk as well. This is exactly what I didn't want to happen! I didn't want to bring my problems to this small town, filled with good and honest people.

I never wanted to be the girl that dragged her baggage with her everywhere she went because she was too scared to ask for help carrying it. They don't deserve to have to deal with the demons of my past because no matter how hard I tried to stay under the radar - he still found me.

Tears stream down my cheeks as I stare at the package, still unable to say or do anything. The suspense must be getting to them too, because Abram snatches the box and begins ripping it open. His fingers cut through the cardboard like melted butter, the need to know what's inside far too important.

The moment the flaps are burst open, color drains from Abram's face. My body feels the way it did the night Grant cut me open, slicing me from my belly button to just under my breasts, hopeless and afraid.

Afraid for my life.

Afraid for my future.

Afraid that he'll never rest, never quit, until he has me in his clutches again.

I don't need to see what's in the box to know it's a message that he's coming for me, that he never stopped. He just wanted me to believe I was safe. Alex is reaching for the box, hoping to see what Abram already knows when the latter's eyes meet mine. Questions swirl in his irises, desperate for any information, any inkling that this is all a joke. I wish I could tell him it's not so bad, that we can figure it out. But the only thing that leaves my mouth is the haunting truth we're all faced with. "He found me."

STOKER

chapter twenty-four

♫

Dynasty • Miia

"Abram!" I hear her scream behind me as I burst through the front door, ready to hop on my bike and tear this goddamn town apart to find the fucker who haunts her dreams. Now he's back to haunting her real life too, and I refuse to allow this man to breathe another day.

"Please," she heaves, grabbing my arm as she tries to turn me to face her. Her voice pauses, deciding what to say, and I feel the first crack in my armor. I've never felt such an insane urge to protect someone the way I do now, not since my mom. I can't stand the idea of someone like Grant coming for her, assuming he has any claim over her. It's bullshit.

Pulling my arm from her grasp, I level her with a stare that has her backing up. "There's nothing you can say right now, nothing that would keep me from finding that fucker and making him suffer. The sooner you let me go, the sooner I can erase this piece of shit from the earth."

Her lip trembles, and I want to suck it between my teeth and bite it until I taste the tang of her blood on my tongue. "I don't want you to get caught, or worse, *hurt*. All because of me and my past coming to haunt us, its not…It's not right."

"I'll just call El-," she cuts in again before I can finish what I was saying. If I wasn't already so riled up, I might have spanked her right here and now for interrupting me.

"No. Abram, this isn't your battle to fight and you're not going to call up your boss and ask him to clean up my mess. I won't agree to that," her voice matches the tremble in her lip and my heart cracks a little more. This woman is breaking down the exterior I've spent years building, I don't know how to stop it and honestly, I don't know if I want to. But it terrifies me nonetheless.

"If you think I'm just going to sit by and watch this man torment you for the foreseeable future, then you really don't me at all," I reply harshly as I begin walking towards my bike again. The air feels crisper today, the colder months creeping up like a chill down your spine. Isolde's face drops and I feel like an asshole for talking to her that way. It's a low blow, considering how many times she's asked me to open up and let her in a little more - to tell her more about myself. But what else is there to tell? I've already allowed her to see the darkest parts of me. What else does she need?

"Would you want me to fight your battles for you?" Her voice comes from right behind me. I was hoping she would let me go, but my little bird isn't dropping this. The part of me that softens for her, and only her, was hoping she wouldn't.

"This is different, and you know it."

"How? Just because I'm a fragile little girl, scared of her past catching up to her and swallowing her whole? Dragging her back to the pits of hell where she thinks she belongs. Because I already know all of that, Abram," her voice is soft, delicate and laced with pain. A pain I can't erase no matter how much I wish I could.

The sick part of me wants to make her bleed, drain her body of any turmoil it's still holding onto. Erasing the fear in her thats taken root so deep into her blood stream the only remedy is to suck her dry. But when I look at those hazel eyes, and see the softness, the vulnerability in them, I just can't. I can't be who I've always been and drive her away because I already have a hole in my chest from the death of my mom. What would happen to me if a second hole opened up and I bled out?

"You're not weak, little bird. I've told you this," I say as I turn to face her, reflecting on our conversation in the woods the other day. For years, Isolde was programmed to think she's not strong enough, not good enough, not worthy enough. If I leave her standing here, pleading me not to fight her battles for her, then I'm saying the same thing essentially. But, that's just not who I am, that's not who *I've* been programmed to be. I know this hurts, but leaving her to defend herself and face her past on her own will hurt more in the end.

As I'm about to remind her that nothing she says will change my mind, her fingers grip my shirt, holding me hostage with her soulful eyes that know how to see into the deepest parts of me. "Abram," her voice descends over me like an invisible mist. The sound echoing around me with a mixture of need and want, a sound I fall prey to every single time. Despite how strong I may be, my armor might as well be a blanket of marshmallows when it comes to Isolde.

I watch her wrestle with her emotions, with the words she desperately wants to say, the words clawing at her throat, begging to be let free. It's like I can read her mind without her having to speak, just by watching her face and the subtle movements she makes she thinks no one else notices. Her soft breaths mix with the breeze floating around us as birds chirp in a tree overhead. I feel like I'm in a fairytale, one where the Princess is already mine, just by how she stares at me with what I can only assume is love.

"I…I love you," she confesses with such ease. The words having been there all along, but were unable to be spoken into existence until now.

Neither of us move, too frozen in the moment to say or do anything that might break the spell. Popping the bubble we've trapped ourselves in - knowing that one wrong word would easily pop it and bring us back to the reality around us.

My body and mind fight with what to do first. Tell her that I've loved her for a long time now and was just waiting for her to catch up, or pull her body flush against mine and kiss her senseless until we forget everything else except the way her lips feel on mine. In any other situation, it would easily be one of the those two things. But given what we're dealing with, I can't let emotions take over right now, I need to remain focused. The reason I've always been the best at my job is because I refuse to let outside thoughts bleed into my mind, clouding me of the task at hand. As much as it kills me to do what I'm about to, I need to cut out any and all distractions so I can find the man lurking in the dark ready to take back what's mine.

"It's sweet that what you think is going on between us is love. I'm not surprised though. You easily gave your heart to the wrong guy once, and now you're trying to give it to two," my words cut into her like shards of glass and her exterior crumbles under the weight of what I just said. As hard as she tries to appear tough, I can see the way my words have affected her. The way her lip trembles once, twice, before biting it to keep the tremors at bay. The way her lashes flutter rapidly, trying to fight off the impending tears ready to flood her flushed cheeks.

What I can't see is the way her heart is breaking under my unchanging gaze, knowing that my face is a mask of stone, attempting to hide my real emotions that are begging to be let free. The beast inside me bangs against it's restraints, but I can't think with my heart right now. I can't let her think I'm the man she wants me to be when the man in front of her can only focus on ripping out the throat of the one who brutalized her for years.

Isolde is my weakness, and if I allow everything that is her to fully seep into my being then she becomes a part of my soul. A part of me irrevocably. The way she smells like sweet flowers, a fragrance so delicate it matches everything about her. The way her soft lips smile at me when she completes something in the manor. The way her eyes soften when I kiss her between her breasts, before sinking into her and molding her body to mine like two puzzles pieces.

A single tear slides down her colorless cheeks, all the blood having left, rushing to her heart that's barely beating as I rip it out of her chest. I wish I could eat the words back up, take them all back and tell her how much I'm in love with her, how she's mine and only mine. I want to tell her I don't want to share her with anyone, especially my bother because the sadistic voice inside me wants her all to myself. I want him and any other man to watch as I claim her, hear how she screams out my name as if I'm the one who makes her fall apart over and over again. I want them to see the scratches down my back from her nails digging into me. Her own way of branding me so every other woman knows I'm not available.

There's nothing I want more than to show her she's it for me. That she's the only one who can tame the beast within me and love me for who I am, broken fragments and all. But a stronger emotion is driving the crazy train, and I have to follow it if I ever want a chance of keeping her all to myself. I just hope she can forgive me eventually.

Turning away from her, knowing there's nothing left to be said, I hop on my bike and ride off down the dirt road. I can feel the heartbreak following me like an invisible string tethered to my heart, trying to bring me back to her. Doing what I do best, I cut the string, letting it fall to the ground and leaving it behind as I focus on what needs to be done. I refuse to let thoughts of her in right now, I can't risk them clouding my focus. Just another job, I say over and over again as I rev my bike and speed down the dirt road, mist coating my face as the winds licks my exposed skin.

Wherever that fucker is, he better be ready for what's coming to him. I didn't just blow up my only chance at real love - in hopes of saving her - just to fail my mission. As soon as I find him and take the pathetic life he's been living away from him, I'll find my little bird and show her everything I feel for her that I was unable to speak.

As soon as I'm far enough away from the property, I pull off to the side of the dirt road and yank my phone out of my jeans. The wind picks up, rustling the trees overhead and I swear I can still smell her. As if her scent follows me like a warning. Reminding me the way I feel for her isn't a blessing - its a curse. The last four years have prepared me for exactly this moment, and if I succeed one more time, then I'll be done with this work. Tell Ellis I've done all I can and show Isolde that this version of me isn't all I am.

I need your help.

The three little dots appear, then disappear as I wait for his response. Ellis has been in this line of work far longer than I have, despite us being close in age. If he can't help me track this guy down, I don't know who can. I won't stop until I find him, though. It's not just for Isolde at this point - its the blood thirty demon inside me that wants nothing more than to skin this man alive and watch as his body radiates a pain even the depths of hell can't deliver.

Whatever you need, my protege.

ISOLDE

chapter twenty-five

Labour (the cacaphony)

• Paris Paloma

My heart is nothing but broken pieces lying on the ground in front of me. I tried to give the whole thing to Abram and instead he took it from my hands and threw it to the ground, watching the pieces of my love splinter and lie lifeless in front of him. Uncaring and unbothered.

Alex chose that moment to emerge from the house, eyes glancing all around, looking for what might have me motionless and staring ahead at nothing. "Baby, what is it?" He asks gently, searching my face for a hint. I can hear his voice faintly, the way his fingers caress my cheek softly, trying to pull my attention to him, but I'm unable to move. My limbs feel like jello, only being held together by my clothes. My body feels hollow, like nothing is left inside me to even care about.

I want so badly to be upset with Abram, to curse his name and swear off men for the rest of my pathetic life. I want to run again, leave behind the only place that's felt like home since I was a kid, hide out and live alone. The pain in my chest expands more each time I inhale, making it harder and harder to breathe or focus. But Alex's voice is still beside me, pulling me back inch by inch as each word seeps in and takes root in my vacant chest cavity.

"It's okay, breathe, gonna be okay, I've got you, baby, love." Words jumble together as Alex consoles me and I feel the wetness soaking his shirt. When did I start crying? Opening my eyes to look at him, I see that we're inside the manor. When the fuck did we get here? A panic begins building, and I try like hell to keep it at bay as I focus on what's real and what's not. Alex is here, I am here, and Abram is *gone*. That's all I can process before I feel my eyelids close again.

The darkness has me in its clutches, squeezing out whatever happiness I thought I found. Having nothing else to hold onto, I let it drag me to the void, allowing the pitch black to swallow me whole and consume whatever is left of my shattered soul. The last thing I feel is a cool hand brushing my hair away from my damp face as something warm envelops me, attempting to push out the bitter cold. Only problem is, the darkness has no limits, has no beginning and no end. Giving myself over to it is easier than trying to fight my way out - and I'm so tired of fighting for things that were never meant to be mine in the first place.

***

When I wake up something feels… off. Like I got smacked in the chest and my breathing feels choppy. Looking around the room, I search for something familiar. The last time I cracked an eye open slightly, I couldn't tell where I was and could barely feel my limbs beneath me. This time, however, I find my dresser along the wall closest to the window that overlooks the park across the street.

I can hear kids playing outside, their laughter rising with the breeze and settling over me like a strange kind of comfort I'm not used to. Judging by the amount of noise coming from outside, and the faint strip of light from under the curtains, I know it's morning. It must have been the middle of the night the last time I attempted to right myself. The darkness held me down though, rendering me immobile and speechless as an ache in my head and chest took root.

My head seems to be more clear, and now that I know I'm at home, I feel slightly at ease. I don't know where Grant is though, and every time I've ever woken up like this it means something bad happened last night.

I can't even remember what we were doing or where we might have gone last night. The only reason I know we weren't home was because I woke up somewhere that wasn't here. Aside from that hazy memory, the last thing I remember was cooking dinner for the two of us.

Needing a few more minutes to gain my bearings, I lay in bed and try like hell to remember any details from last night. I hate waking up feeling lost, knowing it'll just be ammunition for Grant to say I drank too much or some other bullshit excuse. He drugged me again, that much I know for certain if the headache was any indication.

The pain in my chest remains a mystery though.

My heart beats erratically, thumping painfully against my rib cage like it wants out. I know the feeling of pain all too well, but this is different. It feels heavier in a way that has me clutching my chest to make sure I don't have weights strewn across me, keeping me held down and at anyones mercy.

"You're awake, wonderful," Grant says, a little too cheerfully as he makes his

way into the dark room. The shades are drawn so I can't see his face, I can just make out his build as he carries in what appears to be a tray. Setting it in front of me, he lovingly strokes my hair, pulling the knotted mess away from my face and helping me into a sitting position. I'm caught off guard as he fluffs a pillow behind my head, knowing this is wildly out of character for him.

"Are you hungry, baby?" He questions as he positions the folding tray over my lap so that the legs are straddling each side of my thighs. I suppose I am hungry, if the grumbling in my stomach isn't proof enough. Something smells delicious, like freshly brewed coffee and cinnamon buns - my favorite. Grant always calls me Princess, so hearing him call me baby is a little weird, but nothing about this morning feels normal.

Grant is behaving too nice, which already has alarm bells setting off in my mind, and now he's bringing me my favorite breakfast treat - also very unlike him. I'm about to ask him what's going on, daring to hear the answer even if it means getting smacked again. The weirdness is keeping me more on edge than if he just yelled at me and slapped me.

The curtains are opened, and a soft light comes through the window illuminating the bedroom in the manor. The voices from the children across the street are quiet now, replaced by the sounds of trees rustling in the breeze outside. Panic seizes my movements as realization dawns on me. I'm not at Grant's place, I'm here at the manor, in the bedroom I worked so hard to make my own. How could Grant get in here without Alex or someone else seeing him? How is he so calm when Abram is out there searching for him as we speak. Or at least I hope he still is.

Just as I feel a scream ready to burst out me, Alex comes into focus. Standing by the window having just opened the curtains. His smile warms what's left of my heart, the relief that it's just him and not the vile human haunting my every thought. With measured steps, he approaches me, smiling a little too brightly for my current mood.

His eyes are unfocused, his movements becoming almost robotic and his facial features morphing into something more sinister with each passing second. The masculine scent I've grown to love, mixed with sunshine smells all wrong. Bitter and sour, like a bad piece of candy. "I'm here, Princess. Come find me."

This time the scream does barrel out of me, shaking the walls and threatening the hanging pictures to clatter to the floor. Clawing at the blankets covering me, I wrestle my way out of the bed just in time for Alex to run around the corner searching for any signs of danger. He scans the room multiple times before his eyes settle on me. Both hands are held in front of him once he takes in my current state.

"Isolde, baby, its just me," he tries to reassure me, but I'm stuck between what's real and what not again. Struggling to understand if it's really him or just another dream Grant has infiltrated in my mind. "Close your eyes, take a deep breath and focus on me, okay?"

Hesitating for a moment, in case my mind is playing tricks on me, I close my eyes and listen to the sound of his soothing voice. The way it reaches inside me, tickling its way down my spine before settling at my toes. Feeling confident it's him, I reopen my eyes in time to feels tears streaming down my face. Warm arms wrap me in a hug and I finally breathe in the familiar scent that is only Alex. The warmth of sunshine mixed with the woodsy smell of cedar.

He doesn't say anything for several minutes, allowing me to sob into his chest as everything inside me crashes down around us. The fear of Grant being so close, I could practically smell him. The painful reality that Abram heard my confession and chose to leave me anyways. The pain is too much and it makes sense now why I woke up with an ache in my chest. "Talk to me, baby. What happened?"

My sobs have died down, feeling like I poured as much of the emotions in my chest out, I stare into eyes of concern. Despite Abram rejecting me, this amazing man is still here, accepting me for the broken person I am. The part of me I can no longer hide. Every facet of my tattered past has been revealed and laid bare before me. "A d-dream, it was j-just a dream," I mumble into his chest. My forehead resting delicately against his muscled pecks that in any other situation, would have me licking my lips.

Alex rubs circles on my back, soothing me without words. Words wouldn't do anything for the feeling in my chest right now anyways. I'd rather stand here for the foreseeable future and just breathe him in. "Thank you," I whisper when my voice feels strong enough to hold the weight of words.

"I'm here, baby. I've got you." Guiding me back to the bed, we sit back against the headboard and just be in this moment. Alex pulls me against his chest and holds me until my breathing is relaxed and the thumping in my chest settles to a soft thud.

"He left," I admit after a while, the silence having become almost suffocating. The way my mind couldn't calm down from overthinking was loud enough to hear without me having to voice anything. But the admission leaves with ease despite how much my chest splinters in agony at the truth of my words.

"I know," he replies softly. "But he's been looking for Grant, you have to know that. He wouldn't be going to such lengths if he didn't care about you."

"I told him I loved him," I admit weakly. Feeling a little ashamed I'm admitting that to the other man I'm in love with. Alex knows how I feel about both of them and I've expressed my love for him as well. Still, a part of me feels guilty for loving them both, like maybe its not fair to either of them. "He…" I can't admit what happened next, the pain too raw.

"He's an idiot, Isolde. If I know one thing about my brother, it's that he doesn't give a shit about anyone." My chest deflates at his words, knowing that's already the case given the way he dismissed me. My insecurities were already taking over, but I shoved them aside to tell him what I thought he felt too. There's no worse feeling than being discarded and tossed aside like you never meant anything.

"But," Alex begins again, holding my hands in his so he has my attention. I feel it slipping lately, but work to keep it together if only to hear Alex out. "He cares a lot…about *you*."

"I wish that were true, but thank you," I sniffle in his hold, my sobs downgraded to a few tears here and there.

"If he didn't care he wouldn't have been out all night looking for that asshole ex of yours."

"That's literally his job, Alex, to hunt down the men who abuse innocent women and kill them off before they have a chance to do it again."

Alex looks at me, brows pinched before nodding his head, "so I take it he finally told you."

"Yeah, I kind of…saw him in action," I admit sheepishly like its a big secret I'm not aloud to talk about. I guess in a way I'm not, not unless I ever want to be called in as a witness to that mans murder. Whether or not he deserved it, Abram is still murdering people and that may eventually catch up to him.

"Wait, what? You saw him take someone out?" Alex abruptly stands from the bed, staring down at me in disbelief. I don't know if he's expecting me to say just kidding, but it's true and I know the majority of him knows that too. I nod my head and he begins pacing. "Why was he assigned something so close? That doesn't make any sense."

"What do you mean? Why does it matter how close he was?"

"To home, Isolde. It was too close to home," he remarks. Sighing, he sits back down beside me, but his leg jiggles uncontrollably as he prepares what he wants to tell me. "When he first told me about all this, what he does, I hated it. Basically told him he was an idiot who would get caught and thrown in jail for the rest of his life. I knew he had issues since our mom died, but being this reckless seemed unhinged, even for him. He told me he would never take a job too close to home, not wanting to risk someone he knew seeing him."

"Then, why would he agree to that kill, especially since it was right outside the bar I work in?!" Its my turn to stand and pace aimlessly as pieces of the puzzle begin clicking into place. Something isn't right. "Let me get this straight," I say with both hands held in front of me as if I can stop the impending flood of information about to wreak havoc on my mind. "Since finding this job four years ago, Abram has not once taken a job within town limits. I arrive, with a crazy ex boyfriend in tow and all of a sudden he's taking jobs here. That doesn't make any sense unless somehow I'm the reason."

"Why would you be the reason though, baby?" Alex stands next to me, pulling me into him as my body vibrates with anxiety. "I know things are messy right now, but you are not the reason. Okay?" I know he's right, my voice of reason, but I can't help but wonder why the timing of me showing up is too spot on for that not to be the reason.

I need to turn my brain off, put it in sleep mode and focus on something else for the time being. If I don't, all of the what if's will consume me and I fear I'll crumble into little particles of stone. Easily blown away with the lightest breeze.

With strong arms, Alex holds me. The warmth from his body and the sweet smell of sunshine comforting me like the sun itself reached out its arms to hold me. I can't believe I almost turned off the part of me that wanted Alex, the part of me that feared having both of them wouldn't work or that it was selfish. I'm not sure how I would have made a decision between the two, not wanting to even consider the thought of losing one. Selflessly, they allowed me to have them both - something I'm still in awe of.

Turns out I was wrong about one of them. Abram never really wanted me the way Alex does. The way he holds me tenderly and with care. Not like I'm a fragile sheet of glass that could break at any moment, but like his favorite sweater. The one he has to wash with care so the threads don't unravel and ruin what was once beautiful in its own unique way.

I've never been cared for or respected by a man, even in college. Back then I couldn't care less because I too was only after one thing. Getting off and moving on with my day and studies. When Grant came along, it felt too good to be true and turns out, I was right. My gut never said anything bad about Abram. Initially, a little, but that's because I knew nothing about him and all he ever did was leave me with more questions. Every time I was around him I felt nervous, but never in danger. Never once did I think he was the kind of person who would waste his time on someone if he didn't at least like them.

The way Abram looked at me with pity yesterday, stings me somewhere deep in my chest, the image forever branded to me.

I'm tired of fighting these things, the feelings that aren't mine to fight. If he doesn't want me, then fine - I can't make him want me and I don't want to try. Alex wants me, and the growing erection pressed against my stomach is proof of that. Not long ago we stood in this very room as he took me against the window, without a care in the world who saw us. I want that feeling back.

I want him to make me forget the shitstorm surrounding us, and just make me feel *him*.

Reaching between us, I palm him over his jeans. Enjoying the groan of pleasure that leaves him as he rubs himself harder into my hand. "Baby, you can't keep touching me like that." The sound of his voice, the rasp to it, sends a shiver of need down my spine. Settling at my toes that are curling in on themselves. I could die to the sound of his voice, the way his need for me bleeds through his words, soaking into my skin.

Gripping him harder I tease him, "and why not?"

"Because I will bend you over this bed and plow into you until the only thing you can think about is the way I make you feel and the way my name rolls of your tongue."

"Mmm, sounds perfect," I grind into him hoping I've made my point clear. My arousal suddenly feels urgent, pulsing in my veins, the need to be filled becoming too much as I wait for Alex to dive in with me. Ready to drown ourselves in the pleasure, muting the world above us.

I gasp as he shoves me to the bed, my knees bending over the edge as he crawls over me. His fingers dig into the junction of my thighs, pulling them apart so he can settle between them. We rip each others clothes off like we're short on time, like the world is outside the door banging to be let in. Ready to burst our happy little bubble of desire.

Alex peels my leggings down, along with my underwear, as I try to pull his shirt over his head. With one hand, he reaches around and yanks it off while his other works to unclip my bra. Thank God for front clasp bras.

"Fuck, baby, I'll never get used to how perfect you are. How beautiful." Feathering my collarbone with light kisses, I wiggle beneath him.

"I need more, Alex. Don't be gentle with me, not now."

His eyes search mine, looking for any signs I might not mean what I said. But

I need him to show me his desire for me, unhinged and reckless. My heart is barely beating as it is, I don't want to be treated like the breakable little girl I know I still am. All the work I've done to strengthen myself feels pointless at the end of the day - I can't even fight my battles myself. Abram never should have made me believe I'm stronger than I am, because its gotten my nowhere.

"I don't -," I cut him off, covering my hand over his lips. I need to reassure him he won't hurt me, nothing will ever come close to the pain I felt when Abram carelessly walked away from me. I need him to prove his love for me in the only way I'm used to - as fucked up as that may be.

"You won't," I breathe. "You won't hurt me. I just…I need you to be here with *me*. Not the scared, defeated version of me, but the one who is begging you to show me what I mean to you. I need to know I'm not some broken shell of a person carrying around all her baggage on a back that's breaking."

"Is that how you think I see you?"

"It's how I feel everyone sees me, Alex. I tried to run from my past and it followed me here. I'm not strong, but I don't want to feel weak either. I want to feel desired and needed, and you're the only one who can give that to me. You're the only one I want to let go with, so please, wreck me."

His eyes soften for a moment, then suddenly turn avaricious. There's the dark side of Alex I love to see, the one who takes without thought or care. When he allows himself to let go, he becomes the unhinged version of himself he's often too scared to show. I want the beast in him to take and take until I have nothing left to give.

Flipping me over, so my ass is in his face, I feel him run his tongue over the curve in my spine. I arch into him, moaning against the feel of his tongue working its way towards the cleft between my cheeks. I know he won't go there, but a small part of me is hoping he does. I don't want him to think about anything but his pleasure, because that is what will bring me the euphoric feeling I crave.

"If heaven had a taste, it would be you, baby." I shudder at his words, letting the sensation run over the cracked pieces of my mind and body. Loving how it seems to mend the tender parts of my soul. I hear his belt buckle clink as he undoes his jeans and shoves them down his muscular legs. "You're gonna take everything I give you, understand?"

"Yes," I moan into the pillow as I grind myself against him. The feel of his shaft lining up to my entrance has my mouth watering in anticipation. The need to be filled so fully, so wholly is almost unbearable - the feeling indescribable.

Without warning, Alex pushes into me and I scream against the strain. It feels too tight, like I'm literally being shredded from the inside out. My walls desperately trying to stretch to accommodate his size as he moves with short and sharp thrusts. It stings, but in a good way, as he forces my body to comply to his relentless movements.

Within seconds I feel the flood of arousal coating us both and his short painful thrusts glide through me with ease as the pleasure takes over. He begins thrusting into me with rushed aggression, taking every ounce of stress he feels out on me. I welcome it as he plows into me from behind. Each time, he pulls all the way out just to ram himself back in harder than before. My eyes roll back into my skull, my bones feeling like they're rattling against each other as a scream works its way up my throat.

Gripping the back of my neck, Alex holds me down to the mattress as he fucks me without abandon. Tears well in my eyes as my heart beats erratically in my chest, each of my senses so tuned into the moment. The feel of him sliding in and out of me, each ridge of his cock rubbing the most sensitive parts of me - deliciously hitting that spot that tears me apart. The sound of him slamming into me, his balls smacking my clit making me cry out in pleasure. The smell of our mixed arousal permeates the air, almost as if I can taste the way he turns me on.

I feel my orgasm building, like a wave forming in the deepest parts of the ocean, ready to crash at any moment. Alex is close, I can sense it in the way his cock thickens even more, his motions becoming erratic as he races to the finish line alongside me. "Fuck, I'll never get enough of this. Of you," his words come out in a growl, emerging from somewhere deep in his chest.

Leaning down, he wraps a hand around my throat until he's able to pull me up so my back is against his chest. Not letting up, Alex thrusts into me at a new angle that has me breathless. Reaching around, he begins playing with my clit, rubbing firm circles over and over again until I'm certain I see stars. Knowing I'm close, I twist a nipple between two fingers as Alex works my clit. I buck against him as the first tremor breaks free - crying out as wave after wave of bliss consumes me from the inside out.

My moans reverberate off the walls as I come, and a sick part of me hopes Abram came back and can hear the pleasure his brother brings me. I want him to watch and burn in the feeling of jealously as I take everything Alex gives me, riding his cock and milking every last drop of his orgasm from him. I want him to feel the sting of rejection when he realizes I won't let his rejection ruin me the way he wanted it to.

Seconds after my orgasm hits, I feel the first jets of hot cum shoot into me, filling me and spilling out of us as Alex empties himself into me. Like a starved man who hasn't felt the bliss of a woman beneath him in years.

Falling to the mattress, Alex lays on top of me, his heaving breaths mixing with mine, both completely spent. "Fucking hell," I chuckle into the pillows. "I love your dick."

Alex laughs from behind me, his breath tickling the mess of hair falling out of my bun. "I love *you*," he replies softly, though the meaning is much deeper. I don't know what the fuck we're doing or where we go from here - all I know is, this is where I want to be, for however long Alex will have me.

I'm done running. For once in my life I found a place that feels like home. If Grant wants to come and get me, then bring it on. I won't leave without a fight. Because as sick as I am of fighting for things that were never meant to be mine - I *will* fight for the things I know I deserve.

***

I wake to an empty bed. Feeling the sheets beside me, they're cold, which means Alex has been gone a while. They've been working with me and training me for over a week now, so I'm sure he has plenty of work to catch up on. One of the perks of owning your own business is not having to answer to anyone else. Not sure their

334

clients love that too much, but it is what it is.

Making my way downstairs I look around the entryway table for my purse, hoping my cell phone is in there. I'm not sure how long I slept the last two days, but it's been a lot judging by the crick in my neck. I haven't checked my phone since before Abram left. Thankfully I wasn't scheduled for a shift at Pour Performer until tomorrow. I doubt Sasha would have liked my excuse.

Finding my bag, I rifle through it until I find my cell. There's no messages from Abram - shocking - and one from Alex saying he had to leave for a job. As I expected.

The message that catches me off guard and has every hair on my body coming to attention is the one from an Unknown Number again. Every time I see those two words, my heart beats wildly and sweat breaks out on my forehead. I can't help the physical reaction any better than I can help my mind racing with a million scenarios.

On a deep breath, I open the message and feel all the blood drain from my face. Not only did he find me, but he's *here*. My worst nightmare coming to life with no one here to save me but myself.

Come find me.

Under those three words is a pin drop location - the woods behind the manor. Feeling the tremors begin to build, I remember that feeling of being watched the other day during our training. When Abram said no one comes out here I knew it had to be someone from out of town who ignored the private property signs, or Grant.

Fuck! I shouldn't have said anything to Abram, I should have bottled my feelings up until we knew for certain there was no danger lurking around each corner. I don't want to cry, I don't want to hide and I don't want to be scared. But I can't fucking help it when I'm standing here all alone with no idea what his next move is.

Pacing the entryway, I rack my brain for what to do. I could just pick up and leave again - but he would just find me wherever I go next. I could follow his instructions and run around aimlessly in the forest until he finds me - another option that has my skin feeling like paste, melting off my body as the heat from my anxiety lights me on fire from the inside out.

Panic is now bubbling in my chest, my feet feeling like cement blocks around my ankles as I frantically try dialing Alex's number. He doesn't answer and I resist the urge to scream in frustration. The man who always has his phone in his back pocket suddenly can't be reached.

"Shit, shit, shit!" I yell into the empty hallway. My voice echoes around me, intensifying the fact that I'm here all alone. June left town to visit a friend a few days ago, so thankfully she won't be here for Grant to hold over me. He knows exactly how to get me to comply to his wishes - he did it all the time with my parents. Threatening to do something to them if I didn't shut my mouth and be the *'good little wife'* I was expected to be.

The package he sent me catches my eye, still sitting on the bottom shelf of the bookcase by the front door. I stare at it, bile rising in my throat just thinking about glancing inside again. All the horrors of my past bleeding through the cardboard and soaking the floor at my feet. Like an invisible noose wrapped around my neck, I walk blindly towards it and kneel on the floor, hands shaking as I pull it off the shelf.

I didn't have to look thoroughly to know what he sent, seeing the first thing on top was all I needed to know the kind of lengths he would go, just to prove a point. That I will forever be under his thumb as long as he's still breathing.

Images of me, naked and bound to the bed flash before me as I dump the contents of the box on the rug. Hundreds of photos, dozens of thumb drives and more, littler the space before me. He documented every single attack. All of the abuse I suffered over the years, all of it right here in front of me. I could burn it - get rid of all the shameful evidence he's presented to me like a fucking gift. Wrapped in neat bows and placed in photo albums like a happy memory to look back on for years to come.

He got off on this - my pain. The way I would cry and beg for mercy, beg for forgiveness on things I didn't even know would result in his punishments. The littlest things set him off, he used every transgression as an excuse to torture me and he got away with it for *years*. Because I was too afraid to speak up and get help, to try and run from the sadistic man I thought loved me.

Look where it got me now. I did run and instead of getting rid of an abusive ex, I gained a psychotic man who will go to extensive lengths to bring me back where he thinks I belong. At this point I don't think it has anything to do with me as a person. He cheated all the time, getting his fill from God knows how many holes during the years we were together. It's about power for Grant - the need to be in control. As soon as I took that from him, I took his purpose.

He will never stop - not until I'm shackled to a wall, bound in chains - or *dead*.

Honestly, I'd happier with the latter at this point.

Staring down at the pile of proof of my abuse, knowing he has multiple copies somewhere, I'm startled by a ping from my phone. Scrambling to my feet, I reach for it hoping to see a response from Alex. Another text from the Unknown Number, and I might actually vomit this time.

Tick tock, Princess. I wouldn't want to take your sunshine away.

I don't move or even flinch as my phone tumbles from my numb fingers and clatters to the floor, the screen shattering from the impact. It seems almost congruent to my heart - the way it keeps shattering when I thought there was nothing left to break.

It's one thing to fuck with me, it's another thing entirely to hurt the ones I love.

Feeling the fear mixed with unbridled rage settle in my bones, I harness it and prepare for the fight I spent months running from. If he wants me, then he can have me - I'm half dead on the inside as it is. If he tries to take one of the only people I've ever truly loved away from me, then I might as well be buried six feet under alongside them.

Grabbing my running sneakers from the welcome bench, I make quick work of the laces, tying them tight before adjusting my ponytail. My hands tremble as I reach for the front door, and I can't help the way my teeth chatter when I'm terrified. Turning around, I let my gaze wander around the space I worked so hard to bring to life - knowing it might be the last time I set foot in here. Maybe someday someone can enjoy this house for all it has to offer. Looking past all the pain it's harbored on the inside and focusing on it's natural beauty.

Pain explodes in my chest at not seeing June again, or my parents. Wiping away the tears that fall without thought, I have to put them all out of my mind in order to finish this. One way or another, this nightmare ends today.

I just hope I get the satisfaction of putting Grant in a body bag before he has the chance to end me once and for all.

***

As my feet pound into the wooded path, I comfort myself with the familiar scents I've grown to love since living here. This forest has a distinct scent that always brings me a sense of peace. The way the damp earth combined with the sharp smell of pine soothes my racing heart. I choose to focus on the fragrances around me rather than the sickening sense of dread building like a block of ice in my chest.

The leaves began changing a few weeks ago, the entire forest blanketed in beautiful warm shades of red, orange and brown. I can't help but remember the first time I wandered around these woods - enjoying the crisp air around me, breathing it in like a lifeline. Instead of being met with herbal combinations and damp soil and notes of sap, I got that mixed with the sharp aroma of tobacco smoke.

I jog past the spot he tackled me to the ground the first time he chased me through these trees, remembering the way he pushed into me and whispered words of desire. I was so naive to think we would ever be more than two people fucking - passing the time with pleasure.

Alex has always been different - caring in his advancements, aware of my needs not just his own. His words echo in my mind like a beautiful memory - the softness in his tone and the way he's always handled my heart with the utmost care. Even when he lets the beast inside him emerge, he's still calculated to a degree. *"I've got you, baby."*

I can't begin to imagine what I might stumble upon when I finally find Grant -

knowing he has Alex somewhere out here with him. Swallowing down the vomit that keeps threatening to make an appearance, I brush off the side stitch gnawing at my ribcage and push harder. For all I know, Grant already installed cameras out here to watch me run around like a dog chasing its tail just for his own amusement.

When he feels like the dramatic build up is enough for his sadistic games, he'll make himself known. I plan on being ready for that moment.

All the mental prep I planned on making comes to a screeching halt when I catch sight of my worst nightmare. Alex is strapped to the base of a tree, mouth gagged so he can't yell for help. Everything inside begins buzzing at a high frequency it feels like someone is tattooing my brain. Without scanning my surroundings for Grant, I run to Alex frantically trying to untie him. I don't care about anything else as my fingers rush to undo the dozens of knots in place - put there to slow me down, no doubt.

Loud mumbles and unintelligible words groan around the tape across Alex's face, and as much as it kills me, I rip it off so he can tell me what the fuck happened. "Isolde, get the fuck out of here!" He whisper yells, as if he thinks I might actually leave him here like this.

"Are you insane? No! I'm not leaving you here like this," I want to say more but Alex's eyes are pleading as he stares into mine.

"Baby, please go. It's a trap, we both know that. I'm just the bait he used to lure you out here. You need to run, keep running until you hear from either me or Stoker." His name sends a zap of pain through me, the thought of him halting my movements for just a second. A split second was all it took, though. He always knows when to strike, when I'm at my weakest.

"Well *hello*, Princess. I've been waiting on your arrival for some time now." Turning around, I'm face to face with the man who tortured and raped me for years. He checks his watch as if he was timing how long it took for me to get here. The same man who paid off medical staff to erase hospital stays to cover his own ass. The man who documented every rape, every attack he inflicted on me, then mailed to my new residence as if he knew where I was all along.

Reading my mind, and the frozen face of fear I'm wearing, he chuckles. "Yes, I've known where you've been all along, Princess. I was just having so much fun toying with you, allowing you to get comfortable and think you're actually safe," he clicks his tongue and shakes his head against his chest. "So naive."

"Why?" I ask, unable to hold it in any longer. "Why me? You clearly have no issues going out and getting whatever woman you want. Flashing that smile of yours in your expensive suit that drips money. Why do you need me so badly?"

The smile he wore just seconds ago, fades. Replaced with a sinister look that has my shoulders hunching on instinct - ready to submit like I always did. "Because, you stupid whore," he begins and Alex thrashes against his restraints, ready to spew a string of profanities at him before I hold up a hand to make him stop. I need to hear this. "You embarrassed me, know one gets away with that."

"So that's what this is really about, *revenge?* It's never had anything to do with you loving me or even being obsessed with me because you crave control. I did something you deemed unworthy and I quote, *'embarrassed you,'* so you track me down and attempt to collect a debt you feel you're owed. Did I get that right?"

His fists clench at his sides, not happy with my tone of voice, surely, and I have to hold in the smile that threatens to break free. Years of being with him has prepared me for exactly this moment. Working hard to reel in his emotions, he cocks a head to the side, smiling like the maniac he is. "You know," he starts walking towards us slowly, a shark in the water stalking its prey. "I think I've changed my mind."

"What the fu-," my question is cut short when a shot rings out. I barely have enough time to register the gun he pulls from his suit jacket before it goes off. My ears rings and I cover my eyes in hopes I can pretend he's not carrying, realizing both myself and Alex are in far more danger than I ever anticipated.

"I wanted to punish you, and boy did I have some fun plans for us. But, I think I found a way to punish you that will bring me more enjoyment than any previous plan I concocted." Grant lifts his chin up causing me to glance over my shoulder. There against the tree, Alex is slumped over with a hole in his chest, blood pouring out of him at a sickening rate.

All the air in my chest gets stuck in my throat, I can't breathe as I stare at a man I love with everything I am, bleeding out before me. Wounded by a man who never loved me at all, a man who looked at me as a trophy wife not a life partner. Alex's eyes are heavy as he glances around, searching for me, for the comfort we find in each other - needing it now more than ever before.

Blinking rapidly multiple times, I try to push away the sight before me, hoping its all just a bad dream and I'll wake up in bed next to Alex. The bed we shared and fell asleep holding each other just hours before. This can't be real.

Grant's voice comes through the haze, and I feel the rising panic building just as reality threatens to break through. "Well, this has been eventful. But I'm not done with you yet. Run, Princess." And with that, I hear him walking closer to me, gun in hand, ready to pull the trigger on me next.

He wants to play game of cat and mouse, chasing me down and feeding off my fear and adrenaline. The majority of me can't imagine leaving Alex here, but the rational side of me knows I can try and get help if I run fast enough. Grant doesn't know I've been training with the guys - and while I know I'm not marathon quality, I can at least hold my own.

"I'll be back, just hold on for me. Okay?" I whisper against Alex's mouth, sealing our lips with a tender kiss before jumping up and running in the direction of the manor. Never playing fair, Grant immediately starts after me, God forbid he gets embarrassed again by a woman outrunning him. Can't wait to show him just how much fight I still have left in me.

His footsteps sound behind me, thundering into the earth while twigs and leaves snap beneath the soles of his boots. Fear skates over every inch of me as memories play on a loop in my mind. The sick soundtrack of my past mocking me into giving up. A not so subtle reminder that I've never been able to escape him. How could I think now would be any different? Fuck, no. I'll fight until my heart stops beating - even then, I'll haunt him in the afterlife.

I came here looking for a fresh start, a safe haven I could one day make my home. That little voice buried deep down knew better than that though. The weaker part of me knows I'll never truly be free as long as Grant walks this earth. At this point I know it's not because he's in love with me and so lost without me by his side that he's going to such extremes. No. It's entirely about power, control and manipulation. I don't fall in line like I always have, so he wants revenge. I can almost hear the words seeping out of his pores, begging me to give in. Reminding me the longer I play this game, the worse it'll be for me.

My adrenaline kicks into overdrive and I push my legs even faster, I refuse to let the weak little girl in my head win. I don't have much of a chance of outrunning him, but if Abram has taught me anything, it's to never give up. Harnessing that strength he's instilled in me, I work up a plan to get out of this. I know these woods better than I did when I first arrived. The amount of times Abram has stalked and chased me through these very trees borders on crazy, and now's my chance to prove I can outsmart him. If only just this one time.

Turning to chance a peak at how close he is, I see that he's no longer following me - just another tactic to keep me on edge. Always looking over my shoulder, wondering where he is and when he'll strike next. "Fucking sociopath!" I scream into the void, hoping the echoes of my rage reach him in some capacity.

He just needed an excuse to get me away from saving Alex, wasting my time so he bleeds out with each passing second. Grants wants me to feel the pain of losing someone I love, taking everything away from me so he gains more power. I refuse to let him have that, not without trying to save Alex first. Racing back in the direction I came from, I search for where Alex is and stumble to a halt when I see him, face pale and lips turning a sickening shade of blue.

Out of breath from the chase, I make my way back over to him. I see him unmoving and fear clutches my chest at the state he's in. Closing my eyes, I try to hold back the impending tears - a pointless feat. When I open them, the scene is still the same. Alex is bleeding out and I don't know how to do anything to stop it, to try and slow it down. Fuck, I wish Hailey was here. The panic that was rising is here instead, bursting out of me as I let loose the scream I had been holding. I throw every ounce of my energy into the sound, the pain that erupts out of me has my knees buckling to the ground as sticks prick my legs.

"No!" I scream again and again as I scramble towards Alex, placing both hands over his rapidly rising chest, his body working hard to keep the blood pumping - to keep him breathing. I firmly hold the area he was shot, working to keep the bleeding controlled - practically tasting the metallic tang of blood as I breathe in deeply - but it's no use. There's too much blood and we're too far away from the house to call for help. I should have just let Grant shoot me, right here next to Alex where we could have died together. This can't be happening.

"This can't be happening," I say again, out loud this time. With one hand, Alex reaches up to cup my face. I don't even remember untying him - the adrenaline must have taken over. He looks at me with a softness I won't be able to erase for the rest of my life. The blue eyes I've stared into countless times, watching me with a kind of acceptance I can't process right now. I can't stand to think of the light vanishing from those blue depths - the only ocean I would willingly drown in.

"Baby, look at me," he whispers as his fingers lightly play with the strands of hair framing my face.

"I can't," I admit. If I look at him, he's going to tell me everything will be okay. That he loves me and that I'm strong - that I can get through this. But I don't think I can, losing him would be too much. I know Alex better than myself at this point and I know the kind of selflessness he possesses. He makes me want to believe everything will be alright, that he's going to pull through and make it out of this mess. That we can still find Grant and end this once and for all, knowing he's lingering here until he gets me back. But I'm not that naive little girl anymore, this is real life and Alex is dying. Right here, in my arms as I hold him against me, hands still providing pressure to his gunshot wound.

I won't stop until I know I did all I could.

"Please, Isolde," he tries again and my chest cracks open, sobs wracking my body as my eyes meet his again, tears of his own falling. "Don't cry, baby," his voice sounds broken, far away and I know he only has minutes left. His blood is pooled around us, the sight making me dizzy as I try to focus on the outline of his jaw, the smile I've loved since the first time I saw him, under a set of blue lips. The way his eyes crinkle at the corners when he belly laughs and the sound of his laughter when it fills a room, lighting it up.

"I n-need you to k-know," his teeth chatter as he tries to get the words out. My own trembles taking over as I watch him work to speak. "B-because of you, I get to d-die with a smile on my face." My body collapses against his, tears mixing with the blood running down his chest. I've never known a pain like this, nothing can even come close in comparison to the raw agony I'm feeling. His words echoing around inside my nearly hollow chest. A part of my heart went with Abram when he left, and the other part is crumbling before me - destined to stay with Alex until I take my own last breath. I move to kiss him one last time, memorizing the smell of him, that sweet sunshine and cedar tainted now by the scent of blood. The feel of his soft lips against mine like an invisible tattoo.

"Don't leave me, Alex, *please*," I beg. "I love you." He doesn't say it back, and I can't bring myself to look up at him. He always says it back, he always means it or is the one to voice it first. In that moment I know it's over - he's gone.

I stay against him for several minutes, praying to catch the thump of his heartbeat, a rise in his chest that remains painfully still. Begging God to help me, bring him back and escape this nightmare. Crying out to the trees, birds chirping away up above as if my world below isn't crumbling to ash.

And just like the ending credits of a movie, the scene unfolds before me in slow motion. The way his eyes close as the final curtain on everything he's been leading up to in his life, vanishes into nothing. Silence envelops me in a tight hold, stealing what little breath I had. It tumbles out of me in a rush of anguish, my body unable to scream due to the shock wracking my very bones. I want to look away, praying that what I know to be true is just a figment of my mind. A nightmare I'm bound to wake up from but not without being drenched in sweat. I'll wipe the perspiration from my forehead and laugh off the uncomfortable unease in my stomach reminding myself it's not real. One look at his lifeless body tells me this is all too real. I don't feel my knees digging into the forest floor, and all I hear is the stillness of the forest surrounding us in black agony ready to take me under.

STOKER

chapter twenty-six

♫

Prayer • Disturbed

Isolde's scream pierces the silence, causing all the air to whoosh out of me, leaving me near breathless. A flock of birds startle in the trees overhead, flying in the opposite direction of Isolde's yelling. Something is wrong, and I have a gnawing feeling in my gut I never should have left. I thought I was doing the right thing by leaving to hunt down Grant - doing the worst thing I could think of so she'd let me go - but all it did was leave her vulnerable to him. I know my brother loves her, but no one can protect her the way I can. The way I will never stop until she understands the depths I will go to for her and only her.

Breaking out in a sprint, I race towards the sound of her bone chilling screams and hope that I'm not too late. As much as I enjoy her screams of ecstasy, the way her body gives itself over to the euphoric feelings - even when mixed with a touch of pain. The terror in her voice says she's experiencing something devastating.

As I approach the opening of the trail into the woods, I see Ellis walking out casually, whistling to himself. Coming to an abrupt stop, I feel the walls inside me crumbling as a horrific realization comes into focus. "Abram! So good to see you, friend," he calls out to me as he inches closer, not caring that a pained woman was just screaming in the woods he emerged from. The same woods that clearly state private property. Each step has my heart rate accelerating at an alarming rate I'm uncomfortable with.

Stopping a few feet away, he cocks his head to the side as he watches me, silent fascination in his gaze. "What's your first name?" I ask, not realizing my voice actually works considering my tongue feels like its stuck to the roof of my mouth.

Tipping his head back, he laughs manically to the sky. "Wow, took you long enough, don't you think? I thought for sure when we met a few weeks ago you would have pieced it together - little disappointing if I'm being honest."

"Grant," I declare, all the wheels clicking into place.

Clapping his hands together like a little kid getting ready for snack time, he jumps up at the same time, an excited gleam taking over. "Yes! Now you're getting it. Ahh," he rubs his hands together in a warming motion as he moves slowly in a circle around me. I don't dare take my eyes off him as he looks down at his shoes, enjoying the suspense of this moment. "This is just too good, truly. I never anticipated my little game playing out as long as it has. You never asked my first name and she must not have ever mentioned my last name, making this all too perfect. It's like Christmas morning!"

All these years, I've been working for a twisted fuck who gets off on others pain and fear. How could he possibly be in the business of taking out rapists and abusers when he himself is one of the worst ones. I saw everything he did to Isolde, the way he tormented her the majority of their relationship. Tied her to chairs, sodomized her, drugged and raped her - all of it is in that box of horrors he sent to her.

"How did you know she was here?" I ask, still sifting through questions racing around my mind, each one fighting for a chance to be answered.

"I'm so glad you asked," he exclaims. "It's pretty funny, actually. Isolde thought she was so smart, using only what cash she had in her purse to get her this far. Guess she forgot about traffic cams and tolls. Each time she passed a major bridge or toll, her license plate was scanned and I was able to track her direction. Once she got close to Stehekin, it only took a little looking to officially find her."

"How long?"

"How long, what?" He looks at me with a fake puzzled expression. He's enjoying this too much. He also seems to keep forgetting what he trained me to do - the things I'm capable of.

"How fucking long have you known she was here?!"

"Since her first week here," he admits with a misplaced sense of satisfaction. "I let her think she got away for a little while, though. Then I started sending her texts."

What the fuck? She never told me he was sending her messages, and she waited to tell us about the package he sent too. Granted that was only a day, but still. Did she really feel like she couldn't trust us with this information?

"Judging by the look on your face, I'd say you didn't know that," his smiles grows, making me want to knock his teeth out. "Jesus, this is too good," bending over, he slaps his knee like he just heard the best joke.

"Truthfully, I was hoping for a scenario like this but never dreamed someone with your capabilities wouldn't pick up on at least *something*. Makes sense, her pussy is pretty magnificent - I can understand why you were so distracted."

I lunge for him, needing to act on my instincts that are screaming to end this guy, and setting aside my own frustrations for not knowing the kind of person I've been working for. He quickly dodges my advance and clicks his tongue at me before I have a chance to say a word. "Careful, Stoker. Wouldn't want all your criminal activity to be released to the police, now would we?"

He's fucking blackmailing me? As if I actually give a shit about any of that - all I care about is getting Isolde away from this creep who believes in a distorted reality where she actually belongs to him. The unhinged animal in me wants to strap him down and make him watch as I claim her over and over again - force him to listen to the way I make her come and how she screams *my* name.

"You and I both know I don't give a fuck about any of that. Where is she?"

He stops the weird circling his prey in the water thing and stands in front of me, hands clasped over his open suit jacket. "Presumably still crying over the body of her second boyfriend. Gotta hand it to her, didn't think she had it in her to bag two guys - let alone brothers. Guess she really does have a magical cunt."

"What the fuck are you talking about?" I yell, feeling my fists clench by my sides, ready to rip a goddamn tree from the ground, roots and all.

"Oh, sorry, thought I mentioned this already. I shot your brother. He's likely bled out by now," he says with a casual shrug like he didn't just admit to killing my brother. My fucking *brother*! My head starts to feel light, like bees are buzzing around and my vision turns spotty. That can't be what he just said, I refuse to believe that's actually true.

"You're lying," I counter. Praying he's just trying to distract me so he can catch me off guard more than his presence already has.

"Afraid not. That's why your precious girlfriend was screaming like a damn banshee. I had to get out of their before she pierced my damn eardrums."

Grant studies his fingernails, leaving him vulnerable to my blooming rage. He doesn't even see it coming when I put all my weight into my fist and knock him out cold. Should have done that a while ago, the sound of his voice like a cheese grater scraping out pieces of my brain.

I can feel the panic and grief ready to take over, but I shove it down for now. My brother is likely dead, which means Isolde is close to wherever he is. As soon as I get Grant somewhere he can't escape, a place I can come back to and handle him once and for all - I'll find them.

A thought crosses my mind, the panic room Isolde insisted on keeping at the manor. A room that would have come in handy had my mom had enough time to get to it before her life was ripped away from her and us. I never told Isolde this, but it was smart to keep it in the house, as a backup or just a security blanket. Something that made her feel more at ease with what she's been running from. I didn't get it at first, but after everything I've seen and learned about her past, it makes sense why she was adamant about it.

Silently thanking her, I grab Grant by the ankles and begin dragging him across the yard to where the bulkhead door leads to the cellar. The ground is damp and I can't help the smile splitting my cheeks as I watch soil seep into his very expensive, tailored suit. I knew something was strange about him when we met face to face for the first time, but this was the man I had been working under for four years, I couldn't fathom the kind of person he really was underneath all the fancy attire and expensive cologne.

Grant groans as his ass bumps into a few stones sticking out of the ground, hopefully leaving an array of bruises. I plan on covering majority of his body in black and blue - my two favorite colors - by the end of the day.

Once inside, I strap him to a chair against a wall in the panic room. These rooms were added as an extra measure of safety back in the days. I doubt it was ever intended to be used as a room someone actually panics in the way I hope Grant does. I hope he wakes up, feels his body shackled to a chair, wrapped tightly with wire and rope - that's all I had nearby - and feels the fear he so easily inflicted on an innocent woman.

Isolde endured too much of this shit, and I'm more than happy to return the favor tenfold. He doesn't know what's coming, but I'm going to make sure he feels every ounce of torture I intend on inflicting on his worthless existence. Payback for Isolde, and my brother. My eye twitches at the thought of my brother lying in the woods, covered in blood, *dying*. I can't push the image fully out of my mind, as much as I wish I could, already knowing what it must look like.

Focusing my attention back to the task at hand, I look at Grant. All I see is a weak man hiding behind money and false power - just a trust fund kid who got everything handed to him on a silver platter. I thought I enjoyed taking the life of that lawyer in his silk pajamas, I intend on reveling in the feeling of taking Grant's life much more than any other kill.

Satisfied that he can't escape, I race back up the basement stairs and through the backyard towards the woods. I know these trails like the back of my hand - woven through the woods like a series of veins all leading back to the heart of the property.

If I had to guess based on where her screams came from, she's not far from the spot we did our training a few days ago. Everything feels like its happening too fast for me to grasp. Grant showing up here and turning out to be the man I've worked for has my head still spinning. Dizzying my thoughts the way the tress blur by as I run with all my strength. How could we have been out here just a few days ago, preparing to fight for Isolde's freedom? Now I'm racing towards the woman I made feel less than she is and my dying brother.

I never should have left!

The phrase plays over and over in my head like a nail being hammered into my skull - the pain of leaving them both here, unknowing of the danger just outside our backyard. I knew Grant was close and that he was willing to go to great lengths to get what he wanted. But I had no idea the same man we've been training Isolde to fight is the one who taught me how to kill. Had I paid a little more attention, I would have seen that. Ellis was right about one thing, I was too distracted and that allowed him to walk right past my open eyes knowing I was unable to see clearly.

The forest is quiet, eerily so. The only sounds my heavy breathing as I race past trees and through mud patches, narrowly catching myself before busting my ass.

I hear her before I see her, the soft sound of sniffling reaching my ears like the saddest soundtrack. She's not going to want to see me - that much I know - but I have to see my brother, I need to see for myself what that fucker did to one of the only family members I had left. The pain I kept trying to push down, burying it until I'm able to face it fully, threatens to emerge again as I come around the bend and see Isolde.

Her small frame hunched over Alex, his body slumped against a tree trunk. My mouth feels like a desert as I desperately try to swallow the bile in my throat. Blood rushes in my ears, making them hot to the touch as my heart beat races against the blood draining from my face. He's gone. I can see that truth from where I stand, a hundred feet away. I can practically taste the rusty tang of blood as it floats towards me with a soft breeze carrying the sharp scents of the forrest. Reminding me that even the most beautiful things can be tainted by darkness.

My restraint is slipping as I move closer to them, slowly and with measured steps. It's like I can't get to them fast enough while also not wanting to see what I already know. Painfully walking towards a reality I don't want to accept but knowing I'll be forced to as soon as I'm close enough.

Hazel eyes, drowning in tears, look up at me. I can feel her despair leaking out of her as she cries endlessly, searching my eyes for the pinch she needs to wake up from this nightmare. I love when I make her cry - the taste of her tears - but only the ones I inflict, a result of her pain and pleasure mixing together in a beautiful symphony. I'd love nothing more than slapping her ass raw, waking her up from the evil that's found us and tell her the only pain she'll experience is when I'm inside her. None of that is helpful in this moment. None of that matters as I take in the scene before me.

"Get out of here, Stoker!" Her yelling startles me as I flinch back a step. The sound of her turmoil is partnered with unfiltered rage, the need for me to be her punching bag evident. If that's what she needs, then I'll be that.

"Baby, listen to me," I begin but she cuts me off with a slash of her arm through the air. I don't miss the way it's painted crimson with my brothers blood. His eyes are closed, the light in them forever snuffed out.

"Don't call me that!" She screams, fresh tears leaking from her eyes. "You fucking *left* us, you don't get to come back and demand I listen to you now. Do us all a favor and do what you do best, *disappear*." Her words hurt, I can't deny the way they cut little slits in my heart. But I need her to understand I didn't just leave them - I didn't leave *her*.

"Yes, you fucking do, little bird. We need to finish this," I try again, my voice leaving no room for argument. I know she's hurting, I feel it in the way her eyes want to fight me but lack that spark I've grown to love. Just like I heard it in the way her voice cracked against the rage in her chest - the way the anguish of everything crumbling in on her, threatening to pull her under indefinitely.

My mind wanders back to not even an hour ago, when I called Isolde's phone, hoping to explain everything to her. I wasn't expecting Ellis to answer, or the way all the blood in my body practically evaporated when it became clear he had her.

"Isolde and I are going to play a little game, a favorite past time if you will. But thank you so much for calling," he spoke into the receiver with a cheery tone that made me want to gut him while he was still alive - ensuring he felt every ounce of pain.

"If you so much as hurt one inch of her I will slit your throat and force feed you your own blood just to watch it drain out of you a second time," I growled in return. It would be a beautiful sight, as long as I get the opportunity to see it through. No way this sick fucker hurts her again - I'll burn every goddamn thing in my way to the ground until I get her back.

"How poetic," he remarks dryly. "You always did have a flare for theatrics when it came to your work - hence why you've always been the best. But let us not forget who trained you to be this way." The fucking audacity this asshole has - he didn't teach me shit.

"Why do you call me that?" She asks, her voice cutting through the flashback. Her voice is even, the tremors held back for the moment as she watches me, waiting for an answer. Why is that important right now? I want to ask, but the words won't form properly, refusing to leave my mouth as I watch her with the same intensity she's watching me.

"You've been calling me *little bird* since I met you, and I've never understood why. I want to know."

"Now? Isolde, we need to - "

"Finish this, I know," she says as she wipes the tears from her face on the sleeve of her sweater, leaving behind streaks of red. "I'll pull myself together, put aside the fact that I just held your brother as he died. I watched the light in his eyes dim to nothing as he dragged in his last breath, and the way his body released it one final time. I can do all of that, as soon as you tell me why."

Fuck. I don't know how to do this. I don't know how to explain to her what that means and more importantly, what she means to me. I'll fuck it up, just like I do everything when it comes to her. "I…" The words are there, begging to be set free. Released from the chains I've held them by, bound to the deepest parts of myself so I don't get hurt. In the process of protecting my own black heart, I've incinerated hers.

"You make me believe in freedom, Isolde. Like I'm allowed to free myself of my past. All my crimes, my baggage, my grief and pain, all the loss but also everything I've gained." Moving closer to her, I watch as her gentle eyes take me in, the lines of my face, the yearning in my eyes I hope she can feel as they tell her everything I can't. "Birds fly free - creating their own way - but always knowing the way home. When you came here I saw it in you immediately. You were scared, yes. But you had a knowing look in you, as if you knew this was home."

She doesn't say anything, my words feeding something in her heart that can only be spoken through the bond we've built. Yes, I left her and made her feel like she was nothing, but in that moment rage was all I could see, all I could feel. I set aside everything because the only thing I needed was to find the man that hurt her, the one that still haunted her, and take him away so that she could always fly free. The way she's meant to. I needed to show her how much I loved her by setting her free.

"So, you call me that because I remind you of freedom? That doesn't make a lot of sense, Abram."

"Baby, it's the only thing that makes sense to me. You're the key to *my* freedom - you showed me by letting someone in I can free myself of the fear. *You* freed me, little bird, and…I love you." She gasps, the trembles in her body that subsided moments ago, back again. Her lip trembles too, and I want nothing more than to suck it between my teeth and bite it until her taste floods my senses.

"All this time, I've been telling you I love you without you knowing, testing the way it felt and if I could love you the way you need. But I realized you don't need my love to flourish. You are the strongest person I've ever met - you face life's bullshit head on and never let it knock you down. Look at everything you've gone through in your life up until this point. You keep looking for your way home - but baby, *you* are home. You're my home."

"Y-you…you love me? But I thought," I interrupt her before she can voice it. The way I spoke to her as if she meant nothing still kills me. The way her eyes died as I said the words so carelessly.

"Yeah baby, I do. That's why I left like that. I needed you to think I didn't care so that you'd let me go. Knowing how close Grant was, how easily he could get to you - the rage that built inside me was like a volcano ready to burst. I physically couldn't stand to sit back and wait for his attack any longer - I needed to find him. If only I had known that was his plan all along," I recall the feelings I felt as I drove away from her - my heart felt like it was splintering inside my chest, silently warning me not to go.

"Well, you succeeded in that," she laughs humorlessly. "But, I guess I get it. I just," she looks down at Alex, her body still clutching his tightly like she's afraid to let go. I can see her allowing my admission to seep in - the way my truth makes sense now as she stares at him. His body lying eerily still, making my stomach churn with guilt. "I don't know how to let him go," she sobs.

The pain in her chest mirrors my own, and as badly as I want to break down, I can't. This isn't over and I refuse to let Grant Ellis live another hour. He's taken too much from us both as it is, it's time we take it back. But she can't force her eyes to look away from Alex, slumped over on the ground.

He's dead.

My little brother, the sunshine that cut through my darkness, is gone. I know he's dead, and the panic in my chest is rapidly growing - becoming overwhelming. I grab Isolde's face gently, forcing her attention on me. "Baby, look at me. I know you're crumbling, I am too. But we have to finish this, okay? Not just for you anymore, but for him too," I say as I look at my brother fully for the first time. His normally tan skin looks waxy from sweat, almost translucent as the life that once thrived there, leaves us more with each passing second. "We can't let him take anything else from us, understand?"

She nods her head slowly as tears paint her flushed cheeks. The exertion from running mixed with her overwhelming grief has turned her cheeks a beautiful shade of mauve. In any other situation I would drown in her beauty, but I move to stand as she finally shifts away from Alex.

"We'll come back for him, I promise," I tell her as I weave our fingers together - feeling hers coating mine in a dark shade of red.

When she fully stands, her body staggers a little, so I hold her up by her waist until she feels confident she can walk again. Knowing her heart is shattered into tiny fragments, I watch with awe as she pushes it down, readying herself for what's to come. Something tells me I don't need to prepare her for anything, I can see it in the self-assured way she eyes the path ahead - she knows what she wants to do and I'm ready to let her take it.

ISOLDE

chapter twenty-seven

Feel Nothing • The Plot In You

Walking up to the manor, I feel a sense of dread, but also a sense of purpose. Like my body knows how badly I need to see this end. My mind is having a harder time catching up, considering how much has happened in such a short time. I can feel the tremors taking over as Abram opens the bulkhead to the basement. He must have locked Grant in the panic room. *I knew there was a reason I wanted to keep it,* I whisper to myself.

Just behind those doors is the man of my nightmares, asleep and awake. But I'm done running. Because if I've learned anything it's that even if you run from your monsters, they somehow always find you.

"Are you ready?" Abram asks just behind me. He's allowing me to take the lead and a part of me is thankful for that, but the larger part of me is terrified of the control. How will I feel if I take this mans life? Will it bring me peace? Or will it bring me a new kind of hell that I'll live in forever knowing I was capable of ending someone?

I think its a risk I'm willing to take - if not for me, then for Alex.

"Yes," I whisper into the dark hallway before the panic room. I used to be scared of coming down here, now I'm balls out terrified. Instead of letting that consume me, I feed into the fear, just like Abram taught me.

The door opens with an unsettling creak, notifying Grant of our arrival. He's awake, watching me as I slowly enter the small space. A shiver works its way up my spine at the chilling way he smiles at me, like he's enjoying the game far too much. He has to know it won't end well for him, right?

"Princess, I'm so happy to see you," he remarks, and my skin crawls at the nickname. I always hated when he called me that. To everyone around us, they thought it was a sweet term of endearment, when really it was so I knew my place. He told me I would always be a Princess until I learned what it took to be his Queen. Fucking idiot.

"Let's skip the bullshit, shall we?"

Abram chuckles behind me, already enjoying my show of confidence. I want him to see the strong side of me he said I posses, harnessing it and bringing it to life just to end someone else. Taking a step back, he holds a hand out in front of him like I have the floor. "You got this, baby."

I don't miss the way Grant rolls his eyes, he doesn't think I'm capable of inflicting the kind of pain he doused me with for years. He's going to find out just how much I've learned from being with him. How being the quiet scared little girl allowed me to absorb all the trauma, all the pain, and use it against him now.

Grabbing a hunters knife on the table beside where Grant is tied down, I flip it between my fingers - watching the sharpness skate over my exposed fingers. I feel an odd sense of exhilaration that I won't be the one inflicted with pain by this instrument. I finally get to use it against the man who tortured me for far too long.

His eyes widen as he stares at the length of the knife. Abram must have supplied me with tools to use should I have wanted to kill Grant myself. He must have known that if I didn't want to then he could easily end him. I love that he sees I'm strong enough to do this, and that he'll be by my side if it becomes too much to do alone.

"I no longer burn because of you, Grant," I begin, already enjoying the sweat that beads in his hairline. "See that was my mistake all along. I allowed you to brainwash me into thinking the world would go up in flames if I failed to please you," I bring the knife down on his thigh, giggling at the satisfying sound of Grant's scream. Removing it quickly like the swipe of a credit card, I hold it up, admiring the stain of blood dripping down the blade. Grant curses loudly, drawing my attention back to his weak form. I hold the knife right up to the pulsing vein in his neck, enjoying the slight squeal of agony that leaves his lips. "I was recently shown an entirely new way of living."

He spits at my feet, trying and failing to hide his pain. Pain I inflicted on him and will happily continue to do. I don't know where this version of me has been hiding, but she's done being veiled in darkness, hoping not to be seen. This version of myself is alive and thriving, and I fucking revel in it. Now I understand why Abram does what he does. There's a unique beauty in eliminating the world of monsters like Grant.

He fixes me with a sinister smile, the one that used to have my toes curling in my shoes. The same smile he used every fucking time before assaulting me, letting me know what deranged shit went on in his head. But with Abram by my side, letting me take the lead has me feeling stronger than ever. His smile and words don't make me cower anymore, so no matter what he says at this point, I couldn't give two fucks.

"I gave you everything you dumb bitch. What way of life has shown you more than what I did for you?"

As I'm about to plunge the knife back into an area of his body, Abram's fist connects with Grants nose, blood splattering all over us. He chokes and spits out clots of blood pouring out of his face as Abram leans in close, gripping the collar of his shirt to keep him in place.

"Me. Asshole."

I stare at him in shock, wondering how I managed to attract the attention of this man. My core tightens at the sight of him, the things he's willing to do to protect me. I love this man, every unhinged part of him.

"I'm sorry baby, he can't talk to you like that. Not in front of me. I won't step in again," he breathes heavily like it pains him to not do his worst on Grant's face. I smile my thanks at him, winking as he steps back.

Feeling a flare of arousal light within me, I grip his shirt and pull him into me, biting his lower lip that makes him groan in satisfaction. A sick part of me wants Abram to take me, back in the deep parts of the woods under the moonlight while Grant watches. It would be a shame for him to die never knowing how to truly please a woman. He could learn a thing, or twenty, and if there's anything redeeming buried deep inside him, he could use it in the afterlife. Not gonna hold my breath on that though.

"This has always just been the family business, Isolde. Thought you would have figured that out by now," Grant interrupts as blood pours down his face, dripping off his chin. "I've known nothing else my entire life, even my father got off on hurting women. Why wouldn't I?" Nausea rolls through me at that statement. This isn't just about him and his sick desires, he comes from it. It's rooted in the very marrow of his bones and I suddenly want to puke.

Before I can say anything, Abram holds up a hand beside me. "What the fuck do you mean, *'the family business'*?"

Grant throws his head back on a maniacal laugh, causing goosebumps to explode down my arms. Lifting his chin, he directs his next words at Abram and I feel the urge to cover my ears, knowing I won't want to hear whatever he's about to say. "You know, I had you as my right hand man because I thought you were the perfect blend of rough and smart. Turns out you're a bigger idiot than I could have imagined," he snickers almost to himself. "It's bad enough you didn't put two and two together after we met, but this," he laughs again, "this is almost pathetic."

That earns him another punch to the nose, more blood pouring out of his face than before, but still he manages to keep his head up and continue. "All these years you thought you were taking out the bad guys to protect those women and children, when all along you were practically serving them up on a platter to my doorstep." He licks his lips, dragging a thick amount of blood into his mouth making his teeth soaked in crimson. "You see, with the predators out of the way, thanks to your unhinged obsession with eliminating the bad guys," he nods his approval at Abram. "I was able to step in and take what I wanted. I didn't have to get my hands dirty because I had you for that."

I chance a look at Abram and see that his face has gone a ghostly shade of white, all the gears working together, creating an image that actually does cause me to puke this time. I heave onto the concrete floor beneath my feet, feeling like my chest has a boulder weighing it down. I'm not sure I even want to know what Abram is feeling, because if this is how I feel having not had anything to do with any of this, then surely he must feel like every organ is being ripped from his body. His very soul and purpose was to protect people who had been abused like his mother, like me. Only to find out the one man worse than any of the others he's killed, was the man he trusted and worked for.

"Who do you think raped and killed your mother all those years ago? Surely you didn't think it was a coincidence I found and hired you."

Abram stares at him, his own demons threatening to break free. "Wow, you really are just as dumb as she is," he laughs as he tries to point a finger in my direction, still being held back by the twine Abram wrapped around him. "Match made in heaven. Thought I made my point clear when I said it was in the family business."

"You don't mean…" Abram wonders aloud, and the second round of vomit working its way up my throat threatens to paint the floor again.

"Oh, I do. My father is the one who raped and murdered your mother that night all those years ago. Made sure you were there to watch too, isn't that just the icing on the cake!" He thunders with a boisterous laugh that ricochets off the walls. "It wasn't part of the original plan, surely. He wanted your own father there to see her taken away - turns out he didn't give a fuck to begin with. Instead, you got to witness your whore of a mother get held down and raped while tears soaked the carpet beneath her. Ah, if only I had been old enough to tag along that night."

I can't help the scream that erupts out of me as Abram pummels Grants face, over and over and *over* again. I want to stop him, but nothing would get through, not now. Not after Grant admitted the one thing that has haunted Abram since he was nine years old. I thought I needed to let my demons caused by Grant free, turns out Abram and I are linked more than either of us could have ever imagined.

"Abram, wait," I manage to choke out through shuddered sobs.

The sound of my voice halts him, looking back over his shoulder with eyes that almost appear obsidian with the amount of rage burning in them. The soft gray has been replaced by the blackness of his past, taking root and unleashing years of pent up anger. Anger for not being able to save his mom. Anger for saving those women and children from the men who took something from them that was never theirs in the first place, just to be handed off to the man who created this new fucked system.

Appearing like a selfless man on the outside, caring only for the weak and wounded just so he could take from them while they were at their lowest point. The whole thing makes me sick to my stomach, never knowing that the torture he supplied me with, extended to so many others as well.

We both need revenge for our pasts. What better way to bond than to kill the person who single handedly brought us immeasurable amounts of pain?

Holding the knife up, still dripping with blood from Grants thigh, I smile at Abram. Creating my own aura of deranged thinking as I glance back at the man spilling blood like a gossip queen spilling secrets. Abram reads my mind and holds the knife over my hands, our fingers linking together.

"Then it seems only fitting to end your pathetic life in the same place your father took his mother's. An eye for an eye," my heartbeat thrums erratically in my chest, Grant's fear igniting a new kind of excitement within me. It's exhilarating.

Moving in synchronized steps, Abram and I lift the knife together, plunging it deep into Grant's chest, just beneath his breast bone - the same place he stabbed me all those months ago. Holding tightly, we drag the blade down his chest until reaching the sensitive skin of his belly button.

The veins in his forehead pop, his face turning a dark crimson that almost appears purple, he bellows out a string of pained curse words as blood soaks his expensive dress shirt. I've always wanted to ruin one of his expensive suits, its a delightful sight to see now.

His groans turn feral as the blood loss catches up to him - he knows this is the end. Satisfaction at the image before me brings a new sensation I've never known before - control and power. The two things Grant has sought after for as long as I've known him, only difference is I won't allow this feeling to dictate my life. I won't turn into the very monster before me, ruining innocent lives for a taste of that euphoria. Abram kills bad people but that doesn't make him a bad person too. Knowing I'm about to kill one of the most evil men I've ever met, brings me joy and peace like I've never known - but I won't go to sleep tonight itching for another taste. I'll go to bed knowing I eliminated my walking nightmare, and I never have to face him again.

A thought crosses my mind as I turn my attention back to the bleeding figure in the chair, I refuse to even address him at this point. "You were wrong about something," I reflect. His eyes slowly find mine, a touch of defiance still sting back at me. Delusional man, it's so sad.

"I'm not dumb," I state. "I got away from you, and though you may have known where I was all along, I still managed to outsmart you in the end. The only dumb one here, is *you*. You chose to come for me after knowing who I was involved with. The man who as you put it, is the best at what he does. So tell me, Grant, do you feel as dumb as you look right now?"

Rearing back slightly, his lips pucker like he's about to spit. I cover my face from the impending shower of saliva and blood coming my way, but nothing happens. Looking up, I see Abram lodged the knife in Grant's chest, rendering him speechless forever. His voice has been silenced, and I can't help but think - *fucking finally!*

"Sorry, baby," he growls out, eyes not leaving the sight before us. "I didn't feel like he deserved to answer a question that was meant to be rhetorical."

I don't say anything right away, any words I might want to speak are jumbled in my brain, dancing around each other like they don't know who should go first. The room reeks of rust as Grant's blood pools around us on the floor. There's so much of it and as sickened as I am by the sight, I'm also flying. I must be having an out of body experience because I feel practically weightless - for the first time in a very long time.

The weight that was always weighing me down, with it's claws that felt permanently hooked into my shoulders, has vanished. Like it was never there in the first place. My chest loosens as I stare into eyes void of life, the eyes that watched me with disgust, hurt me with nothing but malice. Grant's body sits lifeless, the last of his control bleeding out onto the cement in a silent symphony of my accomplishment - Abram's too. He may have been the one to take his last breath, but I helped him get there. A part of me knows he did it so I wouldn't have the blood on my hands, theoretically, and wouldn't have to carry that weight.

I think I could have done it and been fine with whatever feelings came after, but the part of me that believes in goodness is glad I didn't have to. There's a new darkness in me, I can feel the way it lights up and snakes around my veins, joining the rest of me like it was just waiting for the day to emerge. I'll never act on my impulses the way Abram does, but I feel a confidence in myself - like I'm stronger than I ever thought possible - and I have a feeling I'm going to enjoy this newfound version of myself.

"It's over," I whisper almost to myself, eyes still focused on the knife sticking out of Grant's chest. A small part of me was waiting for him to lunge, like they always do in the movies, but I can see that he's dead. His chest isn't rising any falling in rapid succession the way it was moments before. His body sags against the chair, neck craned in an unnatural way, reminding me of Alex still in the woods.

His soul may have left, gone off to a better place where he can hopefully watch over us and smile knowing we avenged him in some way, but his body remains still. Tears spill over at the memory of his eyes closing one final time, taking my sunshine with him. The lightness I always craved but was too afraid to seek out, was found in Alex. Soul crushing aches fill my chest at the loss and I can't begin to imagine telling June. She too has lost far too much in this life - it seems cruel that yet another person is taken from us too soon.

"It's over," Abram repeats, snaking an arm around my waist to pull me close. "He would be so proud of you, little bird." He doesn't have to say who he means, I know exactly who he's talking about. The one who has the other half of my heart, perpetually.

Feeling the weight of today, my knees buckle under me, almost hitting the floor before Abram catches me and lifts me into his arms bridal style. I want to go to Alex, give him the burial he deserves - but my mind is telling me now is not the time. The trauma of everything I've witnessed is going to take a long, *long*, time to recover from. Guess it's finally time I seek out therapy - nothing wrong with getting some help, June once told me.

Abram places me on the couch before pulling out his phone and sending off a text. "I'm contacting the clean up crew to come and take care of Grant's body," he says as his fingers fly across the keyboard.

"Won't they know its him, though?"

"No one has ever seen him until I met him a few weeks ago. He clearly kept his identity under wraps so that he could indulge in all the things he claimed to be against. To protect the beast hidden beneath the well groomed, well respected gentleman," he snorts, still focused on his phone.

I fake gag, knowing what a hock of shit that is. He was excellent at fooling everyone else, except me. Until today, I may have been the only one who truly saw him for the ugly person that he was. Like he said, this was a part of the family business and I cringe at the mere thought. He came from a man who abused women for fun, and if I could, I would erase every one of them from existence to ensure no one suffers at their hands again. I finally understand why Abram does what he does.

The blow Abram felt when Grant admitted to abusing those women, *after* he killed them, could be felt from the rage emanating from his shaking body. All the work he's done, all the lives he's taken has been for nothing. He made it his mission to torture those who took what didn't belong to them - ruining so many women's lives, children too - just to hand them back to a man who promised them freedom. I'm sure his mind is spinning with everything he's learned tonight, and I don't even know how to help him.

My brain feels like it's drowning inside my head, all the knowledge that's been thrown at me weighing me down and threatening to pull me all the way under. Abram and I both need to find a way through this or we risk losing not only ourselves to the weight of grief, but each other as well.

With his back to me, Abram looks out the window to the back yard where the trails lead into the woods. Trails he's grown up exploring and being a kid, alongside his little brother. Those same woods witnessed the murder of Alex, forever tainting those memories with dark and painful ones. No one should have to witness their mothers death and also deal with the death of their younger brother. Life can be so unfair sometimes and as I watch Abram gaze out at the night sky, I can't help the tears that roll down my cheeks.

I can't help the immense pain I feel for him in this moment - knowing I can never give him back the things he's lost. Thankfully he still has June, and he'll always have me. This place is my home now and I no longer have the fear of looking over my shoulder clouding the happiness I know I deserve. Once the dust settles, the first thing I want to do is call my parents - something that is so long overdue I'm nervous just thinking about it.

On shaky legs, I stand, and make my way over to where Abram leans against the cool glass. His eyes scanning the dark open sky - like he's looking for a shooting star to wish upon or maybe the flash of his brothers spirt making his way up to heaven. I never thought too much about what comes after death - but I love to imagine Alex up there carefree and happy. On the warm days when the sun shines brightly, I'll think of him - my sunshine.

Slipping my arms around Abram, I hold his back to my front, feeling the quiet inhale and exhale of his breaths. I've never seen him cry and probably never will, but this feels a lot like what his tears would look like if he allowed them to fall. "Abram," I whisper against his black t-shirt, that masculine scent that is uniquely him somehow still noticeable despite us being covered in dirt, blood and who knows what else. "Are you going to be okay?" I ask, even though it seems pointless. We're both fucked up right now, it doesn't take a genius to figure that out.

Still, I feel inclined to at least check.

He holds my arms that are wrapped around him, giving them a little squeeze of acknowledgment. No words escape him, no reassurance that he's okay or that he's barely holding it together. Honestly, either response wouldn't surprise me given what I know about him. Sometimes I just wish he would crack open the door and let me at least peak inside. I desperately want to help him - in any way that I can - but I don't know where to begin.

"I've been searching for the one thing in you that could crack this code," I gently tap the spot where his heart thumps beneath his muscled chest. Reveling in the way the organ beats faster when I touch him. "Something to allow me all the way in."

He's quiet for several beats, and I just listen to the steady thrum in his chest, thankful that I still have him with me - darkness and all. When he turns to face me, I don't see the rage he wears so well. I don't see the desperate need for revenge, or the crippling pain of his past. I see light gray eyes that shine back at me with nothing but a softness and the kind of love I've searched my whole goddamn life for.

With a touch so gentle I barely feel it, he slips his hands through the loose strands of my hair, locking them behind my neck and lifting my chin until I'm staring up at him. He licks his lower lip, causing me to focus on the movement before he speaks directly into my soul - the very core of my being. "It's you, little bird."

ISOLDE

chapter twenty-eight

♫

Good Girl • Ruby Darkrose

STOKER

As expected, Alex's funeral was full of joy and laughter - as well as pain and
the kind remembrance we'll all carry with us. The town came together to honor the
man that he was, telling stories about him as a kid and all the work he did alongside
Abram. Sasha hosted the repast at Pour Performer with enough food and drink to
feed the homeless - and as much as June tried, Sasha wouldn't allow her to pay a
cent towards anything.

"We take care of people around here, remember?" Sasha had said to June and I
smiled knowing she couldn't argue with that. This was the woman who took me in
without knowing a single thing about me - opening her heart and home to me when
I had nowhere else to go. Stuck in the idea that I had to hide for the rest of my life,
providing me with the shell until I felt ready to come out.

Telling her about Alex was as bad as one would imagine. Some nights I wake
up covered in sweat, ears ringing like I can still hear the scream that bellowed out of
her. Wishing more than anything I could take the words back and protect her from
that pain.

Eventually things settled down, despite the raw ache of his absence that is now
forever engrained into the fabric of my soul. My lightness, the sunshine in every day,
was gone - and so far nothing close to his warmth has been able to fill the void he
left behind. Not that I would want it to anyways. I've reserved a part of myself for
him and only him for as long as my heart keeps beating - hoping one day I'll see him
again.

"Ready?" Abram calls from the foyer of the manor, the deep timber of his voice
carrying up the steps. He still has his space in the cottage at the back of the property,
but he officially moved back into the manor with me about a month ago - right after
Alex died. The idea of living in this big house alone made my skin crawl - preferring
to live in that tiny bedroom at June's again than here by myself.

It took some adjusting, and intense therapy on both parts to get him to agree to
it - but he's here and that's what counts. Abram is still my darkness, the black parts
of my heart seek out his, like a matching pair destined to thrive as one. "Coming!"
I yell down the stairs as I smooth the lines on my dress. I opted for a long sleeve
black dress for Abram's birthday - it seemed fitting. The sleeves are a see through
mesh and the neckline is a straight cut across the top of my chest, keeping me fully

covered but not leaving much to the imagination.

It took a lot of arm twisting to get Abram to agree to a party, but this is our first chance at hosting something here since we restored the manor. What better occasion than the birth of my dark knight?

As I descend the stairs, I feel Abrams gaze tracking my movements. The way my legs slowly slink over each step in my leather biker boots - a gift from the birthday boy. My cheeks heat in remembrance at the way I tried denying the gift since it was his birthday - earning me a punishment that lasted well past breakfast.

Before reaching the bottom step, a hand snakes out, wrapping around my waist. Giggling into his chest, I palm the muscles beneath his black button down, enjoying the feel of the soft material on my fingers. "Don't start something you can't finish, Stoker," I breath him in, licking my lips as the decadent scent of him envelops my senses.

"You and I both know I can get the job done," he counters. "And what did I say about calling me that?" His grip on my hip tightens, caging me against his body the way he knows I love. Abram was able to open my eyes to how enjoyable sex can be when pleasure is mixed properly with pain. No more being afraid to feel pain, knowing it would always end in bruises or a hospital visit. He's taught me to welcome it, how to harness the pain as it mixes fluidly with pleasure. One in the same, as he always tells me.

"People will be here any minute, so I thought it would be fun to anticipate my punishment all night knowing you can't do anything about it until they all leave," I tease, fixing the buttons on his shirt.

His growls of lust fill my ear, and his length presses into my stomach, showing me just how badly he wants to act on that punishment here and now. Before he has a chance to do anything, I pull away, tugging his hand behind me as I guide him to the kitchen.

"I know all the food is catered and there's a cake for our guests, but I wanted to give you something a little more…special. Just for you," I say, looking over my shoulder with a flare of satisfaction lighting my face.

Abram watches me with wary eyes, but I don't miss the subtle flicker of curiosity as I pull a homemade cake from the fridge. It's frosted with a dark chocolate frosting, and letters spelling out *Stoker* in bright red icing. He stares at me with inscrutable eyes, and for only a second, I second guess my decision on making this cake. What if he hates it? What if it tastes bad?

Nerves take over and before I completely lose my nerve, I light the black candles and sing happy birthday while he watches me with an avaricious glint. Neither of us say anything as I cut into the cake and slide a piece over to him. "If you wanted to kill me you could have found more creative ways than poison," he teases as he takes his first bite.

I watch him carefully, searching for any sign of revulsion, but find none. He eats the entire piece with ease and even licks his fingers when he's done. "That was delicious, baby, thank you."

Warmth unfolds in my chest before the butterflies take flight inside my ribcage. "Well, I included a secret ingredient I didn't think would be suitable for our guests," I shudder. As nervous as I am, lust blooms low in my belly with the way he stares at me - brows arched in anticipation.

"What might that be?"

On an exhale, I close my eyes and rip off the bandaid. "My blood."

My heart beats wildly in my chest, blocking out any other sounds as I wait for his reaction. When my eyes open, I find his on my body. Slowly working their way up my figure until settling back on my face. "You laced the cake with your actual blood?"

"Y-yes," I whisper.

Abruptly, Abram stalks out of the kitchen and down the hall. I peer around the corner when I hear the deadbolt lock at the front door. "What are you doing?" I ask, puzzled and slightly taken back by his lack of response.

Eyes as dark as the night sky sear into mine as he reaches for me, pulling me up so my legs wrap around his waist. "Abram, where are you," lips crash against mine, cutting off my question and my air. His tongue works its way into my mouth and I groan at the feeling of it dancing with mine. I can't tell where we are in the manor until I feel my legs bump into what feels like a table.

Lowering me, Abram leaves me perched on the dining room table as he makes his way to the windows, effectively drawing the curtains closed. "What are you doing?" I manage to ask before he's ripping into the zipper at the back of my dress, pulling it down to expose my breasts.

"I'm going to fuck you right on this table and smile every time I see someone sit here tonight completely unaware that not long beforehand I had my cock buried in this tight cunt."

"Does that mean I did good?" I ask, unable to hold the question in any longer. I had a feeling he would love it because I'm rather certain he was a vampire in a previous life. But there was always the chance I may have taken it too far.

"Little bird, if I could get away with fucking you the rest of the night and not deal with this party, then I would. But I know you worked hard on it for me so I'll make round one fast and hard," his tone is as controlled as it is needy as he unbuckles his belt, letting his pants slip down so his cock can spring free.

"Just the way I like it," I moan into him.

With one swift movement, he has himself sheathed inside me, driving me to the edge I love to dangle from, knowing he'll always be the one to pull me back in. The scent of our arousal mixed together permeates the air, like an aphrodisiac making the entire space around us smell like heaven and sin. Together we sizzle - like fire and ice - giving into the sensations of lust while holding true to the feelings of love we have for each other.

"We better make this quick before my parents and June arrive," I say, breathless against his rough movements. The table legs screech against the floor as he drives into me with rushed thrusts. Racing to get us both to the finish line just so we can do it again later.

"I guess it would be pretty awkward to meet them while I'm buried deep inside your sweet pussy. I doubt June would want her new pottery piece either, knowing where my hands have been," he jokes as he slides a thick finger through my wet center. Toying with my clit the way he knows will bring me to my breaking point.

As if on cue, I feel the wave of my orgasm about to crest just as the doorbell rings. Eyes wide with panic, Abram covers my mouth as he holds me in place, never letting up in the way he pinches my clit while working himself in and out of my tight channel. I scream against his palm, eyes rolling back in my head as the bliss only he can deliver, takes over.

Leaning forward, he bites into my bare shoulder as he comes. His teeth sink into me hard enough he has to stifle my screams again, but not hard enough to draw blood - that would definitely take some explaining.

Panting against one another, Abram slinks the loose strands of my hair behind my ear before kissing me fiercely, unapologetically robbing me of oxygen. Molding his lips to mine with a tight grip around my throat, reminding me who I belong to. I could melt into his touch, spend the rest of my days lost in him knowing I'm as whole as I've ever been because he loves me.

Emotion clogs in my throat, coming out of nowhere as I look at him. "You know I would never hurt you, Abram," I whisper.

Rubbing the soft flesh of my cheek, he watches me with rapt attention. "You're the only one who has enough power to bring me to my knees. To everyone else I'm Stoker, hard as stone, but with you…I'm a damn sheet of glass. At your mercy and ready to break at any moment. You are the *only* one who can hurt me, little bird. And if you do, I'll lose any sense of morality I have left."

"Then it looks like we're on the same page," I smile sweetly, a softness I reserve just for him lighting my eyes.

Slipping my arms back through my sleeves and zippering me up, he glances down at my exposed thighs. "I'm going to enjoy knowing my cum will be leaking out of you all night long. No one else will know," he says, a dark playfulness in his expression. "But I will."

And with that he walks to the front door to let our guests in - leaving me still collecting myself on the dining room table.

He's still very much unhinged - especially when it comes to me - not that I'm complaining.

As he welcomes in the first few guests, their happy chatter echoing down the hall, I look down at the scrip tattoo scrawled on the inside of my ring finger, my first tattoo. It's not a marriage proposal - something neither of us is thinking of or ready for - but its the next best kind of commitment.

In black ink, the words *til death* decorate the delicate skin on my finger, given to me by the only darkness I allow in my life anymore. I came here for a fresh start, a place to hide from the demons of my past, never expecting to find what I have in this place - with these people. Sometimes you have to adjust to the darkness to see clearly - and that's exactly how I found my light again.

thank you

for reading